Mad
About You

Also by Mhairi McFarlane

You Had Me at Hello

Here's Looking at You

It's Not Me, It's You

Who's That Girl?

Don't You Forget About Me

If I Never Met You

Just Last Night

A NOVEL

Mhairi McFarlane

AVON
An Imprint of HarperCollins*Publishers*

This is a work of fiction. Names, characters, places, and incidents are products of the author's imagination or are used fictitiously and are not to be construed as real. Any resemblance to actual events, locales, organizations, or persons, living or dead, is entirely coincidental.

Originally published as *Mad About You* in Great Britain in 2022 by HarperCollins Publishers.

FIRST U.S. EDITION

Designed by Diahann Sturge

Library of Congress Cataloging-in-Publication Data has been applied for.

ISBN 978-0-06-311794-5 (paperback)
ISBN 978-0-06-311796-9 (international edition)

22 23 24 25 26 LSC 10 9 8 7 6 5 4 3 2 1

For Shelley Summers & Jennifer Lee
soulmates

All the days that you get to have are big . . .

—Self Esteem

Prologue

"Hi, you're the best man? Is it Sam? I'm Harriet, I'm the photographer today." She raised the Nikon D850, around her neck on a strap, by way of unnecessary corroboration. "Is the groom around?"

The best man looked at her with an expression of taut desperation. He was coated in a pastry glaze of sweat, like he'd been brushed with an egg wash and would form a golden crust at 180 degrees.

A very awkward pause ensued, where Harriet wondered if he could speak.

"He's gone, Harriet," Sam croaked, eventually, with wild eyes. He uttered it with the kind of brokenness and weight people usually reserved for when they meant: *passed to the other side*.

"Who's gone?"

"*The groom!*" The best man gestured with both arms outstretched at the empty space next to him.

Harriet checked her watch. Ten minutes to the official kickoff.

"Get him back, pronto, or she'll arrive without him here," she whispered urgently.

"That's the idea," said Sam, who looked as if he were having an anesthesia-free foot amputation aboard a haunted boat in a storm. "He's *gone*-gone. For good."

"What? *Gone?* As in . . . ?"

"As in has departed the premises, is declining to get married," Sam said under his breath, eyes bulging.

"What the fuck!" Harriet hissed. "Did he . . . say why?"

"I told him he didn't have to do this if he wasn't sure, sort of as a JOKE, and he said, 'Seriously, do you mean that?' and I said, 'Why?' He said, 'Because I don't want to do this,' and I said, 'Is this nerves?' and he said, 'No, did you mean it when you said I didn't have to do it?' And I had to say, 'Well, yeah, I guess so?' and he said, 'OK, I'm going then, please say I'm sorry.'"

Sam said this all in one galloping breath and had to pause to suck in air. He put a steadying palm on his chest, on his pristine white shirt, and when he moved it there was a tragicomic sweaty handprint on the cotton.

"I'm going to have to tell Kit he's jilted her. Oh my fucking life!"

"He's definitely not coming back?" Harriet said.

Sam said, closing his eyes, clearly wishing himself able to teleport from this church in the Gothic revival style on the outskirts of Leeds: "Nope."

Harriet had no protocols for this whatsoever. She was hired to take pictures, from the soup to nuts of bridal prep through to the first dance. It didn't always go to plan—best men got so drunk they slurred the speech, DJs played the uncensored version of the track, and a chocolate fountain once broke and appeared to be pumping out a mixture of kibble and raw sewage. But the knot always got tied. A runaway prospective husband-to-be was off the map, as far as crises went.

"Did he tell the vicar?" Harriet said in hushed tones, through a placeholder gritted smile, in case they were under observation.

"Yes. He told him at least," Sam said.

"Where's the vicar now?"

"Round the back, having a cigarette."

"*What?* Are vicars even allowed to smoke?"

"I don't know, but under the circumstances, I didn't feel I could tell him not to."

Harriet nodded. One for God to judge.

"Did I cause this? With my stupid line about how he didn't have to do it?"

Sam genuinely looked like he might cry.

"No!" Harriet said, in an emphatic whisper. "This isn't exactly something you'd do purely through the power of suggestion."

"I should walk out to meet her, shouldn't I?" Sam said. "It'll be worse if she gets to the door?"

"Oh God—definitely," Harriet said. The public humiliation would surely be unbearable if everyone saw her in her finery. If they realized at the same time she realized. The Kristina who'd hired Harriet didn't seem the type to take any disappointment well, let alone catastrophe. She was doll-tiny, with jet-black hair and a self-assured, borderline haughty demeanor. The groom had been too busy to meet Harriet during the standard planning stages, and now she was wondering if that was significant.

"If he's definitely, *definitely* not coming back?"

Sam's face was panic and agony. "He's not."

"I can't believe he's done this to you. And to her," Harriet said, aware that it was a slightly odd statement given she didn't know the tosser. *I can't believe [a total stranger] would behave this way!*

She glanced at the good-natured, expectant hubbub behind them, feeling crushed on their behalf.

"I'll walk out with you," she said, and Sam nodded *thank you* in gratitude.

Heads down, they strode purposefully down the aisle, out into the churchyard and down the path, among the mossy gravestones. As they neared the road, Harriet saw a beribboned white Rolls-Royce slide up alongside the pavement and felt physically sick. Poor, poor Kristina.

And poor Sam. He blew his cheeks out and exhaled, windily, stuck his fingers into his wild mop of curly hair, then seemed to remember it was tamped down with gel.

"It's not your fault," Harriet said, and Sam nodded, no longer able to communicate.

"Wish me luck," he said eventually, in a pinched voice, as he left Harriet's side.

"Good luck," Harriet said, quietly, though as the words hung in the air they sounded violently tasteless.

She realized she couldn't bear to even look, to see the moment the bride crumpled, and it was clear Harriet's contribution to the day was over. She strode briskly in the opposite direction, staring down at her cherry-red Doc Martens in the fallen cherry blossom on the pavement, silently counting the steps to busy her mind, *One—two—three—four—five—si—*

Harriet heard a scream rip through the air and stopped dead in her tracks, her heart pounding.

She turned to see Sam being punched square in the face by a five-foot, four-inch woman in an exquisite mermaid gown of ivory satin.

Sam reeled back, clutching a bleeding nose. The father of the bride exited the car like a gorilla escaping a safari park, and the shouting began.

1

One month later

"Read me the menu again, would you? I've totally forgotten what we're having for the main course," Jonathan said, swinging his gleaming silver Mercedes lustily around a corner, precariously close to a drystone wall.

It always took Harriet aback that Jon's driving was completely out of step with every other aspect of his demeanor. Put a steering wheel in his hands, and mild-mannered, cautious Jon became flamboyant, even cocky.

Harriet unlocked her phone, scrolled to the relevant page, and read aloud.

". . . Aged Yorkshire venison . . . heritage carrot . . . ramson . . . miso cashew cream."

"What's a ramson when it's at home? And I'm pretty vague on the properties of miso cashew cream, truth be told."

"To think you work in the food industry."

"Not at the miso cashew cream end."

Harriet prodded at the handset to google it, briefly bracing her free palm on the car door to ward off motion sickness.

"It is a 'bulbous perennial flowering plant in the amaryllis family.' Garlicky, by the sounds of it."

"Good-oh. And we told them about my special condition?"

Allergic to lettuce. Harriet sometimes thought that was Jon in three words. Who on earth is allergic to lettuce? Imagine the shame at the inquest. Cause of Death: Radicchio.

"Your mum said she'd do it."

And if she decides she didn't say that, I have the texts as receipts.

Harriet treated dealings with her in-laws like running Churchill's War Rooms. You napped with one eye open around Jacqueline Barraclough.

Harriet pushed her phone back into her handbag and fiddled with the volume on "Missing" by Everything but the Girl.

"Actually, can we have it off, please, Hats? I'm getting one of my headaches," Jon said.

"Sure, pull over in a lay-by."

"What?"

"*Have it off.* Never mind."

Jon threw her a baffled glance. He was one of those people who thought he had a great sense of humor. His GSOH was more like a burglar alarm: might work if he turned it on, but he often forgot.

"John F. Kennedy had to have sex several times a day or else he got headaches, you know," Harriet said.

"Inconvenient, given his workload. Would ibuprofen not do the job?" Jon said.

"Nope, had to be Marilyn Monroe."

"Ah."

Harriet could tell she was irritating him slightly. She couldn't say this sort of thing in front of his tightly wound parents, and they were close to entering their planetary atmosphere. Jon, already on his guard, wanted Harriet to behave accordingly. Like an actor getting into character on set, before they shouted, *Action*.

"Presume they're whipping up chicken nugs and chips for Joffrey Baratheon?" Harriet said.

Jon gave her a sideways look and tutted. "Oh, he's not that bad. He's twelve soon, entering adulthood! We're all allowed a grotty phase as a kid."

Harriet said nothing more because Jon's mother, Jackie; his father, Martin Senior; elder brother, Martin Junior; his wife, Melissa; and their eleven-year-old son, Barty (Bartholomew for tellings-off, which Harriet thought were all too scarce), were all in one big rolling grotty phase.

Jon dwelt in an odd mental space, as regards his family—he never denied they behaved like absolute menaces, because it was pretty hard to pretend otherwise. But he could never go so far as to attribute malice to them either, which Harriet thought left him a day late and a dollar short in terms of having their measure.

They always *meant well.*

This wishful claim of Jon's had [citation needed] after it. It was as if their true personalities had locked-in syndrome, in Jon's analysis, given their tragic inability to make their inherent kindness known.

"Nearly there." Jon looked at the clock on the dash. "An hour to shower and change, I reckon, and then a gin and tonic in the bar."

"Sounds good to me," said Harriet, in tacit peace-making, and Jon beamed.

In typically generous fashion, Jon had booked dinner and an overnight stay for all of them at a country house hotel in the Dales for his parents' fortieth wedding anniversary.

Harriet had agreed to it with the usual sense of dread, but, you know, you couldn't pick your boyfriend's family. You also couldn't stop Jon from spending his considerable salary in such expansive ways.

"No roof racks on hearses, Hats," he'd say, riffling her hair.

He was MD of a division of a supermarket chain, developing upmarket ready meals. Harriet's best friends, Lorna and Roxy, called him Captain Gravy, a nickname he didn't find funny.

"It's not just gravy I've got responsibility for—it's all sauces and luxury pouched condiments!" he'd lightly fume, bewildered to be increasing their mirth.

Harriet had never experienced money the way Jonathan had money. It landed in huge snowdrifts in his account every month and could build up to unwieldy, drain-clogging fatberg size if not dealt with efficiently by splurging on Parker Knoll furniture, spendy meals, and five-star weekends away.

Despite his protestations, Harriet had always given him proper rent since she moved into his mansion in Roundhay. She'd maintained a basic hygiene and not let him pay for most things—she had her own income, a lifestyle she could afford, and self-respect, but with Jon's profligacy, it was like sharing a bathtub and trying to keep the hot water separate.

Dating him for the last two years had been an education in good living. Maybe money couldn't buy you happiness; however, it was still a mood-altering, life-changing, addictive substance. It could purchase you not only pleasure, Harriet had discovered, but ease, patience, convenience. A kind of sunny outlook and frictionless existence where your path through any difficulties could always be smoothed by its liberal application.

In choosing the original venue for this celebration, for example, Martin and Mel had carped about the awkward location, and his father had objected to the trendy "plant-forward" cuisine ("The photos looked like things they'd fling at monkeys at Chester Zoo!"). And Jon simply flipped the booking to another hotel without even checking how much it cost. Everyone should be pleased, that was Jon's religion, and Jon could facilitate that pleasing, so he did.

He was, Harriet always said to herself and others, an incredibly, ludicrously nice guy. So, given her increasing doubts, what did that make her?

2

They pulled through gateposts that owls perched upon and followed a gently twisting drive to park up in front of a sprawling stone country house hotel. Warm yellow light flowed from leaded pane windows onto an immaculate lawn dotted with white canopied picnic tables, in the crisp early dusk.

Jon's mother emerged from the main door and walked out to meet them, Harriet's heart sinking at the inevitability of their having arrived first. Jon's dad was someone who would leave at dawn for any journey.

Jacqueline was in a candy-pink-striped shirt with upturned collar, pearls, and white jeans, pushing her bouncy salon blow-dry out of her face with her fresh manicure, fingertips like shiny coral beetles. She was always groomed to within an inch of her life, the snowy Mallen streak in her blonded silver hair giving her a pleasingly appropriate look of Disney villainess, to Harriet's eyes. In turn, her dismay at Harriet's "curiously tomboy style" (© Jacqueline) was barely concealed.

After Harriet had met them for the first time, she was sitting next to Jonathan when he got a text from his mum. It was very

Jon to have neither the deviousness nor the common sense to not open it in Harriet's eyeline.

We thought Harriet was a lovely girl, JJ. Terribly pretty face, like the sidekick girl from the detective show where he's lame with a cleft palate. But why on earth does she wear those awful glasses?! Last seen on Eric Morecambe! Such a shame. Given contact lenses are widely available, you presume she's making some sort of cross feminist statement.

"What the . . . !" Harriet had exclaimed, cupping her hand to stop herself from spitting BBQ-flavored Walkers Bugles. "What's wrong with my glasses, and why say something like that?"

"She thinks you're beautiful!" Jon said, blushing, with what Harriet at first took as embarrassment and later realized was in fact a swoon at what he'd taken as straight praise from his mother.

"She's only saying that so she can go in hard on the 'four-eyed feminazi frump' angle, Jon. That's a 'paying twenty pence so you can use the toilet' move."

"You really can't cope with compliments, can you?" Jon had said, absurdly fondly. Harriet gave up trying to translate it for him. Like trying to wake a sleepwalker.

"At last!" Jacqueline said, as they climbed out of the seats, straightening stiffened limbs and grinning awkwardly. "We were about to send out the search parties!"

Jon and Harriet weren't late.

"Hit a sticky bit of traffic on the B6160," Jon said. "Hi, Mum, how are the digs? Acceptable?"

"Fine, though your brother asked them to change the pillows on his bed, they're like rocks."

Of course he did. Martin Junior, a chest-puffed humorless little pigeon of a man, always led with a complaint, to make it clear he was superior to his surroundings. Harriet suspected he liked Jon picking up the bill but was also hugely insecure about it.

"Harriet, how ARE you?" Jackie cooed, with that oddly sarcastic intonation that passed for good manners among affected people.

"Very well, thanks. And you?"

"Oh, you know. Can't complain."

Bet you do, though.

Harriet had really tried to bond with Jackie, at the start. She once told her over too much wine in girl talk that she had irregular periods. The following week, Jackie rang Jon and told him that he should send Harriet for a fertility test.

"We're going to check in, head up to change, and meet you in the bar at six?" Jon said.

"I should hope you *are* going to change!" Jacqueline said, in fake merriment, giving Harriet's standard T-shirt and jeans and Doc Martens an up-and-down pained look. "Tell me you've packed something smart!"

"I'm always smart-casual, Mum!" Jon said, imagining this was maternal fussing, rather than a blatant gibe at Harriet that Jacqueline was very thinly disguising by pretending she was referring to the pair of them.

Somehow, no matter how much she remembered that Jon's family were a trial, their manifold horrors always dazzled her afresh in person. A thunderous measure of Bombay Sapphire could not come fast enough.

THEIR "ESTATE ROOM" was more hipster than Harriet had anticipated for the Dales, a collision of countryside and town—William Morris Strawberry Thief–print quilt on the bed, Edison bulbs hanging on a cluster of cables as a modern chandelier. There was a vast freestanding copper tub with matching jug near a marble fireplace, as a whimsical cosplay of the privations of a previous century. The walls were a dramatic shade of Farrow & Ball smoky gray against toothpaste-white cornicing.

Harriet was a veteran of fancy hotels thanks to her job, and this one still stood out as exceptionally luxe. The kind of scene you were near obliged to put on Instagram with a moody filter, captioned #dontmindifIdo or #todaysoffice. (Harriet was an Instagram refusenik. "Busman's holiday!" she told her best friends, Lorna and Roxy, when they exhorted her to join in.)

"Bloody hell, Jon, this must have cost a fortune," Harriet blurted as she twirled her trolley case to a halt, then regretted her words as a bit crass and grasping, rather than grateful. It must have, though.

"It's not Travelodge prices, but, then again, it's not every day you're forty years married!"

Harriet tensed as she watched him do that thing—where he saw tissues on the bedside table and immediately had to seize one, and start blowing his nose astonishingly loudly, like he was trying to bring brain matter out through his nostrils. Her stomach churned, like it was mixing a Slush Puppie of freezing cement.

"I'm so glad you're here," Jon said, folding Harriet into a hug, and she squeezed back, mumbling, "Thank you for inviting me."

"Dur, of course I invited you! You make it sound like you're an optional extra. You're one of the family. You're more my family than they are."

"Hah, I hope not," Harriet said, disentangling from an octopus grasp. "That would make this incest. I'm going to have a shower, if that's all right?"

"Have at it!" Jon said, accepting her subtle noncompliance with the moment he wanted.

He began prodding at the remote control for the television. What was the unspoken rule that all men in hotel rooms had to immediately put CNN on at a slightly-too-loud volume and lie on their bed watching it in their socks? Harriet had so often found herself brushing her teeth in a gorgeous suite, listening to a newsreader booming, "The violence and looting continued through the night as community leaders appealed for calm," through the door.

She unzipped her case and riffled through it for her eveningwear and her clean bra and knickers, silently cursing the way Jackie made her want to mulishly reappear in the same T-shirt. Actually, no, reappear in a T-shirt with the slogan BEAST MODE: ACTIVATED and a pair of Union Jack Crocs.

In the floor-to-ceiling white metro-tiled bathroom, like a sexy sanitorium, Harriet stood under a showerhead the size of a dinner plate, in a pleasingly scalding gush of water. Her hair was gathered off her face into a drooping bun. Harriet had an incredibly thick strawberry-blond mane, which some might think a blessing, but it meant it was unmanageable worn any other way than up in her trademark long, high bell pull of a plait. She'd tried cutting it short in her teens, but it stuck out from her head like a box hedge. In a science class at school, they'd examined strands plucked from their own scalps under the microscope, and hers looked like an ear of wheat.

Once dry and in her underwear, she picked up her dress from the armchair upholstered in chinoiserie fabric in the corner. Bathrooms with armchairs: mad fancy.

Harriet didn't buy many dresses, but this one had called to her from the window of a boutique in a picturesque village, a few months back. She'd had an hour and a half to kill before Andy and Annette said "I do" and had gone in to touch the fabric. Naturally, she was swooped upon by a bored assistant who was adamant Harriet would look "absolutely stunning in it," and that was that.

It was a deep emerald-green dress that buttoned high at the neck and clung so tightly to her calves it meant she had to take baby steps. She'd not necessarily wanted to wear something so showy to tonight's dinner, but she also had few options in her wardrobe, and it had cost her almost £200.

She also had to concede her beloved black-rimmed spectacles didn't really go with it. Harriet would have to infuriatingly oblige Jacqueline and wear contacts. She gingerly applied mascara to her exposed eyes and wound colossal handfuls of hair into a bun, securing it with bobby pins. She turned her head from side to side to check her handiwork. It looked like she had a huge cinnamon pastry on her head, but it would have to do. She dropped the necklace she always wore, with the small key, down her neckline.

As she exited the bathroom, she saw Jon standing naked in the tub, dousing his head with the jug, spluttering as he swallowed water. She hadn't expected to come face-to-face with a penis this early in the evening and let out a small yelp, covering her eyes.

"And good evening to you too!" she said.

"You have seen it before!" Jon said, in jolly fashion, and set about aggressively towel drying his hair, so his face was obscured while his member flapped gently at her, like a windsock in a weak breeze.

Jon was the image of a solid catch—solvent, dependable. He had a catalog-model handsomeness, tall, with neatly clippered dark brown hair, unthreatening and well ironed, and a slim build softening around the edges. And that was a perfectly adequate size of penis. As Lorna always said, the extra-large ones were only a recipe for constant cystitis.

What kind of monster wouldn't be satisfied with a man like Jonathan Barraclough?

"Wow!" Jonathan cried, mercifully having wrapped the towel around his waist by the time he'd blinked away sufficient water that Harriet swum into view. "My girlfriend, the supermodel!"

"Hah. Thanks," Harriet said, tugging black velvet heels on, which were otherwise only used for funerals. She'd never worked out why comfy flats were disrespectful to the departed. "Not too much?"

"Not at all, seriously, you look stunning," Jon said, staring as he stepped out of the tub with some effort, given it was the size of Gibraltar. "Really. *Wow.* I don't know why you don't dress up more often, given you're such a knockout."

"It's not really me."

"It is you; you just can't see yourself the way others do. Stand up, I want a proper look at you."

Harriet embarrassedly got to her feet, while Jon whistled and waggled an imaginary Groucho Marx cigar.

"I'm the luckiest guy in the world!"

3

". . . And I tell you this, I wouldn't live in Bristol if you paid me to. A hotbed of troublemakers and scruffy malcontents." Jonathan's father, Martin Senior, was holding forth with characteristic vim as Jon and Harriet found them in the private dining room, which had tartan shot-silk curtains and a mounted stag's head.

"Evening all!" Jon said. "Is Dad off on one already?"

"Your cousin's moving to Temple Mea—oh my God! Harriet, can that be you?" said Jacqueline, clutching her chest and reeling back in simulation of a heart attack, while Martin Senior said, "Well! Wonders will never cease!"

Jacqueline leaped up from her seat to come and tug at the fabric on Harriet's hips, twitching it into place. Harriet went stiff at the uninvited physical interference.

"There! Perfect." She added, "*So* nice to see you in a frock for once."

The "see the praise you get when you actually make the effort" triumphalism in his mother's tone made Harriet wish she'd made a cross feminist statement in stout trousers after all. You don't negotiate with terrorists.

"Thank you. Happy anniversary." Harriet smiled at Jacqueline and then Martin Senior, who looked right through her. He was a husband and a consigliere, with the flushed House of Lords look of someone who had dined and drunk well for many decades. His main role in matrimony seemed to be sinking expensive booze and muttering, "Quite right, Jackie, absolutely abysmal behavior," to punctuate any of Jacqueline's stories about the many wrongs they had been done.

Jonathan's brother, Martin Junior, and his wife, Mel, walked in behind them, with a scowling, skinny Barty in shirt and tie. He went to a private school, and his parents dressed him so smartly he looked like a kid from another era, who might buy sweets with shillings and play conkers.

"My goodness, Harriet?! I didn't recognize you! I thought Jon had a new woman!" Martin Junior said, double taking.

"Isn't it extraordinary!" Jacqueline chimed in.

It?

"Seeing you in a dress is so unfamiliar it's like . . . like you're in *drag*," he said, chortling, and Harriet was momentarily speechless at the rudeness, as everyone fell about.

"Yes, doesn't she look incredible?" Jon said, deploying his selective hearing. Why did she feel so undermined by Jon? *I'm not asking for their approval.*

"Why is Aunt Harriet in fancy dress?" Barty said, looking up at his mother, and everyone whooped at this precocious wit.

The standard Barty MO was to direct borderline offensive questions about the company to his parents. "Why don't Uncle Jon and Aunt Harriet have children?" was a supposedly innocent query last Christmas, over the prawn cocktail starter.

"Because they're not married" was the snaky answer from Barty's grandmother, which Harriet itched to correct. Harriet had no moral objection to marriage; she just had no interest either. Doing it purely as a favor to someone else, and to meet society's expectations, seemed wrong. She'd been quite clear with Jon on this from the start, before he got the chance to start dropping hints. And whenever the subject came up again, she reiterated her stance: *Nope, not for me.* Not now. Not ever. It wasn't personal to Jon, but it was personal to her.

"Harriet says you told them about the green threat," Jon said to his mum, as they took their seats and marbled ham hock terrines were placed in front of them, Jon's absent of its decorative leaf of Little Gem.

"Oh, so it's blame Mother if they forget, is it?" Jacqueline chortled in more faux merriment, shooting Harriet a look.

"Jon asked me if I'd told them and I said you said you'd do it," Harriet said.

"I'm only joking, goodness!" Jacqueline chided, waving her hand at Harriet as the waiter topped her glass up. Sniping passed off as humor, Harriet characterized as oversensitive if she defended herself? The Jacqueline Barraclough bingo card would be fully dabbered tonight.

"A toast, I think!" Jon said, picking up his malbec, once everyone had theirs, and Barty was noisily sucking on a Coke with a straw. "To our wonderful mother and father and their marvelous achievement of forty years of happy marriage. Your ruby anniversary! May we all be so fortunate. And so patient, hahahaha."

As they raised their glasses, Harriet could see Martin Junior's slapped-bum face at his brother hogging the limelight.

"Perhaps *Dad* wants to say a few words?" Martin Junior said, pointedly, but his father paused in swilling the grog to say, "My wife speaks for me, that's how we've made it forty years," so his gambit failed.

"Thank you for organizing this. I have such wonderful sons!" Jacqueline said.

"Time for our gift, I think?" Martin said, and gestured with a head nod at Barty. "Go on!"

Barty looked stubbornly blank until Melissa leaned down and whispered urgently in his ear. Barty slid off his seat, walked to the back of the room, and collected a gift-ribboned shiny rectangular package. Amid much cooing, he handed it over silently to his grandmother.

"For me?!" Jackie said.

"What do you say, Barty?!" Mel trilled from the far end of the table.

"Happy anniversary, Grandma," Barty mumbled sullenly, before stomping back to his chair.

She tore the paper off to reveal a framed photograph of their wedding day, a young Martin and Jacqueline standing on registry office steps. Martin with a thatch of hair, then dark brown; Jacqueline in an unusually tasteful, simple eighties wedding dress in pale mocha satin, a long veil fixed to her head with an Alice band.

"Oh, Marty! Melly! And Bartholomew, of course. You shouldn't have!"

Barty looked like he agreed.

"Look, look what they did for us," Jacqueline said, turning the picture to face Jon and Harriet, as if they didn't witness the gift-giving.

Harriet said, "You look gorgeous! That dress really suited you," glad to be able to be both honest and positive.

"You'd have loved my going-away outfit, Melissa, I had this super little swing coat," Jacqueline said, to make it clear she had only one stylish daughter-in-law.

"Yes, didn't Mum look bloody smashing on her big day?" Jon said, and put his hand over Harriet's, looking at her with proprietorial adoration.

That was the moment Harriet felt a whisper of strange foreboding, a psychic disquiet, that she chose to ignore in favor of more wine.

4

They made it to a chocolate marquise in raspberry coulis with a quenelle of tonka bean ice cream without controversy, until Martin Junior said, "How's the *wedding photography* going, Harriet?"

His tone put scare quotes around "wedding photography," as if it were an implausible front for escorting. Perhaps it was all the nice red wine, but Harriet could feel her diplomacy waning by degrees: many of the times she'd thought she was at the end of her tether with her in-laws, she was actually somewhere in the middle of her tether.

Two years of being fastidiously polite to them all, and for what? She was as much a disliked outsider as ever. Whatever the code was to crack their safe and become accepted by the Barracloughs, the magic numbers stubbornly eluded Harriet.

"Good, thank you," Harriet said.

"Busy? Lots of bookings? Business booming?"

"Yep. People are determined to keep marrying. The soaring divorce rate never puts anyone off."

"That's a rather cynical observation," Martin said, pouncing. *There it is,* Harriet thought.

"I was joking. I think it's romantic that it doesn't put anyone off."

"You never seem very keen on weddings, to say you've made your career out of them."

"You'd probably not love them either if you went to two a week."

He swilled the wine in his glass, holding the stem between forefingers, as if he were considering the grape on a vineyard tasting tour.

"Why do it, if you don't have a passion for it?"

"I don't think that's Harriet's attitude, actually," Jon interjected limply, and was ignored.

"I am passionate; I'm passionate about doing a good job for the couple." Harriet paused. "You're in property, it doesn't mean you want to move house every month."

"Tell them about the wedding last month, Hats," Jon said, slightly desperately. "The groom who legged it." He looked around the room. "Seriously. Everyone was there at the church, the bride pulls up in her Roller, only to be told he's been and gone and done a Lord Lucan. Minus murdering a nanny. Dreadful! Can you imagine?"

Melissa gasped. Harriet squirmed at using someone else's ordeal as a thrilling anecdote to dig herself out of an unpopularity hole.

"That was it really, I don't know much more," she said, carefully. "He got to the church, changed his mind, and left. The bride was told when she arrived. I've no idea what happened or why he went."

"What an absolute *creature,*" Jon said (he never swore in front of his parents), "shattering a young woman's life like that."

"Presumably they lost a lot of money on it too," said Jon's dad. "You'd not get refunds, canceling on the day."

Everyone nodded, sadly, and murmured: "Terrible."

"Why would you change your mind at that moment?" Melissa said. "It's so . . ." She grasped for what Harriet thought might be insight. ". . . *random*?"

It was the very opposite of "random," Harriet thought, it was an utterly intentional and conscious decision based on a specific prospect. Which is why it was so hurtful. Harriet couldn't stop wondering about how ruthless you'd need to be, how *heartless,* to abandon someone you were supposed to love like that. To set them up for a fall from that height.

"Perhaps it was like that film," Jacqueline said. "What's it called, you know. The old one, with Dustin Hoffman?"

"*Rain Man*?" Martin Junior said.

"No, the one where he runs in and stops the girl getting married . . . *The Graduate,* that's it!"

"I didn't see anyone else," Harriet said. Although maybe the someone else wasn't physically there, but the groom couldn't stop thinking about her? Or him? No, don't dignify a horrifying episode by giving the man some sort of high-concept romantic comedy motivation.

Had Kristina ceremonially burned her wedding dress, watched it go up like a white flag in the garden? You'd have to aggressively own an experience like that in order to conquer it. Like incorporating a pirate scar.

The dessert dishes had been cleared away and she saw Jonathan making emphatic faces at someone in the doorway.

He'd not told her of any cake presentation or similar, and she wondered if he and his brother would now be locked into escalating displays of devotion. They'd be frog-marched outside to watch a biplane fly past with a banner.

The room fell silent as a waiter strode up to Harriet and, with exaggerated ceremony, placed a plate in front of her, covered by a silver salver. Harriet glanced around. No one else had one?

He leaned down, whipped the cover away. On a large white plate sat a small, square royal-blue velvet box.

Harriet frowned. She looked up. Not only did no one else have Weird Plate with Tiny Velvet Box, they were all riveted upon her in a way that suggested they weren't similarly confused.

"What's this?" she said.

"Open it!" Jon said, practically vibrating with gleeful anticipation, and Harriet felt woozily nauseated. It was impossible that Jon could be this reckless, this tactless, this INSANE? Please no, please God no: What was happening?

She picked up the box and pushed; it snapped open heavily. A diamond ring sat on a white silk lining—one square gem flanked by two smaller ones, set on a platinum band.

There was a beat of silence, which felt to Harriet like a yawning void she could tumble right into.

"It's a ring?" she said, because she had no other words, and the held breath of the room erupted in hysterical laughter.

"Not much gets past Harriet!" Martin Junior whooped.

"It's a ring," Jon agreed, his eyes scanning her face for reassurance in her response. "Let's do this properly."

He took the box from her damp, lifeless hand and pulled his chair away from the table to create the necessary space to go down on one knee.

"Oh, JJ!" bleated Jackie in the background as he steadied himself on the carpet, overjoyed to see her youngest play Mr. Darcy.

Looking at Jon's earnest expression, Harriet honestly wanted to be sick. Imagine that. Imagine responding to a proposal by vomiting on someone. Eat your heart out, runaway groom.

Her head was spinning and her heart was pounding, and not in the good way.

"Harriet Hatley, you already make me the happiest man in the world. Will you make me this happy for the rest of my life, and agree to marry me?"

The two silent seconds that followed this question felt like a whole cultural era had passed. Harriet desperately calculated what to do for the best, what she *should* do, with no time to do so.

"Yes," she squeaked, eventually, in a minuscule and defeated voice. "Yes, of course."

The moments that followed were a blur, the small thunder of the room's applause, of Jon landing a clumsy kiss, half on her lips and half on her cheek, of Martin Junior bellowing, "*Well, this calls for champagne!*" and picking up a brass bell and jangling it—a sound that resonated inside Harriet like an alarm—to summon minions, so he could demonstrate his largesse by sticking bottles of Moët on Jon's tab.

Jon grabbed Harriet's left hand and slid the ring onto her finger, gabbling: "Do you like it? It was my grandmother's. Maternal grandmother's. Mum found it by chance in the attic two months ago and got it restored. It's Mum you have to thank for giving me the idea I could use it, in fact!"

Oh, I bet.

"Overcome your aversion to weddings now, eh!" gloated her father-in-law-to-be, pointing at the ring, and before Harriet could reply, Jon said, "It's different when it's your own. Right, Hats?"

Was Harriet a voiceless chattel from a bygone age?

Harriet glanced over at her mother-in-law-to-be, who was smiling at her like a large pedigree cat who'd eaten a crow.

"Yes, it's beautiful. Thank you, Jacqueline."

"Welcome to the family, Harriet."

5

Over the next hour, Harriet clung to the phrase *There's so much to think about!* like a life raft. Like a barrel going over Niagara Falls.

"Where will you look for a dress?" Jacqueline demanded. *No idea, so much to think about!*

"Would you prefer a reception venue in the city, or out in the countryside?" Jon's dad asked. *Ooh, I don't know, so much to think about!*

There really was so much to think about. Like, what if she'd said no? She internally remonstrated with herself for her cowardice—but even if she'd been prepared to make that scene and deal with the fallout, she now knew for sure that it was only half the size of the conversation she and Jon needed to have anyway.

She had no choice but to perjure herself for the next hour and a half, repeatedly and fulsomely. To agree she was now a fortunate woman with a sky's-the-limit budget to plan her society nuptials, and wasn't Jonathan's gesture tonight wonderful?

"I'd guessed he was going to pop the question," Martin Junior offered. "Well, you're *thirty-four,* aren't you? Thirty-five, it's a watershed." He tapped his nose, glancing at her stomach, and Harriet truly wanted to throw her champagne in his face.

At least she could honestly say she'd had no premonition that Jonathan was going to use this evening to propose. She left out the part where she'd failed to anticipate it because she'd thought there was no way he was so off his rocker to think that doing it in front of his parents, brother, sister-in-law, and nephew was remotely fair, romantic, or appropriate.

"It's so lovely to think your wedding anniversary is our engagement date," Jonathan said to his mother, practically simpering, and Harriet wondered if what she'd seen as dutiful benevolence was in fact appalling arse-licking. She'd been dealt such a blow she couldn't tell what was analysis and what was raw anger.

As they finally all started yawning and agreeing *well, what an incredible evening, but maybe time to turn in,* Harriet didn't know how to feel. What had happened was torrid; what was to come was likely worse.

"I keep catching sight of the ring on your finger and my heart explodes," Jon said to her, grabbing her hand to hold it as they walked up thickly carpeted, shallow stairs to their bedroom.

She was quaking at the prospect of what she was building up to do—it was going to be unutterably awful, but he'd really left her no other options. Harriet didn't even have the comfort of feeling one dominant, defining emotion—fury at Jonathan and pity for him were fighting a tumultuous war inside of her. However much he deserved what was coming next, he didn't deserve what was coming next.

Harriet had a fear that he would try to kiss her, and she'd have to push him away, so she dropped his hand, swiped the key card, and strode assertively through the door. She moved swiftly across the room, sliding the ring from her finger and placing it on a French chest of drawers, then turned and folded her arms. Jon, seeing this, looked unperturbed.

"Don't fret about safety?" he said. "It's worth a bundle, but I've already put it on the home contents, which would see us covered for loss or damage here too. So put it back on and come here, my stunning *fiancée*."

He looked like a kid at Chessington World of Adventures who'd been told the rides were free.

"Jon," Harriet said, in a voice so low and grim, it didn't sound like her own. "What the hell did you do that for?"

Jon's expression changed abruptly, and yet he remained motionless, scenting for danger like a vole sensing a predator in the undergrowth.

". . . Should I not have agreed with my mother she could be involved in the dress fittings? I will rein her in if you'd find it too much, don't you worry. I know you don't like fuss."

"No!" Harriet shrieked in disbelief he'd still not grasped what he'd done, and Jon recoiled. She realized she'd have to keep her emotions in some check in case they were overheard. "I mean, why did you propose? In front of your bloody family?!"

"That'd be because I very much want to marry you," he said, balancing one elbow on the mantelpiece, the smile creeping back onto his face. She could tell that he was fairly drunk, and so elated, so awestruck at the idea he was looking at the future Mrs. Barraclough (Junior) that he had enough happiness for her too. Her fussing would not be able to withstand the juggernaut that was Jonathan's joy. Surely she couldn't help but be infected with his ecstatic certainty of their bliss? As if infatuation were a communicable disease.

"I've always said that I'd never want my own wedding. You know that. I didn't leave it in any doubt?"

"Errrr. Then . . . why did you say yes?" Jon said, and even though Harriet guessed this was coming, she still had to dig her fingernails into her palms to stop herself from shouting.

"Are you serious? What choice did you give me? In front of your PARENTS? Have you got any idea how agonizing that was?!"

Jon stood up straighter, processing this. But Harriet could see he was also frantically assessing: OK, she's really upset, Work Brain Mode, conflict resolution, how do I apologize sufficiently for misjudging the manner of proposal and soothe her, make her feel heard? Until we can make up, spoon in bed, and perhaps even chuckle about it? *What am I like!*

"Oh God, sorry, Hats. You're completely right. I'd not thought of how that might feel. I got so excited that my mother had the ring, she said she'd give it to me *here,* and of course I couldn't wait, and a plan formed. My mum was insistent it wouldn't be stealing their thunder, bless her."

The incaution of praising his mum for her key role in this shitshow was typical Jon. Jackie wasn't guileless like her son, she'd have known it was interfering, taking family ownership of what should be a private event. She had no doubt hatched the plan as soon as she found the ring, and stage directing her son wasn't difficult. If Barty was Joffrey in their *Game of*

Thrones, Jacqueline was Lady Olenna Tyrell. *Tell Harriet. I want her to know it was me.*

"It was a bit of a runaway train. I see now that you feel you've been put on the spot."

"I don't 'feel' it, I *was* put on the spot. I don't want to get married! You know that about me. We've had explicit conversations about it?"

"Yes, but . . ." He raised and dropped his arms in a gesture of baffled futility. "People say things all the time, don't they? I say I'm going to pack my job in to become a paddle sport instructor every summer. I thought you were being irreverently witty! You'd got a bit jaded about them because of your work. I thought if you could do a wedding *your way,* that—"

"My way? You mean once you'd offered to pay for one, I'd grab it? My convictions are that shallow?"

"No!"

He did, he thought his wealth carried all before him. That if he was prepared to roll out the red carpet, in return he could have what he wanted. Jon wasn't a cynical person, but this was the calculation.

"You thought once I was permitted to plan a party, all my silly little feminine objections would magically fly away? It was one of those little lady ideas that don't really matter in real actual life?"

"Come on, Hats, I'd never think your opinion doesn't matter, you know that. You're being a bit mischievous here," Jon said, and she tried not to scream. "I suppose I thought . . . As ridiculous as it sounds, I thought, *No harm in asking. Shy bairns get nowt.* That you could say no."

"Except, if you ask with an audience, Jon, that's not quite true, is it?"

A hostile audience, at that.

This, more than anything, seemed to pierce his bubble of satisfaction, and he took a step toward her, hands up, beseeching.

"No, no. Oh, fucking hell. I've made a pig's ear of this."

Harriet said nothing. It still didn't sound or look like real contrition to her. She didn't think he even believed her. Harriet had presented him with a hurdle he'd have to navigate, that was all. If they left it here, by tomorrow, the fantasy would have reasserted itself, such was its power. He'd be cheerfully whistling and secretly scheming how to incorporate an expurgated version of their exchange tonight into his speech. *What was I like!*

"So . . . Do you want to officially break off the engagement, or simply put the idea on hold, say we're doing a long engagement? *Please* keep the ring, though. It looks perfect on you. We can call it a commitment symbol or something."

The ring. After everything she'd said, he was fretting about a piece of jewelry. Harriet felt an electric prickle up her spine and, for the second time today, roller-coaster-drop nauseated. How did she end up here? *What was she like?* And suddenly she knew, with crystal clarity. The thing that her gut had been telling her for a while. She'd been letting those messages accumulate like unopened bills, and now the bailiff was at the door.

She took a deep breath into her lungs.

"I don't want to be with you anymore. This is over, Jon."

6

He stared at her, eyes wide, skin turning a terrible lime-white color, chalky, like the paintwork. It was his spirit dying, in real time.

Eventually he said, "You can't be serious . . . ? You're breaking up with me?"

"Yes."

". . . Because I botched a proposal?! Harriet, this is ridiculous. You're quite right to be angry but let's not turn this into a full-tilt drama." He paused. "I don't need any more punishment to understand how upset you are."

She hard-gulped, as the tears surged up. "I'd hardly say this and not mean it, to punish you. That would be vile."

"Then why say it now?"

Harriet said, thickly, "You've kind of forced the issue tonight."

"So you weren't happy before I proposed?"

Deep breath. *Say it.*

"No."

Jon said, "Really?" in a broken voice, which was a small stab to her heart.

"Yes."

"You don't love me?"

Harriet closed her eyes. "Not in the way I need to."

"What the hell does *that* mean?"

"Just . . . what I said." She opened them again. It was as if Jon was shrinking inside his clothes. She hated herself.

"How do you love me then? Like a hamster?"

". . . I feel this has run its course."

"Oh, all the lazy clichés coming out tonight! What's up next, you love me but you're not *in love* with me?"

Harriet said nothing.

She realized she had on some level known that this conversation would be barely any less traumatic for her, which was partly why she'd never looked directly at it. Harriet was not skilled at antagonism.

Yet it was still even worse than she could have imagined. The version in her head didn't have this ugly, hollow quality to the air around them, as if the oxygen levels had plummeted.

Jon walked across the room and sat on the bed, head in hands. When he looked up again, his eyes were red.

"A moment ago, I was getting married to the love of my life. This can't be happening."

"You weren't getting married," Harriet said, quietly, rubbing a hand across her eyes. In the face of Jon's pain, it felt manipulative to cry, so she pushed it down as far as it could go.

"No. No, seems I wasn't. Fucking hell."

He held his hands out in exasperation.

"I don't understand, we were happy. You seemed perfectly happy? What the *fuck,* Harriet?"

"I was happy! I was happy loads. I don't regret our time together." That wasn't entirely true, but compassionate lying had its place. "But we're very different people, Jon. Tonight proved that."

"What can I do, what can I say to persuade you not to do this?"

Deep breath: *Say it.*

"Nothing." Harriet tried to say this gently, though obviously it wasn't gentle. "I'm going to pack and get an Uber home, if there's any near enough."

Jon's head snapped up. "Oh no, at this hour? Don't be ridiculous! I can sleep on the floor if you want." Harriet couldn't decide if his insistence on this was gentlemanly or martyrdom—either way, it made her grit her teeth.

"I very much do not want to see your family tomorrow," Harriet said.

Jon paused, clearly realizing he was going to have to face them too, and despite their shared misery, Harriet still felt some vindication that he finally comprehended how demented it was to involve them.

"We could leave very early tomorrow morning," Jon said.

Harriet paused. It made more sense than trying to run from the middle of nowhere at midnight. But the trouble with Jon's plan was that it meant many more hours in his company. He'd use them to press her to change her mind, and even if he didn't, being in a small space with someone you'd broken up with—possibly simply broken—for many hours was a grueling prospect. However, it'd be worse to find no taxi could get to her and then, shabbily, take Jon up on his offer. And fleeing the scene of the crime was an illusion—she'd only be going to his house, to sleep in his spare room. Proximity to Jon couldn't be avoided, for the time being.

"OK," she said at last. "But I'll sleep on the floor."

"Don't be daft," Jon said, and she knew his chivalry wouldn't allow it.

Examination of the bedding revealed there wasn't any way to disassemble it that made any sense, but the bed itself was vast, so they agreed to share it. It also humiliatingly revealed that Jonathan had apparently tasked someone with scattering rose petals on it. Harriet had to wordlessly brush them away as if they were lint. They took turns changing in the bathroom, then lay stiffly in the dark, bolster pillow between them, trying to breathe silently, the room filled with the cacophony of their thoughts.

HARRIET WOKE TO the sound of the toilet flushing at dawn, thin gray sunshine seeping in at the edges of the brocade curtains. The gruesome script of their breakup had kept her awake, replaying its lowlights, and her skin still prickled in the aftermath. She pushed herself up on her elbows as Jon came out of the bathroom. Only now, in the gloom, she saw there was a bottle of champagne on a side table that had clearly been delivered while they ate dinner, unopened in its tin bucket of melted ice, two spotless flutes.

"Harriet. Please don't leave me."

She focused on Jon's face in the half darkness, which was shining wet with tears.

"Please. I'm begging you. This is breaking my heart. I can't imagine life without you, Harriet. Please. Stay."

Harriet said, her voice hoarse, "I can't. I'm sorry."

"What if we agreed to some time apart, had a break?"

"It wouldn't change anything."

"Is there someone else?"

"One hundred percent no."

Jon gasped back a sob.

"Do you know, I almost wished there was. Because then there'd be a reason. A person I could compete with . . ."

"Jon," Harriet said, as softly as she could, a hot tear sliding down her own cheek. "You haven't done anything wrong. Apart from the proposal."

"Apart from not being who you want."

He put a palm over his face and cried, the kind of crying that rattles your rib cage. She couldn't hold him; the contact would feel wrong. For the first time since the door had closed on them last night, she allowed her own sobbing, drying her face roughly with her pajama sleeve.

It was completely harrowing to choose to shatter another person like this. It wasn't a choice, she told herself—except it was, because it was within her gift to not break up. She kept her weeping silent, bit it back, because it felt like giving him false hope that she was going to regret her decision—agreeing that it might be a mistake.

She was scared of her decision—scared at passing up someone who cared for her so much, scared of the loneliness on the other side, of having to go back to dating, of being single at thirty-four and what that might mean. But even in the teeth of that fear, she knew no part of it was second thoughts. The only upside to spending so long in an emotional limbo was the value she could now place on her certainty. As terrible as doing this was, knowing and avoiding that she needed to do it was worse.

"How long have you been unhappy?" Jon said, when he could speak again.

Harriet was ashamed of the truth, of the first incontrovertible sign. *Coming back from our first holiday together in Barcelona, and you made a joke about how we'd return in twenty years and I had to stop myself from physically flinching at the idea.* Stop being such a pathetic commitment-phobe, she'd told herself. Happiness wasn't a constant with anyone, it was an elusive, nebulous, fluctuating thing. She'd told herself she couldn't accurately gauge it. No one splits up with anyone the second they feel conflicted or bored. Or maybe they do, but it makes them Warren Beatty in the 1970s.

"I don't know. A few months?"

"Months?! Why not tell me before? Say to me you were having doubts?"

"I had to know my doubts were real, first."

"When would you have said something, if I hadn't proposed last night?"

She looked away. "I don't know."

"You knew you were going to finish this, *break my heart,* and yet you were coming to weekends like this?"

"I didn't know what to say and when to say it. When is the best time to break someone's heart?"

Jon shook his head in disbelief. He gave an answer that was both quintessentially managerial Jon and, she feared, infinitely wise.

"As soon as possible."

7

You get what you pay for, and at the hotel Jonathan had paid for, they got discreet, supposedly incurious serenity at the sight of the newly (un)engaged couple doing a flit—Harriet didn't doubt the staff recognized them, given Jonathan's extensive arrangements.

They might've imagined it was some sort of amorous impulsiveness, like they were about to floor it to Gretna Green, except for the fact Jon and Harriet were both as edgy during the checkout as a pair of bank robbers waiting for the cashier to empty the till.

What on earth is going on there? the staff would say, as soon as Jon's Merc scrunched away with a spray of gravel.

As they dragged their trolley cases past the dining room, Jon said, "Right, it's inclusive, so if we move like lightning . . ."

"You're not seriously suggesting we have breakfast?" Harriet hissed. "It's already seven a.m.!"

Every minute he'd spent in the shower this morning had felt like he was trolling her. Jon's promise of a "very early" departure was now, timewise, well into overlapping on the Venn diagram with "The kind of hour that sixty-somethings get up and potter around with the *Telegraph* over a decaf coffee."

The thought of Jacqueline appearing around a corner, wreathed in Jo Malone English Pear & Freesia and schadenfreude, was making Harriet ill.

"I've got to grab *something* or else it could provoke a migraine," Jonathan hissed. "I'll wrap a croissant in a napkin."

Harriet suppressed fury. "If you must."

For "migraine" he meant *a bit of a headache*—headaches always conveniently and passively aggressively brought on by anything in his environment not entirely to his liking. The way he finicked over his own health needs had always given Harriet a slight shudder. She once saw him tell a waiter in the Wolseley, "No fresh orange juice for me thanks, it's gastric carnage an hour later. Like a Roman candle. Something to do with the acidity."

Harriet didn't want to accompany Jon to the buffet, but she sure as hell didn't want to risk an encounter with anyone they knew while standing on her own, so she followed him through.

They both stopped dead in the doorway at the sight of Barty, alone, calmly picking his way through an absolutely gigantic full English, with three fat sausages, extra granary toast, and a fruit salad on the side.

"Why are you here?!" Jon blurted, and for once, Harriet had to allow that the insolent Barty comeback of "Why are *you* here?" was justified.

Even in the nasty shock of discovery, Harriet spent a split second admiring Barty's audacity. He was surely going down for three counts of "Conspiracy to Defraud" and one of "Impersonating a Sheikh" at the Old Bailey in the future.

In the turmoil of the previous evening and the agony of this morning, neither Jon nor Harriet had strategized for running into his family and their asking where and why they were going.

"I woke up and I was hungry," Barty said, boredly, looking back at a banquet spread that Harriet now saw included two pain au chocolat.

There was a brief yet painful pause.

"Same here! Fancied an early brekkers," Jon said, leaning over to playfully muss his hair, which made Barty wriggle away.

"With your luggage?" Barty said, skeptically.

"Oh, ah . . . no harm in being organized," Jon said, shakily, and they all stared at one another in a Mexican standoff involving blatant lies instead of guns.

"I'm eleven, I'm not an idiot," Barty said, succinctly, and Harriet felt belatedly vindicated that the near-mute who asked his parents to explain everything was indeed a malicious persona.

"Are you trying to avoid seeing my parents and grandparents?" he added, clearly enjoying tearing off the mask to reveal Clever Barty. Barty Poirot.

Harriet, desperate to be gone, said, "Yes, we're doing a runner."

"Why?"

"Jon and I have broken up because I don't want to get married."

"You did say you didn't like weddings," Barty said, insouciantly, and returned to cutting up his hash browns. Finally, a Barraclough who listened to her!

"True enough. Bye then," Harriet said, and saw that Jon looked like he was having a heart attack. She nudged him and gestured to the croissants.

As soon as the car door slammed outside, Jon rounded on Harriet: "Don't you think I have the right to tell my parents before that little berk does?!"

She knew he must be genuinely incandescent, to be slandering his nephew.

"Jon, I know, but we'd been caught red-handed."

"We could've fobbed him off!"

"How? I couldn't think of a single innocuous reason why we'd be legging it at this hour, could you?"

"Well, if you'd given me a chance, before blabbing, *Oh, I dumped him, I dumped his ass, he dwells alone in a hovel in Dumpstown.*"

Harriet said nothing, having forgotten that Jon trying to speak "street" was worse than him telling waiters about his bowel movements.

"I'm really sorry. I did say we shouldn't risk the dining room."

"They'll be ringing me in ten minutes' time now! Demanding explanations! And guess what, I don't really have any? Turns out Harriet doesn't love me and the thought of marrying me is like an EARLY DEATH!"

". . . Do you want me to speak to them?"

"NO, I FUCKING DON'T! THAT WOULD BE REALLY WEIRD."

He was port colored, working himself to hysteria, and Harriet didn't know what she could do other than stay calm. She wasn't insured to drive the Mercedes either. She really needed Jon to make good on his promises or she'd be waiting for an Uber, concealed in a ditch. She imagined pin-dropping her location in a roadside bush.

Eventually, breathing heavily, Jon resentfully thrust his key in the ignition and roared out of the hotel grounds as if he were in the Grand Prix. Harriet inwardly let out a huge sigh.

It was an odd thought, but as they tore through leafy country lanes full of cow parsley, she wondered if Jon now regretted agreeing to their (partially) successful bolt. After all, they were leaving behind the four people—minus her new pal, Barty the sausage gannet—who'd be appalled at Jon's reasonless mistreatment, at the inconceivable arrogance and stupidity of rejecting him. Jon always wanted to protect and promote Harriet's reputation with his loved ones, but had that expired abruptly, like insurance cover? She had terminated her policy and stopped paying the premiums.

They drove in threatening, unbroken silence back to Leeds. At first, Harriet felt she should say something, but as it continued, she felt respecting his not wanting a conversation was wise.

"You can stay as long as you like until you find somewhere," Jon finally said, with wounded gallantry, as they passed through the electric gates to his house. It seemed a semblance of Jon normality had returned. "If you're genuinely determined to do this."

"Thank you," she said, ignoring the last part.

As they got out of the car, Harriet noticed the uneaten squashed pastry in the map pocket of the driver's car door.

In the hallway, Jon checked his phone, scowled, said nothing, and strode off to make calls in the garden.

8

In the atmospheric, dimly lit gloaming of the deserted restaurant dining room in Headingley, Harriet's friend Lorna leaped from her seat, pushing her chair back with a loud scrape and theatrically clutching her collarbones.

"Oh FUCK YES! I thought you were going to tell me you were MARRYING THE CLOWN. OH GOD, THE RELIEF. I'm shaking here, I'm shaking, look at me!"

Lorna held out her hands for inspection of the tremors and Harriet blinked in surprise, momentarily speechless.

She'd told Lorna she wanted to tell her something, and Lorna had said guardedly, "All right, will our usual Thursday night date at my place do?" They pretty much always met for weeknight lock-in drinks at Lorna's restaurant, Harriet's job preventing most Friday and Saturday plans.

Lorna had looked wary on Harriet's arrival, and Harriet felt she *saw* her brace as she made her announcement. However, at the words, "I've left Jon," Lorna exploded like a ticker-tape parade. *Clown?*

"You . . . didn't like Jon?" Harriet turned this idea over in her mind while she worked out how she felt about it. She didn't think she'd been rosy spectacled in this matter—she had judged Lorna's feelings toward Jon as hovering somewhere around "good-natured, mild contempt." Yet this level of jubilation had really startled her.

Harriet decided she was three-quarters intrigued and a quarter defensive of Jon, mostly out of guilt.

Lorna sat down again. "I mean also, sorry for your loss or whatever I'm supposed to say"—Harriet belly-laughed at this—"but it was one hundred percent completely the right decision, you know that?"

Harriet nodded, sadly. "I feel awful that I hurt him so much, though. I should've done it ages ago, not let it drift until he imagined we were going to get married."

Obviously, having kids stayed as an unformed, hazy expectation too. Unlike marriage, Harriet had no objection, though equally they'd never discussed it. She suspected Jon's family wouldn't like pregnancies among unweds, so he thought he'd fix A to move smoothly to B. It was amazing the size of icebergs you could mutually ignore, really.

"Did I *like* Jon . . . ?" Lorna continued. "I didn't actively loathe him or anything. But . . . I felt his effect on you was pernicious and he was completely wrong for you. The longer your relationship went on, the less time I had for him. Yes, all right, there's sufficient material there to say dislike. You could certainly make a miniskirt from the amount of fabric of my dislike."

"So if I had been saying I was marrying Jon, I'd have gone

the rest of my life not knowing my best friend detested my husband?"

"Oh no." Lorna barked a laugh. "I'd have told you. I'd have risked it. I thought I was going to have to tonight, that's why I was absolutely bricking it."

Ah. The adrenaline powering Lorna's rejoicing was principally due to avoiding what she'd anticipated might be a traumatic falling out.

"This calls for the good wine and the better music," Lorna said, jumping up again to first stab at her phone to play George Michael on her duck-egg-blue Roberts Beacon Bluetooth speaker (everything in the place was high-end hipster kitsch), then marching over to authoritatively riffle through the illuminated fridges behind the bar.

In a previous lifetime, Lorna had worked for a mobile phone company and hated it. In her late twenties, she got a big compensation payout when she broke her leg falling into an uncovered manhole. ("They didn't need to know I'd had a party pack of Desperados and was doing the *Pulp Fiction* dance with Gethin from IT in order to get off with him. Needless to say, I got no fucking action with my leg in traction, he didn't even call.")

She used both the recuperation period and the cash to relaunch her life as the owner of Divertimento, a bistro-bar serving Mediterranean dishes. The Dive, as she always called it, was her baby, and "much like a parent, I spend all my time stressed and knackered by it, yet somehow never loving it any less."

Lorna plonked a bottle of orange wine between them, and as she poured it out, Harriet described the ring-box-on-a-plate farrago.

Lorna's mouth fell open. "You call that misjudgment; know what I call it? Massively selfish. Only someone who didn't really care about the *actual qualities of the person he was proposing to* would pull such shit. He treated you like a prize pet pig. Feeding you acorns and taking you to show."

"He isn't that bad! He isn't callous. He'd not think of it that way."

"If he's only treating you as a vacuous trophy by accident, Hatley, and he's not *intending* to do it . . . what's the meaningful difference in outcome anyway? He's still doing it."

"Hmmm."

She'd never thought of Jon in these philosophical terms before. If you blithely assume everything should go your way, is it that different from fixing it in your favor? If he forgot to consider Harriet's feelings, was it a world away from not caring what they were?

She had dwelled since on how completely absent her wishes had to have been from his accounting. The mental process must've gone: I Love Harriet ✍ I Love My Family ✍ I Love the Idea of Marrying Her = Bingo, It's All Love. Yet without noticing "I" prefixed every aspect.

"And I had an issue with the money," Lorna said, after taking a hearty swig of her wine. "I never said anything because I know you're not materialistic. He bought you, and what's more, he knew full well he was doing it."

This was clearly Lorna at last breathing out, getting comfy, after two years in a constrictive corset. (And Lorna might be in a literal corset; tonight she was wearing a banana-yellow chiffon prom dress and hot-pink Birkenstocks. Divertimento was known for the wild fashion of its bleached-blond owner-proprietor. Jon once said everything Lorna wore looked like "She lost a bet," which wasn't said in approval and yet actually described the thrill of her style brilliantly. Except she'd always won the bet, in Harriet's opinion.)

"So . . . that suggests I was for sale, which is my fault?" Harriet said.

"No. It was more insidious than that. Whenever you were in danger of coming to your senses in a period of quiet reflection, it was 'How about a weekend in Reykjavik!' or 'Let's go to this incredible place in York to try the tasting menu,' or 'Have your friends round for dinner in my palace and I'll chuck my wine cellar around.'"

Eesh, Harriet had forgot that. Jon had produced a bottle worth a grand when everyone was in their cups. It looked flash but put everyone on edge, suddenly having to switch from post-prandial, carefree raucousness to mumbling their polite appreciation as he somewhat pompously talked them through its "cherry and blackcurrant nose." They'd had tense words afterward, Jon confused that largesse could ever be taken badly.

"If he'd worked in Specsavers, the Barraclough grift would've been much shorter," Lorna concluded.

"I don't see how that isn't on me, though, if you're saying I wouldn't have stayed if he was skint?"

"It wasn't that you wanted him to spend money on you, but . . . He created gratitude in you. Constantly. You felt gratitude that he was so obsessed with you, and gratitude at all his mad spoiling to demonstrate it, and that gratitude made you think you owed him the relationship. He used his spending to *oblige* you and control things. It wasn't generosity, it was a messed-up power dynamic."

Harriet grimaced. She'd have to think on this, but she didn't see how she could be innocent. Then again, she remembered times when trying to go Dutch with Jon caused such a fraught showdown, she gave up. It was, she realized with hindsight, disempowering.

"Nor did he remotely pass my Day Three at Glastonbury test," Lorna said. "Which is foolproof, in my opinion."

"What's that again?"

"It's the third day of the festival. It's a rainy, muddy year, someone in the chemical truck that cleans the Portaloos has pressed the wrong button and sprayed gallons of actual human shit straight into the dance tent, covering both of you. You're subsisting on those foil trays of compacted noodles that have three slivers of greasy onion in them, the cider hangover's kicking you like a donkey. Toploader are the Sunday headliner. But. Are you having a laugh about it?"

"That is a harsh test, Lorna."

"Born of much experience. If it's right, terrible adversity somehow makes your chemistry shine brighter. That's when you find out if it's genuine joy in each other's company: if it can make the worst times good or reveal if your relationship relies on all the trappings."

"I'm never going to meet anyone that makes me think not being coated in feces is a 'trapping.'"

They looked at each other and both collapsed in laughter. Harriet felt a pang of guilt at Jon's disgust if he witnessed the scene.

"Apologies, I know I'm being Lorna Plus tonight. I'm so glad you've seen the light. Also," Lorna spoke more quickly, "you wanted kindness, and I know why. I'm sure it *felt* kind."

Their eyes met and Harriet's throat felt tight. They rarely spoke about Before Jon, but somehow it was always there, like a sleep paralysis demon squatting in the bedroom shadows.

Lorna returned to a lighter tone: "I was starting to get seriously worried. I gave you and him eighteen months, tops. This is why, if you'd told me you'd said yes this weekend, I was going to have to put our friendship on the line to say, *Oh no you fucking don't.* Good women are not a rewards system for silly men."

Harriet hooted. "It wouldn't have put it on the line."

"Might've ruled me out as a bridesmaid, though, huh?" Lorna said. "How's living in Jon's spare room going? Was it a headache choosing which one?"

"It's . . . bad," Harriet said. "But only because I feel so bad about it. Jon's being nice and giving me space. Of which there's lots anyway, as you say."

"Is he now. We need you out sharpish, then. Rox will have somewhere." Their friend Roxanne was an estate agent for a company that did rentals as well as sales. She normally completed what Lorna called their "Dark Triad" but had an unmissable work event that evening, if drinking acidic warm white wine with honking bros in Hackett shirts was unmissable.

"I'm also relieved that you didn't marry Jon, buy a house with him, have kids, and only then come to your senses," Lorna said. "He was super nice as a partner, but I predict he'd be one hell of a vindictive ex if you had to unentangle anything."

"Jon?! No." Harriet laughed, and she was gratified to be completely sure of herself for once in this conversation. "He couldn't be more considerate and respectful. I was even surprised he swore at me in the conversation when I finished it."

"Harriet, you only know Boyfriend Jon, not Business Jon. I doubt Captain Gravy got to be MD by cuddling everyone."

Harriet laughed again, shaking her head. "He's currently trying to develop a macaroni and cheese with kale, he's not Tony Soprano."

"As I say, I'm glad he has no hooks in you, so we're never going to find out."

An hour and a half later, feeling the most stable she'd felt in days thanks to Lorna's support, Harriet got back to Jon's house and found a note stuck to the fridge:

H (only if you want to!) pots labelled 1, 2, and 3 are a baba ganoush recipe we're trying out, let me know which you like? Pretty sure 2 is shower grout, not to unduly influence the results. Jx

Lorna was right about so much, but wrong about Jon.

9

Jon had been the final date in a string of about a dozen woeful encounters, transacted via an app to find your soul mate. It trumpeted that it was "designed to be deleted." Harriet certainly agreed with this description, as time went on.

Aged thirty-two, she should've ignored the wholly concocted peril of "having passed thirty while single."

Harriet knew Jon was the end of this particular road before she met him. She'd had second thoughts on the day, along the lines of *I can't face another night like the others.* She was folding her cards and leaving the casino, and therefore, tried to cancel on him.

She thought the tricky "it's not you, it's me (and how can it be you, I've not even met you yet)" exchange deserved the respect and nuance of a phone call, however awkward that might be. But when she rang, she got the dead tone of a phone that had been switched off. An exploratory WhatsApp was left on Unread.

She later found out Jon had been deep in the warren of a factory testing hot water crust pastry for a cheese and pineapple pie. ("Misconceived," he said later.) Harriet never told him why she'd been trying to get through. Perhaps the fault in their stars had been there from the outset. They were the cheese and pineapple pie.

Given her conscience wouldn't let her no-show, Harriet got her closest thing to glad rags on, a gray woolen dress that looked nice with red lipstick, which she rubbed off in the taxi, worrying it was too provocative a signal. She girded her loins for another evening of working out how many drinks were polite—but not to the point of misleadingly encouraging—and took up a seat in her beloved Alfred Bar.

Harriet was hopeless at internet dating. Really, just shit at it. She didn't sell herself well, didn't choose well. By contrast, Lorna and Roxy were both masters, always habitually seeing someone or other for lighthearted larks, queuing offers up like hits on a playlist. At first, Harriet bought into their encouragement that she simply wasn't confident enough. She would be sensational once she hit her stride! *Nope.*

Harriet ended up wondering at how unassertive she must be, or how desperate she must've seemed, given the distaste and outrage her post-date polite rejections met with. She wasn't remotely prepared for the volley of passive aggression a simple "exercising of her right to choose her sexual partners" met with.

Oh come on, Harriet!! You've not given this a chance. How about we try next week?

Yeah I know I said I wanted a second date but when I thought about it, I realised I wasn't bothered either actually. Onwards & upwards eh, have a nice life

What exactly is a "spark" and would you really expect to find one after an hour and a half?

That's a shame I thought we had a great time. tbh getting really worn down by the way women say they're looking for a nice man then bin you off for vague reasons.

Dave is typing . . .

Dave is typing . . .

Dave is typing . . .

Dave is typing . . .

Dave is typing . . .

OK whatever.

"I see the issue here," Lorna said. "You don't do casual. Every encounter ends up having meaning for you. What Dave Is Typing thought of me would live in my brain for a fraction of a microsecond. You always care what people think of you, which is wonderful, but sometimes to your detriment."

Roxy—usually more circumspect than Lorna, though to be honest "more circumspect than Lorna" was a most fragrant goat prize—concurred. "Block them and move on."

Lorna had offered an absolutely on-the-money description of Harriet's psychological makeup, except Harriet wanted a boyfriend, not therapy breakthroughs.

Actually, the app had made her wonder if she *did* want a boyfriend.

Singlehood had a lot to recommend it, she realized, even if the rent on her city flat was fairly crippling. She was skint, but complete. Thanks, app. She long-pressed the image on the phone screen so the icons wobbled and clicked the X to rid herself of it. She had only the formality of this Jonathan Barraclough with the uncontactable phone to endure. With one bound, she'd be free.

So there was Harriet, on one last job before retirement, swinging her feet, sipping a red wine, under Alfred Bar's ceiling jangle of mismatched pendant lights. He was twenty minutes late, and although she didn't know this man, something in his fastidiously polite and grammatical correspondence made her think this was unusual.

A bloke who looked like the spitting image of that tennis player crashed through the doors and roared, "HAVE YOU GOT AN ICE BUCKET OR SOME SORT OF SIMILAR RECEPTACLE?!" at the frightened bar staff, who surrendered a washing-up bowl, and proceeded to puke violently into it, observed by the stunned clientele.

One of the bartenders handed him a napkin and he dabbed at his mouth.

"Food poisoning," he gasped to the general company, when he got alternative use of his throat muscles back. "Occupational hazard. I'm so sorry." Louder: "Never eat a Scotch egg made by a Chelsea fan!"

The room erupted in a light smattering of applause, and he gave a small courtly bow. He darted off to the men's room, insisting he'd rinse the washing-up bowl ("No, no," he insisted, "you can't be dealing with that, you're not paid enough!").

Harriet pondered what had happened; at least this would be the shortest date yet. She finished her wine and prepared to leave. What was the etiquette here? Would he prefer her to simply disappear, like she hadn't seen the vomiting?

She opted to stay and do the proper goodbyes and "get well soons." Though she wouldn't have blamed him if he hid in the loos until she'd gone.

To her surprise, an impressively unrumpled man reappeared by her table.

"I think it's fair to say that's the worst possible first impression I could've made. Like Tony Blair in 1997, at least I can say things can only get better."

They both laughed, Harriet with a surprised delight.

"I work in recipe testing, so I always carry a toothbrush, toothpaste, and mouthwash with me," he said, slapping a canvas kit out of his pocket and unrolling it on the table by way of proof, as if he were Crocodile Dundee showing a Sheila his knives. "I'm still good to go if you are."

"Aren't you too unwell?!" Harriet said, in wonder.

"Oh no. I'm used to this in my line of work, one and done." He paused, obviously realizing that bragging about your prowess at regurgitation wasn't very sexy. "Not that it happens often! But even with the best health and safety, with the number of factories I visit, sooner or later you encounter something a bit whiffy. The tragedy here is it was only the office potluck to raise money for Guide Dogs for the Blind. What were you drinking?"

Jonathan went to get the round—now something of a celebrity in Alfred's, he got them comped—and Harriet had to admire his sangfroid.

Despite this date being a total No Hoper from the get-go—and that was before the man honked up his lunch—it had an unexpected advantage: it was unburdened of any expectations. It really didn't matter how it went. Harriet started to genuinely enjoy herself, and it was that double-plus sort of enjoyment you feel when it's come out of left field.

She warmed to Jon. He wasn't someone she'd usually find herself with, and that started to become attractive in itself.

Harriet liked how he had no qualms at admitting his sensitivities, and how he listened intently to her speak, laughing heartily and properly at her attempts at humor. She'd been taken aback by how many men would only offer a quick tight smile of appreciative tolerance, that conveyed, *I see what you're trying to do, and if I had time, I would give you notes on the effort.*

Jonathan had been so badly bullied at his all-boys private school he'd moved to a public school at his request, where he became popular and happy.

"I kind of reinvented myself. It taught me a lot of life skills, a lot of coping mechanisms that have served me well," he said. "It's possibly left me more shy around the opposite sex than I might be."

She could see how his personality had been molded: the impeccable manners and slightly upright, older-than-his-years bearing, the eagerness to please. Harriet even found herself feeling a whisper of protectiveness.

Inevitably, the question came from Jon: "What about your parents?"

"They're both dead."

"Gosh, I'm sorry. Do you mind if I ask how?"

"They both died of cancer within a year of each other, by the time I was six years old."

"Oh my God!"

"I can't really remember it, obviously. My grandparents brought me up. My mum's parents. In Huddersfield."

"Oh, that's so hard. I'm so sorry," Jon said.

"Hey, Huddersfield's not that bad!" Harriet said, yet Jon's expression remained bleak.

"Are your grandparents still with us?"

"No, they died by the time I was in my mid-twenties."

"Oh God."

"It was very sad but it wasn't unexpected, they made good ages. They were grandparents."

"Yet you're all alone?"

"I have good friends. I have aunts and uncles and cousins, loads on my dad's side in Ireland. I don't feel alone."

Jon shook his head. "Poor thing," he muttered.

"Thank you, but I'm not a poor thing," Harriet said, in an unusual moment of being forthright. She'd tucked away quite a lot of wine on an empty stomach. "Please don't look sad for me, as if I'm now a Thomas Hardy heroine. My upbringing was different, but it wasn't sad. It was actually a really good childhood. Pitying me feels like a bit of a value judgment on my life, although I know that's not how it's intended."

"Fair enough," Jon said, looking rather startled. "Pity certainly isn't what I've been feeling this evening." After a long pause he said, "I could absolutely destroy a curry, could you?"

Harriet laughed. "Definitely."

They went on for dinner, and at the end of the night Jon said, making no move whatsoever and handing her into a taxi, "I'd love to see you again, if you wanted to?" and Harriet said yes, without hesitation.

She would describe her evenings with Jon from then on as easy. Harriet's rejected suitors might be irked to know that she'd dispensed with "the spark" as criteria. Jon had spent a full thirty-five minutes explaining why David Gray's *White Ladder* was his favorite album and scoffed at Harriet liking "trendy obscure stuff." (Tindersticks weren't that obscure, surely.) There was no spark. But sparks caused fires.

It was four dates until Jon suggested "dinner at his."

He'd never mentioned being such a swaglord. Harriet was quietly impressed he'd not revealed this earlier. Turned out that Jon's place overlooked tennis courts, had electric gates and a specific fridge for chilling wine, and—unrelatedly—he asked endlessly what you'd like him to do in his super-king-size, top-of-the-range memory foam bed. (*Maybe stop asking that constantly* was Harriet's unspoken response.)

He felt like a tour guide to a different life, one who was prepared to work very hard for his five-star customer review. And God, he seemed smitten with Harriet. She'd catch him looking at her sometimes, a sappy expression on his face, simply worshipping the fact she existed.

Harriet didn't think she was a narcissist, but in those early days of novelty, it was hard not to be affected by how intoxicated he was by her. She wasn't enough of a narcissist to think she'd ever be idolized like that again.

10

Harriet awoke early to the unwelcome sound of water spattering on the Velux window in Jonathan's spare room on Saturday, and by the time she was on the M62, it was a wipers-on-full-speed, pavement-rinsing downpour. It was the kind of rain from a slate-gray sky that had fully settled in for the day and *might* think about easing off by the evening, if you were good. She had a longer journey than usual to the Radisson Blu in Manchester, and Harriet prayed the marrying couple, Rhian and Al, would laugh the inconvenience off.

Hopes of such resilience were dashed as she was shown into the spacious bridal suite. Rhian was starfished and sobbing, facedown on the bed, still in her tartan flannel pajamas, her mum anxiously holding her hair back so that the expensively salon-glossed curls didn't get mussed. The makeup artist was solemnly unpacking her kit for a second time, accepting her previous efforts had been for naught.

"This is a storm to bring the bones of the lepers up," commented Rhian's Nana Pat, who, it must be said, wasn't helping. Nana Pat seemed very much a woman to embrace any misfortune.

"*God's sake, Mum!*" Rhian's mother, Lynn, mouthed at her furiously, making a zipping-lips gesture, at which Nana Pat shrugged and returned to sipping what turned out to be Harveys Bristol Cream in a teacup.

"It's like . . . calming app rain, the sleep app rain," Rhian said, lifting her face briefly from the duvet, before resuming her howling.

Harriet thought better than to say, *That's ironic,* and busied herself taking photographs of the gauzy, sparkled bridal gown on its hanger. When she was done, Lynn discreetly suggested she leave them alone while she talked Rhian around. "If she doesn't pull herself together soon it's thirty-five grand down the chute."

Harriet never said this, obviously, but so many weddings seemed to come with such dizzyingly elevated hopes of being a Hashtag PerfectDay that they could only end in squabbling and misery. Not only did being a Mrs. Someone not appeal to her, but she didn't want the stress. Harriet had once seen a couple have a meltdown over whether their personalized coasters were round or square. By the time you were bellowing, "*THE TILE SHAPE LOOKS LIKE SOMETHING FROM A GREENE KING PUB, YOU TWAT!*" at your furious fiancé, you'd drifted quite a long way from the point of it all.

Harriet ended up outside in the hotel reception's grand stone entranceway, eating a hash brown roll wrapped in a paper napkin with the three bridesmaids. They observed the monsoon in the dry, from only an arm's length distance, as if they were under a waterfall.

Hollie, Katie, and Jo had foam rollers on their heads and strong Yorkshire accents. They were smoking Marlboro Lights held aloft in French manicured hands, hotel dressing gowns thrown over the stretchy flesh-colored tubing that provided the foundation for today's outfits, fluffy slippers on their feet. Harriet always liked the "chrysalis to butterfly" of the preparations, and the trio cheerfully agreed to a snap in an archway, the torrent as background, as if they were still in wardrobe on the set of a dramatic music video. Harriet might not desire a wedding herself, but she still loved photographing people who did enjoy them.

"I know she's raging that her tarot reader told her she should choose today," said Hollie, flicking ash onto the ground. "But it's fuckin' Manchester? What are the chances? Not a million to one, is it? If you're this bothered about rain, go abroad?"

Harriet thought this was a fair point and that it was also terrible luck to have stumbled onto an unreliable tarot reader. You should always check that a tarot reader was professionally quality accredited in their field before taking their advice. Otherwise you could so easily end up with any old fraud with a pack of cards and a silk turban they bought off eBay, making stuff up for money. She made a mental note to tell Lorna this and realized she'd never made mental notes to tell Jon funny things. He'd have completely missed the point, slow blinked, and said, Are *there validated tarot readers?*

"She did look at Cyprus, but her Nana Pat wouldn't travel any further than Manchester, she wouldn't even come to Harrogate because she doesn't like the food," said Jo. Ha. Nana

Pat being the architect of this chaos felt about right. Plus, it was the first Harriet had heard of a Harrogate cuisine.

"You've just got to get on with it, haven't you?" said Katie. "My cousin got a stress rash on her neck on the day so bad that she had to wear a bolero jacket over a strapless Marchesa dress, and she'd had her tits done specially. Total waste."

"Not a total waste. The same tits went on the honeymoon," Jo said, stubbing her cigarette out, and Harriet was so taken with their sorority, she almost wished she smoked. Imagine if she had married Jon. Country house hotel. Lorna looking resigned yet dejected in her bridesmaid dress, Roxy preening delightedly in hers. Jon, in a cravat and in his element. It wasn't a kindness to accept a proposal from someone you weren't in love with, however much rejection felt like wanton cruelty.

"Are you married, Harriet?" said Hollie, pleasantly.

"No, and I dumped my long-term boyfriend last weekend. I'm living in his spare room."

"Oh, that's brutal, sorry," Hollie said. "There's eight ushers today, though, so plenty to go around, hahahaha."

Oh God. Harriet had forgot Al was a madcap-lad groom, no doubt she'd have to do an ushers' "squad strut" photo with Peroni bottles. There was a lot to be said for the calm and order of unpopular introverts.

"Do not touch Bruce, whatever you do," Jo said. "Awful in bed, like riding a mechanical bull."

"So gorgeous he doesn't think he has to try, that's why," Hollie said. "Also avoid Batley Chris."

"Why is he called Batley Chris?"

"The other Chris isn't from Batley," Jo said.

"No Bruce or Chrises from Batley," Harriet agreed.

"Right, do we reckon she's rallied?" Katie said. "Let's get a bottle of bubbles from the bar and take it up. She needs to be told it doesn't matter if it's shitting it down, the human spirit is bigger than this."

"Yes!" said Hollie. "We'll do a preshow prayer huddle with her. Time to find her Sasha Fierce."

"See you there," Harriet said. Were these three always this entertaining? She'd like to book them for funerals.

Harriet feared the worst in the bridal suite, heading back with camera lowered in anticipation, but moments later Lynn threw the door open to her with a grit-teeth smile and made a fingers-crossed signal in front of her body.

Inside the suite, a composed Rhian in a cotton robe was sat daintily drinking a V&T through a straw as the makeup artist primped at her repaired face with a tiny brush and "We Found Love" pumped away motivationally in the background.

Apparently, an encouraging FaceTime with the groom, a stiff drink, and some Rihanna on the stereo had done wonders, her mum explained, under her breath.

"Knock knock," Hollie called from the hallway, and then she, Jo, and Katie conga-danced into the room, to much squealing delight from the bride. "Turn the music UP! We found love IN A RAINY PLACE!"

Lynn gamely joined the conga, and Harriet tried to get a few photos, though she doubted they'd win any awards.

"C'mon, Nana Pat!" Katie shrieked, and hoisted her unsteadily to her feet. "And you, Harriet! Put the camera down!"

Harriet consented to join the back of the conga, which did two awkward laps of the bed and went into the bathroom before realizing they couldn't execute a turn and backed out again, Hollie yelling in an automated voice: "THIS VEHICLE IS REVERSING."

As they disbanded, Nana Pat announced, "If one of us falls here we all go down like nine pins. That's what took my friend Oonagh's husband, Roy Plomley."

"A conga line?" Harriet said.

"A fall!"

"Mum, can you try to think positive, please?" Lynn hissed, and Pat said, "There's nothing positive about the way he went, they removed the feeding tube."

Nana Pat aside, the mood seemed to have swung wildly upward.

"Thanks for bearing with us," Lynn said to Harriet. "Sorry for this fuss. You must've seen it all by now?"

"Every wedding is unique," Harriet said, smiling. "This is uniquer than most."

The strangest thing about her job was how you had an intense, access-all-areas pass to a stranger's world, this tiny, intimate snapshot of lives in progress at a crucial point. Then you never saw them again.

It was quite bittersweet, in a way.

She could probably forgo the pleasure of tons more Nana Pat, though.

DURING THE SECOND, and what she feared wouldn't be the last, conga line of the day, Harriet saw her phone flashing with a call from Roxy and excused herself into the corridor—away from the decibels of Rihanna's "Umbrella"—to answer it. The bridesmaids had made alcoholic lemonade from lemons.

"Have I got a house for you!"

"Have you?"

"New listing today. Proper beautiful semi in Meanwood, a quiet street, one of my faves. It's a very reasonable rent because he's looking to fill the room quickly, and *you should see* your en suite bedroom and the garden."

". . . *My* en suite . . . ?"

"But call him now, absolutely NOW, to arrange your visit! It'll go in a heartbeat when I put it online in an hour."

Harriet's heart sank. She'd instructed Roxy she'd rather have a place to herself, even though she knew the cost would be punishing. Hell is other people. In usual Roxy fashion, she'd listened, discarded this information as burdensome, and plowed on with her better ideas.

"*He?* The other tenant's a man?"

"It's the twenty-first century. Men can be people too. Plus you've got an en suite. No bathroom sharing. That is key to housemate harmony, in my professional opinion."

"Why's he looking to fill the room fast?"

"Apparently there were problems with the last one, so he booted him and wants someone in ASAP. Can't have it empty because his mortgage is a bitch, I'm guessing."

"The other occupant is also the landlord?"

"Yeah, he owns it."

"Why did he buy a house that's too big for him?"

"Harriet, I am the letting agent, not his official biographer."

Living with her own landlord? What could be more appealing? He'd be having cold rage fits at every coffee cup ring.

Harriet thanked Roxy for her discovery, thinking it'd be easier to deter her via messaging, and rang off. Her WhatsApp pinged with a set of photos. She leaned against the wall of the corridor and clicked through them, as the champagne-laced squawking continued in the bridal suite.

All right, it *was* lovely. Aesthetic splendor was not a thing Harriet expected or wanted in her stopgap rental, and she was surprised to be so carried away by it.

The house was at the end of a row, a handsome box in proper old gray Yorkshire stone, covered in Virginia creeper. The door was a vibrant glossy orange. The interiors were an exercise in discreet peacockery—lots of dramatic yet dusty wall colors, fashionable appliances, and potted palms. Lorna would approve.

Not to stereotype, but if this was a straight man, he was one with an arty design job. Harriet had never known one who'd choose a Coca-Cola-red Smeg fridge, or the star pendant light in the front room, or the sleigh bed in the master bedroom.

The garden was abundant with roses, and there was a swing seat at the far end. Off to the side, a long picnic table had a canopy of fairy lights strung above it. Every setting implored you to fill it. It said *Insert Your Life Here*. Not that Harriet had much of one.

Damn you, Roxy. She'd found something that was nothing like the brief and somehow exactly what Harriet wanted.

Another ping. A business card for a "Cal Clarke" and a text.

Seriously H call him because I fully expect this to disappear in the blink of an eye. Check out the master suite bathroom. I want a copper bath, a chandelier, and that blue-black paint 😍

Actually that'd been the only element of the decor to give Harriet pause. It was chic but also a bit "sex people." That said, she'd not be using his quarters. As long as he didn't have sex in it too loudly.

Sod it, she'd ring Mr. Cal Clarke, she'd find out he somehow had seven informal visits lined up for Monday already and it'd not be worth being the eighth, and that'd be that. She didn't want to ignore Roxy's find as she could be petulant as well as impetuous—she might take it badly if Harriet didn't follow it up.

A youthful, confident-sounding man answered after two rings.

"Hello, this is Cal."

"Hi, I'm Harriet Hatley. I'm interested in the room you're letting and wonder if I could make an appointment at the start of next week to view it?"

Was there anything worse than cold-calling a stranger?

"Oh, hi. That was fast! The ad's not even live yet, is it?"

Harriet squirmed and hummed and ahhed noncommittally. She had a very different constitution to Roxy.

"I'm busy Monday and Tuesday with work, actually. I've got something on Wednesday too. I should've thought of this when I chucked the listing up, shouldn't I?"

"Ah, OK. Maybe Thursday?"

"Thursday is . . . sod it, do you know, I've got to be honest, I hate this rigmarole. The last guy spent an hour chatting on my sofa and got through two cups of tea and a flapjack, and I still failed to spot the fact he was a loon. We could just do this on the phone, now?"

"OK . . . I haven't seen the house?"

"You've got the link?"

"Yep."

"That's pretty much the deal. Fully furnished. There's no rising damp or car up on bricks we maneuvered the photos around, it's a nice-looking place in good nick. You've got the second bedroom with an en suite, and I work long hours so I won't be competing with you for the kitchen much either. Rent is bills included and that covers the cleaner too."

Ooh. Financially, Harriet couldn't fault it. It *would* be nice to have spare income . . .

"That's very fair. What do you do for a living?"

"I'm a politics reporter for the *Yorkshire Post.*"

"Oh!" With that information, Harriet's most basic sort of apprehensiveness at having not met this Cal faded away. Not only did she stereotype men who could do interiors well as gay, but it seemed she also stereotyped men doing white-collar, respectable-sounding jobs as Not Murderers. As if there was any solid precedent for thinking that. What was a murder-y job, anyway?

A pause. "What's that noise?" Cal said, as the hens clattered loudly past the suite door shrieking harmonies to Calvin Harris.

"Oh, I'm a photographer." Harriet moved slightly farther down the corridor. She had no idea why she spontaneously omitted the "wedding"; that was an air and grace she'd had at the start of her career—"I don't want to be pigeonholed!"—that she'd long ago dispensed with. Maybe because Cal was quite well-spoken, and she felt Yorkshire-accented common.

"Right. That must be . . . fun?"

"On and off," said Harriet, conscious that he could probably now make out the offstage lusty shouting along to Guns N' Roses' "November Rain."

"How old are you, if that's not an impolite question?" Cal said, and Harriet felt sure this was because he could overhear it. "Only I'm thinking if you're twenty-four, your 'having parties' interest might be higher than mine at thirty-two, and we're probably best off knowing that up front."

"An ancient thirty-four and antisocial as hell, to be honest."

"Brilliant news. So, to summarize, you're not a guy, so that's got to be a head start. You're a thirty-four-year-old loner. Have you got a habit of walking around completely naked and watching *SNL* clips at ear-splitting volume on your laptop? And not even the good ones. The weird ones where the studio audience are all having heart attacks laughing and you're too British to work out what could possibly be that funny."

Harriet smiled into her handset. "None of that sounds like me."

"And final question, sorry to be indelicate but I've got some PTSD to manage. Do you have a habit of using the downstairs loo with the door open?"

Harriet laughed. "No. Oh God. Does anyone really do that in a shared house?"

"It turns out they do. And he had the en suite, the animal."

Harriet guffawed again.

"So, unless there's anything else you want to ask me, the room's yours, if you want it," Cal concluded.

Harriet felt unprepared for this. Not only could she not think of a reason to refuse, more important, she couldn't think how she'd phrase refusal. *I'll think about it* would sound pompous and, from what little she could tell of the nature of Cal Clarke and the terms of this impromptu offer, would result in a polite yet firm farewell.

"Yes, thank you. I will take it."

They agreed to the sending and signing of a six-month contract and moving in next weekend. Harriet rang off not knowing whether to feel exhilarated at being so decisive or slightly idiotic at being hustled into it, and settled on both.

11

When Harriet got back to Jon's, she was exhausted. She picked up the mood of weddings by osmosis, so, even sober, she felt as if she'd been through the emotional wringer.

Jon wandered out of the front room, holding a large glass of red wine, Sting playing in the background. He was in a striped shirt—one Harriet had once said she liked—with two buttons undone, and she got a disconcerting feeling he was trying to look enticing.

"Join me?" he said, raising his glass.

"Oh, thanks, but no. I want a shower and my bed. It's been a day."

"Ah, well. If you change your mind, I made lamb shanks with mash. There's plenty left in the slow cooker."

He was definitely trying to contrive a date night ambience.

"Thank you," Harriet said.

As she turned the corner, she said, "Oh, Jon. I've found a place to rent in Meanwood, I move in next Saturday."

She expected this to be taken with minor dismay, but Jon's jaw dropped.

"What?! It'll have been two weeks?"

"Roxy was helpful," Harriet said.

"Amazing. Some indecent haste. You really can't bear to be around me, can you?" Jon said, the jazzy atmosphere disappearing in a puff of smoke.

Harriet was too tired to be diplomatic. "What do you think separating means?"

"I didn't think it meant you rushing out so fast there were tire marks on my driveway."

"Was I supposed to stay in your spare room for months?"

". . . Are you on dating sites yet?" Jon said, hesitantly.

"*What?* Are you serious?"

"Yes."

Harriet did a double take. "Yes, Jon, I'm already on five of them and telling the dates I'm not having to not come back to my place, which is your place."

He sniffed. "Just checking."

"What the hell? Why would I be dating days after we ended?"

"How am I meant to understand any of this, Harriet? You seem to think there's a rule book. I'd love to see it if so, because I'm at a loss."

She frowned.

Earlier in the week, Jon had gone out for a game of squash and obviously a heart-to-heart with his friend Gavin. Gav was someone she'd always kept at arm's length, finding him friendly enough, but perfumed with heady base notes of chauvinism and snobbery. She knew Gavin thought she was a scrubber of undistinguished origins who had lucked out in snaring Jon. He'd have gloried in all this, and likely pumped Jon full of

There will definitely be Someone Else, my friend, sorry to break the news, that's women for you.

"I told you there wasn't anyone else."

"What a learning curve this is proving to be," Jon said, gnomically, after a pause, and stalked back to the front room, which seemed a twattish statement, given he'd learned nothing.

It was ironic that in tearing into Harriet for going, Jon had only confirmed to Harriet that it was the right decision.

Dating sites? You don't really land a blow by accusing someone of something ridiculous, she thought, *you only make yourself look ridiculous.* Jon was drifting into paranoia.

Harriet knew why he wanted her to stay longer: he thought he was vividly demonstrating how wrong she'd been. For her to come home to the domestic idyll of lamb shanks and expensive Bordeaux and "Fields of Gold" and start to wonder if she'd been gripped by some skittish madness at the hotel in the Dales. Did he have a fundamental inability to take her seriously? Harriet pulled her shoes off and lay down on the bed.

As she stared at the ceiling, the strangest of messages arrived on her phone.

Jacqueline Barraclough

Now I know Jon said you were having a long engagement but no harm in being prepared. This boutique is absolutely delicious and she has appointments free the week after next . . .

Harriet sat bolt upright and reread the words three times, then a fourth, while she tried in vain to invent a context that made sense of it. What the . . . ? She checked the time and date, in case it had been logjammed in the system for ages. It hadn't, and the "long engagement" detail was distinctly bizarre. That was what Jon offered her during their breakup?

She sprang from the bed and ran into the sitting room, where Jon was on the sofa, staring morosely into the middle distance rather than at the television, wineglass topped to the brim. Many tea lights flickered in his decorative tea light tower.

"Jon," Harriet said, quivering with the adrenaline of the incipient clash, "why have I had a text from your mum suggesting we go bridal dress shopping?"

She held the iPhone up, as if he needed to be reminded what a mobile was.

"Oh. I haven't told them yet." That Jon didn't react with the slightest embarrassment told Harriet that he was in a major huff.

"Uhm, *why*?"

"I decided to put them off until I felt ready to discuss it. That's my right with my family, isn't it? Or did I lose *all* rights here?"

Harriet stiffened at the evident nastiness in his tone, felt an old familiar fear. She forced herself to mimic confidence.

"It's not your right to lie about me, no, nor not to warn me. I'm fielding messages about a wedding that isn't happening from your mum? What the hell am I supposed to say?"

"Ignore her. Fob her off. You've managed it well enough when it suited you."

Jon took a large swig of wine.

"What the fuck is that meant to mean?!"

Jon ignored her.

"You're acting as if I wasn't allowed to make a choice here?" Harriet continued. She was taken aback at how unreasonable he was being. Reason was one of the keynote Jon qualities.

"Oh, you had one. You made it. The bad news is that I get choices too."

Harriet put a palm to her forehead in frustration. "Can you stop enigmatically pronouncing like some sort of Obi-Wan of scorned men and actually discuss this like a human being? It's not OK to put me in a position where I have to lie, is it? I presume you don't want me to reply, 'Sorry, Jackie, has he not said we've split up?'" Harriet waved her phone by way of illustration, but also as a threat.

"I'm seeing them next week at their barbecue, I'll tell them then," Jon said sullenly, and Harriet sensed her implied threat had done the job. "Just ignore it."

Urgh. The Barracloughs' annual barbecue at their sprawling manor in Ilkley, she'd forgotten about that calendar fixture. Jackie made jugs of Pimm's, and Martin Senior manned a top-of-the-range outdoor oven called a Broil King. One time Harriet had timidly asked for a semi-raw sausage to get another few minutes' cooking, and Martin Senior acted as if she'd ridiculed his exposed manhood. "Nonsense, that's the correct texture!" he said, inspecting its Barbie-pink innards. "They're not fairground-quality bangers, you know," he added, to make it clear Harriet was too common to understand an artisanal meat product.

Never having to suffer his parents again was a joyous bonus of leaving Jon, no doubt about it.

Yet Harriet was blindsided by the oddness of Jon's reluctance to tell them. What on earth was he doing?

"What did you tell them to explain why we'd left so early? I thought Barty knew anyway?"

"I told them you had a stomach flu and we were only joshing with Barty. Felt good to undermine the little turd, to be honest. I'm damned if he's going to be town crier of my private business."

So much for Barty being entitled to a grotty phase.

Jon must've gone really all out with the ingratiating bluster to allay their suspicions, after Barty dropped his exclusive bombshell and the happily engaged couple were nowhere to be seen.

"'Stomach flu' the morning after a boozy night is only going to be interpreted as 'hanging out of her arse,' isn't it?" Harriet said, frowning.

"No, I don't think they thought that . . ." Jon said vaguely, which meant: *I didn't think about whether they thought that.*

"This is crazy. When you tell them the truth, they're going to realize you made my illness up?"

"For me to worry about, isn't it?"

It wasn't. As Harriet climbed the stairs, having concluded she'd get no sense out of Jon, she felt the mediocre disgrace of it smeared all over her. It was bad enough she'd ditched the beloved younger son of the Barraclough family, but when it was revealed they'd been bullshitted—and Barty had been right, the poor lamb!—the whole thing would be a scandal.

No doubt they'd take it as proof of how deeply distraught Jon was that he'd do such an out-of-character, desperate thing, and it would intensify their disgust at her.

Oh well. Aside from receiving death stares in chance meetings in department stores, she'd never have to face any of them again.

If there was one thing she was sure of, the Barracloughs weren't the types to offer any *bon voyage!* fond farewells. By leaving Jonathan, she'd made herself a Bad Person. They were one of those families who were hard enough to marry into but would be even worse to divorce out of.

Back in the spare room, Harriet marveled at the stupidity of Jon telling such short-termist, pointless, self-defeating lies. He'd now have the mortification of copping to them over a corn on the cob from the Broil King, probably in earshot of Ilkley's braying high society.

When the answer dawned on her, it was as though she actually had the phantom stomach flu.

Her departure had screwed up a secret timetable.

Jon had gambled he'd have persuaded Harriet to stay by then.

12

The next morning, Harriet walked into the kitchen to find a vision of domesticity: a plate on the island heaped with assorted pastries, a bunch of lilac stocks in a vase, the smell of fresh coffee, Radio 4 trickling out in the background.

"Peace offering," Jon said, from a vantage point behind a newspaper at the far end. "There's more than a cup left in the French press."

"Thanks," she said, neutrally, and helped herself.

The stage management of the scene meant Harriet could only think of Lorna's voice in her head. *He bought you, and what's more, he knew he was doing it.*

"Do you want any help moving? Two cars are better than one."

"It's fine, I can manage," she said. "Thank you, though."

She hoisted herself onto a stool at the island and chose a bun that looked like it was wearing a toupee of grated cheese. It felt rude to decline Jon's provisions and rude to carry anything out of the room, so she was stuck picking at it in the tense atmosphere, wearing the false-insouciant air of a teenager who'd come in well past curfew last night and certainly wasn't going to mention it if her parents didn't. As Harriet tried to chew silently, she considered that was probably the motive behind its purchase: forcing her to have breakfast with Jon. He no doubt meant well, but these minor manipulations were making her even more desperate to be free.

"From the Bakehouse?" she asked. "Really good."

She nearly added she'd miss Roundhay, then knew it would sound like a gibe that she wouldn't miss Jon. She would miss Jon. Just not enough.

"Harriet," Jon said after a minute or so, and she tensed, having suspected something was coming. "Can I say something?"

She nodded while chewing: *Yes, of course.* And thinking: *Here's the price of the baked goods.*

"I'm not proud of what I did with my family. Not telling them up front, I mean. Or how I behaved last night. I've been quite shell-shocked by our finishing, but it's not an excuse."

Pause.

"On my deathbed, I won't want any of this to be playing in the highlights reel. I've taken a step back and looked at myself harder."

He smiled to indicate "joke," and Harriet gave a reciprocal tight smile. She could feel a big fat "but" coming. Coming in the air this morning, as Jon's hero Phil Collins almost had it.

"I laid awake most of last night thinking about us, about what went wrong."

". . . OK," Harriet said. *Please don't let this be another attempt to appeal her decision.* She had empathy for Jon's pain but no way to fix it.

"The thing is—and not in a nasty way, I hasten to add—you think I'm a bit daft, a bit self-parodic. Or un-self-aware at least," Jon said. Harriet swallowed hard and opened her mouth to argue, and he motioned for her to stop. "Let me get to the end. I know you do, most people do. It's partly my own fault for actively giving that impression. It's a protective layer I developed, I think. Being something of an apprentice Alan Partridge. But be careful who you pretend to be, you are who you pretend to be, and all that."

He cleared his throat.

"What I'm saying is, I know I can seem . . . straight-edged and even foolish, but I'm not."

Harriet nodded, not sure what to make of this speech, what move it was in the game of Breakup Battleship.

". . . Because I'm not stupid, I know there's some part of you that you won't let me near. I don't know what it is. I don't know if it's to do with the loss of your parents, or why you're so deliberately vague about most of your twenties. Or if it's to do with that jewelry box you won't let out of your sight."

Harriet remained rigid and impassive, but her skin felt numb.

". . . But by keeping it secret from me—I don't think you realize that it set me up for failure with you from the start. I wish you hadn't. If you'd let me help, I would have done everything I could to help. For whatever reason, you wouldn't or couldn't allow me to try. I think it's a huge loss for both of us. If you ever change your mind and want to talk, even if there's no way back for the two of us, I'll be there for you. Even if . . ." Jon took a shaky breath. "Even if it's some point in the currently unimaginable future for me, where either or both of us are with other people."

Pause.

"That's it. That's all I wanted to say."

Harriet said nothing because she was fairly stunned by this and couldn't begin to work out how to respond.

"I'm guessing you want to go this week without a brouhaha or speeches, so other than this one, I will respect that," Jon said, into the ensuing silence.

"Thank you," Harriet said eventually, in a slightly hoarse voice, wishing she wasn't so dumbly inarticulate in these moments.

She could've contradicted Jon. He deserved better than her lies.

IN THE YEAR she'd lived at Jon's, in their two-year span together, Harriet occasionally felt somewhat Surrendered Wife about the fact that there'd been no way to stamp her personality on it. Everything was so top-of-the-range and European-brand lustrous in his detached residence that there was no reason or space to buy a stick of furniture or a white good (or, to fit with the look, a brushed-steel good). Their taste didn't overlap: Harriet tried putting up some blue fairy lights, and Jon had said they looked like "luminol for blood spray" and taken them down. They had also given him *one of his headaches,* natch.

As she stuffed her car with another black sack of her clothes on the day she left, Harriet was finally grateful for the built-in kitchen, built-in wardrobes, everything-from-Heal's bachelor-pad sterility. Much better not to be working out how to put a sofa or a bed into storage, not to be cramming a five-foot-tall fern into her Golf. It was pathetic really, but the fact virtually nothing here was hers felt like vindication that she was right to go. Or perhaps it was an indictment of her failure to try.

Harriet wondered if her subconscious was way ahead of her—it knew, long before she'd accepted it, she'd never really be long-term mistress of Roundhay. *Hold off on buying the Etsy knickknacks,* it must have whispered.

She could've done with Jon making himself scarce today, but of course he didn't, he hung around twitchily, waiting to make their final goodbye. He was the man who endlessly asked what she wanted yet somehow never thought about what she wanted.

As Harriet slammed the boot on her junk, he strode out onto the driveway in his Penn State University sweatshirt and moccasin slippers, hands jammed in pockets. It wasn't Jon's fault that he was fast becoming an entirely alien creature to her; it was hers for messing with a boy from the right side of the tracks. Preposterous idea.

"This is it, then?"

"Think so," Harriet said, casting a look at her car, feigning to think he meant packing. It had been an effort, with her camera kit, but putting the seats down, she had got everything in. She brushed her hair away from her face and tucked it behind her ears, tightened the band on her plait.

"Will you give me a forwarding address for your mail?"

"Sure. Easiest for me to message you with it," Harriet said.

Jon shielded his eyes against the intense June sun. "Feels like we should have some words befitting the occasion, doesn't it? Not 'see ya.'"

Harriet's chest felt as if it had a concrete block resting on it. She'd not considered, until this second, what she should say in parting. Being a grown-up was so strange. In someone's life and their bed constantly for two years, and then suddenly unable to offer them so much intimacy as a coffee.

"We'll see each other again," Harriet said.

"When?"

"Barty's trial," she said, and this only raised a weak smile.

"Should we shake hands?" Jon looked like he was going to cry; Harriet prayed that he wouldn't.

She stepped forward and put her arms around him, mumbling, "Take care, Jon."

He gripped her tightly and clung on, pushing his face hotly into her shoulder. As they parted, Harriet was careful not to meet his eyes. She knew it was cowardly, but she rationalized that making this more excruciating helped no one, least of all Jon.

"Goodbye, Harriet."

"Bye."

Her heart was blocking her throat as she pulled out of his drive and studiously avoided looking at the immobile figure in the rearview mirror. *Goodbye, Jon. Sorry I hurt you. Sorry our two years ended up only setting you back two years on the wife and mother-of-your-kids hunt.* She didn't mean that unkindly: he wanted that, and she wanted it for him.

As she drove to Meanwood, postcode punched into the GPS, Harriet remembered telling Jon she didn't feel alone on that first date at Alfred.

Was it true now? Had it been true at the time? Her answers were: no and probably not. Harriet had confused her refusal to admit to loneliness for not being lonely.

Who was she kidding? She was on her way to a house she'd never set foot inside before, at the wheel of a hatchback full of her worldly possessions, soul in transit. She gripped the wheel tightly, letting her nails dig into the plastic as she blinked back tears.

Maybe she was cursed to never belong anywhere. "Orphan": a strange word wreathed in tragedy that belonged in old novels, a descriptor that Harriet steadfastly refused to apply to herself. Yet leaving one man's house and moving into a stranger's, she felt it. She let herself say it in her head: *Mum and Dad's.* Imagine having a mum and dad to flee to. She genuinely couldn't. The sentence sounded peculiarly foreign to her; it was a phrase she'd rarely had cause to speak aloud. She remembered finding court letters pronouncing her "a minor bereft of the usual legal guardians."

Harriet shook herself out of the unhelpful wallowing. This was what was called a "hard reset," that was all, and hard resets were hard. She had to shed her existential Freshers' Week flu. Toughen up.

Perhaps her spell in Cal Clarke's party-ready house, in which he never held parties, was going to be transformative. Perhaps the very meaning of her life was contained behind that tangerine door in Meanwood. She'd accept a working washing machine and a separate bin for recycling.

13

There was space on the house's drive for Harriet to park, but she didn't want to seem presumptuous and pulled up on the curb instead. She made a note to self to negotiate terms of access with Cal. She was belatedly remembering how when you moved in with someone, you took on their oddities and peculiarities. She'd not done a flat share since her early twenties, when the other girl got blazing mad if the cereal boxes were turned "the wrong way" in the cupboard and kept an empty pet carrier in her bedroom with teddy bears in it.

She checked her reflection: pale, bug-eyed, and tired. Some people looked older in fatigue; Harriet worried she resembled an angry baby in glasses, like an internet meme.

It was a muggy summer day with the smell of smoldering charcoal briquettes and sputtering sausages on the air, the heaviness of the heat making Harriet long for a chilled drink with condensation on the glass.

She didn't want to make a poor first impression as a hobo clutching a trash bag and decided to make her introductions before unloading. Especially as the foliage-clad house was even more enchanting in person: imagine actually owning a place like this. She belatedly wondered how a newspaper reporter afforded it. She pressed the old-fashioned brass bell, and the door opened, held by a young man in a white T-shirt, washed-out gray jeans, and navy Converse boots. He looked younger than thirty-two, so maybe he wasn't the owner. He looked like the lad you'd call from TaskRabbit to put your shelves up, who'd arrive on a skateboard. (Lorna had shagged a Task-Rabbit helper of this precise description. "It was a task I needed help with, and we were like rabbits.")

"Harriet? Hello," he said, extending a hand for her to shake.

"Cal?" she said, uncertainly, and was taken aback when he nodded. This somehow wasn't the Cal Clarke she had built in her head, who she didn't even know was there until this second.

The real version was average height and medium build and had short dirty-blond hair, the volume on top teased upward like it was thinking about becoming a quiff, and a neat beard, a shade darker than the hair on his head. His pale green eyes were sharp and intense, and he was unarguably good-looking in an "actor in a cop movie playing the fresh-faced recruit from Quantico who'd soon learn what the job was *really* like" way. Harriet was somewhat dismayed by this. She didn't need the weird tension of a prom king preening and imagining himself being crushed on. Zero sexual psychodrama with an on-premises landlord, please. The same way you didn't want a hot doctor for a pap smear.

"Did you drive here?" Cal said, craning to look.

"Yeah."

"Feel free to park outside the house, I don't have a car."

"Oh, thanks!"

He ushered her indoors. The house smelled of berry-scented cleaning products, so he must've made an effort; then she recalled he had a cleaner.

"Your quarters are at the end of the landing upstairs, but maybe you want to have a look round first?" he said, gesturing for her to step into the front room.

"Sure. Thank you," she said. The look was old-meets-new, preserved period features, copper light shade, and crayon-bright furniture in front of an old, tiled fireplace. An immaculate, oyster-colored carpet said, *We don't have kids or pets.*

"You have really good taste," Harriet said, taking in the gilt mirror on the mantelpiece and a velvet sofa the color of the inside of a pomegranate. It was nice to be somewhere where everything wasn't box shaped, up lit, and a shade of pebble or mud.

"Ah, I don't deserve the credit, mostly my ex's efforts," Cal said, and Harriet thought, *Aha.*

"Have you been here a while?"

"Two and a half years. Where have you come from?" Cal said. "Today, I mean."

"Roundhay."

"Ooh-la-la." He grinned.

"Ooh-la-no," Harriet said, smiling back. "Breakup. It wasn't my house."

"Ah. Sorry."

There was a clunky pause, and Harriet considered it might have been rash of them not to meet beforehand. This felt like a lot of pressure, now that they were committed.

The doorbell rang and Cal went to answer it, Harriet glad of the interruption.

She heard a jocular male voice, offstage. He apparently knew Cal well enough not to do hellos.

"Fuck's sake, get rid of the apocalypse beard. It makes you look guilty."

"How can a beard look guilty?"

"I don't know but you've managed it. Real 'arrested on the border stating your intention to join the insurgency' sensations."

Harriet laughed, quietly.

"Come and meet my new lodger," Cal said, mainly to warn his friend they weren't alone, she thought.

A tall man with a springing mass of curly hair walked in. Harriet had a moment of *Oh, he looks exactly like . . . wait—he IS him?*

"Sam?!"

He stopped, mouth slightly open.

"Wait . . . don't tell me! Harriet?" he said, equally startled.

"Yes!" Harriet was touched the best man from the wedding-that-wasn't remembered her. They both broke into broad smiles. She supposed, although their encounter was brief, it had been a pretty memorable occasion.

Cal, behind them, said, "You two know each other?"

"We met at a wedding. Sam was the best man," Harriet said, joyfully. She'd been so adrift in the world, moments ago, and here she was with an instant reference point. She'd really warmed to Sam. "It was quite an experience, that one."

The anticipated curiosity from Cal was not forthcoming. Instead, the three of them stared at one another in turn, in a suddenly deathly silence. Sam studiously inspected his socks-with-pool-slides-clad feet. Cal looked at Harriet like he'd seen her drown a kitten in a tin of paint.

"Er, Cal was there too," Sam said. "For *a bit* . . ."

"Oh, were you . . . ?" Harriet trailed off.

She met Cal's heavy gaze from under his brow. Oh. Fuck. No. *What? WHAT?*

This was the bastard of myth and legend, made flesh? CAL was the runaway groom?!

14

"Why . . . were you there?" Cal said, in a strangled way that suggested he'd been desperately trying to find the right formulation of words for what ought to be a banal inquiry.

"I was the photographer."

"You're a wedding photographer?"

"Yes."

"You told me you were a photographer," Cal said.

"I am. I do a lot of weddings."

"You didn't know this was Harriet from your . . . from the wedding?" Sam said, in wonder, and Cal looked at him like he was now suppressing a scream.

"No. We've not met before," Cal said, with some effort. "We've only spoken on the phone, last week, about the spare room."

There followed a conversational abyss, during which none of them could find a thing to say to make it less excruciating. A dog barked in the distance and an ice-cream van chimed, on an otherwise normal summer's day.

Coincidences were usually casually remarkable things, not cataclysmically awkward. Harriet and Cal were trying not to meet each other's eyes while they both internally wailed, *WHAT ARE THE FUCKING CHANCES?!*

However, this mess was down to Cal, Harriet told herself, never mind "you told me you were a photographer." Harriet would have Cal's forename on a sodding schedule somewhere on her laptop, but only Kristina's had felt relevant. A bride who took up a lot of the acreage of a wedding could sometimes cast the groom in the shade. Once the job was canceled, Harriet had no reason to revisit her notes. The precipitous nature of their arrangement, not to mention his precipitous departure from his own wedding day: one hundred percent on Cal Clarke.

"Well. This feels like something we shouldn't discuss ever again!" said Sam, eventually.

Harriet forced a pained smile, and Cal, scowling in explicit discomfort, was so preoccupied that he couldn't even manage that.

As Cal, monosyllabic, showed her around the kitchen and garden, Harriet's brain whirred. Her first instinct was what Jon would call a "field triage maneuver"—say it was an unfortunate mistake, she'd not bother bringing her things through the door, such is life, regretful face-pulling all round. She knew if she were better at difficult conversations, someone like Lorna for example, that's exactly what she'd do.

Harriet also didn't much want to be a traitor to her sex by paying rent to the Gone Groom of folklore—if he could treat his bride like that, what chance did anyone else have? She was equally certain he didn't want a reminder of that day cohabiting his property, judging him in her misandrist silence while they cooked their pasta and pesto of an evening.

Nevertheless, as she worded this merciful no-contest, amicable divorce between them in her head, she realized that she wanted to die at the thought of pulling back up in Jon's driveway, begging his pardon while she searched for a few more weeks. Jon would make a meal of it, and both Lorna and Roxy only had sofas to offer. Harriet was aged thirty-four, with a VW Golf brimful of her possessions. She couldn't quite bring herself to crash like a student with a sleeping bag.

Unless Cal told her to leave at once—and though he appeared deeply afflicted by the turn of events, it didn't feel as if he was going to go that far—the better approach was to move in and immediately start looking for an alternative. She had a feeling Cal would gladly waive the contract breach.

"How about we give you a hand in with your stuff?" Sam said as the tour ended, and Harriet felt she had to say a graceful thank-you even though she cringed at how paltry her belongings were and the fact they were presented as refuse.

It took barely any time with the three of them all marching up and down the seagrass-matting stairs, Harriet and Sam at one point exchanging *Can You Believe It!* knowing glances as they passed each other. She was grateful Sam seemed sane and kind. There might be an opportunity for him to explain what went on, at some point—interesting that the friendship had survived. Sam must be an incredibly forbearing person. Though Harriet wasn't sure she wanted the R-rated version of what happened at the wedding. She'd grasped the essentials.

"We're going to have a beer in the garden, if you fancy joining us?" Cal said, with excessive good manners, given this must be the last thing he wanted.

Harriet pasted on a smile. "Thanks, but I'm going to do some unpacking instead."

Cal nodded tightly, with what Harriet read as equal parts relief and resentment in his eyes.

She shut the door of her spacious room and sagged. There was a key and she turned it, feeling reassured by the click of the lock snapping, though she wasn't sure why. Cal would hardly be seeking her company out.

The room had varnished floorboards the color of honey, walls in a color that Harriet had learned through weddings was called "eau de Nil," and a large paper light shade like a wasp's nest. The surfaces had clearly been vigorously fumigated in anticipation of her arrival. Harriet had the childlike homesickness of an unfamiliar-smelling environment. She pulled the jewelry box from her handbag and put it by the bed.

She plunged about in her luggage to find two framed photos and placed them on the windowsill. One was of her grandfather in his dressing gown, water-gunning pigeons from the roof of his house with a luminous water pistol, and the other was one of herself and Lorna as over-sugared young teenagers, mugging in tinsel disco wigs and cheap lipstick. Neither picture had been allowed at Jon's; he'd quietly moved them out of sight. When she demanded to know why, he'd said, "I'm sure they have great sentimental value, Hats, but displayed prominently, they make us look a little batty, don't you think?"

Harriet loved these photos, they instantly transported her back to when they were taken. She could hear her grandad cackling delightedly when he got a direct hit, could taste the cherryade she and Lorna were drinking. Roxy had arrived later, in sixth form college, when the cherryade became plastic bottles with vodka.

She pulled her Doc Martens off and lay down on the double bed, under the window. From Jon's spare bed to Cal's. (Callum? Calumny? Calamity?)

It was extremely comfortable, pillows like clouds: Cal's ex couldn't be faulted. Jesus Christ—his ex, as in Kristina. She pictured the diminutive woman with the oil-slick-black hair wafting around that bridal suite, brandishing a coupe of Pol Roger, with no idea of what was in store for her next. She'd left this beautiful home too? Did Cal chase her out at the end of a pointy stick, held by a lawyer?

Harriet felt treacherous. Imagine if Kristina could see her here. It would look as if she'd used her failed wedding as an opportunity to network.

"What the fuck just happened?!" Cal Clarke said, at a low yet perfectly audible volume, somewhere beyond the room. "Tell me that didn't happen."

"Only you could achieve this," Sam replied. "It's like you've decided to turn your life into a sitcom."

"Sitcom? Horror movie."

Harriet sat up, vibrating with self-consciousness. The tenor of a conversation not intended for her ears was unmistakable. She could now hear squeaks of mirth that clearly weren't coming from Cal.

"This isn't funny! This is hell."

"How the fuck have you moved your wedding photographer in without knowing that's who she was?!"

"I didn't meet her, did I? Kit booked her."

"OK, how did she not know who *you* were?"

"Like I said, we didn't meet before today. I was so traumatized by Ned the Frequently Naked that I thought, *Oh fuck it, might as well pick names from a hat.* She rang me as soon as the room was advertised and I thought, *Well, Ned proves I don't have a functioning radar for wild eccentrics with Prince Alberts and tattooed arse cheeks anyway. Might as well take a punt.*"

Harriet momentarily wondered if perhaps she was *supposed to* overhear this, some brutal bullying move to provoke her to go? But more likely: Cal had never slept in his own back bedroom, and had made the erroneous calculation that she was upstairs and indoors and he was outdoors and at ground level. In reality, they were a few feet and one single glazed window apart.

"She's probably nice. She was really sweet to me actually, she calmed me down and walked me to the car," Sam said.

"OH GREAT," Cal hissed, with forceful sarcasm.

"What?"

"She'll be even more Team Kit then, won't she."

"Everyone who attended that day is Team Kit. There aren't two teams. That's like saying, 'I hope she's not one of the people who came away from *Star Wars* with a poor opinion of Darth Vader.'"

"I could really do with you enjoying this a bit less!"

"Mate, I got punched in the face for you. I still see her dad calling me 'Sideshow Bob Twat' in my nightmares. So, I will enjoy this exactly as much as I want." Pause. "Harriet's nice, and also, fit . . . ?"

"No! Absolutely not!" Cal said, which Harriet, cringing, chose to take as blunt denial of Sam's right to approve of her.

She briefly imagined appearing at the window, a reverse Cathy in *Wuthering Heights,* and causing them a fright.

"Don't rile me even more," Cal continued.

"You know the cute librarian thing is my wheelhouse."

"You are not to make any approaches! The one thing—the *only* thing—that could make this even bloody worse is having to listen to you in the act. Then you'd settle down with her, to keep her in my life and spite me."

"If you're this bothered, why not ask her to leave?"

"I can't, the contract says six months. Fuck. I'm going to feel every second of it." Cal dropped to a whisper, a whisper that Harriet could still hear. "Also, why's she got so few things? Isn't that quite weird? She's thirty-four."

"Is there some rule on how much you should own by thirty-four?"

"No, but . . . thirty-four. We're not kids. My mum had me and was pregnant with Erin by then."

"Are you saying thirty-something women without husbands and kids are aberrant?"

"Obviously not, I'm saying it's unusual to have four rubbish bags of clothes, a massive pile of photography gear, and a box of shoes to your name. Makes me think she's running from something. Or someone."

Harriet started, like she'd been slapped. She'd not asked them to pick her bags up, and here she was, being judged and mocked. It was also a devastatingly perceptive snap judgment. *That's* why she'd had so few things at Jon's. Ease of fleeing. Of course.

They got distracted by something on Sam's phone, from what Harriet could make out, and the conversation moved on.

She folded up one of her towels to protect the pillowcase from mascara, took her glasses off, pushed her face into it, and wept, silently.

As she blearily wiped away the tears later and her eyes settled on the patch of wall just in front of her, four small words, written in soft pencil, became legible.

I HATE CAL CLARKE

She was tempted to cosign.

15

Harriet was unsurprised to find that Roxanne did not consider her landlord's identity reveal to be either here or there. Lorna low-whistled, but Roxy, the inadvertent matchmaker of this blind date from hell, was thoroughly indifferent.

"Did *you* do something wrong at the wedding?" Roxy said, plunging around with a spoon in a Kilner jar of ice-cream sundae so crammed with Cadbury Flakes, strawberries, and marshmallows that it looked like some sort of edible terrarium.

They'd decided to spend Sunday afternoon watching a hangover comfort film staple, *Top Gun,* at the Everyman Cinema. It was exactly the soothing relief Harriet needed—camaraderie, quiet, and velvet seats, with prosecco bussed to their tiny seat-tables. Like being first class on a plane but with no jet lag or latent fear of going nose cone into a mountain range.

"Nothing other than witness it."

Roxy licked the back of her spoon. "It's one hundred percent for him to feel bad then, isn't it? Enjoy your en suite."

". . . Yes, I suppose." Harriet sighed. Being so very much not wanted as a tenant had made her feel responsible, somehow.

"Are you making other people's feelings your problem again?" Lorna said.

As she spoke, a message from Jon dinged on her mobile screen and she opened it. *Can I have your address?* Harriet couldn't remember the postcode off the top of her head.

"I overheard a chat with his best mate which made it clear he irrationally resented me for it," she said, as she fiddled with her phone, making sure it was on silent. "Plus he said I was a suspicious tramp lady due to my lack of owning furniture by my grand age."

"Ask him why he's not got a wife by his age," Lorna said.

"The house is great?" Roxy asked.

"The house is great," Harriet conceded. "I am very pleased with that part." She didn't want to sound ungrateful, although she was.

One thing was for sure: if Harriet moved on, she'd not involve Roxy and break the news tactfully.

Harriet had seen very little of Cal in the weekend since she overheard the "Sam in garden" contretemps. He made a comment about how he'd not seen a Breville sandwich toastie-maker like hers since his childhood, in a way that implied she was the dowdy pensioner of the parish. "I do a mean Nutella one," she'd said, and he looked revolted. Otherwise, they exchanged courteous, terse exchanges about whether the other wanted a cup of tea or coffee, given they were making some (they never did).

Every time Harriet looked at him, she heard the tone in which he'd spoken about her. *And I will feel every second of it.* She shivered anew.

As the lights dimmed, a man approached their seats, doing the crab-like scuttle beloved of roadies trying to remove something unwanted from a stage while the gig was under way. The *if I bend over, no one can see me* stance.

"Lorna? Lorna Everett! I knew it was you!" he said.

He knelt down in front of them. He was thirty-something and attractive, in a careless sort of way: mid-length brown hair pushed back from his face, five o'clock shadow, jeans with trailing hems.

". . . *Gethin?*" Lorna said, putting her drink down with a bump. "Oh my God! How are you?"

"Good, thanks! I've not seen you since the accident!"

"The one where I fell down a manhole, broke my leg in three places, and chipped my kneecap?"

"Yes! Oof. Hope it's healed now?"

"My career in the Royal Ballet was over, but yes, I can walk."

"Fuck, that's awful. I felt so responsible as we were both messing around at the time," Gethin said.

"So responsible you failed to visit me in hospital," Lorna snorted.

Hmm. It must've really bothered Lorna, as she wasn't the resentful type.

"I did come to visit you." Gethin frowned.

". . . What?"

"I came to see you on the ward!"

"Bollocks you did! Did you . . . ?"

Harriet and Roxy sipped their prosecco with wide eyes.

Gethin lowered his voice further out of deference to the adverts starting.

"You seemed quite out of it. You'd had a lot of morphine. You told me you were Catherine of Aragon, Henry the Eighth's first wife. You accused me of being infatuated with Anne Boleyn and plotting to behead you. Then you screamed at the nurse for more 'special syrup' and told me to fuck off."

Harriet and Roxy stifled considerable laughter, and Lorna appeared temporarily, and deeply uncharacteristically, speechless.

"Ah . . ." Lorna said, after a pause. "While obviously I was not a Tudor queen, had I been Catherine and had you been Henry, this would have been correct."

"It was Leeds General Infirmary, but yes, your grip on the 1500s was sound. I did try to message as well, but your phone got smashed in the fall and I assume you had a different number afterward? Or blocked me, hah. For my wife-murdering."

Oh dear. Harriet could see Gethin from IT—who'd legendarily disgracefully withheld a shag and then pastoral care—might have been misrepresented. A revised history must be written.

"Oh . . . this is a cock-up," Lorna said, weakly.

"You run a restaurant, I heard on the grapevine? Stalked you on Twitter, if I'm honest."

Ooh, Harriet thought.

"Yeah." It was hard to tell in this light, but was Lorna . . . blushing? "Divertimento up on Otley Road in Headingley."

"That is so cool. It's yours? You're the owner?"

"The debt-ridden owner, but yes, it's mine."

"Wow! I'm still doing shitty corporate IT jobs. You are really living your dream."

"Come! Bring your wife and kids."

"I don't have a wife and kids. It's only me and my wee pal Bubbles Hussein."

"Your pet name for your penis?"

Harriet and Roxy were now gripping the seat arms.

"That is my *rescue Chihuahua,* thank you very much. Half old lady's treasure, half fearsome dictator."

"Well, you and Bubbles Hussein are very welcome."

"In that case I'll be straight in there! Great to see you again."

"And you," Lorna said.

He crept back to his seat.

A slightly tense silence settled among the three of them afterward, entirely unrelated to the trailer for the "spine-chilling psychological thriller of the year" that was booming out.

"Really nice of him to come and say hello, given what had in fact transpired," Harriet said, in a loud whisper.

Lorna hoarse-whispered back: "No. That was a passive-aggressive charge sheet disguised as a *hi, how are you.*"

Harriet grinned. Lorna didn't mean a word of that.

"Fuck, I knew I was high as a kite, but to have had visitors I don't remember?!" Lorna continued. "Fuck the NHS! Someone must lose their job over this."

"You were very stoned, early on," Roxy said. "You kept asking me and Harriet if they'd been able to save your leg, and we'd point at it in the sling and you'd say, 'Where's the other one?'"

"Unbelievable," Lorna huffed. Harriet sensed her furiously processing this alternative version of Gethin.

"Thank God I've had my roots done. And am, obviously, ravishing," she whispered, only to Harriet, as Roxy was sat on the other side of Harriet and would've at this stage required too much projecting of voice. "Though I'm not sure this was the right outfit."

This was how Lorna admitted feelings for men, only by implication.

"I love that outfit, it's one of my favorites," Harriet said. It was a black high-necked dress, with black-and-white-striped tights and red shoes, as a reference to the Wicked Witch in *The Wizard of Oz*.

"'Is that your pet name for your penis,'" Harriet repeated, and started shaking with laughter again. "Poor Gethin."

"I knew I needed to take it down by at least twenty-six percent, but I was startled," Lorna said.

Harriet felt excited on Lorna's behalf. She'd not seen her this discomposed by a member of the opposite sex for a very long time, and from what she'd seen, Gethin was a worthy sparring partner.

As the film began, Harriet saw another WhatsApp from Jon ding noiselessly on her phone screen.

Read, but no reply. Is there any reason you're avoiding me?

Harriet scowled and switched her mobile off completely, in a snap of irritation. What was this creepy, resentful tone about?

She wasn't sure she understood Jon anymore. Perhaps she never had.

16

"Do you think I'm an idiot?!"

"I don't think anything about you at all, mate, what with not knowing you."

"I'm not your mate."

"No shit!"

As Harriet's taxi dropped her off at Cal's, she heard raised male voices that seemed to be concerningly nearby and worryingly familiar. As she approached, she saw the front door was open and discovered the altercation was happening in the hallway. She reached the door to see Jon blocking the space, Cal glimpsed beyond.

"Jon!?"

He turned to see Harriet.

"Oh, thank God," Cal said, at the sight of her.

"Jon, what are you doing here?"

"Hi, honey, I'm home," Jon singsonged. He looked unsteady; even from this distance Harriet could see he was smashed. "When were you going to tell me you'd moved in with the other guy you haven't told me about? Or, *let me guess,* you weren't."

"He's my landlord!" Harriet said. "I pay Cal rent!"

"Yeah, and the rest."

Cal's eyes opened wide in distaste, and Harriet was mortified. She had a feeling Jon wouldn't remember this in the morning, he was so far gone, but she had no such comfort. It was playing out in front of judgmental Cal Clarke too. Infinity fuck's sake. She had no choice but to take charge and claw back some meager amount of dignity.

"I can see you're pissed, but this is BEYOND. Get out of Cal's house."

"The love nest," Jon said, with a leery smile. Harriet felt the remaining regard she had for her ex-boyfriend shrivel up and die.

"Listen, you heard her. We're not sleeping together," Cal said, and then quietly, but not quite quietly enough, "Psycho ex."

Jon pivoted on his heel, drew back a fist, and punched Cal in the face, Cal letting out a surprised yelp and staggering backward, half sitting, half falling down, landing with a heavy thud on the staircase. Harriet let out a cry of shock and disbelief. Thankfully, Cal looked stunned but not aggressive, or likely to thump Jon back.

"What the fuck, Jon!" Harriet shouted, incredulity overriding her fear of causing more aggro. "What have you done?"

Cal, dazed, put a hand to his forehead. Blood trickled out from under his palm.

"Are you OK?" she said. Cal gave her a *what do you think?* look in the upward swivel from his visible eye.

Jon turned back to Harriet with the glazed, triumphant, and slightly unfocused gaze of the temporarily deranged and totally wankered.

"I did say I'd fight for you."

Harriet lunged forward and grabbed Jon by the shirt, bundling him through the doorway and out of the house. She could smell the alcohol on him, but she didn't think he'd lay a finger on her, even in this state.

"You realize you committed assault, right? And being drunk is no defense?"

"If you aren't having sex with him, why hide where you live?" Jon said. Harriet cringed at this blunt accusation in front of Cal. She betted the neighbors, this quiet summer evening, were having a ball.

She now easily imagined the buildup to this scene: Jon spending an hour or two firming his fevered jealous suspicions into cold certainties, helped along by his wine cellar, and eventually deciding to seek her (and him) out for a full confrontation and proof. Catching them at it. But how *did* he get her address?

"I wasn't avoiding anything; I've been gone two days. You've totally lost the plot."

"You didn't tell me you were moving in with a man!" Jon said.

"Why does it matter?"

"Women don't move in with men they don't know, do they?"

"Well, I have."

"You must've desperately wanted to get shot of me," Jon said.

Cal muttered, "Can't imagine why," behind them, and Jon spun on his heel.

"*What did you say?*"

Before he could attempt another brawl, Harriet pulled the front door near shut.

"Go home and sober up." She hesitated. "Have you got your phone?"

Jon absently patted his trouser pocket. "Yeah."

"Right, walk this off for a while, then call an Uber."

"Harriet."

"What?"

"I love you."

"Fucking hell."

Jon made a fingers-to-head salute that turned into the V sign as his gaze went over Harriet's shoulder toward Cal, then he turned and staggered off, on legs that appeared to be part mechanical.

When Harriet reentered the house, Cal was in the kitchen, dabbing at his wound with a screw of paper towel. He'd been clean-shaven since their first meeting; Sam's comments must've hit home.

"Fuck I am so, *so* sorry. How are you?" she said.

"I've been better," he said, briskly, making it clear her sympathy wasn't particularly welcome.

Harriet grimaced. *Jon, you absolutely mad arsehole.* She pushed painful thoughts away: How could she have got him so wrong? How could she have got it so wrong, again? What was wrong with her? She knew from experience there would be plenty of time for that. The self-disgust.

"It would've been helpful if you'd explained your circumstances rather than to leave me to answer the door to him. He was hammering away like he was being chased by a bear, and if I knew there was a looming threat in your life like that, I'd have known to keep it shut."

"Honestly, this is as much a shock to me as it is to you," Harriet said.

"No offense, but I doubt that. 'Breakup' didn't quite cover it, did it?" Cal said. "Bad breakup might've at least hinted at it."

"It wasn't a bad breakup, that's what's so impossible to add up," Harriet said.

"Could've fooled me."

It took Harriet some seconds to realize she was visibly and uncontrollably shaking, with Cal realizing this at the same time.

He narrowed his eyes at her, assessing. Then, appearing to almost resent the necessity of asking, said, "Are you all right?"

Harriet nodded and gripped her elbows with her hands. It was a surge of fight or flight, that was all; from experience she knew she just had to ride it out. With her teeth chattering.

She saw a look cross Cal's face and could almost read the thoughts like a news break caption scroll. *Oh my God, you verbally attacked HER over HIS behavior! YOU are the ogre!*

"Shit, Harriet. I blurted that without thinking. Obviously this isn't your fault. At all."

Harriet nodded, feeling the shaking abate slightly. Jon had triggered a panic response in her, stirred up feelings she'd not experienced for a long time.

Cal put his paper towel down and gripped her shoulder.

"It's OK. He's gone now."

After a moment's hesitation he hugged her, and Harriet submitted to it, thinking how surreal her life had become. Cal was very warm, probably sweating with the shock. She appreciated the gesture, but somehow, being clasped in guilt by the man who didn't want her in his house wasn't much reassurance. Neither she nor Cal wanted consolation from the other.

"Don't be scared. We'll get him sent to Horny Jail."

"I'm not scared of him," Harriet said, laughing weakly, as they stepped back. Cal raised his eyebrows.

"You should probably start," he said, pointing at his forehead.

Harriet thought he was being relatively chill, really, given he'd been cracked in the face.

"I assume this is why you ran out with the clothes on your back, and were calling me the second the room went online?" Cal added.

Harriet had the full power of speech back as her heart rate slowed. "No! Jon's house was so top-of-the-range and he was so opinionated about decor, I had no reason to buy things. He's not aggressive; he won't even swear when he's cut off by another driver. Since I ended it a few weeks ago, he's gone off the rails. I've never seen him so much as angry in two years. This is completely out of character."

"Oh," Cal said, frowning. "Lucky me, I suppose."

"Have you got any antiseptic cream for that?" Harriet said, peering at the graze on his brow.

"Yeah, I think so."

Cal banged about in the cupboards. "This sort of thing?"

He held up Savlon, and Harriet nodded.

"What does he do for a living?" Cal said, squeezing the liquid onto his finger, patting it on, and wincing as it made contact with broken skin.

Harriet explained Jon was Captain Gravy, both senior and well paid.

"Good, he won't want to be fired then. Please tell him if I see him anywhere near this house again, I'll call the police *and* his employer. I won't do anything about this, for my sake and your sake, rather than his."

"I will do. Thanks," Harriet said, gratitude washing through her. "He'll be crippled by shame in tomorrow's hangover, seriously."

Cal looked dubious about this. He had perhaps started to wonder if Harriet was doing a dynamite job at covering for him.

"You sure this isn't a pattern? He's never raised his hand to you? Or other men?"

"He's never even been slightly intimidating in his life. He'd not complain the order was wrong in a Michelin-starred restaurant."

"Well. Wow."

Harriet was in a slight bind: the more she emphasized it was extraordinary, the more it implied Cal ought to be less bothered about being on the receiving end. Great news, there are no other victims!

"What's his name again?"

"Jon."

"Iron Jon, eh. Travel Iron Jon."

Harriet snorted.

". . . Want a drink?" Cal said.

Harriet hesitated. She couldn't see why Cal would want to socialize with her, given the hellfire she'd brought through his door, never mind her presence at his almost-wedding. The expression in his eyes was sincere, however.

"There's no catch?" he added, with a small smile.

She let out a breath.

"Then a world of yes please."

17

At Cal's suggestion, they carried their bottle of white to the picnic table in the garden. The steamy atmosphere on a late summer evening was unexpectedly potent, and her senses were heightened by the last half hour's ordeal.

Cal was dressed like Tom Hiddleston in *The Night Manager* (she'd overheard this ridicule from Sam—"I'd not let you manage my night"—and liked it): pale blue linen shirt with rolled-up sleeves and, now, sunglasses. The effect was only enhanced by the way he looked like he'd been roughed up by spy drama heavies.

As Harriet sat down, she took it all in: the bees buzzing groggily in the flowers as the light faded, the scent of honeysuckle, the damp, muggy air, the fairy lights glowing amber like fireflies as the solar power kicked in. She was enjoying her fridge-cold glass of chenin blanc more than any wine she could remember. Cal had upended a bag of crisps into a bowl, and Harriet was struck by the endearing idea he had unselfconsciously copied a parental habit.

"After I've been beaten up, I always like to reflect with wine and Waitrose nibbles," Cal said, as he moved the bowl toward her. "A thrashing, and a finger savory. A perfect Sunday."

Harriet smiled into her wine. He talked like someone who read and wrote a lot.

"Is this the right flavor pairing?" Harriet said. "I'm a wine-crisp sommelier. Like, a hearty beef crisp goes with a robust red."

"Ready salted and"—he consulted the bottle's label—"floral aromas, assertive apple, and pear."

"Ideal," she said. She gestured to his face while taking a crisp. "You seem to have taken it in your stride."

"I haven't been hit like that since one time at school, and it turns out my survival mechanism is the same: hope they don't do it again."

Cal had a very sophisticated form of confidence, Harriet thought, the kind where it can play dress-up as qualities such as self-deprecation and vulnerability. You needed to be pretty sure of yourself to have sailed through the last half hour with no apparent fear, combativeness, embarrassment, or bravado.

"Do you mind me giving you some unasked-for advice?" Cal said after a pause.

"I can't really say no, while gazing upon your ruined face," Harriet said, taking another crisp. *Mmm, crisps.*

"There's no chance of you and Jon getting back together, right?" Cal said.

Harriet crunched, and shuddered. "Uh, no. There wasn't before tonight." She conjured up a Lorna-ism. "I would rather eat aquarium gravel."

Cal laughed, then wiped at his face, serious again. "Tell him that, once and for all. Maybe not the gravel part. It's nice, you caring about whether he has his phone on him to get home. But trust me, someone in that state is clinging to anything as hope that there's still a way. Cut him off. Don't even politely entertain any further bullshit."

Harriet frowned. "But I've moved out? He surely knew that we were over."

"He's ranting on about fighting for you, so no, I don't think he does."

"I feel like such a shit for hurting him so much, is the problem."

"Yes, and I'm afraid he knows that. That's the weakness he'll exploit, your guilt. But you asserting yourself doesn't make you cruel."

Harriet nodded, writhing slightly. It was hard to imagine a less appropriate relationship advice coach. (And surely this was the moment he should tell her to leave—he hadn't wanted her here since Sam's reveal, and now she'd given him a solid reason for booting her out? She wondered if he felt too guilty, now that he'd got a look at who she'd left.)

Nevertheless, cold Cal seemed to be hitting nails on heads, and she couldn't help but appreciate a different perspective. He had faced Jon down, but neither did he stoop to his level nor gratify him with any display of anger in return. Perhaps she could do with borrowing some of that strategy and attitude.

"I'm so baffled by this. Ever since I finished it, this whole side to him has emerged that I never knew was there. I feel quite freaked out and very stupid for not being aware of it."

Harriet remembered what Lorna said about Jon being a bad person to break up with. The more she thought about it, the more she was slightly frightened by the extent of Lorna's prescience. In her many years of knowing her, Lorna's instincts had never been wrong. Another person's attitude that Harriet should borrow.

Cal grimaced. "Some people don't let you leave well, I'm afraid. They don't do easy endings."

Harriet nodded. They exchanged a look of understanding that they'd not be discussing his aborted nuptials. In this moment, Harriet couldn't fit that episode together with what she'd seen of Cal so far tonight, whatsoever. Unconfrontational, able to wisecrack under pressure, and annoyingly . . . pleasant. But then, how did she expect a bride-jilter to behave? Given her track record for understanding male behavior, and the fact it was none of her business, she decided not to try.

"Is there another lad this was meant for?" Cal said, pulling his shades down to squint while pointing at his damaged forehead.

Harriet cringed. "Oh God—no! It's as if Jon wants there to be someone else, so I can be the scarlet woman, and he can duel."

Harriet knew that this jealousy hadn't come *entirely* from nowhere. She'd simply not needed to notice it, before. For example, a running joke, if she was going out without him, was Jon asking, "Cui bono?"—*Who benefits?*—at the sight of her outfit, Harriet always replying, "No, Zara," or similar. The idea there had to be a male admirer for any effort she made was, on review, overwrought. She'd chalked up too much to an ex–all boys' school, creaky outmodedness. It wasn't school, it was Jon.

"Then are you sure Jon's not seeing someone, and this is all displacement?" Cal said, looking studiously into his glass.

"I seriously doubt it. Our split was very recent, and Jon's not the womanizing type."

"Hmmm. Counterintuitively, I've found being excessively paranoid and a cheater tends to go together. They're judging you by their own standards."

This felt true; in fact, Harriet knew it to be true in her own past: the flex of accusing someone of your own bad behavior. Still, she failed to imagine Jon doing such a thing, even if he'd not been so in love with her. He was a moral person who had a very developed sense of what was "not on." On a practical level, he was barely on social media, never seemed to cling to his phone, so unless he was having it off with someone at work over the range cooker in the kitchen, chances to meet other women were scarce.

"I think it's more that he didn't see this coming, didn't really understand me in the first place." Harriet let out a sad sigh, thinking this was as much her fault for not really trying to be understood. "Instead of figuring it out by spending some time in his own head, he's spun off into some movie idea of how he thinks a heartbroken ex would behave. He thinks I'm going to realize he must really love me, to go this far. I feel so bad for him, but . . ."

Harriet paused; this was pretty insensitive when Cal had been hit by him. Worse was the way Cal was looking at her, as a sort of pitiable curiosity.

"Also," she said, in a "reasserting herself" tone, "next week I'll start looking for somewhere else to live. First the wedding coincidence, now this. I don't think we were meant to house share."

Cal's eyebrows shot up. "Er . . ." He hesitated in that precise way people do when offered something they definitely want, but seizing upon it is unseemly. "If you're sure?"

That was all the hint Harriet required.

"Yes, absolutely," she said, firmly. "No hard feelings. We weren't to know Leeds was this small, hah."

"No rush," Cal said. "I won't advertise the room until you're set to go."

"Thanks."

Harriet sensed him casting about for something to soften the fact she'd said, *I'll leave,* and Cal had said, *Ooh, yes please.*

"Hmmm . . . so far in my landlording career, I've encountered nudity and violence. What's left on the R-rating criteria?" he said, after a pause.

"Injury detail," Harriet said, pointing at Cal's face.

He winced. "Scenes of a sexual nature from the next one? Oh God."

They smiled, an easing between them.

Her promising to go had lifted the curse of awkwardness, although in the following seconds she remembered Kristina's scream and hardened again. It would've been so much better for both of them if she'd never known about that. Never mind.

A bat flitted past in the blue dusk.

"What is Cal short for, by the way? Callum? I realize I don't know," Harriet said, as they walked back into the house.

"Calvin," he said, taking his shades off, rolling those intense pale green eyes. "Want to know why? It's fucking shameful."

"Go on . . . ?"

"My mum loves *Back to the Future,* especially the bit where Marty gets called Calvin because he's in Calvin Klein underpants."

She broke into a wide grin. "That's great."

"Is it, though?" Cal said. "It's also a film where the mum crushes on her son. *Cool.*"

"Calvin. I like it."

"Forgive me if I don't trust your taste," Cal said, with a smile, and she felt a little chill in his palpable disdain at her grubby life.

DUVET DRAWN UP to her chin in bed, Harriet scrolled down to the Fleaslags group on her WhatsApp and typed.

Jon turned up at my house uninvited, claiming I was hiding my location from him, and PUNCHED the house mate / landlord, Cal, accusing us of having an affair. A SUNDAY MOOD.

Lorna

YOU WHAT

Roxy

???!!! Are you joking??

Harriet

Sadly not. Luckily Cal isn't pressing charges. Jon was absolutely off his head, ranting about us shagging, had clearly been drinking.

Lorna

Woah

Roxy

OMFG

Harriet

What I don't understand is, how did Jon find out where I lived?

Roxy

Uhm . . . sorry that was me. After the film. He made it seem like it wasn't a thing ☹

Harriet

How did he explain away that he was asking you, not me??

Roxy

You know Jon, it was all fiddlesticks and whoops butterfingers and Harriet said she'd give me it and keeps forgetting, would you mind ever so? I didn't think he'd punch anyone! I didn't even think you'd mind him having it or I'd not have given it to him 😬

Harriet

You weren't to know. I really hope he's so ashamed tomorrow he comes to his senses

Lorna

Imagine if you actually HAD left him for someone else. Presume Jon would be being fingerprinted under arrest for murder right now

Harriet

What's got into him?! Two years together and no sign of this stuff in his nature whatsoever?

Lorna

You say that but he did have a thing about Second World War films. He once told me every man of his generation feels guilt at never having faced a Nazi

Roxy

He must be so madly in love with you he's lost his mind.

Lorna

Don't make this some male passion "nice guy snapped" shit, Rox. If this was a woman we'd have no problem saying she was a vindictive scary banshee

Roxy

I WASN'T! ☹

Lorna

I admit I'm struggling to picture Mark Corrigan from Peep Show turning into The Punisher, can you act it out when you see us next, H?

Harriet

NOT LOL

18

Harriet had claimed Jon would be broken with contrition after attacking Cal, and she was half right. She was right-ish. Lorna would've called it "wrong."

Jon appeared with dark circled eyes—it had clearly been enough of a sesh to still be lingering by the summit that Harriet called in Laynes' Espresso bar on Tuesday morning. He'd taken the week off work—whether that was in emergency recovery or planned, Harriet didn't know, and didn't trust him to tell her the truth anyway. He was downcast, very subdued at first, but not without lingering defiance. His Merc keys were slung as a casual status symbol next to his flat white, and Harriet was struck anew that she had been in a relationship with someone who refused to get public transport even when it was far easier than driving.

"I'm horrified at what I did, it's not me," Jon said, with a certain rehearsed fluency, not seeming horrified enough for Harriet's liking. Was he . . . secretly proud at his laddish escapade? The likes of Gavin his squash partner would applaud. Gav's profile picture on Facebook was Joaquin Phoenix dancing on the steps as the Joker.

"I can't remember much of it," Jon continued, "except a lot of shouting the odds, and then lamping that cocky man when he insulted me."

"Cocky?! You barged in and were threatening him in *his* house, wrongly accusing him of banging your ex-girlfriend," Harriet said. "I think he had the right to be *a bit put out*? I think being *a little sassy* could be excused?"

"I was out of order, no question," Jon said. "Can't you see how it looked, though? Not telling me where you were, I go round and a bloke answers the door?"

"I don't care how it *looked*. I don't have to make it look any certain way." God, the Barraclough family mentality.

"All I'm saying is, had I been forewarned your housemate was male, it would've helped."

"If you hadn't tricked my address out of my friend and turned up unannounced, that would've helped too?"

Harriet was moderating her voice, partly to keep a lid on the scene, and partly as she didn't want to startle the attractive young couple at the next table, who she suspected were listening rapt to every word nevertheless.

"Fair point. I've been a real dickhead."

Harriet twinged with annoyance as an unexpected black pudding hash on toast with fried eggs was set down in front of Jon. "Medical necessity, Hats. Let the healing begin!" They'd said coffee, not brunch. It indicated a lack of real shame. You weren't all that tormented if you were plowing into a pair of sunny-side-up Burford Browns. She narrowed her eyes.

"If he goes to the police, I hope your bosses are understanding about giving you a day off for the trial."

Jon, grinding a pepper mill over his dish, stopped. "Is he going to the police?"

"Probably. Why shouldn't he?" Harriet said. Jon needed a good healthy scare, and she'd do some white lying to help it along.

"Oh . . . well . . . I mean, come on. It was completely shit on my part and I will grovel my apology, but do we honestly need a day in court over one right hook?" He paused. "It'd drag you into it as well, as witness."

Oh, so the effect on her was suddenly occurring to Jon, coincidentally right when raising it could benefit him? Oddly, this was what she needed to hear, to prove to herself that her heartbroken ex could be manipulative and selfish. She'd been feeling so guilty, but it was time to toughen up. Rather belatedly, she caught on that Cal kicking her out would've been, if not the intention, at least an unexpected bonus to Jon. *So, so sorry, Hats, free bed and board at mine until you can find an alternative is the least I can do.*

"I'll speak to Cal about his pursuing this and see if I can persuade him not to. But I need to make it absolutely clear: there's no reason for you to be coming round and you have no rights over me. Even if I had been involved with Cal, that would be my business."

Jon paused again, fork midway to mouth. "*Are* you?"

"Jesus Christ, NO. I'm asking you," she enunciated clearly, "to accept that we've separated and to behave accordingly. Don't appear on my doorstep again. Don't contact me. Respect my decision that we are over . . . and that's not going to change."

Harriet had broken into a light sweat at the harshness of spelling it out, yet this was vital clarity.

Jon said nothing, putting his cutlery down as if he'd abruptly lost his appetite.

"It'd be simply 'your business' if you were seeing someone, mere days after you gave me an engagement ring back? I'd not have rights to be upset, and wonder when it started?"

Harriet took a deep breath and remembered Cal's advice. Do not equivocate or wrangle with what-ifs.

"Yes. You don't get to carry on making demands of me and setting rules. You don't seem to understand that my telling you where I was living was up to me. I don't have ongoing obligations to you."

"It's not that you have obligations to me . . . It's that you don't seem bothered, Harriet. *At all.* You just declared you were on a new course, that night in the hotel, and set sail without me. It leaves me wondering what this was all about, if you ever loved me. I don't know who you are."

"It's funny you say that, as right now I'm not massively sure of who you are."

"Oh, come on, don't be so disingenuous. I've not covered myself in glory, but I'm flailing. I'm in bits, my heart is broken. Whereas not only is your heart clearly fully intact, you don't seem to have had a moment's pain over us finishing."

Her mouth fell open at this. She was damned if she'd soul-bare after the way he'd behaved. He now wanted her to describe her sense of loss, prove she cared?

"I have. Sorry. I don't know how this is relevant to what you did."

"No. Clearly."

Jon stared at her intently.

The idea here was she left him with no hope of a way back. How had she been sidetracked into apologizing?

"You're *sorry,*" Jon said. "It's like you scraped my paintwork or dumped trash in my bin. You used me, didn't you?"

"Used you for what?"

"Used me to get over something. Or someone."

It occurred to her that Jon was saying the exact same thing she'd overheard Cal remarking to Sam in the garden, about her lack of possessions suggesting she was running away. Harriet never so much as hinted at the figure in her history, and yet somehow, they all knew he was there. She balled her trembling fingers into a fist under the table, out of sight.

"D. H. Lawrence said, 'Women in their nature are like giantesses. They will break through everything and go on with their own lives.' I never knew what he meant until now."

Harriet rolled her eyes. At least he sounded more like himself. Classic Jon-ing.

"Did he now. Sounds sexist. I'm not here to have another fight, Jon."

"OK, understood," Jon said, jutting his chin out. "You're a free agent, and so am I. Message fully received, Harriet. Remember that's what you said."

"How are you turning this into a threat?"

"I'm merely reiterating that the same rules apply for all. You only hear a threat if you think we're not equal."

"We are equal."

Harriet stood up to leave, putting a five-pound note down for her coffee and a tip.

"Have you told your parents we've separated?" she said. She'd had no further texts from Jacqueline, and despite the impossible position Jon had put her in, she disliked how rude it had felt to ignore her. She wondered if Jacqueline raised it with Jon and, if so, what was said.

"No, not yet, only because the barbecue was *teeming*. I will tell them this afternoon, I think, in fact."

"OK. Enjoy your brunch."

Jon looked contemptuous. He was no doubt made ratty by her ill manners in not staying until he'd finished the food he'd not said he'd ordered, and listening to more accusations of her emotional frigidity. Harriet said bye to a stony countenance.

As she walked back through the city center, she saw a missed call from Lorna. She called back.

"Listen to this. Gethin's booked a table at the Dive this Saturday. Keen, right?"

"Yep."

"WRONG, he's bringing two friends. Two!"

"Is this less keen?"

"One friend is a wingman, and to be expected. Two is three lads total, which is a gang. It says, *Don't get any ideas*."

"Let me ask you this: If Gethin had a restaurant and had invited you, wouldn't you take us, on your first visit? Hedge your bets?"

"Yes, but."

"What?"

"You can prove anything with this sort of smart-arsery, Hatley! I don't need it; I need your help. You and Roxy have to come in that night. Please tell me you don't have a wedding."

"You're in luck, this week's is a fashionable Friday at the town hall and reception at Issho."

"Yasssssss! You and Roxy have a table, also at around half eight, nine, and then if things go well, all six of us do a lock-in. That way, if I'm being mugged off here, I didn't act like I had any expectations."

"It sounds like he wants dinner and you're casting for *West Side Story*. Is it not a little bit obvious if you've got us in at the same time he's got them in?"

"It would've been, had I not had the reactions of a ninja and as soon as he said he was bringing pals I said smoothly, 'Oh, that's a coincidence, this'll be fun, my mates are in that night too.' Gethin is not dealing with an amateur."

"Haha. Lucky I could make it then."

"Seriously, though, this is bringing it all rushing back. All the flirting and the signals, then suddenly a big air horn of nope."

"Wasn't the air horn you falling down a manhole, thinking he'd ghosted you, when in fact you'd ghosted him?"

"I knew you'd throw that 'fact' in my face."

Harriet updated Lorna on her meeting with Jon, and how he started quoting literary greats on the perfidy of women.

"Unbelievable. He is a possessive shit in bad denim who has never really respected you. That's from Jane Austen."

"I know. I mean, I appreciate he's really cut up and didn't see our breakup coming . . ."

"Stop making excuses for him. Punching your landlord isn't OK. Accusing you of infidelity based on nothing isn't OK. Proposing to you as a form of entrapment isn't OK. He is misaligned."

Harriet couldn't find an error in this.

"You've got to stop planning for the Jon you thought you had and start dealing with the Jon you actually have. Who appears to be an absolute danger."

It was no good—indicting Jon always led Harriet to the same place.

"Lorna . . ."

"Yes."

"Is this definitive proof I have the worst judgment in men?"

"No, you don't. What you have is trust that has been abused. Men aren't your fault."

19

It couldn't possibly be Jacqueline Barraclough's "little town runaround" sports car that was backing into the drive early that evening, boxing Harriet's Golf in, could it? Why would she be here? How could she be here?

Harriet's stomach went on spin as a familiar silver-blond head emerged from the driver's side. Harriet had no time to escape: she was visible through the front room's bay window.

The doorbell bing-bonged, and a gut-churned Harriet opened the door to Jacqueline, wearing an imperious expression. Sunglasses with rhinestone-encrusted arms were pushed up into her hair, and she was clad in a seashell-pink silk jersey sweater, thrown over a starched white shirt with turned-up collar. She was wearing a rose-gold locket, which she'd once shown Harriet contained infant photos of Jon and Martin Junior: "My babies, always near my heart."

Harriet sensed she was not about to be asked how she was settling in.

"Hello, Harriet."

"Hi."

"Aren't you going to ask me inside?" Jacqueline said, in a combative tone that suggested the imminent rinsing might be better behind closed doors. Harriet led Jacqueline through to the front room, wondering if she'd just stupidly invited the vampire across the threshold when she could've simply shut the door on her. Why didn't being wholly innocent feel more powerful? It was an ambush and Harriet was unprepared.

Jacqueline glanced around at the furnishings, to make it clear that Harriet was being judged. "Jon says you're renting a room that you found online."

"Yes, that's right," Harriet said.

Jacqueline looked back at her with a triumphal pony-shake of her head, as if the fittings proved a point. "You've walked out on Jon to *crash* in a stranger's spare room. I hope she likes having you here."

Harriet briefly wondered why Jon hadn't added, *And she is dwelling with a MAN,* to the list of charges, then thought, *Ah, it was because it'd lead to confessing to lamping him.*

"How did you get my address?" Harriet said, as if she didn't already know the answer.

"Jon gave it to me. Lest you attack him for that, he's still so protective he'd not have handed it over had I told him the truth. He thinks I'm here to see if I could talk you round, persuade you to give him another chance. I think we both know that's not going to happen. This is more some woman-to-woman honesty."

Oh, what a fucking HERO. He'd immediately unleashed his mum on Harriet, on the outside chance it might get him what he wanted. And Jacqueline genuinely thought that gave him nobility?!

Jon didn't overlook his familial vices; Harriet had been woefully naive on that score. He gave them a pass in the certainty they'd do the same for him—all in it together, co-enablers. Somewhere there was a Barraclough family crest with a Latin motto that translated as *Eat Shit Losers.* He knew perfectly well his mother was a nuclear warhead in Hobbs occasion wear, but she was never going to raze *his* village.

Harriet finally accepted the truth of everything Lorna had said that night when she'd told her about his proposal. It was ruthlessness. Ruthlessness using a telephone voice, in chinos.

He gave himself a psychological comfort zone of willful ignorance. When you confronted him, tried to make him take responsibility for the consequences, he slithered through your hand like a bar of soap. *He meant no harm!* He'd simply not spent a second considering or caring if he would do harm, which actually was the same thing.

Offstage, Harriet heard the front door open and close and wished, fervently, that Cal Clarke hadn't got home from the *Yorkshire Post* this very second. He'd now hear all of this. Jacqueline had the sort of voice that cut through.

"I'll get straight to the point," Jacqueline said. "I wasn't going to bother with you, but then I thought, no—someone needs to force you to look at what you've done. And it sure as hell won't be your victim: my distraught, loyal son."

He was loyal all right, loyal to his own interests.

"You are not a mother, Harriet. If you were, you might have some idea how it felt to see my youngest son, broken, sobbing, asking, 'Why doesn't she love me, Mum? What did I do wrong, Mum?' The shame he felt in confessing to YOUR behavior was devastating. You have humiliated and shattered him."

"I'm sorry if Jon is hurt, but—"

"I will finish, thank you!" Jacqueline barked, with a vehemence that startled Harriet into silence.

"I never thought you appreciated him, and it was agonizing to watch. I could see him striving, so hard, for you to love him the way he loved you. I could see the effort he made that you didn't reciprocate. You made him feel like he wasn't worthy of you, like he wasn't *enough for you*. In fact it was quite the opposite way round, but of course, a besotted man cannot see this. But even I could never have anticipated the *sheer viciousness* required to throw that ring back in his face, on the same night you accepted his proposal in front of his entire family."

Harriet wished she hadn't blushed a shade of nectarine. "That situation was chosen by Jon. Would it have been better if I'd said no on the spot and let him down with you all as an audience?"

"I think anything is better than telling a man you will marry him, and then withdrawing that an hour and a half later, Harriet, yes. Falsely accepting a proposal is plain hideous."

Harriet could see how this version would effortlessly make her the gaudy whore of Ilkley boomers' wine clubs and book groups. It was one of those anecdotes where no one would spoil it by asking themselves precisely what Harriet had: What was the good girl's option here? Marrying someone you didn't want to, because it was ill-mannered otherwise?

"Sorry, but that's total rubbish," Harriet said, with a force she didn't quite feel, and saw the sour satisfaction pass across Jacqueline's face. She should remember the law of being goaded: you losing your temper was a victory for them. It was proof of who you really were. "My crime is breaking up with Jon, the end. You'd hate me however it happened."

Harriet feared she'd not heard Cal go upstairs. Please God, don't be listening. She couldn't reasonably object, if he was—Jon had provided Cal with a legitimate interest in the Barraclough family, and after all, this was his house.

Considering that she'd moved in with a man with a scandalous love life, so far, Harriet hadn't exactly pulled off "low-key" in this department either.

"Irrespective of the precise degree of brutality with which you've treated Jon, you've made the biggest mistake of your life, I'm afraid. You peaked with my son," Jacqueline said. "Women will be queuing round the block to date JJ."

Ewww. Bragging about your single son's sexual prospects? Harriet hoped if she was ever a mother, she didn't tell herself this sort of thing was "lioness with her cubs" behavior. Seemed a very gendered sort of brag, too. Harriet couldn't imagine a father saying of his dumped daughter, *She'll be all right as she'll get mad amounts of dick.*

"He's handsome, he's successful, and you could not ask for a kinder, more devoted man. He can't see it yet, but he who laughs last, laughs the longest. And he will be laughing long, long, after you've stopped, my girl."

Jacqueline cast another appraising look at their surroundings. Given the house was nice, Harriet took the implication to be: *Meh, none of this is yours.*

"I haven't split up with Jon to look for an upgrade. I'm not replacing an iPhone. Relationships are about being right for each other, being happy."

Jacqueline snorted. "And he couldn't make you happy, could he? No matter how much money and attention he lavished on you, or how much praise he gave you . . . No. Not enough."

She simper-smiled poisonously, like she had a coat made of dalmatians, and Harriet decided that, in fact, enough *was* enough. What had Cal said? Asserting yourself doesn't make you cruel, and by that same measure, setting a boundary didn't make you rude. Jon's mother, however, was very rude.

"Jacqueline, you've obviously created a mythical hate figure in my memory, a conceited gold digger who set out to hurt your son. She's not real or anything to do with me, but feel free to hate her, she sounds awful. In reality, Jon and I are two people who had a relationship that ran its course. You being gratuitously nasty to me after the fact is completely unnecessary."

Harriet was quite pleased at that succinct summary, given her animal terror at facing off with a woman twice her age whom all her social conditioning had told her to try desperately to please.

"It didn't '*run its course*.'" Jacqueline did air quote marks. "You were happy enough bumping along with the fancy holidays right until he wanted serious commitment. At that point you had to come clean that you always thought you could do better than him."

Harriet twinged. She *had* strung Jon along, to some extent. These European minibreaks, where Jon wouldn't let her pay for so much as an apricot Danish at the airport Pret a Manger, were not her finest hours.

No point now in saying Jon had insisted, acting as if her financial contribution were some sort of emasculation. Another vindication for Lorna's take—those indulgences, as Jacqueline now made clear, were down payments on a future together. Harriet had defaulted on her debt; she was on trial. She had *gained pecuniary advantage by deception*.

Meanwhile, Jacqueline's indignance was reaching a crescendo.

"I hope you enjoyed Antigua and the Cotswolds, Miss Hatley, because there's not going to be a lot of that in your future."

"Isn't there?" Was Jon keeper of her passport and the RAC road map?

"Who do you think will be rushing to commit to a woman on the wrong side of thirty, who won't run a comb through her hair and dresses like a surly teenager? Do you imagine you're a femme fatale? You should SEE the young lady who Jon took to prom."

Harriet mentally filed the last line to quote to Lorna and Roxy, to send them into paroxysms.

"If we've reached the personal insults stage, I think you need to go," Harriet said, satisfied to hear no wobble in her voice. "I don't give a rat's arse what you think about my appearance."

She could hear how flatly Yorkshire-accented she sounded, in ire, and Jacqueline would no doubt revel in this too.

Jacqueline bristled. "One final point. You need to return the jewelry that Jon gave you, while you were together."

"*What?*"

Jon had a habit of buying Harriet sparkly trinkets from Berry's, which weren't her taste and for which she thanked him profusely. She kept them neatly stacked, resting on their little silk beds in boxes, and rarely wore them. She'd never investigated their worth, as she guessed it'd give her vertigo.

A polite knock at the living room door sounded while she was still boggling at this.

"Excuse me, I'm ever so sorry for interrupting." Cal ducked into the room. He was wearing a smart blue oxford work shirt, rolling up the sleeves as if he'd been summoned to give a presentation in a meeting. "I want to help here. Think of me as a mediator."

They both looked at him in confusion.

"Who are you?" Jacqueline said.

"Cal. I own this house. Carry on," he said, making a gesture toward Harriet. "She should return the jewelry . . . ?" He waved his hand.

Jacqueline jutted her chin. "Yes, she should."

"They were gifts," Harriet said.

"Accepted under false pretenses."

"What false pretense?"

"That you weren't going to treat him like ignominious dirt."

Cal turned to Harriet, who was shaking her head and on the verge of laughter.

"Harriet, what are your feelings on being told you should give your personal property away, based on etiquette guidelines that sound like something from the 1800s?"

"I think she's taking the bare piss," Harriet said, flatly.

"You're taking the bare piss, Jacqueline," Cal said.

"You've got nothing to do with this!" Jacqueline said to him. "You have no idea what went on between these two. Stay out of it."

"Sounds like a perfect description of your own situation," Cal said.

"I know plenty, thank you," Jacqueline said, returning her basilisk stare to Harriet.

"Do you know your son committed common assault on me the other day?" Cal said.

Jacqueline's face dropped. "What on earth do you mean?"

"Point made, I think. Harriet, you've told Jacqueline you have no interest in her opinions or willingness to do what she says. Do you want her in your house?"

Harriet steeled herself to look Jacqueline in the eye. She was an arachnophobe being forced to fondle a tarantula.

"Nope."

"Right. Jacqueline. You heard her. Go, please."

Cal gestured to the doorway, and Jacqueline huffed through it.

"You should be ashamed of yourself," she spat at Harriet, as a parting shot. Perhaps Harriet should, in some ways, but Jacqueline was never going to be the one to tell her how.

Cal closed the front door firmly behind her and returned to Harriet's side as they watched Jacqueline back out of the driveway, glowering, with one hand over the adjoining head rest as she reversed.

"Thanks for that, Cal." Oof. Yet more humiliating spectacles. This man would surely be throwing a celebratory ceilidh once she was out of his property.

"Sorry to have barged in. You were holding your own, but she was being so disrespectful to you that I snapped. Did *Jon* let her talk to you like that?"

Her throat thickened. "She wasn't usually as blatant, but more or less."

"Wow."

Harriet got a little ache as she thought, *So, this is what it feels like when someone's on your side.* She watched his face closely, expecting to see that confused pity again. Instead, he looked . . . amused?

"What *on earth,* though?" Cal laughed, a release of endorphins following the face-off. "What century is she in? She sounded like one of those costume dramas. *Now you have slighted my son you will never make an advantageous match!* She knows this is suburban Leeds and not *Bridgerton,* right?"

"Maybe it's a very-well-off-person thing. It antiquates you. Jacqueline has always been a lot, but even I am blown away by that tirade."

"I genuinely thought you handled her with aplomb," Cal said. "Total harridan."

"Oh. Well. Thank you."

A beat where apparently neither of them knew what to say.

"Look, I'm off to meet Sam at Zucco in a minute. Want to join us? If anyone ever needed an Aperol Spritz the size of a baby's head, it's you."

"Oh . . ." She felt wrong-footed again. "Won't I get in the way of you-and-Sam time?"

"Sam and I have known each other since junior school. We couldn't be more pleased at someone getting in the way of our time."

As they walked to the restaurant, Harriet considered that an unintended side effect of Cal's involvement would be to bolster Jon's suspicions. At hearing Cal had white-knighted her, he'd go up like Jeff Bezos's cock rocket, surely.

This time, she really, definitely didn't care. Setting his rabid mother loose on her was evidence of real malice, and it had finally snapped Harriet's patience and expired her goodwill.

How perfect if it rebounded on Jon, not her.

20

Sam was fifteen minutes late, and so they sat in the hubbub of the black-and-white-tiled dining room with untouched menus, an Aperol Spritz, and a Negroni. Harriet had expected this to feel awkward, but the buzz of voices and the residual hysteria from vanquishing the witch seemed to carry them through ordering and waiting for drinks to be delivered.

"Dunno how anyone can drink those things. A Fanta-flavored migraine in a glass," Cal said, affably, nodding to Harriet's Aperol.

"You suggested it!"

"Ladies like 'em," Cal said, injecting enough irony into it to get away with it. "So," he added, "the real question is: Did you really say yes to marrying that man and then change your mind?"

"Oh," Harriet said, starting to sweat a little. "I didn't change my mind." She'd not dwelt till now on the extent of what Cal had just learned. She outlined being ambushed in the Dales.

"Gruesome. That's not 'will you marry me?' as a question. That's someone who thinks your 'yes' is a mere formality, if you've not even gamed a no."

Cal had got it in one.

Harriet couldn't believe it had taken until now to comprehend: had she agreed to a wedding under duress, and then felt committed to go through with it—newsflash—Jon would've been fine with that. *That's amore!*

Harriet was yearning to ask about Cal's proposal but didn't dare. For all she knew, it'd snap them out of the friendly mood like she'd fired a gun. She was quite enjoying becoming some variant of honorary, pretend friend to Cal Clarke tonight. She felt she knew why she'd scored an invite, despite his initial misgivings—it was the more surprising, interesting choice.

The funny thing about going to so many weddings is you got to observe society's archetypes, and she instinctively felt she knew Cal's—the social media Gatsbys. If they didn't marry in Italy or Ibiza, they wed in their hometown in a repurposed brewery or swimming pool or cinema.

Glossily attractive, raucously fun, their gaggle of friends was always as upwardly mobile and photogenic as they were. They didn't apparently operate a brutal caste system, they weren't mean girls or boys, but equally they didn't consort much with the ordinary.

Their attitude was "why not?" They bowled into work straight off the Eurostar after weekend bacchanals, they asked unabashedly for promotions, took chances with reckless abandon, and moved on without remorse. They had that knack for making life sparkle, for silvering its edges, as her gran used to say.

They usually had a large disposable income, but were a tribe distinct from the ex–public schoolies who dressed like young royals. They weren't the rich kids, they were high-profile through force of personality—gregarious, bright, ambitious.

You'd think parenthood would slow them down, but it usually didn't: they'd be the couple at the wedding shoehorned into narrow designer outfits, who still looked twenty-seven, doing a sneaky line in the loos anyway and last on the dance floor after obliging in-laws whisked Rafe or Coco back to the hotel for them.

Taking the lodger out to dinner and getting the lowdown on her romantic dramas—it was charming, it was gracious, and it might be entertaining. *Why not?* The one thing social media Gatsbys detested was being normie and boring.

When he arrived, Sam looked gratifyingly pleased at the sight of Harriet, and she was similarly pleased, then recalled she was considered "fit." She'd have to be wary: she liked the loose-limbed, garrulous Sam, but she didn't want to be a notch on the spare room bedpost or an unwanted complication to her landlord during her brief stay either. A period of celibate wilderness suited her fine. Nil by woo.

But Harriet didn't imagine she'd be an object of interest for very long. She was a shade too old, and a touch too Trad Yorkshire Lass dull, for either of these two. Cal had an upcoming birthday, and Harriet had overheard Sam compiling an invite list that was full of hot girl names, like Ashley and Mia.

Over plates of fritto misto, pizzetta, and lasagna, Sam got the tale of Hurricane Jacqueline. Even though Cal's barging in had been a risk, it had perhaps been a more finely judged one than it initially looked. If Harriet had hotly objected to his interference in her private life—if it *had* struck the wrong note, backfired—Cal could've pointed to the fact he'd written off Jon's assault as a favor recently. She'd bet he was a very good political journalist. He probably had an incredible second-act career as a spin doctor.

"Far be it for me to be the bluebottle in the carbonara," Sam said, and Harriet could spot the schoolfriend DNA with Cal in the way they sounded alike, "if you've insulted his mum, isn't this making the likelihood he's going to punch you again very high?"

Cal put his head on one side and chewed, nodding reflectively. How refreshing for his self-interest to come second.

"I'd not actually thought of that," Cal said, after swallowing. "Harriet, do I need to hire a bodyguard? I'd quite like to turn up at the *Post* with a six-foot-four man in sunglasses called Trey."

"I think Jon's going to be fuming, but I also raised legal action and job peril when I saw him after last time. On balance, I don't think Jon will dare turn up again."

The last week or so had proved that yes, Jon was capable of losing control, but not when his livelihood was at stake. That said something about how much of a loss of control it really was.

"If you say so. I might check out the front window whenever the doorbell goes, all the same."

"Astute."

Sam and Cal were from a nice bit of North Yorkshire, it turned out, but went to a public school. This satisfyingly confirmed Harriet's assessment of them: more well-to-do than her, as implied by their lack of strong accents, but not other-worldly so. Sam worked in some sort of troubleshooting role for Leeds City Council.

"Any weddings coming up, Harriet?" Sam said, and Cal looked determinedly at the rubble of some deep-fried zucchini.

"Danny and Fergus, this Friday, at Leeds Town Hall."

"Nice. Here's hoping both grooms stay all day," Sam said, doing a fingers-crossed, teeth-grit gesture.

Harriet laughed, while not knowing if she should, and Cal rolled his eyes.

"Oh, hah hah. We all know I've got the section of my Wikipedia subheaded 'Controversy' covered. If the waiter comes while I'm in the gents, I'll have an espresso, thanks."

Timely call of the bladder, Harriet thought.

"Notice that our Calvin assumes he'll have a Wikipedia," Sam said, once Cal had gone, and Harriet properly laughed this time. "In fairness here, I should tell you he's not that guy."

"What guy?"

"The one who traumatized a woman for life, in public."

"Ah." Harriet didn't know what to say and hesitated. "He kind of *is* that guy, though?"

"Technically yes, he IS that guy. But he's not that *kind* of guy."

Harriet felt this might be an argument of creeps the world over. Yes, I Did the Thing but I'm Not Defined by the Thing, Like Those Other Guys Who Also Did the Thing.

"The unfortunate thing is, he's a hopeless romantic," Sam continued. "Or more of a hopeful romantic, I guess. He has cherished ideals."

Oh sure. Seeing a wedding day through not among them.

"Was he hopeless or hopeful that day?"

"Heh. Both?"

"I wouldn't presume to know what went on, obviously," Harriet said, checking herself. She didn't want to lose what was left of her bed and board.

"You're not curious?" Sam said.

"Erm . . . yes, of course, but also not really. It feels too much like glorying in the worst day of someone else's life, to be honest."

"You're very principled," Sam said. "Gossip doesn't usually involve celebrating people's best days."

"True. Except the story about a lad called Errol at my school who got caught in flagrante delicto with a crossing guard in an empty office. She left her sign propped outside the door. STOP. Haha."

"There's probably a joke here about being 'hi-viz,' but I'm too classy to make it," Sam said.

"I thought you were brave that day, for what it's worth," Harriet added. "I'm not sure I could've done it. You're a good friend to accept that being visited upon you."

"He did offer to stay and tell her himself, to be fair to him," Sam said. "I knew it'd be a hundred times worse if he did. I brought it on myself, to some extent."

"Oh, right!" Reality, as usual, turned out to be a shade more complicated than it looked. "I thought Cal just informed you he was off?"

"He did, once we'd agreed I was the better messenger." Sam hesitated. "I was probably keeping explanations brief, at the time. Have you met Kit?"

"Only when she hired me and during the bridal shoot; she was pretty preoccupied."

Sam glanced up, warily, and muttered, "Like Errol, we best stop."

A second passed, then Cal pulled out his seat.

"No espresso, and my ears burning. As I expected."

Harriet smiled thinly and thought, *You are a very unknown quantity.* All in all, she was happy for him to stay that way.

21

Every wedding came with its idiosyncrasies, and so far, Danny and Fergus's was that they didn't want the "getting ready" sequence of snaps—a great rarity, given Harriet's price included it, and Yorkshire was known for its thrift.

"You're sure? Even in smaller weddings it's often such a nice part of the storytelling of the day. I don't want you to regret not having them later?" Harriet had said, when she met them for the planning session over pints and a charcuterie board at Friends of Ham.

"First of all, don't you usually photograph the bride?" Danny said. "The bride here is me, so Fergus will sulk."

"Actually, I agree, you're the bride," Fergus said.

"To me, the whole point is us looking incredible at the ceremony," Danny continued. "The magic is ruined once you know how the sausage is made."

"I hope you're writing all this down, Harriet," said Fergus, in his gentle, refined Aberdeenshire brogue, which somehow made his dryness funnier. "Gay wedding, but sausage magic must stay secret."

"Totally," Harriet said. "Obviously it's never a warts-and-all prep session. The wet shave angles as if you're in an aftershave ad, adjusting your bow tie. But the customers are always right. You know your own minds."

"Danny knows our own minds," Fergus said.

Therefore, on Friday afternoon, Harriet arrived at the town hall at the same time as the guests, three p.m., under instructions that they pretty much only wanted candids, mingling, and "general atmosphere" captured.

The grand Victorian building with its handsome colonnades was an old friend, Harriet must've done scores of weddings here. She ran off frames of the clock tower, smoky stone against the overcast sky, testing the exposure. The forecast said they were in for a balmy evening, which was just as well given the reception venue had an outdoor terrace.

The car pulled up, and Harriet caught the moment that the couple emerged and walked up the steep steps, to cheers. They each had bespoke three-piece suits—Fergus in Harris tweed, Danny in sand-colored wool—and succulents as boutonnieres. The cake later was a giant pork pie.

She weaved and bobbed among the throng to get the shots of the grooms greeting their guests. It really helped in her line of work to be a not-center-of-attention kind of person. She naturally moved around in a way that avoided notice. One of her local rivals, Bryn, was a lovely Welsh guy and a very good photographer, but six foot two and with a voice that could blow the froth off coffee, two tables away. She'd personally not want someone who turned your wedding into a football match where he was the Brian Clough–style manager. You are recording the event, not directing it; you were a documentary maker, not a creator of fictions. (Unless the bride and groom asked for comic photos of her pulling him along by his tie like a dog with a lead, or double taking at cupcakes bearing photos of their faces in their wedding breakfast, which Harriet had occasionally been asked to do. She had to summon a lot of "customer is always right" Zen to go through with it.)

"Harriet! This is my best woman," Fergus said, snagging her arm as she ducked past. "Isla."

Harriet shook the hand of a large-bosomed woman in her fifties in a vermillion fascinator.

"Let me get Danny's best man . . ." Fergus said, standing on the balls of his feet to get a bird's-eye view of the hairstyles and hats. "There he is!" He made an arm-waving and pointing gesture. "This is Scott."

Harriet heard the name, turned, and made eye contact with the thirty-something man who'd been pushed to the fore of the melee to greet her.

Time slowed and then stopped completely, in the way that the seconds before a car crash were supposed to elongate into a small eternity. The collision was in her consciousness: the thought, as she heard the name, that it might be him barely had time to form before it flew smack bang into the visual evidence that it *was* him.

Harriet blinked, stunned.

It had always been a risk, living in the same city, doing her job, but a bullet she'd dodged for so long she'd forgot to worry about it anymore. If *she* didn't know the marrying couple, then *he* wouldn't, went the shaky logic, as if they still shared an era. Harriet had started to indulge herself with the belief that he'd moved away. Or better still, gone to prison.

And yet.

"Harriet, the photographer today!" Fergus was exclaiming, somewhere at the other end of a tunnel.

Scott didn't look surprised, which meant he'd seen her from afar already and had the jump on her being here. Scott being a few steps ahead, *plus ça* fucking *change*. His expression was a mixture of amused contempt and unspoken challenge. *Go on. I dare ya.*

He looked a little older, in the pin-sharp HD of daylight—more fine pencil sketch lines around his eyes and on his forehead, but otherwise unchanged. It was like exhuming an old photograph, one where you regretted not holding a lighter to its corner. He reminded her of a previous version of herself, one she hated.

"Hiya, Harriet," he said, in that cocky rock star drawl that, once upon a time, made the hair on the back of Harriet's neck prickle. Turned out it still did, but in a very different way. "Nice to meet you."

"Likewise," she said, with a dry mouth. She'd have liked to include his name, but she couldn't manage it. With trembling hands, she raised her camera again, as a combination of mask and weapon.

"Picture of the four of you?" she said briskly yet sweetly, to reassert herself, to drown out the raging storm inside her.

"Yes! C'mon, Daniel!" Fergus said.

The quartet assembled in a line on the steps, Harriet slightly below them, steadying her weight on her back leg.

As she looked through the viewfinder, she saw the malevolent thrill on Scott's face.

HARRIET FIERCELY RECANTED ever thinking fondly of modest, compact weddings. How she longed for this one to be in a tent so huge that half the attendees were obscured by the curvature of the Earth. She wished Danny and Fergus had known so many people, the wedding would have been like marshaling the cast of an old Hollywood epic, complete with spear carriers.

Instead, here they were in a Japanese restaurant, sound echoing off a hard floor and industrial fittings, with nowhere to hide unless you ducked behind a decorative plum blossom tree. There were only forty-nine people available, minus the staff, to distract from the fiftieth one: her ex-boyfriend Scott Dyer.

Barmen poured and rattled cocktails, bottles of sake held high with a flourish; waitresses circled with platters of gyoza; and people holding full glasses drifted onto the decking outside to take in the view of city rooftops. The happy couple had their first date here, so it had sentimental significance, and Danny and Fergus had hired the whole place.

Their generosity and style were making things abundantly worse—the contrast between the glamour of it all and the horror of it for Harriet, as if she alone were being set up. There was no first dance but there were speeches, to be bathed in the early-evening glow as the sun went down.

The environment for the next two hours or so was an accidental hellscape of a blissful union, Harriet constantly trying to calculate how many times she needed to pass by the knot of guests that contained Scott. Looking like she was avoiding him was untenable; seeming as if she had a special interest was intolerable.

Scott's title of "best man" was more than a little satirical. How few men had Danny met, if this was the best one he knew? However, Harriet was unsurprised that Scott was best manning someone he'd not known in their years together. Scott thrived on being a novelty, buzzed on being the latest, greatest person you'd met. He poured his energies into winning new acquaintances over like a top salesman with his most potentially lucrative client. He'd have effectively been auditioning as a future best man from their first handshake, whether he got the gig or not. Scott, she had realized only with hindsight, liked to overwhelm people.

Every so often, when the crowd parted and Harriet was sure he'd not see, she allowed herself a moment's scrutiny. Scott was chatting animatedly and winningly, in his slim-cut violet suit, and still with the expensively ruffled, mop top hair. Harriet knew the maintenance that went into the unkempt lead guitarist look.

At his side was a petite girl with brilliant blond hair in a blunt shag cut and sticky, raspberry-bright lips. The combination of her big blue eyes, framed with sooty eyelashes, and high forehead gave her the look of Tweety from *Looney Tunes*.

Her presence was a given, to Harriet: Scott wasn't the type to be without a partner. He always had an eye for a pretty girl.

She was in a lilac dress—she and Scott had coordinated—with diaphanous lace panels that stretched tight across her hips, and Scott had a proprietorial arm draped around them. Her killer metallic heels were so high that Harriet would be weeping for the relief of removing them after five minutes, but she never saw her so much as shift from leg to leg, no sign of wincing or complaining whatsoever.

Scott was doing the talking, and as time went on, in Harriet's covert snatched surveillance, it started to become a point of fascination: When would she say something? A polite *no thank you* head shake to the tray of lollipop prawns was all Harriet could catch, as the blonde decorously sipped her Passionfruit Something or Other.

It took a lot of deep breaths, and a quantity of valiant guts that Harriet didn't quite know she possessed, to stride over at a natural juncture.

"Could I get a quick group photo?"

Everyone acquiesced, Scott pulling his girlfriend (wife? fiancée? Harriet hadn't seen rings, but also had not allowed her gaze to linger long enough at any one moment to be sure) sharply to his side, in unspoken taunt, or defiance, a mocking kind of lopsided grin on his face.

"Fantastic, thank you," Harriet said, with a fake smile, moving on, feeling the sweaty heat under her clothes.

Eventually everyone was ushered inside for the sit-down meal, and Harriet had the scheduled hour's grace to find something to eat herself.

She took the lift down several floors and emerged into the deserted Victoria Gate shopping center. It was oddly atmospheric out of hours, the monochrome, zigzagged tiled floor splattered with moody illumination from up-lit shop windows: like the holodeck of some spaceship vast enough to provide designer stores with undulating windows for its passengers.

She should find food, but she had no appetite. Harriet remembered the kindly nurse, when her grandfather died, telling her eating when not hungry—but traumatized—was nevertheless essential: "Emotional and physical energy aren't separate things." KFC it was. She could absently gnaw on hot wings while imagining Scott falling over that balcony.

As she walked down the arcade, she heard the din of heels on a hard surface behind her and turned to see Scott's partner also exiting the lift. Shouldn't she be busy with the wedding meal?

Blond Girlfriend pulled the vertiginous shoes off, one after another, and rubbed her feet, grimacing. She stood barefoot as she riffled in her tiny bag for a cigarette, which she lit with unsteady hands. Harriet had once heard the term "restraint collapse" to describe kids who are good as gold at school and naughty once home. Blond Girlfriend seemed to be relaxing into her own restraint collapse—after several deep restorative drags on her Marlboro Light, head thrown back, she began scrolling her white iPhone with one hand, while massaging alternate feet with the other. Harriet was pretty sure that her left ring finger bore a showy sparkler that could only be an engagement ring. Her cigarette was gripped in her mouth like Betty Draper when firing the shotgun. The tableau felt like it featured a different woman from the one Harriet had seen upstairs.

She looked up and saw Harriet watching, at a small distance. Harriet didn't know what to say, or what expression to make, to transform the interaction from spying on what Blond Girlfriend thought was an unobserved moment into something socially understood as mundane and acceptable. After a few seconds of blinking at each other, both transfixed and mute, Harriet turned and continued on, camera bag on shoulder.

She couldn't stop mentally pulling apart, dissecting and analyzing, what she'd witnessed, as she picked at fries.

Afterward, she wiped her hands on paper napkins and hurried back, not out of fear of being late, but because she didn't want to lose the courage it took to walk back in.

Harriet fired off aggressively frequent frames of Scott giving his best man's speech. *Clack clack clack. Whirr, clack.* In the quiet of the room, it sounded like the clatter of shutters you got in the somber hush of press conferences. *Too many! Pump your brakes, Hatley.* She needed to calm down before she gave herself away, the same way people who gabbled too much thought they were hiding their nerves.

Scott had the audience in the palm of his hand. He was telling the story of how he and Danny bonded on the hilariously disastrous bachelor party of a mutual friend in Cologne—half the men fell out and flew home, Scott and Danny discovered a joint love of the divisive local speciality, Mettbrötchen, then the relationship had deepened further back home, when Scott helped Danny through the loss of his mum.

Danny broke down and leaped up to hug Scott, Scott embracing him and rubbing his back, notecards for his speech gripped in his hand.

"It's all right, man. She's here. She's here," Scott said.

Several onlookers openly wept.

Harriet took more photographs, in lieu of feeling the right feelings. Yeah, that was Scott. Always great in your crisis. Always exploiting an opportunity.

Once again, Harriet found herself lost in the lonely chasm between who Scott Dyer was supposed to be and who he actually was; the sole person burdened with the dissonance, doubting herself. She hated this wedding for forcing her back there, against her will. She hated everyone in this room.

The Ministry of Ideal Weddings could use the minutes that Scott was speaking as a textbook example of How to Give a Best Man's Speech. It was flawless. He was witty, but also sincere: the tribute so well judged in its obligatory embarrassing disclosures and gentle mockery, but laden with much touching, genuine praise. There was the sad part, honoring Danny's missing mother. When he had his audience sniffling, he brought it back to laughter and relief, riding in to the emotional rescue and providing catharsis. It was as if Scott were playing them like a musical instrument, knowing when to ramp up tension, then relax the pressure—a virtuoso performance.

Scott built toward his summing up, describing the great joy of seeing Danny find his equal match and balance in Fergus. How lucky everyone here today was to share in this occasion. How loved the marrying couple were. Having Harriet as spectator clearly didn't bother Scott in the slightest, didn't throw him even slightly off-balance. Of course not: he'd have to care what she thought for that.

Scott had given an A-plus performance of the perfect pal, the dream hire best man. Richard Curtis himself would cast him. It was as if the collective crush that had developed was tangible. *Swoon,* he's so caring, so funny, and hey—quite gorgeous, which never hurts? There was a maiden blush on the cheeks of Fergus's trio of beautiful Celtic teenage nieces.

If Harriet didn't know Scott, no doubt she'd be as enamored of him as everyone else.

"When myself and Marianne tie the knot next month"—Scott paused to squeeze the shoulder of his intended, who glanced up and gave him a quick, tight smile—"Danny is returning the favor and being my best man. I can't wait. Just don't get your own back in grand style, eh?"

Laughter.

"Ladies and gentlemen, I ask you to charge your glasses to the wonderful Danny and his incredible husband, Fergus!"

Thunderous applause. Harriet's Nikon crosshairs zeroed in on Marianne, whose smile while clapping looked . . . strained. If Harriet didn't fear projecting, she'd even say anguished. Marrying Scott Dyer. Becoming Mrs. Dyer. Did she know what she had let herself in for yet? Had he changed? Was that possible? Was Harriet a very bad chemical reaction?

The light was fading, and Harriet's job would now be handed over to the vagaries of iPhones wielded in candlelight by amateur enthusiasts, cross-eyed on Taittinger rosé.

After suitable promises to Danny and Fergus that the album would be sensational and she had everything she needed—apart from the number of a reliable and affordable hit man—Harriet fled the building like it was on fire.

Outside in the city, she took deep gulps of fresh air, flagged a taxi, and repeated the mantra: *I'm free. He is history. He's Marianne the Blonde's problem now.*

He's someone else's problem.

And even as she thought the thought, she knew that was why he was still *her* problem.

22

"What looks good?" Roxy said, scanning the menu, and added: "That's my new line on dates, by the way. They always say it on American dramas. It's sophisticated, like you care what the catch of the day is and aren't going to have the burger like you always do."

Harriet laughed and filled their water glasses. "Not to sound like Chris de Burgh, but I've never seen you looking as lovely as you do tonight, and you look lovely a lot," she said, enveloped in the bosky aroma of the expensive tobacco perfume that Roxy favored.

Harriet was in a chambray pinafore dress and red lipstick. She'd imagined she'd made a special effort, until Roxy arrived in something silky-strappy, bosoms pointing aloft without any identifiable means of support. Harriet felt like the plain, low-born companion employed to carry Roxy's bags on a trip to Monte Carlo.

Roxy snorted and patted her chignon.

"Ta. Just a hun with a messy bun, getting things done. I don't look like that one from the Peru Two, do I?"

"No! Haha."

"I can't do the lock-in, by the way. I've got two viewings tomorrow morning and I don't want to repeat the puking-in-a-planter PreggoGate hangover."

This had been Roxy's worst event of the previous year and Lorna and Harriet's favorite. She'd got to a house she was showing, a £1.2 million mansion at that, early. Rough as arse-holes thanks to a night in her local pub and unable to keep her breakfast down, she treated herself to a healing vomit in an empty pot on the terrace. Unfortunately the interested buyers, with their young kids, turned up while Roxy was crouched down on her knees, stilettos up, barking into the bowl making animalistic *nnnnhhhunnnngh* noises.

Always enterprising when in a fix, Roxy said she was pregnant and had morning sickness, in a single stroke transforming their judgmental disgust into warm sympathy. Naturally, they bought the house, and throughout the purchase process Roxy had to work out how far along she was meant to be when they asked after her and the baby's health.

"For Roxanne, a son: Gregg Bean-Melt," Lorna had said, and she and Harriet had been rendered incapable of speech for several minutes.

Tonight, getting a meal at the Dive was a tremendous novelty, and Harriet was determined to make the most of it.

It wasn't that Lorna disliked them being there, more that it never made sense to socialize in a situation where Lorna was, by necessity, mostly absent. She had a head chef, but as she'd said: "Leaving your restaurant to look after itself is a bit like leaving builders to work in your house. You can do it, but chances are you're going to wish you'd overseen it."

She and Roxy waved at Gethin's table, which Lorna had cannily placed on the far side of the room, making their joint presence look less like the setup it was.

Lorna breezed past from time to time in a halterneck Pucci dress and snakeskin heels, and Harriet reminded herself to tell her later what a great outfit it was. She liked that Lorna's mate-attractant outfits were even more Lorna-ish, and not chosen for the male gaze.

"Have the heirloom tomatoes with whipped feta," she said, scribbling their order down. "Roxy, we've been over the fact that is not code for old tomatoes."

The food was great as per usual, the cocktails were great as per usual, but as for the company, Harriet felt Roxy was distracted.

Eventually she started talking about work, and it became clear why—her colleague Marsha was leaving to start her own firm and wanted Roxy to come on board as partner. The hour to become a self-employed entrepreneur seemed to have arrived, and Roxy was in a quandary: go with her, it tanks, and she'd have lost a handsome salary. Stay where she was, and if Marsha's agency took off, she'd be laden with regret.

"Is Marsha good?"

"Shit hot," Roxy said, making as emphatic a face as was possible concurrent with a mouthful of vodka rigatoni.

"You're shit hot," Harriet said. "This seems like a good bet? Shit and Hot PLC."

"I don't have any savings," Roxy said, which wouldn't come as a huge surprise to her closest friends. Every year, Roxy and her sister spent a fortnight at the exclusive Nikki Beach in Marbella. When Harriet and Lorna nearly fainted at the cost, she said, "It's a signature white mattress resort with poolside cabanas!" and Lorna said, "Is it, aye," as if either of them knew what on earth that meant.

"If we mess up, I literally can't pay my mortgage," Roxy said. "I don't mean 'would have to wind my neck in,' I literally mean I literally couldn't pay it. Literally."

"Could you tell her you'll join her in a year, then save like mad?"

"I could, but to be honest, Marsha's nobody's fool, and after a year, if she's doing great she won't want me as equal partner anymore. I can't blame her; I'd be the same."

"Tricky. All I can say is in all the time I've known you, you've sold houses like they're cold beers on the hottest day of the year."

"Aw, thanks, Harry." Roxy smiled, but she still seemed slightly out to sea somehow, mind further away from the substance of their conversation than Harriet's was.

Lorna conveyed by WhatsApp that Gethin's companion Tom had to head back, but he and Ste might be up for a late one; Ste was waiting on a pass out.

Rox has to get off. Do you want me to find a reason to go with her? Harriet messaged Lorna, who replied from the kitchen:

NO NO NO. NO. x 10 NO. Plus I'd already said you could stay out. It's a legal quagmire.

Unfortunately, Ste didn't get his pass out, and Harriet was left worrying she was a third wheel.

"This place is out of this world, well done," Gethin said to Lorna, once service had wound down and she was off the clock.

Gethin was easy to have around. He seemed far more interested in others than talking about himself, always a positive sign in a man, Harriet thought.

"I can't tell you how much I admire you for taking the plunge," he said. "While I'm still Mr. Have You Tried Turning It On and Off Again."

"Thank you, I do love it. It's not the whole life plan, though," Lorna said.

"Oh yes?" Gethin said.

"At some point I want to buy a dilapidated rectory with acres of land, for a song. I'll live in a motorhome outside in the grounds while I do it up."

"Oh no, not the dilapidated rectory. She's *that* many drinks in, is she?" Harriet said, and Gethin hooted.

"The dilapidated rectory dream is real, you hater."

"Apart from the fact it's a dream," Harriet said.

"I would not live in a motorhome," Gethin said, and Harriet clinked glasses with him.

"Nor would I, and pertinently, nor would Lorna."

"Are you DIY handy then?" he asked Lorna.

"Ish. No, not really. How hard can it be though? A few YouTube tutorials and I'd be rewiring a poltergeist-ridden castle, no problems."

Harriet enjoyed watching Gethin respond to Lorna, impressed by her but not at all intimidated. Gethin eventually announced his intention to get home "before I disgrace myself" and insisted he should leave cash for his liqueurs.

"It's on me," Lorna said, to his voluble objections.

"Why should you pay?!" Gethin said.

"Because I'm rich and fun."

Then, with Harriet feeling agonized to be in the way of a more private conversation, Gethin added: "I'd really like to see you again, Lorna. On a night when you don't have to cook, as great as that was."

"You're on," Lorna said. After a pause, where Harriet held her breath, she added: "I would like that."

LORNA POURED OUT more shots.

"Did I reek of sincerity?" she asked, as soon as Gethin had gone.

"Yes, you did!"

"It took considerable effort. *No nervous jokes if he asks me out,* I had told myself. What's the catch here then? I like him, he seems to like me. I can't wait for God's great prank to be revealed."

"There isn't one. You already know about Bubbles Hussein. Secret wife and kids?"

"Doubtful. I've investigated him so much online it was practically a colonoscopy."

"Scott was at the wedding I did yesterday," Harriet said, gasping through the mouth burn from the Limoncello, the only way she felt able to force the words past her lips. "He was the best man."

Lorna's eyes widened. "Scott as in your ex?"

"Yes."

The mood was immediately extinguished, as if they'd snuffed a candle by pinching the flame with wet forefinger and thumb. There was a reason Harriet had held this back until the bitter end, and it wasn't just because she wanted to be hammered. He was still a sore topic between them, one they avoided. They had no other conversational no-go zones as friends, but Scott was uniquely poisonous to the mood.

"We didn't speak other than to do hellos, as if we didn't know each other. He was with his fiancée, who looked terrorized."

"No doubt," Lorna said quietly.

Harriet grimaced. "I've been stewing on what I'm going to do about it for twenty-four hours and I've made up my mind."

"Do about it?" Lorna said, skeptical. "There's something to do?"

Harriet explained her very simple, powerful, and necessary course of action, to deepening furrows in Lorna's brow as she spoke.

Afterward, Lorna shook her head, firmly. "Two things. One, that is mad. Secondly, I am too drunk to deal with this articulately. I'll drive over tomorrow at midday for a walk in the park, and we'll discuss why you won't do this. Deal?"

"Deal to the walk, at least."

Harriet might be drunk too, but the previous night she had lain awake until three a.m. thinking it through. Eventually, she'd got out of bed and written nonstop until five a.m. She had been a woman possessed. She had got so absorbed in it, it looked like an epic once she'd finished, yet she couldn't and wouldn't edit it either. Whole truth and nothing but the truth.

Harriet was absolutely sure of one thing: she would send this letter to Scott's fiancée.

23

Harriet was still brushing her teeth when Lorna rang the doorbell at ten to twelve the next day—she wasn't usually punctual, let alone early, and Harriet feared this was an ominous sign about Lorna's fervor for her mission.

She heard Cal let her in and decided that, as Lorna was being attended to, she'd do her mascara and find her bits and pieces for their excursion.

Minutes later, as Harriet came down the stairs, Lorna was laughing, and—rather disconcertingly—it was Lorna's *real* laugh, earthy and guttural. Harriet had been so sure that Lorna would disapprove of Cal, she'd not even considered it could be otherwise. God's sake, did Cal Clarke's ability to beguile never end? Well, yes. Once you were in a white gown, in sight of a vicar.

"You've got a friend! Who hasn't punched me!" Cal said, ready for a run, headphones around his neck, looking as fresh in his white T-shirt as a cleanly cut apple.

"I was thinking about it, I won't lie," Lorna said, hands in the pockets of her dungarees, and she and Cal giggled conspiratorially together again.

For fuck's sake.

"Just checking I've got it right. Otley Road? The green frontage with the bay trees?" Cal said.

Why was she encouraging him to go to her restaurant?!

"That's the one. If you don't see me when you're in, mention to the waitstaff, and if I'm in the kitchen, I'll come out and say hi."

"Sounds great. Expect me soon, in my special bib."

"Shall we get off, then?" Harriet said pertly to Lorna.

"Nice to meet you," Cal said, as Harriet shepherded Lorna out of the house.

"Ooh, he's, dare I say, rather *acceptable,* isn't he?" Lorna said, behind a stagey raised palm, as they wove around Harriet's car on the driveway.

"Hmmm, yes, he's personable but also the bastard jilter who wants me out, remember?"

That was a point she'd done next to nothing to expedite. Cal didn't seem bothered, but if she let it drag much longer it'd look like an empty promise.

"Is there any context we don't have, that could make him not *guilty*-guilty of running out on his own wedding? I'm suddenly keen to find exoneration. Let us not rush to judgment. It is only Christian."

"The fact I can't think of what that could possibly be suggests no, don't you think?"

"Dismaying," Lorna said. "Very hard to find nonproblematic crushes these days."

Harriet had thought on what Cal's acceptable reasons might be, after that conversation with Sam at Zucco, and concluded: (1) Of course his best friend said he was a nice guy, that is really the job description of a best friend; and (2) There couldn't be something Cal didn't know, regards his decision to wed, until minutes before the vows. Even if Kristina was a nightmare, he still chose to (almost) marry her. It's not as if grooms are picking up their phone messages, at that point. It was a cold-feet bolt-spooking that showed when push came to shove. Behind the seductive facade, Calvin Clarke could be incredibly ruthless. *I hate Cal Clarke.* Who has hostile graffiti in their own house?

It was a temperate day and they passed many artisan bakeries and bistros, people lunching on folding tables. Lorna huffed and Harriet braced for the standard tirade.

"I understand sidewalk café culture in Paris, or Barcelona," Lorna started, and Harriet suppressed a smile. "Even Soho at a push. Not in Leeds on an arterial route with an Eddie Stobart wide load rumbling past, and a load of cigarette ash flying into my eggs Benedict."

"As soon as the Dive gets a license for a few tables, you'll be right into it."

"Of course, but that's capitalism, which has nothing to do with good taste."

Harriet had been mildly dreading this talking-to, so a combination of Lorna's humor, sunshine, and light exercise had put her in an unexpectedly positive frame of mind.

"How do you do this?" Lorna said, flushed and frowning at Harriet's face, after they'd gone two hundred yards into the park. "You look like roses and soft-serve vanilla ice cream, and I look like a sex case having a coronary outside court."

Harriet hooted with laughter and then said, "Wait, wait—this is to butter me up before you have a right go, isn't it?"

"Yes, it is. All right, run me through why you think writing to Scott's fiancée telling her not to marry him isn't completely fucking mad?"

"It's a moral obligation. It's solidarity with other women. And I'm not telling her not to marry him. I'm enlightening her about him, before she does."

"That's not how she's going to see it, though, is it? Before we even get on to how *he'll* see it. What are you going to say?"

"I'm telling her my story. Telling her the truth of what happened between me and Scott. No one ever told me what he was like. She deserves the warning I never got. Because I don't doubt there were ones before me."

"It's not like the mysteries of the human heart can be solved by leaving a stinker on Yelp, though, is it? You think you're going to pen her a letter saying her fiancé is a monster, and she's going to write back first class and say, *Aw, thanks for the heads-up, doll, consider him binned*?"

"No. Of course not. I think she'll more likely be angry and hate me for a while."

Lorna frowned. "Glad some reality is intruding."

"But once she gets over that, she might start matching up my description with her experiences. It might be the encouragement she needs. You should've *seen* her outside that wedding, Lorna. She's a hostage. She was me."

"You know how advice works, don't you? The only advice people ever take is the advice they want to hear."

"So she doesn't take it. Maybe it'll be a year, five years down the line, and she'll remember my letter, and it'll count. It'll give her the backup she needs to have faith in her own judgment. Honestly, I cannot emphasize how much he screws with that."

"I dunno." Lorna looked away, and Harriet saw the pinched look of skepticism on her best friend's face. "Look, Harriet, I can't argue with your strength of feeling and I admire you wanting to protect her. If I may be brutal, however, would such a letter have worked on you?"

Harriet kicked at a stone underfoot. "I don't know. I think so. Maybe not immediately. It would've by the end."

"The end was the end anyway. That's why."

They both reached a natural pause and had to hold fire to let a gang of students in activewear and jelly shoes past before they could resume debate.

"You don't think this is some scheme to split them up and get him back?" Harriet said, with considerable difficulty. She didn't want to ask this, but it had to be addressed to be dismissed. She didn't want to know and yet couldn't not know how badly compromised Lorna still thought she was. Her years with Scott had stripped her of credibility. "I promise you I'd not go near Scott Dyer again in a million more lifetimes."

"Uh . . ." Lorna considered this, and Harriet squirmed, as she'd hoped for an emphatic *Of course not!* The trouble with best friends who tell you the truth is that they tell you the truth. "I don't know, to be honest. That whole period of your life was impenetrable to me. How hard you fell, how fast you fell. How impossible you were to reach during."

Lorna welled up all of a sudden, and Harriet put her hand on her arm. Lorna wiped at her eyes. "It was like the way people talk about loved ones in an addiction spiral. The addicts pass a point where you can't help them, they won't let you. All you can do is watch and wait and hope to God they decide to save themselves. It made me truly understand what it means to feel helpless."

"I'm so sorry for what I put you through," Harriet said, thickly, starting to tear up as well, and swallowing it back.

Lorna said brusquely: "Don't be. You weren't the one putting me through it. It took balls to get out. Right. Where were we . . . ? No, OK, this isn't about the risk of you falling for Scott again. It's because this is one huge wasp's nest and every instinct I have says don't poke a stick in it, to no obvious benefit whatsoever. Is this revenge? I get it, if so, but it's going to rebound. He has to live the rest of his life as Scott Dyer, that's his punishment."

"It's not revenge. Helping his fiancée, now that I'm on the outside . . . it's an exorcism for me."

"Could be more like a savior complex."

"Courage calls to courage everywhere," Harriet said.

"I know that's a neat slogan on a Tatty Devine necklace, but I'm not sure it has tons of practical application," Lorna said.

"It's from a suffragette's speech!"

"And this is the horse you're throwing yourself under."

"Seriously, Lorna." Harriet stopped, to catch her breath, and to make sure the family with the young kids on scooters had passed. "Who stops these men? How do we stop them? Scott never hit me, he never physically attacked me or hurt me in any way where I can point to a scar. But he demolished me. If I could go to the police, I would."

"I think you can go to the police over what he did now."

"Not five years after the fact. Not with my job either, probably. 'Associated with scandal' isn't what people want from a wedding photographer. All we really have is warning each other. Who am I, if I don't warn this woman? Ultimately, it's as much for me as for her. If I leave another woman to suffer Scott Dyer because I'm frightened of intervening, then nothing has really changed. If I don't do it, Lorna, then I'm still scared of him. That's just a fact."

Lorna exhaled, heavily, and a light breeze whipped at their hair.

"I guess I see that. I also see you've made up your mind and it will eat away at you if you don't do it."

"Thank you."

"Let's say you send this letter, and his fiancée leaves him. You think if Scott knows you're the cause, he'll take that lying down?"

"Maybe not, but what can he do? I don't have a fiancé for him to cost me."

"Mmm. Does he have any photos of you that you'd not want posted publicly? Or videos?"

"Oh, no! You know me, I like to take the pictures, not be in them. There was nothing like that at all. I'm glad to say that was never Scott's thing."

"Good. I'm surprised you told me beforehand, by the way. You're a victim of your own honesty. You could've posted your letter and said, *Guess what!* while I roared."

Harriet laughed. "I'm honest and . . . to send it, I need your help."

"Oh, for fu—I'm not a pigeon."

"It's easy. I'll only be able to find details for the fiancée through social media. I'm sure Scott is on Facebook and he's got me blocked. He won't have blocked you. If you can look him up, maybe you can find out her last name from what you can see on his profile?"

Lorna opened her phone and found the app. "Scott Dyer . . . D-Y-E-R, right?" she murmured. "Here we go. Six Mutual Friends. Fucking hell. Six people who need to get a fucking clue . . . In a Relationship With . . . Marianne Wharmby."

"That's her!"

"This look like who you saw?"

Lorna held her phone up and Harriet inspected Scott's profile photo—him and Leeds's answer to Reese Witherspoon. They were in bowler hats, holding handlebar mustaches on sticks up against their upper lips, at some fancy-dress party or wedding photobooth.

"Yup, that's her."

Nevertheless, the larky image gave Harriet a moment's doubt. What if they *were* happy? She told herself: *Were the photographs online of you and Scott representative of any private truth?* If they're happy, Scott can spend an unpleasant evening owning up to his past, and they'll move on. If nothing in the letter rings a bell for her, it'll have a hugely diminished impact.

Lorna frowned and did some more tapping. "Let's see how much Marianne has set public . . ."

"Remember not to accidentally Like anything," Harriet said, nervously.

"I'm not going to accidentally Like anything, I am not a nana . . . Oh, you are IN LUCK. Or completely unlucky, depending on the wisdom of your foolish plan to contact her.

She's a senior stylist at Estilo. That new salon up on that side street by Waterstones, isn't it?"

"I think so . . . Roxy will know."

"I guess you book in for a style consultation and say, *Never mind choppy layers to create a sense of movement, your boy's a cunt*?"

They both laughed, and then Lorna's face fell to deadpan.

"Seriously, though, I still think this is mad."

"You know what's most likely to happen? Absolutely nothing."

"Believe it when I don't see it."

24

You know what's most likely to happen? Absolutely nothing.

Ya reckon, babe? Fuck around and find out, drawled a phantom Scott Dyer.

Harriet was clinging to her own words, as she stared into the cocoa-powder-dusted heart on her cappuccino in the Waterstones café. They rang increasingly hollow. After all her pugnacity with Lorna, on the brink of going through with this, she was doubtful.

Harriet was reminded of a tactic of her grandparents, when she harangued them relentlessly to get her way—there was nothing so humbling as getting her way.

She'd told Lorna it wasn't revenge, but perhaps that wasn't the case. She hated Scott with a force she'd never known. It was his denial of responsibility that was so hard to stomach. You could forgive many things, if the person looked you in the eye and said sorry. Scott's refusal to acknowledge his damage, his arrogance, and, most of all, his way of placing the blame and shame back on her: it was enraging, it was disgusting. It was so deeply unjust. It made her feel like she was in one of those nightmares where you scream and no sound comes out. Harriet never had her day in court, metaphorically or otherwise. He got the last word. More people believed his version than even knew hers.

Yes, she was angry. She hated him so much it was practically cardio. Harriet wasn't over it. Without seeing Scott again, she could live in the patched-up halfway house of her imagination, where he was suffering in some way. Seeing him swaggering around tore it all open again.

Harriet looked at the envelope in her hand with *Marianne* written on it and the haphazard Sellotape on the back. If Marianne slung it on a shelf while she finished her workday, Harriet didn't want it drifting open, pages falling out, and having the whole team at Estilo passing installments around on their afternoon break: *Give me the bit you've got, I think she's broken up with him in mine.*

But such notions of modesty and privacy were ridiculous, Harriet knew, like the doctor who's been inside you up to the elbow leaving the room while you put your clothes back on. Harriet was throwing herself on the mercy of a total stranger, who could do with this information whatever she wished.

Of course, if she chose to use it against Harriet, she'd also be indicting Scott. Harriet had weighed up Marianne publishing it to the world, on some platform, and thought it wasn't for her to fear the abasement of the contents. If Marianne did that, so be it. Harriet would stand by it.

She accepted she wasn't going to drink this now-tepid coffee, pocketed the envelope, got up, and walked, drenched in trepidation, to Estilo. Argh, what if Scott had come to meet her or something, and she bumped into both of them? Then she'd be going to book a haircut. That's right. How would she know where Marianne worked, after all?

Harriet wrenched open the heavy glass door with the name etched in cursive font and inhaled the aroma of a salon. Scented mousse and serums were carried on the warm wind of a half a dozen hair dryers and the standard loud R&B was playing.

"Is Marianne working today?" Harriet asked the woman with a mop of Pop Art sapphire-blue curls at reception.

"She's with a client right now. Do you have an appointment?"

"No. I wanted a quick word . . ." Harriet trailed off, tense with having no better way to phrase it. The woman blinked at her, while chewing gum.

"She's with a client, she's doing a color. She won't be done for forty-five minutes." She looked up at the clock. "Come back then?"

"What is it?" said a voice to their right, and Harriet saw Marianne from the wedding, without the makeup or the heels. She looked much younger and smaller, claw hair clips attached to the arm of her T-shirt and a paddle brush in one hand.

Harriet was momentarily speechless.

"Aren't you . . . aren't you the photographer from Dan and Ferg's wedding?" Marianne said.

"Yes," Harriet said, smiling awkwardly, wishing she'd not had that face-off with Marianne outside the venue. She needed to not seem like a flake right now, and frankly, she wasn't doing a great job. "I wanted to give you this letter."

She held it out and Marianne took it, squinting in justified confusion at her forename in ballpoint on the envelope.

"That's all," Harriet said, and turned to leave, perfectly able to picture Marianne and Blue Curls staring at her, stunned, as she left.

All the way back to her bus, she comforted herself: *There, done, over, you did your bit. Congratulations on your clear conscience! That was hard, but it's over.*

Unfortunately, now that it was irrevocable, she finally grasped what Lorna was saying to her. It wasn't a letter, it was taking the pin out of a grenade and lobbing it over a high wall. It was all very well saying she'd got the nerve to do it, but she couldn't see *what* she was doing. She had no way of predicting the fallout.

You know what's most likely to happen? Absolutely nothing.

She'd said that on Sunday in casual, dismissive confidence and, if she was honest, mild disappointment: whatever happened, chances were Harriet would never know, she'd be denied any closure. Now, she'd grab that outcome with both hands.

25

Dear Marianne,

I'm sorry for the weirdness of pushing this letter into your hands. It was a difficult decision to write it, and I know it will be very difficult to read. I'm sorry for any pain it causes you. I felt I had to. Hopefully, by the end, you might understand why.

I'm going to give you the whole story, because if I start to leave parts out, I won't know which parts to leave in.

I'm an ex-girlfriend of your fiancé, Scott. We met when I was twenty-five and were together until I was twenty-nine, and lived together for most of those four years. I look back now, nearly ten years on from when we met, and realise how young and inexperienced I was.

I wasn't myself yet, if you know what I mean: I was a bundle of ideas and intentions, untried and untested. But like most twenty-five-year-olds, I didn't think there was anything I didn't know.

I met Scott at a dinner party. A friend of a friend liked to host them in a networking supper club kind of way.

It was the first time I'd been and I was intimidated. I knew no one, beyond nodding acquaintance, and the hostess was busy. I drank a sugary cocktail, fast. Quite buzzed, I found myself sitting at a long trestle table opposite a slender lad with a broad Manchester accent and messy, rock-star-in-waiting hair. He had a sly grin and made dry remarks. He fastened his attention on me and asked rapid-fire questions about myself, his response to my answers a very northern "aw, right." He had a way of looking at me from under his brow that suggested I was the only one in the room who was on his wavelength, and vice versa.

We clicked. Not any old click either, the magic click. The click there are films and songs about, that you spend your adolescence dreaming of.

I went from What the hell am I doing here? *to feeling a kind of confident, joyful belonging in the room that I hadn't known before, and it wasn't coming from Bacardi served in Moroccan tea glasses. We swapped numbers as we left: "Cos it's always nice to make a new friend, Harriet Hatley."*

I don't remember Scott ever asking me out on a date. He was keen, it was obvious I was too, he told me when gigs were happening that he'd also be at. We were soon intertwined on benches at pub garden tables, him introducing me to his friends in that languid drawl as "my girl Harriet."

My name in his mouth sounded like a miracle. Our love was like a spell. I didn't walk down the street anymore, I bounced on air. I stayed awake to watch him sleep; we moved in together within months. I was flooded with brain chemicals that made me slightly mad. I put the "dope" in "dopamine."

There was only one unexpected flaw in the rosy picture: my friends weren't enthusiastic. They made the right noises, in a muted way. Then my best friend Lorna said: "He's a little bit full of himself! You're in love with him and so is he, haha." My friend Roxy thought he was great, but: "It did happen very fast, between you two?"

I was caught off guard. Maybe he had a little swagger, but Scott was surely entitled to be full of himself. He was fascinating, opinionated, creative, so sure of his convictions. Charisma to spare. He was the leader of his pack, wreathed in a special aura, the kind of character who blazes through life like a comet.

I once ventured some edited version of this stuff about his extraordinary presence to Lorna, who burst out laughing. "He's an egotistical lush, not Lord Byron."

I sometimes watched other women react to him. They'd fall by visible degree, with their faux-grudging smiles and sparkle in their eyes as he teased them. Then they'd remember my presence and give me a guilty glance, and I'd respond with a confident smile that said, Yep, I know I'm lucky.

I decided: Lorna's jealous. She maybe even fancies him a little herself. Ditto Roxy. They want him for themselves, but they know that's a traitorous thought, so they're taking the edge off their envy by nitpicking. *With hindsight, I realise, this was the moment I crossed the line from girlfriend to a delusional member of a personality cult. Anyone criticising him must be in bad faith, or at least have bad taste.*

All of this was the early hazing phase. I had to be in a state of bedazzled worship, where he was all the points on my compass and my heart's only desire, as preparation for his destabilising me. I had to have pushed my poker chips across the green baize and gone all in.

At first, it was subtle. It could be written off as bumpy young love. I still remember the jolt, the cold shock, the first time he lost his temper at me. There's a photograph of us earlier the same day, sat on the grass at some concert, all bucket hats and face glitter and giddily wasted on plastic pints. He has both arms wrapped around me and I'm grinning, delirious. I look back now and I see how much of a warning it is. His embrace like a cage, staking a claim. Me thinking that his possession is my paradise.

We got home to our flat, sun stroked, woozy with cheap cooking lager and me fancying a takeaway. I threw my house keys with a clatter to the table and yawned. "Want a Chinese?" *I turned and saw his face like a gathering thunder.*

"Why did you say that fucking thing to Lorna?"

My stomach dropped like a stone.

"What thing?"

"You know 'what thing.' Your stupid jokes about how my job is easy—how dare you make me feel that small?"

Scott worked as a sales rep for a drinks company. I'd made some throwaway remark about how you never had to work hard to overserve Brits in a holiday mood. It wasn't about Scott, it was a general chat about how none of us stayed within our recommended units.

He launched into a rant about how dismissive Lorna was to him, how I always colluded, how trivialised he felt among my friends.

I was horrified I'd made him feel that way and grovelled my apologies. I would never do it again. It would never happen again. I would never let THEM make him feel that way again.

Next came the jealousies over other men. Never mind the fact that Scott was a champion flirt himself. It was as if the face of every woman he met was a mirror; he was constantly needing to see his attractiveness reflected and reaffirmed. Yet if there was a man around, I was under immediate suspicion of inviting undue attentions.

One night I walked in on him scrolling my phone's camera roll. He had demanded the passcode in a fight, a week earlier.

"There's something fucked up going on if you don't want your partner to have your passcode. If there's nothing you wouldn't mind me seeing, why refuse to give it to me?"

It was easier to comply. Incredibly, I found his controlling nature proof we were passionate, at first. On my phone, he found photos of me in a shop changing room: I couldn't decide whether to buy a dress and wanted to ponder it later.

"Who did you send this to?"

I explained: no one.

"Bullshit, that's for a bloke, look at the stupid face you're pulling with that much cleavage out. Even if you didn't send it, you were planning to. How do you expect me to feel when you constantly fucking lie, Harriet? Do you know how shit that makes me feel? Do you even CARE?"

He didn't speak to me for twenty-four hours.

The next night, after several beers, he played the Lennon version of "Jealous Guy" and conceded selfies weren't necessarily proof of infidelity. He said, sloppy-drunk and amorous: "You know this overreaction is because I'm obsessed with you, don't you?" I threw my arms around his neck and promised him he had nothing to worry about. If he was insecure, I would fix him with my faithfulness.

When you're so grateful to get a reprieve—from the only person with the power to grant it, the only one who can make you feel better—you never question your good fortune. I craved his approval like a drug, and I never knew when he'd throw me into sudden withdrawal.

Under this onslaught of hatchet job reviews of my behaviour, the vicious hyper-scrutiny, I started to change. Adapt to survive. I became withdrawn, tense, on edge. I lost a stone and a half. Out of nerves, and because he'd mentioned how much he liked skinny girls. He said: "You, you're well covered, though, aren't you? No, I don't mean it in a bad way. You like your food a bit too much, but so do loads of us."

I stopped liking food so much.

He laughingly reported his friend said I looked "like a cartoon chipmunk. You would, but you don't know if you should."

Mortified, I objected.

"Haha, I obviously don't mind, do I! You're my girl! He clearly thinks you're punching, but I don't."

"Punching?" I said, aghast.

"Oh God, Harriet," Scott said, pinching the bridge of his nose, in great exhaustion. "Please don't kick off. Not again. I thought you'd laugh it off, it's nothing."

After that, Scott often relayed put-downs by third parties, insisting he'd leapt to my defence. I was always alarmed and upset they were, bafflingly, from people I thought I got on fine with. In retrospect, I can see such lying is an exercise in power. Making you mistrust everyone else but them, is power.

I turned down most social invitations, and when we were in company, I stayed quiet for fear of saying the wrong thing. Scott's friends would joke with me and I would grit-smile, respond in monosyllables, worried that I would be accused of inappropriate reactions, or saying something that could be taken to embarrass Scott. None of this had to be explicitly demanded by him, anymore—I had learned to treat the earth as if it were full of land mines, and pick my way gingerly through it.

Scott drew the circle I had to live inside smaller and smaller. The harder he made me strive, the more I was absolutely determined to pass the test, to show him I was worthy of his love. To get back to where we were in those early months. It had been perfect, and somehow, I had ruined it.

Our lives were ruled by his moods. The devil-may-care, wise-cracking lad-about-town I'd started seeing had been replaced by a miserable snipe, given to volcanic eruptions of fury.

It became a theme, a definitive characterisation—I was casually cruel, I had no respect for his feelings, "bull in a fucking china shop, you are." He said losing both my parents young had left me with deep problems, and because I'd not been to therapy, my unresolved issues were being taken out mercilessly on him. "You really need to see someone," he'd say, after he'd forgiven me another of my trespasses.

Even as I write this, I find it hard to accept: he turned the death of my parents into another weapon.

Now we call it "gaslighting," but at the time I had no terminology, no map for this upside-down place I'd stumbled into where I was the aggressor, and my dependence on him had made me prisoner. If someone who loved me this much, and seen me at my most vulnerable, thought my soul was disfigured and ugly, then it must be.

Increasingly broken, and unsure of him, I cried, wheedled, begged, and manipulated to get him to show affection. I played games. In a sordid, unhealthy relationship, you become sordid and unhealthy too. People who tell you to Just Leave, as if it's clean and simple, right and wrong, they don't understand. They don't understand you've become accomplice as well as victim.

My job was my only time out of the atmosphere, the only part of my life that existed independently of his influence. Scott said I was throwing my talent away. He constantly needled me about quitting, under the guise of being the guy on my side, my cheerleader who wanted me to realise my potential, until it became a symbol of my lethargy and hypocrisy that I'd not comply. I see now that I was supposed to stop working precisely because it floated free of his control. Had I done it, it would also be more proof of my failure and dysfunction. He wanted me to fall apart, become isolated. He would be my carer and rescuer to the outside world, while turning the screws even tighter.

One day, my friend Lorna confronted me. She didn't give me time to scheme my way out of it—she was "in the area" and did I fancy a coffee. I asked Scott to come, he was playing Grand Theft Auto.

"I need her attitude like I need a hole in the head."

Lorna and I sat, tense, talking over lattes like a couple of colleagues on a training weekend.

She blurted: "What's going on at home, are you all right? Is he mistreating you?"

I reacted with stung indignance. "WHAT? What do you mean? Of course not! Why would you say that?"

Lorna described my agitated, downcast demeanour and my striking weight loss, and above all, how hard it was to see me without Scott present. That I seemed to spend all my time with his friends and "doing what he wants."

"He's always with you, not like he's accompanying you, but shadowing you, watching over you."

I retorted that I liked my lifestyle, actually, and she shouldn't be so "clingy." I actually called her clingy. Then I stormed out of the café so fast that, given she couldn't do a runner on the bill, she couldn't follow.

When I got in, she had sent me a text. I stood in the hallway, opened it, and stared at it with dread.

Harriet, look. Firstly you need to know I love you . . .

Scott saw me, and sensing something was up, grabbed the phone from me. He frowned momentarily at the screen, then swiped and deleted the message, unread.

"There, fixed it for you, deleted and blocked her. I told you she was poison, right from the off. You shoulda listened. But you're always right, huh? We always have to do it the hard way."

So, how it ended. I wish I could say I had a self-generated epiphany. Instead, it was the most trivial thing. It haunts me where I'd be now, had it not happened. Maybe that's not uncommon. Maybe when you've reached your limit, you don't know it—you need something to spring the padlock open, like the last correct number aligning on the combination.

It was Saturday morning, and we'd gone to B&Q to buy some replacement bulbs for a lamp. I'd knocked it over the night before, when I'd got in at the decadent hour of 10.30 p.m. from seeing a film that Scott wasn't bothered about. I'd gone with the girlfriend of one of his closest mates, thinking that was "safe," and she'd insisted on a couple of drinks after. I'd texted to tell him and got no response, which was a clear warning I'd pay for it. To this day, if someone forgets to reply to a message, I get that icy feeling in my gut, thinking they're furious with me.

In B&Q, we were browsing those broad, open shelves which have other customers on the opposite side of them.

We couldn't find the right kind of bulb. I felt a familiar panicky sweat rise on my skin. Why couldn't the bulb be there, why did it have to let me down? My shoulders tensed as I waited for the diatribe.

"Well, there we are, lamp's knackered. Fucking hell, Harriet, you are so fucking selfish, why don't you ever think of anyone else before you go and get pissed?"

I muttered I was sorry. I knew better than to make my punishment worse by pointing out I wasn't wasted, that—God forbid—he was also to blame for turning off the other lights, that it was a £6 light bulb we could order online instead. Facts never had anything to do with Scott's feelings.

"Yeah, sorry's no good to me, is it. If you genuinely cared, you'd stop doing stuff like this."

"I do care."

"You always say you do, and your actions prove different."

He didn't realise there was a young woman, maybe twenty-one or so, on the other side of the shelf, who'd heard every word as clearly as if she'd been the intended audience.

She stiffened as if she'd had a small electric shock and stared at him in amazement, her hand frozen on whatever she'd been reaching for. The venomous aggression. Over a lamp. Over anything.

Then her eyes met mine. I saw in them a mixture of incredulity and pity that I will remember for as long as I live.

She hurried away, before we polluted any more of her pleasant weekend, before she had to think about the strange, depressing couples you encounter in B&Q of a morning. If Scott had noticed her, it didn't show.

Right there in the Lighting & Lighting Accessories aisle, I saw myself. Soon turning thirty, in a relationship with someone who spoke to me in a way that alarmed and repulsed a younger woman. For once, I saw a reaction to his behaviour from someone that Scott couldn't demonise or dismiss, a casual observer with no stake in our lives. It woke me up like a syringe of adrenaline to an unresponsive heart.

As we left the store, walking into the fresh air, I turned to Scott: "This is over. I don't want to carry on. If you can move out today, I'll pay this month's rent."

Scott took a moment to take this in, then nodded. "Yeah. Your attitude has said as much for long enough. Good you can finally admit it."

The incredible thing is—when the switch had flicked, when I wouldn't take another minute of it—it was so *simple. I knew it, but amazingly, he knew it too. Once I revoked my permission to be treated that way, what did he have left? He was an emotional terrorist but not violent, there weren't going to be threats to my safety.*

When we got home, I waited in the front room while he packed a couple of bags. I didn't quite believe he'd go. He eventually emerged and hefted his belongings onto the back seat of his car. Our only shared possessions were kitchen things and a pine bed. "I'll pay you for them," *I said, but he sneered at me.*

"Keep your fucking money."

He came back into the front room, once the car was loaded.

"Get some help, Harriet. I mean it. You need it. Get it for your sake, and before you put someone else through this."

I looked at his angular face that I'd once thought was so beautiful and saw only ugliness. You can't easily love someone you're scared of; I knew I hadn't loved him for years. His way of leaving, his incapacity to say a single caring thing: it finally confirmed what I'd known but spent years trying not to face. He wasn't the love of my life; he was an abuser. To confuse the two things seemed impossible.

I later found out that he'd told everyone we knew that he'd left me, made up a story about me throwing the lamp at him and breaking it, how he'd been hiding for years that I was a nasty drunk. I didn't care. I really didn't care. I was free.

His friends melted away immediately, his family took his side and cut me dead. They know Scott, but they don't know him. The thing with abusers is they're a percentage of a nice person. If the nice percentage is the only part their friends ever see, they don't know he's other things as well. If the abuser gets accused, they reflexively defend them, as any good friend would, if they hear something that doesn't chime with their experience. No, no way, not Scott, he's sound!

They're right, they know the nice part and the nice part is *nice. No one is seduced by someone showing their worst traits up front. Scott is a showman, and a con artist. His friends don't realise that they're part of the show, and the con.*

I don't doubt I've been erased from Scott's history. His sister once referred to a "bad breakup" that predated me, and Scott gave her a look like he was going to strangle her. He scrubs us from the record. It's supposed to be, I think, an act of extreme scorn, but to me it might be the one sign he knows he has victims, not exes.

Why write to you and tell you all this, instead of hope Scott might've changed, that he's different, that you're different, that you're happy? After all, your life is a complete unknown to me. I was going to. Believe me, involving myself with Scott Dyer's life again is the thing in the world I least want to do.

Then I saw you, and it was like seeing a past version of myself, seeing myself the way others must've once seen me. Maybe you are a reserved person, I don't know you. But when I saw you, outside the reception, it was like you were sticking your head out of water to gasp a breath.

I know that feeling.

Please understand I'm not telling you what to do regards the man you want to marry. I only want you to know all this before you do. And that if you have been made a victim of Scott Dyer, you're not alone.

Best wishes,
Harriet

26

There was a throb of light and music coming from the house as Harriet pulled into the drive, in the dusk. She belatedly remembered it was Cal's birthday tonight. He'd asked her if it was all right with her to have "a do" in a very punctilious manner, given it was his house, his thirty-third birthday, and entirely not for Harriet to veto. He'd also said she was welcome, and she was relieved to say thanks, but she was covering a steampunk Goth wedding in Whitby and would be late back.

She slotted her key in the door as quietly as possible and hoped to slope upstairs and disappear into her room, unseen. She'd put her noise-canceling headphones on, read her Kindle for a bit, and drift off to sleep in the cocoon of her duvet, like a content old pensioner. It had been almost a full week since she handed over the letter. If she made it to a fortnight without reverberations, she had arbitrarily decided, that would mean she didn't have to worry. RIP, the memory of Scott Dyer.

"Harriet? Harriet!" Sam bellowed from the kitchen, with the unmistakable brio of the half drunk. "Join us!"

"Hi, Sam!" she said, stopping with her hand on the banister, ducking her head to the side so she could see them in the kitchen. Multiple curious faces behind Sam's looked on. "I'm all right, thank you."

"Let her be, Sam," Cal said, appearing next to him. "Harriet has her own Saturday night to be having."

This was kind, if obviously untrue.

"Happy birthday, Cal," Harriet said, and he raised his glass to her, winked.

"Aw, no way, you can't go sit up there on your own, that's tragic!" Sam said. He held up his glass: "One of my margaritas! C'mon! Just one, then I'll let you go!"

Cal mouthed, "Sorry," behind his back and grinned his leading-man grin. Harriet weakened.

"OK, down in a sec."

After a minor makeup touch-up and brushing her teeth, she found them still in the kitchen. The back door was open to the garden, where young women were shimmying half-heartedly around a portable Sonos playing Haim. Harriet could've changed out of her jeans, but everyone knew she'd got in from work, so why bother.

Sam poured her a gray drink in a glass with a salted rim, and Harriet did the rounds of "hi, nice to meet yous" with attractive people whose names she wouldn't remember. They seemed to be a mixture of *Yorkshire Post* staff, city council colleagues, and miscellaneous shiny individuals, in the age twenty-seven to thirty-four bracket.

Approximately four drinks behind everyone else, Harriet was free to observe the dynamics. Cal, while one of four men present, was clearly the prime object of female interest. There was a lot of coy pawing of his shirt and squealing in mock offense in his vicinity. Although you'd expect a birthday boy to be key to proceedings, she felt their orbiting around him, performing for his attention. Clearly, his treatment of wives-to-be was no deterrent.

Sam was also flirting hard.

"I'm from a small place outside Richmond. Tougher area than Cal's," he told Mia, who was in leather trousers so closely fitting they looked like body paint.

"Your village won Britain in Bloom seven times, Dr. Dre," Cal said, and Harriet had to put her hand over her mouth so she didn't spit her drink.

They were a slickly amusing double act, she'd give them that.

Harriet accepted a second marg and marveled at alcohol's ability to bear you aloft on its tide. You stopped feeling out of sync and unwilling and became generally happy to bob around in your metaphorical water wings.

A sudden shower of rain pushed them indoors, to the front room, and Sam conspired with a couple of others to put karaoke up on the television.

"Oh God, Sam, no, not the karaoke. You PROMISED," Cal said, sitting down and groaning as the lyrics to "Waterloo" danced across the screen. Cal picked up a cushion and pressed it onto his face as the room was thronged with partygoers caroling ABBA.

Harriet, the other non-karaoker, snuck a sly look at Cal.

There was no one feature you could alight on and say, *There, that's why he's so good-looking,* unless you counted the laser-clear pale green eyes.

Like some very fancied women Harriet had known, the beauty wasn't in any detail but in the way the whole hung together. Everything in proportion, everything working in harmony. Harriet often felt like a jumble of bits that weren't quite meant to be juxtaposed. Cal's neat nose was clearly meant to go with those lips, which looked exactly right set in that jaw.

There was something else appealing about him too, something undefinable. She vaguely wanted to wipe the easy smile off his face and see those eyes darken as they focused on her. No, she couldn't and wouldn't be any more specific about how she might achieve that. (*Ugh, Hatley, get a grip! How much tequila, and you think you're dirty?*) But she betted there were a few people here who knew what she meant.

The karaoke enthusiasts cycled through "I Want It That Way," an admittedly very poor B-52s' "Love Shack," and a workmanlike Spice Girls' "Say You'll Be There."

Repeated attempts to get Cal up and singing failed miserably.

He was someone who drew all the attention he wanted without trying, Harriet thought, with no need to make himself the center of it.

"Harriet, Harriet, come on!" Sam pestered, after each turn was complete.

Eventually, fired by Sam's belief she'd "smash it," Harriet sighed and stood up: "I'll have a look what there is."

"Yes! Count HH onto the dance floor!"

After skeptical song flipping, Harriet said, "'Dancing in the Dark,' Bruce Springsteen. OK, I'll do my best."

She pulled a dubious face as it struck up, and Cal said, "Oh, thank God, I thought you said 'Dancing in the Moonlight,'" and made a forehead-chest-shoulder-touching prayer sign, which relaxed her into giggling as she began singing.

Harriet was glad she'd not tried a feminine-yodel type of ballad, and actually, the song was quite a good one for an ordinary voice to carry.

Harriet's confidence grew, and by the time she was bellowing the chorus, she was well into it. She knew what Bruce meant.

She stuck her hand out to Sam, who put his drink down, grabbed it, stood up, and took the other microphone, keeping hold of Harriet while they both sang the lyrics together. Was she flirting? She didn't know, but she felt briefly happy, and that was enough of a miracle for her not to really care.

Cal was looking at her strangely when she sat down again, flushed and rather triumphant.

Yeah, I know what you're worried about—I'll settle down with him to spite you.

Multiple females entreated Cal—"C'mon, c'mon, ONE"—and he consented to join a toneless group sing-along of "Get Lucky," mugging with a finger in one ear.

As a result, only Harriet heard the doorbell. Whoever it was really meant business too, holding it down for seconds at a time, so that when you tuned in to its frequency, it was like a piercing alarm. Uh-oh. Furious neighbors?

"Isn't that the door?" Harriet said, to no response.

She got up to answer it and pulled it open to see a stunning, diminutive, and distinctly grumpy woman, with long black hair pulled back from her face.

"Kristina?" Harriet blurted, in the disinhibition of margaritas.

27

"Hi. Is Cal in? Wait, you used my name? Where do I know you from?"

"The photographer. From the wedding. I'm Cal's lodger."

Things had grown so surreal that Harriet wasn't anything like as abashed as she thought she'd be, confessing to this. Embrace the farce.

Cal emerged from the din of the front room and looked no less startled to see his ex-fiancée than Harriet had been.

Kristina was wearing—wearing the heck out of, in fact—a long, simple black cotton wrap coat-or-dress, Harriet wasn't sure; it ended mid-calf, with a ropelike leather belt that tied in a bow like a shoelace. It was the sort of outfit that Harriet had only ever seen on famous people, on the red carpet. Her legs were bare, and her feet were shod in pointed black satin ankle boots. She looked like she'd walked out of *Mission Impossible* and could pull a hair pin out of her low bun that would turn out to be a lethal poison dart.

"You moved our wedding photographer in?" Kristina said to Cal, as if Harriet weren't there. "Classy."

"I didn't know that's what she was when I moved her in."

"You weren't exactly *all across the details* of that event, I guess," Kristina said, icily, and Harriet couldn't work out if she idolized her, feared her, or wanted to be her.

"Can I help you, Kit?" Cal said. "I'm in the middle of my birthday do."

"Can we talk?"

Cal looked pretty stormy as he led Kristina out to the garden.

The word must've gone around that the ex was here, because the music shut off as if they were at a bar trying to kick out stragglers. Although it wasn't intended to be a full stop to the fun, only a pause while they assessed what was what, everyone looked deflated and there was a general confusion about whether the party was still under way. When one of the guests took the initiative and got themselves an Uber that arrived in a minute flat, three more piled in, and then there was an exodus.

"She really is something," Sam said to Harriet, meaning Kit. "I'm going to get off, I don't want to be punched again. Don't let him get back with her, please?"

"Is that likely?" she said, startled. "Does *she* want to get back together?"

"Oh, fuck knows. I've given up trying to predict the pair of them," Sam said. He put out his hand and Harriet shook it.

After the house emptied, Harriet couldn't resist heading up to her room, which both got her out of their way and offered the chance to listen in on the garden conference. Would Cal sound brokenly contrite?

She sat down silently on the bed and tuned in.

"It wasn't an admin error, and it says everything you'd call it that," she heard Cal saying. "Turning up on my birthday, at this hour? It's not on. Don't do aggressive things like this."

Nope, not contrite. Wow.

"I didn't want to upset you by crashing in, but you didn't return my calls."

"There's a reason for that; it's because I didn't want to talk to you."

Whoa!

"If I can get over what happened, then you certainly can," Kit said.

"That's not how human beings work."

"We're not finished business and you know we're not. I brought you a gift," Kit said.

"I'd rather you—"

"Here's your gift."

There were soft, muffled noises, and Harriet wondered if Kit had jumped him.

"Fucking hell, put that back on!" she heard Cal say, and Harriet at once made a connection between the bare legs and one-piece outfit and Cal's response, and had to clap a palm over her mouth to stop herself from snorting.

"Why?"

"Because being nude in public isn't the done thing? I've got a houseful of people . . . !"

Had, Harriet thought.

"If you mind them seeing, maybe that tells you something."

"It tells me I'm wired fairly normally, thanks. Seriously, Kit! Put it back on!"

Harriet put a pillow over her face to muffle her giggling, and when she removed it, the action seemed to have moved abruptly to the hallway, where she could only make out the heightened tone but not the words.

Eventually the front door closed, and there was the sound of a car ignition and retreating exhaust.

Harriet couldn't detect any more footsteps on the hallway tiles. She had a hunch that the scene was Cal standing dejected and alone, on his birthday, realizing that everyone had left. It pulled at her heartstrings, even if the scorned woman stripper was his fault.

She opened the bedroom door carefully and tiptoed along the landing. Cal was, exactly as she'd pictured, stood with his hands in his pockets.

"Er. Hi. Want a hand clearing up?" she said.

Cal's head turned and his strained expression softened. "That's really nice of you. Clear up, then a quick nightcap? It's a bit of a shit note to end on, this, isn't it?"

"Sure." She smiled, and his look of genuine gratitude gave Harriet a philanthropic glow.

It didn't take the two of them long, and when they'd finished, they both gravitated to the living room, with its burgundy sofa and the warm glow of the karaoke screen, blinking.

"Operation Trash His Birthday was a resounding success," Cal said, as they sat down with bottles of beer, and Harriet didn't know what to say to that, in light of historical crimes.

"God Almighty, she was naked," he continued. Harriet feigned not knowing what he meant. "Under that coat. She was doing the flasher-mac, booty-call thing. I didn't think that happened in real life."

"Lucky you," Harriet said, smiling tightly. "She wants you back?"

(*Wowzers,* she thought. *Takes all sorts.*)

"No. She doesn't. Kristina just wants to know she *could* have me back, if she wanted. It's all a power struggle for dominance, all the time." Cal put a hand to his forehead. "I need her to leave me alone now. I've had my fill of incidents."

"She's forgiven you, then?"

Cal's brow furrowed. "In what way?"

Harriet knew they were both quite smashed, but she thought this was spectacularly obtuse, all the same.

"For running out of the church?"

"Haven't you had chapter and verse on that from Sam?"

Harriet shook her head.

"I'm amazed, Sam bloody loves retelling this lurid yarn. That goes double when his listener's pretty."

Harriet remained impassive, while suppressing an involuntary thrill at the compliment.

"I think he tried, but I wasn't very receptive to him telling me, to be fair," Harriet said. "I didn't want to be . . . what's the word. Prurient."

"Hah. All right, well, if you're asking if Kit's forgiven me, I feel like the time has come for the story of the wedding that wasn't. Are you ready?"

"Hit me," Harriet said. She was actually dying to make sense of it, at this point. He didn't sound at all abashed, and Harriet wondered if he really was about to exonerate himself, or finally confirm her worst suspicions.

28

"Where to start . . . all right, so. By the time of the wedding, I'd been with Kit nearly three years."

"Can I ask a stupid, minor question?" Harriet said. "When I met Kristina she told me she was always Kristina, 'never Kris or Krissy,' but you and Sam call her Kit?"

"Haha, did she? Well, there you go. That's Kit in what she calls her 'corporate psychopath' mode. Telling you that you had to call her by her full name was a power play, that's all. Making it clear she's in charge. She's Kit to everyone."

"Ah. Carry on."

"OK, so. Eighteen months ago, we went on holiday to Portofino." Cal paused. "Have you been to the Italian Riviera?"

There was a beat of silence, and then Harriet, knackered, pissed, nearly shrieked before collapsing into incapable laughter.

"What?!" Cal said, laughing because she was laughing.

When she got the power of speech back, Harriet gasped: "'Have you been to the Italian Riviera,' ahahahaha!"

"WHAT?! I didn't know if you had!"

"Literally only you would pause to ask that. Before I go on, *have you tried the divine spritzes at Caffè Florian in Venice . . .*"

"Your disrespect here is staggering," Cal said, but she could see he was enjoying himself too. "Look, I asked because I didn't want to mansplain Liguria to you, but clearly, I will be mocked either way."

Harriet gurgled.

"My point is: Portofino is like falling into an F. Scott Fitzgerald novel or something. When it's lit up at night in shades of soft blue and you're on a pink bougainvillea-filled terrace carved out of the mountain rock . . . I'm setting the scene to explain that, even though I knew things between Kit and I were going badly wrong, and I didn't feel what I should feel—when she asked me to marry her, it seemed like the greatest idea that evening. Watching yachts coming into the harbor, drinking cold wine, it's like crack cocaine for romantic feelings. There should be laws against accepting proposals on that terrace. There should be a cooling-off clause."

Harriet was reminded of Lorna's Day Three of Glastonbury rule. *Is it their company, or is it all the trappings?*

"The ridiculous thing is, I agreed to get married *because* I knew we were going wrong. The fabled Band-Aid. Yeah, what this failing relationship needs is a big act of committing to it!"

He looked at her, and Harriet nodded, with an expression of sympathy. If he thought *so I went along with it half-heartedly thanks to her proposing on a nice holiday* was much of an excuse, however . . .

"Kit took over the wedding planning. She's one of those hyper-effective ruthless types in business . . . Out of laziness, out of my ambivalence, I let her run the show. Which is why I never met you, I guess."

"Right."

"But, after we got engaged, something else was going on. There's this guy at her work, Sebastian, Seb, who she starts mentioning all the time. She doesn't realize she's mentioning him, as people with crushes generally don't. Or that she's getting a silly look on her face, telling me banal stuff. 'Oh yes, Seb said that restaurant gets busy,' and so on. I'm not super-suspicious, but I have registered it."

Harriet sat up straighter.

"Kit goes off on a week's training course in Gloucester. Kit wears a Fitbit. The Fitbit is linked up to the iPad we both use, that's still at home."

Harriet said quietly, ". . . Oh . . . God."

"Yeah," Cal said, taking a swig of beer. "My fiancée gets back from Gloucester. The biggest chump you've ever met, me, says entirely not intending anything: 'The hotel had a twenty-four-hour gym then? Useful.'"

Harriet hissed, "*Fuuuuuuuu—!*" under her breath.

"Kit said, 'No, why do you say that?' I said, 'You were clocking up some seriously athletic heart rates after ten every night?'"

"Oh my God!"

"It would be incredibly funny if, at the time, it wasn't also so awful. She stands there looking absolutely mortified as I catch onto what strenuous activity was actually winning her gold medals. I said, 'Let me guess, the person next to you on the nocturnal cross trainer was called Sebastian?' Then she burst out crying. Howling-crying."

Harriet could only make murmurs of astonishment. Fair to say this rivaled accepting and then unaccepting Jon's proposal.

"Another beer, before I continue?" Cal said. Harriet nodded. If ever there was a two-beer-worthy story.

Cal returned with the beers and flopped back onto the sofa, next to her.

"Where was I? Oh yes. *It was a mistake, she had commitment nerves, one last fling before decades of marital monogamy. She'd never do it to me again! Please, please don't leave her, not now. The wedding would be the best day of both our lives.*"

"Oof."

"By the by, Seb is 'obsessed' with her and has begged her to call off the wedding, but she won't, because I'm The One."

Cal swigged his beer and sighed, picked at the label.

"That was it. That was the moment any remotely sensible person would say, *No, let's not, eh?* The writing is on the wall, Banksy-size. She prostrated herself on the floor and wept on my feet. It was as if holding her to account for the affair would be an act of great cruelty on my part."

Harriet gritted her teeth. She had seen for herself that Kit had some strange and powerful charisma. Like the tractor-beam pull for an enemy spacecraft.

"You already know the next part of KitBitOnTheSideGate: we stayed together. The wedding was paid for and planned out. Do you know why I didn't call it off? Apart from that canceling it would've been a social ordeal and a lot of spending down the drain?" He sighed. "I wanted to win. I'm so fucking ashamed of that. Above all, that is the part I hate myself most for."

"Win . . . ?"

"Seb wanted her to leave me. If we'd split up, he'd be right in there. He'd know he caused it. I have absolutely no excuse for myself here other than I was in a state of shock. But still. Bit of toxic masculinity intruded. I wasn't going to have a bloke who wears Oakley sunglasses call my wedding off for me."

"Then on the day, you couldn't go through with it?"

"Oh no. I'd have actually gone through with it. A thought that chills my blood."

Harriet frowned in confusion.

"I'm stood there, in the church, wondering how to psychologically handle this completely hollow, grotesque sham that my stupidity, weakness, and vanity have got me into. You know when you realize you want to get off the ride, but it's right after they've slammed the safety bar down? It's started moving, and it's dangerous to let you off? It was that. I finally came to my senses at the point of no return. I got dressed that morning, feeling sick. Then who should swagger in and take his place in the pew in church, but Mr. Skyscraper Climb Badge himself, Sebastian."

"What?!"

"Yep. She invited him. Her piece of ass. And yes, the invites to her colleagues went out *after* Hotel Fitbit. It's not as if I double checked with her that he wasn't being invited, because who would DO that?!"

Harriet gasped.

"Quite," Cal said. "I saw Sebastian, and in that instant, I truly knew Kristina. I mean, I already knew Kristina, but that was so sociopathic as to be unreal. I never wanted to be near her again, let alone marry her."

Harriet genuinely couldn't find the words.

"The universe had already offered me a respectable and eminently intelligent moment to walk away. What moment do I choose instead? The one that's a huge fucking public disgrace and when my aunt and uncle have wasted the price of a Travelodge. When everyone thinks I'm the ice-cold shit. Sam—who never liked her—said, 'Look, mate, you don't have to do this, you know.' Half in jest. He didn't know Sebastian had arrived. But that was it."

There was silence in the sitting room as Harriet absorbed this. That Cal Clarke could've had a reason for doing what he did, a sound reason, was a huge adjustment. She had declared it impossible. She thought Jacqueline was dreadful for cherry-picking her facts, stripping them of context, and making Harriet a two-dimensional brute, yet it turned out Harriet was capable of this too.

"That is . . . I don't know what to say, Cal. Unreal."

"One for the grandkids, as they say."

Harriet was still trying to make sense of Kit's machinations.

"What was her excuse for inviting Sebastian?"

"Oh, she'd drawn up the invites before the cheating, forgot to set it aside when she was posting them out. I don't think as you're merrily putting the stiffy in the envelope—no pun—you forget that it's the Other Guy? Laughable."

"Why invite him at all?!"

"I've been over and over this in my head. I think it boils down to this. Kit is a narcissist. She wanted to bait Seb, to see if he'd turn up on her big day, witness her marry his rival. She thrives on inhabiting a diva spotlight."

"She must've known you'd be incandescent?"

"Yeah, but Kit thought, *When Cal clocks him, by then, we'll be Mr. and Mrs. Clarke,* or very nearly. She didn't think I'd have the nerve to walk out."

"She'd designed a trap. Like Jon did with my proposal," Harriet said.

"Exactly! Perhaps she thought I was so in her thrall, it'd only mean a sulky couple of days on the honeymoon? Truth be told, I've stopped trying to work out how she thinks. Bear in mind if it wasn't for the technology fail, I'd never have known about the infidelity. She's . . . brutal."

Harriet nodded, wincing. "Exceptionally so."

"That's my type, I'm afraid."

"Is it?"

"Yeah. I have form for picking Hot Thatchers."

She choked on her mouthful of beer. "Hot what?"

"Sam says every girlfriend of mine is, I quote, 'Margaret Thatcher's personality in the body of a babe.'"

Harriet started laughing again. "This isn't my fault," she gasped out, pointing at herself. "You need to be less funny while telling me terrible things."

"I mean it's finding a balance, isn't it? Equally I'm not inclined to go for girls who buy ornaments of moon-gazing hares or try crafting with cat hair," Cal said, throwing her an *I've cheered up now, serious bit's over* smirk.

"Smart-arse," she said.

"True. Ugh, I am so wasted," Cal said, rubbing his eyes. "Mind if I lie on the floor?"

"Pardon?" Harriet said.

"Remember in school, the laminated safety poster with the fire bell procedure? If there was a roomful of smoke, you're supposed to get underneath it? That's how I feel when pissed."

He wriggled off the sofa and lay down on the carpet, hands on his stomach.

"Better."

"Really?"

"Try it. You won't go back."

Harriet put her beer aside and lay down next to him, heads alongside each other. They both stared at the star-shaped ceiling pendant, its bulb the only illumination in the gloaming.

"I still feel drunk," Harriet said, after a minute.

"That'll be the alcohol."

"Why did Kit leave all the house stuff? And the house, for that matter?"

"Because I paid for it all."

"Oh."

"A sizable inheritance from my gran, right after I met Kit. It was too soon for joint mortgages, but she was all, 'Put it into property!' I had the credit card and she had the vision."

"Did you pay for the wedding?"

"Yup. Twenty-five grand to remain single."

"Ouch."

"Worth every penny when her dad came to see me afterward. Imagine owing it to your Not-In-Laws."

"Ouch."

"Did you tell them why you cut and ran?"

"No. Beyond some 'ask your daughter' enigmatic stuff that went down like a lead balloon. I told my parents, who to be fair said I was well off out. Might've helped that they already couldn't stand Kit."

Cal sat up, back against the sofa, and picked up the remote for the karaoke.

"Remember being bright, shiny, and hopeful about love and relationships, thinking we'd not make the same messes our parents' generation did?"

Harriet remembered Sam calling Cal a hopeless/hopeful romantic. She still couldn't quite see it, though it made more sense than it did before.

"Did your parents make a mess?"

Cal checked his watch. "Another time. For tonight, pass. Did yours?"

"Pass."

They sat up together, backs leaning against the sofa, time starting to stretch and blur as Cal scrolled the karaoke options in indifference. They knew they should go to bed, but they were too tired to move.

As they listened to a percussion-only version of "Dancing in the Dark," Cal fell asleep on her shoulder, his phone dropping from his hand and rolling onto the carpet.

Harriet picked it up for him. The lock screen bore opening lines of WhatsApp messages from multiple women: Ashley, Bonnie, Mia, Frances. They mostly looked to be apologizing for "running out," and she would bet they were designed to discover if Kit was back in his life. She laughed out loud. Cal twitched at the sound and opened his eyes.

"You filthy womanizer," she said, handing it back. "It fell out of your hand. I didn't grab it."

Cal blinked blearily at the handset.

"I know you won't believe me, but my encouragement is nonexistent. I've got no appetite for any of it," he said.

"I don't believe you, you're right," Harriet said, and Cal gave her a lazy-drunk, seductive, *well, what can I do about that?* half smile.

Annoyingly, she totally believed him.

29

It had been nearly a fortnight since the Marianne letter handover at Estilo, and sure enough, zero blowback. *What a drama llama I've been,* Harriet thought, as she allowed herself to breathe out. Her confidence that nothing was coming had grown with every day.

You know what? Scott's fiancée, Marianne, probably read the first few paragraphs, said, *Oh, a bitter ex, is it,* skimmed the rest, and shoved it unceremoniously in a bin full of discarded till receipts and hanks of hair.

Anything was possible, in the off-world colonies that were the private lives of others. Maybe Harriet had been Scott's reckoning, and he'd never dared to treat a woman that badly again—Marianne couldn't reconcile him with the portrait of a belligerent man in his twenties. He'd mellowed beyond recognition. (Harriet knew this wasn't true, from her merest brush with him, but rule nothing out.)

Maybe—whisper it—maybe Marianne was another Scott, who gave as bad as she got. Maybe a bottle of toner got spilled on the letter and Marianne was left forever wondering what the pale photographer with the plait thought she ought to know.

Maybe she simply thought Harriet was a malignant fantasist.

Maybe maybe maybe.

The point was, Harriet had done her duty to another woman when the universe sent her a test.

She hadn't realized how much the potential consequences of her act had weighed on her until she approached her imaginary safe-by date, and her shoulders dropped by half an inch. Her years with Scott Dyer were ones she never revisited. Even when her mind wandered, she stopped herself.

Writing that letter was like drinking hemlock, or thrusting her hand into a crackling bonfire.

Hence Harriet was in an unexpectedly bouncy mood when the doorbell rang late morning Sunday, a week since Cal's curtailed party. She ran down the stairs to answer it. The man of the house was in the shower, or he had been fifteen minutes ago, according to the squeak and hiss of the water pipes that she'd overheard as she made coffee.

Her housemate was her friend now. She didn't have to offset every pleasant interaction with Cal with: *But remember he's a creep. That* readjustment had floored her. In the seven days since she'd learned the truth, every day had brought small but friendly interactions, even when they were doing boring chores.

The thing about Cal Clarke was, he was fun. She'd not realized how much she had missed fun. Whenever they chatted, he made her laugh. He managed to be always upbeat without ever being unserious. She'd put her key in the lock and find herself hoping he was home.

On the other side of the door stood a middle-aged deliveryman in a flat cap with a friendly face; in the crook of his arm, a spectacular bouquet of pink-and-white lilies.

The lusted-after and eligible Cal seemed the more obvious flower-receiver in the home, yet he said, "Ms. Aitch Hatley?"

"Oh! Yes."

Harriet never expected thanks from weddings she photographed, but it was always gratifying to know she'd been appreciated. The responsibility of her job was that you knew you were creating an album they'd keep forever, bar bitter separations. She knew of only one wedding she'd covered where she learned that the ex-wife had set the album ablaze at her divorce party. ("It's all on a memory stick, but it's nice to do something symbolic, isn't it?" she'd told Harriet, when she ran into her in BrewDog.)

"You don't own a cat, do you?" the courier said, while she was signing the electronic delivery receipt with the plastic wand. "These can be fatal to cats, you know."

"No cats," Harriet said, beaming.

Cal appeared on the stairs with damp hair, as Harriet, a slightly smug expression on her face, conveyed the huge bushel of flowers to the kitchen.

"Whoa! An admirer?" he said.

"A wedding thank-you," she said, "I assume."

She was proud of the Danny and Ferg gallery, now that she thought about it. And they weren't to know she was toiling under duress.

As she said it, an extraordinary alternative occurred to her.

Marianne. Harriet had never, for a moment, imagined Marianne might be grateful to her. If that emotion ever arrived, it'd be a long way off. Even then, Harriet doubted that the woman who warned you off your intended was ever very likely to be close to your affections. Harsh, but there it was.

The prospect was so peculiar and exhilarating that whomever the flowers were from, she knew she'd be slightly disappointed if it wasn't Marianne now.

She pulled the card from the box and opened it.

Two words, in capitals, in the foreign, feminine handwriting of some anonymous florist shop assistant.

GAME ON.

Harriet blinked at it. "Game On"? What . . . ? Was this a misdelivery?

The few seconds where it dawned on her that this wasn't a gesture of affection, but one of hostility, were sufficiently sickening that she knew her sender had got his money's worth. It would've been queasily intimidating no matter what, but her opening that card eagerly was the real coup de grâce.

"Who's it from, then?" Cal said.

"Couple from last week," Harriet said, concealing her shakiness, stuffing the card into her jeans pocket.

"The Goths?"

"What?"

"In Whitby?"

"Oh yeah."

"You must've smashed it."

"Mmm-hmmm."

Harriet's heart was clanging like a kid bashing a cymbal. WAIT: Scott had her address? HOW? *Think, think . . .* Was it him? It had to be him.

The doorbell went again.

"These'll be my flowers," Cal said, and Harriet forced a smile.

The kitchen was suddenly full of Mr. and Mrs. Clarke Senior, and Harriet remembered Cal had mentioned his parents were coming to take him out for lunch, as a delayed birthday visit.

"Hello, you must be Harriet!" said a gray-haired sixty-something man, a scaled-up version of Cal, with a fleshier nose and broader build. Actually, he shared a jawline with his father, but she could see Cal's features more closely resembled his slight, fair mother. (She was reminded of a Lorna complaint about vapid Facebook comments: "'Child looks like both of its parents'—shocker.")

"I'm Andrew and this is Sandie, it's lovely to meet you."

"Nice to meet you too."

"I've heard a lot about you!"

He looked excessively delighted to meet Harriet, as if the discovery of a woman in his son's kitchen was the treasure of the Sierra Madre. He was one of those men who wore lashings of an expensive, spicy aftershave, its scent now filling the room and eclipsing the lilies. Good.

"That makes me sound weird, Dad," Cal said, grimacing. "Harriet, he's not heard a lot about you, he's heard a few things about you. An appropriate amount about you."

Harriet smiled.

How did Scott Dyer get her address?!

"You're a photographer, Cal says. A really talented one."

Whether this was hyperbole or not, Harriet didn't know, but accepted it with gratitude.

"Thank you, that's very kind. Only a wedding photographer. I don't win awards. Well, maybe wedding industry ones, occasionally." Her brain was flying on autopilot, operating her mouth.

"Game On." What does that mean?

"Fabulous. If our daughter ever gets her act together you can do hers. Might be waiting longer on this one, though, he can't make up his mind even when the Motown band is tuning up and vol-au-vents are being heated through," he said, nodding toward his son.

Cal checked his watch and said, "A new record."

Cal's dad continued dazzling a smile at her, and Harriet wondered if he'd mistaken her for a girlfriend in the ascendant, such was the torrent of attention and positivity. She felt a little shy, in fact.

What if he turns up here?

"We're taking boy wonder out for lunch, would you like to come?"

"Dad . . ." Cal said in the background. "Let Harriet enjoy her weekend . . ."

"Only pub grub, our treat. Sandie and I would love for you to join us, wouldn't we, Sandie?"

Cal's mum, who seemed a woman of fewer words than her husband, said, "Yes! Do come, Harriet."

"Come on, what else do you have in for lunch?" Cal's dad said, looking toward the fridge, as if Harriet might throw it open to reveal a cartoon turkey, with paper frills on its legs.

"Um, nothing, but . . . I don't want to intrude on your family occasion! Thank you, though," Harriet said.

She sensed the fact she was being given no choice, and although she was sure it was well intended, it felt slightly suffocating. That said, being home alone with the flowers didn't appeal either.

"You're not intruding on anything!"

"Dad," Cal hissed, and said, "Sorry," to Harriet.

"Really, you three should be able to talk family shop," she said, and Andrew made dissenting sounds.

"No, no—not at all. I'm bored of family shop, haha. It's agreed then, our treat," he said. "I'll drive if you give me directions then, Calvin."

Harriet opened and closed her mouth in realization she'd been completely railroaded. She sensed Cal sag in defeat at this turn of events, which she understood: it changed the nature of it, with her spectating. She felt culpable and yet powerless. Had she known this invitation was remotely likely she could've prepared a watertight excuse. She'd not thought renting a room from their son would give her status as anything other than a person of passing, minimal interest. Clearly Cal had got his sociable gene from somewhere.

"Heard anything more from Kristina?" asked Cal's mum, after they got into the Clarkes' huge off-roader.

Cal, in the front passenger seat, swung a sidelong look at Harriet on the back seat and widened his eyes, which she presumed to convey: *Don't mention the visit.*

"Nope, thank God. Mutual friends tell me she mainly puts

up Instagram Stories of lifting kettle bells in Sweaty Betty leggings and clinking espresso martinis with Kanye's 'Stronger' playing."

"I wish I understood a word of that," his mum chuckled, and Cal said, eyes back on the road: "Be glad you don't, Mum."

ON THE WAY into the city, Clarke family chat keeping the other occupants of the car occupied, Harriet messaged Lorna.

I've had a bouquet with a note saying GAME ON. That is 100% Scott's sense of "humour." I guess he's seen the letter. 😐 How did he get my address, is what's panicking me?

Ugh. I wasn't going to say, but I sussed that he knew about the letter, because he's blocked me

Harriet felt her stomach drop through her pelvis.

Blocked YOU? Why would he do that?

He must've worked out where you got the information to contact Marianne from, I guess? Or be battening down all hatches. I only know as when I checked back, he'd disappeared, and so I looked him up on The Dive account. And there he still was. Don't fret too much, he's waving his guns because he can't really do anything. As you say, he can't write to your fiancé. Sit tight and don't panic. It's what he wants. Xx

Harriet thanked Lorna, while knowing the very fact she had changed her tune was a terrible sign. Lorna wasn't going to kick Harriet when she was down: the letter had been sent and the shots had been fired. There was nothing to do but reassure Harriet and hope for the best. It was the advice-giving equivalent of moving from reflective vests, dire warnings, hard hats, and clear instructions about handrails, to simply lighting a scented candle and handing you a glass of wine.

"Game On."

Harriet had priced Marianne betraying her into the policy; she'd declared it more likely than not. Marianne would be under Scott's thumb, as she once was. It still hurt. No matter how many times she'd said this good turn wouldn't deserve or provoke another, it was a lot to get her head around. Marianne had read those words and rejected them. At a deep level, Harriet had been convinced her truth would out.

Harriet rationalized, rehearsed, the mental equivalent of rubbing worry beads: What did she have in this world she cared about? Her friends: who knew the deal with Scott. Her work: unless he got hold of a list of her upcoming bookings, which would require hacking her laptop, hard to see how he could destroy that. Property: no, she had a rented back bedroom in Meanwood. A love life? Hahaha. Revenge porn: he had no material to work with, so that was out, unless he was any good at making deepfakes.

Maybe trying to unnerve her was all he had. *Maybe* again. All her previous maybes had been wrong.

By the time they parked up in town, she'd figured out how Scott could have found out where she lived. She'd invoiced Danny and Fergus both by email and with a hard copy that had her address on it. There's no way they'd suspect foul play from the world's *best*-best man, so all he'd have to do is call them and say, *Hey, Marianne borrowed a lipstick or found a scarf that belonged to their wedding photographer, and would they know where he should post it?* Danny and Fergus had told her they were only doing a "mini moon" before a lavish winter trip, so they'd be at home to look up the paperwork. She could contact them and confirm that was what had happened, in an innocuous way, if she needed to know for sure.

Call her a coward, she wasn't sure she wanted to. If it wasn't Danny and Fergus, she was out of alternative possibilities.

Should she tell Cal? She looked at the back of his dark blond head. He'd said she should've warned him about Jon, except she didn't know Jon required a warning. She absolutely did know that Scott required one, but not the sort where he was likely to turn up in person. Jon had mistaken Cal for Harriet's boyfriend, but she didn't see how Scott would make the same error—and even if he did, what could he do?

And what was she supposed to say to Cal? *I might've stirred something up with another ex who might also be a threat, in ways I can't predict?*

It was both pointless and unfair to ask Cal to feel agitation at something so vague; it was burdening him without any constructive purpose. She shouldn't do it. Yet the painfully obvious threat still remained.

It wasn't going to stop at the flowers.

30

"What about your parents, Harriet, are they in Leeds?" Cal's mum said, pleasantly, as the mains were cleared away.

Harriet wished she had been in a better condition to enjoy an indulgent blowout at the Reliance—Bicicletta cocktail, bruschetta, roast beef, and red wine. Cal was putting on a brave front, but Harriet suspected she knew why he was so discomfited: whatever gloss was put on it, it was far too much like her being his date. Cal's dad had bombarded her with so many questions, she feared he thought she *was* the new girl, and Cal was simply being coy.

"No, they're both no longer with us," she said, with a small smile. She was so used to this conversation, she knew its beats by heart. Cal's head snapped up and he looked at her intently, as if this were something he should've known. Lodgers were hardly likely to have brought up their origins story, surely.

"Oh, I am sorry," his mum said.

"Thank you, it's OK."

"You're young to have neither parent around," said Cal's dad, putting his hand over hers, and leaving it there a moment too long for Harriet's comfort. She glanced at Cal, and he looked silently aghast: She was an unwanted invader, and now she was pulling their heartstrings with tragedy? She was making other people's feelings her problem again, but surely Cal could see she'd not intended any of this?

"Yes. Not everyone's as fortunate as Cal," she said, with a smile toward him, trying to lighten things. His brow was still furrowed in consternation.

"Hah. Not sure that's how he sees it." Andrew laughed.

"Do you mind me asking, did you lose them in recent years?" Sandie asked, and Cal admonished, "*Mum!*" through gritted teeth.

"It's fine. My dad died when I was five and my mum when I was six," Harriet said. "Cancer in both cases. My late grandparents—on my mum's side—raised me."

"Oh my goodness! Oh, Harriet," said Sandie, and now she rubbed her arm.

Cal said nothing.

"Do you have a boyfriend, someone looking after you?" Andrew said, in a gruffly paternal manner.

"Not at the moment. My best friend Lorna, who I've known since school, is a force of nature and the value of three and a half boyfriends, I think." ("Like a bullmastiff in Ruby Woo" was how Lorna liked to self-describe, in fact, but probably best to omit that.)

Cal's parents laughed and said "Awww" in unison, and Harriet was glad to have defused the tension.

"You've got my son's company," his dad said, changing the subject, and Cal rubbed his temples.

"Cal, I meant to say, I should've found a room by now," Harriet said, in a snap of self-consciousness at having said she'd go, and instead tagging along for free Yorkshire puddings. "Apologies. I'll sort some places to view from tomorrow."

"No fuss, whenever," he said, tightly.

"What, you're off, Harriet?" his dad said, putting his dessert spoon down.

"Yes." Oh. She'd stupidly blurted this without considering neither of them wanted to discuss the backstory as to why. "Thought I'd . . . uh . . . give Cal space."

"You don't like the house?"

"I love it."

"You'd still be renting? In the city?"

". . . Yes."

Harriet, you idiot.

"Stay with Calvin, then! It's a good deal and he's not too much of a pain to live with, I should know. Haha. We had our ups and downs, didn't we? When you brought too many girls back."

Cal cast a Satanic look at his dad.

"Let them work it out, Andrew," Cal's mum chided.

"Oh well," he said. "You two will stay in touch either way, I'm sure?"

They both muttered, "Of course, of course!" while their faces said, *Good God, no.*

HARRIET WAS SUFFICIENTLY agonized that she texted Cal on the journey home.

So sorry. Didn't think a step ahead. Of course I'm going, I'm just disorganised. Didn't mean to make that a thing! ☹

Honestly, totally fine! You don't have to go, I mean it. x

Having worried he was fuming at her, she felt the kiss was nice.

Back at the house, after strenuous thanks for the Clarkes' kindness and hopes to see them again at some unspecified time, Harriet excused herself to her room. It was, rather poignantly, half packed up already, in anticipation of her departure.

She wished she hadn't gone up, when the curse of the garden acoustics visited her soon after. It even began fast enough she had no time to put the radio on, as she'd planned.

"What a gorgeous, good-natured lass. Very fresh faced, isn't she," she heard Cal's dad say.

"Next time, can you check with me before you invite people on the spur of the moment like that?" Cal hissed.

Oof. Harriet understood why it wasn't what Cal wanted—family time is for the family—but it was still rather agonizing to hear it starkly confirmed.

"What's your problem? She was a delight!"

"She might be, but she's my lodger, it's a business relationship. You landed me in it over her moving out too."

"You're being somewhat churlish," Cal's dad said. "Her losing her parents. Imagine being an orphan as a little 'un."

"So sad!" Cal's mum agreed.

"Again, not the point. Don't put me in the position of having to say I wanted her to stay."

Harriet, after a tough day, felt a stab of physical pain at this. She lay there feeling hurt, and foolish, and, when those emotions abated, also angry. He had tricked her into thinking they had a connection, even a spark. Why exploit someone like that? What was the point?

She'd started the day thinking Scott Dyer was no longer a bad guy she need worry about, and Cal Clarke was a good guy she could count as a friend.

She should resign from the predictions business.

31

Harriet heard Cal's parents' gas-guzzler leaving and looked out the window for their son. She saw Cal sat on the swing seat at the far end of the garden, lost in thought.

It was high time Cal discovered he shouldn't chat shit in his enchanting shrubberies. Harriet was smarting too much to pretend she'd not heard what she'd heard. She still had the text in her phone, with a slimy kiss, telling her an outright lie. He needed to know he hadn't fooled her.

"Hi," Harriet said, as she walked toward him.

"Hi. I'm meant to—"

"I've overheard you slagging me off for things that aren't my fault before and I didn't say anything. This time it was too much," she interrupted. "I'm sorry you didn't want me at that lunch, but it was hardly my fault. Your dad didn't leave me much of a choice."

"What?" Cal's jaw fell. "I didn't say I didn't want you there."

"That's exactly what you said. 'She's my lodger, it's a business relationship,'" Harriet quoted. "You're so two-faced. 'Don't put me in the position of having to say I wanted her to stay.' You weren't in that position. I'd offered to go."

"No, wait—this is—"

"I didn't ask to be your pal, you're the one who dragged me into things you were doing. I don't know why you have this *vanity* about being liked by people who don't mean anything to you. Popularity is your drug, isn't it?"

Cal looked both shocked and crushed at this. Admittedly, Harriet hadn't intended to deliver a wide-ranging character assassination based on partial information. Still, screw him.

"Let's be clear that I'm only here to pay rent until I go. You can knock the chummy 'come out for an Aperol Spritz, babes' stuff on the head. Cheers."

She needed a gesture that acted as a full stop, so she turned and marched back to the house. Good grief, where had all THAT come from? Harriet sounded well Huddersfield. Cal leaped up and followed her, catching her arm to make her stop.

"Harriet, Harriet! Wait. You don't have the context. That conversation wasn't about you."

"Pretty sure it was."

"It was the easiest way of phrasing *back off.* I was embarrassed about my dad's behavior around you today."

Harriet frowned and twitched her arm out of his grasp.

"Why? Your parents were being nice."

"My mum was being nice. My dad wasn't only being nice . . ." Cal paused. She saw a flush that she'd never seen before creep up his neck, one she had to admit he couldn't be faking. "He was hitting on you. It's what he does."

Cal's expression was a rictus of embarrassment. Even when Kristina walked in, he'd never looked as rattled as he did now.

"*Hitting* on me?" Harriet snorted. "I don't think so."

"Yeah, I know. The idea's so ridiculous it wouldn't even occur to you. Unfortunately, it's never too ridiculous an idea for him."

Harriet tried to make sense of this. She'd not got predatory vibes from Mr. Clarke Senior. She supposed he was over-familiar and slightly too tactile, but men of his age sometimes were.

"It wasn't that I didn't want you there. I love your company," Cal carried on. "I didn't want to be let down by his behavior and look like a dick in front of you. I was trying to point out he'd crossed a line of familiarity with you. With my mum there, I was hardly going to say, *Stop fancying my friends.*"

"Your mum seemed fine with it?"

"My mum seeming fine with it is a whole different . . . part of why I had therapy."

"Oh," Harriet said. She'd not anticipated any of this response and couldn't help but wonder if Cal was a master of nimble diversions. "Being forced to say 'I want her to stay' still seemed pretty definitive. No one had a gun to your head to say that."

"I was pointing out he'd interfered, not that the outcome was unwelcome. I hate you thinking I've been two-faced. Of course you're not business. We've become friends. I hope."

Harriet said nothing. She wanted to believe Cal, but she'd been here before.

"I also heard you telling Sam it was hell to have me move in."

"When?"

"When I moved in. 'I'm going to feel every second of . . .'" Harriet realized this sounded dubious, and lamely concluded, "'. . . it.'"

Cal's mouth opened and then he allowed himself a smile.

"Fuck's sake, you've earwigged every last thing out here, haven't you? Yes, I freaked out somewhat. I wasn't to know I'd get on so well with you, at that point. I don't recall you seeming overjoyed I was the homeowner either, Princess Pigtail."

Harriet rewarded his risk at levity with a reluctant smile.

"I didn't get the feeling your dad was . . . hitting on me, as you put it."

"No. You wouldn't. You know why?"

"No?"

"Because he's extremely good at it."

Harriet folded her arms and tried to decide whether she believed him. "I've got to get my head around this. Your dad is inappropriate with your friends? He'd never act on it, though?"

"Oh yes. He would."

"What!? Has he ever . . . ?"

"Slept with one of my friends? Yup."

"Oh my God."

"It's not confined to my friends. It just isn't boundaried before them either. You've heard of Médecins Sans Frontières, meet Andrew Sans Frontières."

"Haha. Whoa."

Harriet thought she was a woman of the world, but omnishagger sixty-year-old dads using their sons as an introductions service was new to her.

"Would he think he could slide me his phone number during a family Sunday lunch?"

"Oh, he'd not be that up front and crass. At least I hope not. He doesn't take risks like that; he mainly wanted an attractive woman to goggle at. He's never 'off,' if you know what I mean."

"And he actually did it with one of your mates?"

Cal exhaled. "The last thing I wanted to have to do is tell you the longer version and probably the last thing you want is the longer version, yet now I think we're going to have to do the longer version. Take a seat? After the KitFitbit story I fear you're going to think my life is a very black comedy."

He ushered Harriet back to where he'd been.

"If we're going to start at the beginning regards my dad, it's got to be my childhood terror of Halloween."

"Before you go on," Harriet said, "have you ever been to Portofino?"

Cal burst out laughing and Harriet laughed too. It washed away any remaining awkwardness between them.

"Twat," Cal said. "Here's me, about to lay myself totally bare before your pitiless gaze."

Wait while I get my camera. Bloody hell, where did that thought come from? Cal must have superpowers, because with one thing and another, Harriet's passion had been in deep freeze for some time. Yet here she was, pondering whether he looked as good out of clothes as he did in them, pondering it quite intently. She hoped her face remained impassive.

Cal continued: "I had a fear of Halloween, which everyone thought was funny when I was a little kid. When I got to my teens, I realized that little boys are allowed to gibber and cry at the sight of plastic skeletons and trick-or-treaters in hoods, but society judges grown men for that far more harshly. I honestly used to dread it, though."

"Was it anything in particular?"

"I didn't think so at the time, it just seemed to be all the paraphernalia. I had some awful association with it, the way you can never eat a certain food once it's given you poisoning. Aged about twenty-five, having to make up excuses to my then girlfriend about why I nearly *burst into tears* when she thought it was funny to leap out from a cupboard on October thirty-first, while wearing a bedsheet . . ."

Harriet put a hand over her mouth to stifle a laugh and said, "Sorry."

"It is funny, I know. I went to counseling, as CBT wasn't as much of a thing then. To my amazement, we discovered that I'd been repressing a memory from when I was seven. Of a pumpkin lantern in the back of a static trailer." He paused. "The counselor's talking me through this, and as we dissect the scene—I forbid you to laugh at this—we find that the trailer with the pumpkin is rocking."

Harriet wince-laughed. "Yikes."

"Yeah, yikes. What I've blocked out is that when I was seven years old, my dad took me on a 'camping holiday,' and instead we went to a trailer park where his then mistress was also staying. He dumps me with board games and bags of cheese puffs and spends the whole time at hers. On Halloween, I'd got nervous being by myself and gone wandering the site, looking for him. Obviously I was too young to understand the implications of any of it. Why my dad disappeared for hours at a time, why there was a pleasant woman staying there who seemed to know him and gave me sweets. Or why, on the way home, he wanted me to rehearse a story about the fishing we'd not done." Cal shook his head. "Looking at the pumpkin, I knew bad things were happening that I couldn't give a name to. Therefore, the terrible associations. Unnamed fears are the worst fears, I think."

He sighed, and Harriet committed that line to memory, for later examination.

"By the age I was in counseling, I knew my dad was chronically faithless. Finding out I'd been directly exposed to it and used as an alibi, while he neglected me, gave me a whole new level of rage and disgust."

Harriet grimaced. "That's horrific. What if something had happened in the trailer he'd left a seven-year-old alone in?"

"Oh, totally. The revelation cured me of my pumpkin aversion, however. Carve all the gourds you want; I will not flinch."

Harriet smiled and wondered how much of the unruffled Cal she knew had been shaped by this. He'd seemed like someone very unfazed by life to her, until now.

"Have you ever confronted him?"

"Yes, we had a huge fight after he shagged my mate Lily when I was twenty, and didn't speak for months. She was someone from a summer job in a pub I had. My dad gave her a lift home when she'd been round mine, and wouldn't you know it! He took ages. Turns out he'd had a 'breakdown.' I waited up for him, and when he gave me the AA callout spiel I said, 'Oh, they dispense Viagra now, do they?' All hell broke loose. We had a gigantic row. I didn't move home after university as a result."

"Did he deny it?"

"Oh, of course. Then when I made other accusations, I got lots of deflecting. Lots of 'That's not what happened,' and 'Life is complicated,' and 'I don't owe you an explanation of myself.'

He knows it's indefensible, so you don't get any sense out of him. Futile."

"I can't believe he shagged a friend of yours! Ugh!"

"It's actually worse than that . . ." Cal rubbed his temples. "I'm going to say this very fast so I've said it, and then we can never think about it again. *I'd-slept-with-her-too*—aaaaaaargh."

"Oh God!" Harriet said.

But instead of it only being discomfiting to him, it landed entirely differently from how Harriet expected: she got an undeniable pang of possessiveness at this information.

It was as if a mist had lifted and the last hour's events revealed themselves fully to her: Harriet wasn't simply offended on a point of honor at overhearing Cal say he wanted her to go. It was personal. She'd, against sense and logic, developed some kind of feelings for him. What an idiot. She bloody knew that having a heartbreakingly handsome landlord would come to no good. She definitely had to move out soon, for the opposite reason he thought.

"Don't look at me like that," Cal said.

"Like what?" Harriet said, startled. She very much hoped her specific emotions weren't on display.

"Like you think I should be dipped in Clorox."

"Ah, well." Harriet cleared her throat. "At least you went first?"

"*Argh.* It's not going to be the thing you think of when you think of me from now on, is it?" Cal said, looking genuinely rather upset.

"Definitely not," Harriet responded, unable to say that what she'd just learned about herself bothered her more.

"Where is your mum in all this?" Harriet asked, thinking they both needed to move on from Lily's multilayered psychological impact.

"My mum ignores it. She pretends it's not happening. She's like Tom Jones's wife, except my dad's not sold a hundred million records. At least Melinda got the Los Angeles mansion out of it."

"Your poor mum."

"Yeah. He had a dalliance with one of her friends when we were young, and I think there was a proper bust-up over that; otherwise it's a blind eye. I don't know what it is, if she won't be alone? Self-esteem thing? I got quite furious with her in my angry-young-man years. I wanted to know why she'd not leave him or at least call him out on it. She said, 'Your father and I are happy,' and I was blowing up some old indiscretion into more than it was. I said, 'Oh, come on, he's been in more beds than a traveling mattress salesman and you know it.' She looked devastated by that. I felt like a complete shit. I added to her humiliation."

"You were saying it out of protectiveness."

"Yeah, but also frustration with her. Dad's cheating meant he lost a lot of my respect. The ugly truth is, Harriet, Mum putting up with it lost a lot too. I'd like to tell you I feel nothing but compassion and there's no contempt, but it'd be a lie. I feel racked with guilt about that, but I can't make myself not feel it."

Harriet nodded. Someone of Cal's confidence and forward motion probably would find abject passivity a tough one to empathize with.

"In many ways they're happy, and we had a happy childhood. Erin, my sister, is much less bothered by it than I am. But it's very much not an example of marriage I want to follow. It makes me sad."

"Are you worried you'll turn into him?"

"Oh no. Not at all. I've never found fidelity difficult. I don't think I've ever had his love of the chase."

Also, I bet you've never had to chase.

Odd that in light of this, Cal gave Kit's infidelity a pass. Unless . . .

"What if you're not like him, but you keep dating him?"

"You what now?"

"The Hot Thatchers. You're replaying the dynamic, except you're in your mum's role. You're being the version of your mum who would stand up for herself. *I will tame this person!*"

"Hahahaha, oh God . . . There could be something in that. When Sam's wondered about why I consistently pick nightmares, I always say, 'But you have to have a challenge. I'd be bored with a pushover.'"

"I don't think 'a challenge' and 'remorselessly daunting' are the same thing," Harriet said. She liked the version of herself she was with him.

"At the great age of thirty-three, with your help, I think I've finally worked that out."

They smiled at each other, then both glanced away. Harriet went back to gazing at the butterflies in next door's buddleia.

"God, sorry. You were having a sunny Sunday with bouquets from your customers, and then the Clarkes crash into it."

Cal looked authentically ashamed, but Harriet realized the highs and lows of the last few hours had been a fine distraction from the utter wtf-ness of Scott's attack.

"Hah. It's fine."

"Nice necklace," Cal said, spotting the small key on the chain.

"Thank you."

"Does the key fit any lock in particular?"

Bloody journalists. Harriet smiled. Nearly everyone figured it was merely decorative.

"A jewelry box."

"Ah. Family diamonds?"

"It contains a letter from my mum."

Cal's smile softened. "I can imagine that has extraordinary value. Much more so than stones."

"It does. Although I've never opened it. The letter, I mean, not the box. Obviously I opened that when I put it inside."

She'd not told Jon this, and she felt the betrayal in blurting it straight out to Cal. Jon had also directly asked, and Harriet had dissembled: "It's private."

Yet she knew why she'd told Cal, and never Jon. The stakes were lower. Jon would've demanded they read it together, and when she'd declined, he'd have pecked at her over it, saying it was something she (they) had to do. Jon, she had come to realize, couldn't help but make everything about him, even at moments when he thought he was being exceptionally caring.

"You have a letter from your mum you've never read?"

"Yes. My grandad gave it to me on my thirteenth birthday, and somehow, I've never steeled myself. I know it sounds insane. Or heartless."

"It doesn't sound that way."

"It became a straightaway or on-my-own-deathbed deal. It snowballed into this thing I couldn't do. Now, the moment is never right."

"Are you worried about what it says?"

"Not exactly. It's just . . . I've built it up too much. I don't know what I fear, really. Crying a lot, obviously. Missing her. Which I do anyway, always, at some level. In my head the letter needs to say everything, and how can it, when I don't even know what 'everything' is? If it's *be polite to your grandparents and work hard in your exams, lots of love,* I'll be . . . I don't know. And I'm reading it over twenty years late, which I know is awful."

"No, it's not, stop beating yourself up about that. You were a kid. You were doing what felt right. How do you know if it's the wrong decision, until the day you read it?"

"Thanks."

". . . What if it's not what's written in the letter that matters to you?"

"How do you mean?"

"Until you've read it, there's always one more thing to be said, something left between you."

Harriet swallowed and felt something shift inside her. She knew this was true. It was powerful for someone else to say it.

She didn't know she was crying until she felt the tears drip off her chin.

"Oh shit!" Cal said, with the unmistakable blind panic of a man who's made a woman cry. He looked like he thought he was going to have to explain himself in his line manager's office. "I didn't want to upset you!" He reached over and held her shoulder. The warmth of his reassurance steadied her and made her feel more vulnerable, at the same time.

Harriet said in a strangled voice, "It's OK, it's all right, honestly. You're right. I've never admitted that to myself. It's good to have someone else's thoughts." She sat forward, on the pretense of digging for a tissue, but with the desired effect of dislodging his hand. She couldn't cope with the flirt-jangles while crying.

"Oh God, I feel absolutely awful," Cal said. "Trying to show off I've had counseling, after all your perceptive observations, and completely overdoing it."

Harriet gasp-laughed, wiping the tears away. "It's fine! I like having that insight. It makes me feel better. I'm saving it as our last thing."

"I'm sorry I'd never asked about your parents."

"Hah, don't worry! Why would you?"

"You were raised by your grandparents?"

"Yes. They were a very characterful pair." She sniffed and laughed. She couldn't do more agony, right now. "They did a great job in difficult circumstances."

"Evidently."

All things considered, on a fraught day, Harriet decided to accept that with a "Thank you."

"What were they called? Your parents, and your grandparents?"

Harriet paused. "That's . . . that's the kindest question."

"Is it? I thought I was being nosy."

"Yeah, it is. My mum and dad were Stephen and Rose, and my grandparents were Frank and Mary."

They sat in a peaceable silence, underscored by a loud mower a few gardens away.

"I know I'm a very shit Yoda, but about your letter. Let the time to read it arrive. Maybe it'll be the night before you get married or something. But it'll come. You don't need to force it."

"If you're Yoda shouldn't you say, *Come, it will*?"

"I don't want you to actually slap me."

They laughed, as much in relief at moving on from the heavy stuff.

"Thank you, Cal. That's comforting. Except I'm never getting married."

"You and me both, sweetheart," Cal said. "I honestly can't ever imagine feeling whatever I'd need to feel, to want to try that again."

"Exactly same."

He held up his palm for her to high-five. "Cup of tea?"

They got up, Cal stretched—Harriet sneaking a glimpse at the flat stomach revealed as his arms went over his head—and walked back into the house.

When they were in Zucco, and Cal was getting the bill, Sam had said to Harriet, "The thing about Cal, the big surprise, the plot twist is: he's genuinely, incredibly nice. He can get anyone or anything he wants by batting those eyelashes and so you itch to hate him. People search for the lurking conceited arsehole or the dark side, or, in some cases, try to torture it out of him. It isn't there."

At the time, Harriet had said, "Right," and thought, *What a bros-before-hoes, male-centric whitewash of a bride-ditcher.*

As Cal filled the kettle over the sink, she had to admit every word might've been pure truth.

He was so superficially attractive that believing his fundamentals were rotten had been a helpful safeguard. She got out her phone and fired up a Zillow.

32

In the end, Scott's revenge arrived quietly—it slunk in like a robber gripping a knife inside their coat, or the way that in a horror film, the tiny, menacing *drip-drip-drip* of an unseen liquid turns out to be blood coming through a floorboard.

Ten days after the flowers, on an otherwise quiet Thursday, Harriet got an unusual number of notifications on her phone. She had finished a bagel in the sitting room, musing that "the flow of the rooms" was an invention of the property market and posh people, but something about the environment of Cal's house was so spirit-lifting.

She'd finally seen a few rooms at the start of the week, and none of them were a patch on it. They likely didn't contain men who gave her stomach fireworks when sighted briefly on the first-floor landing without his shirt, though, so pluses and minuses.

PING. Someone has commented on Harriet Hatley Photography.

PING and again.

PING and again.

And again.

This was irregular. Harriet didn't use social media much, but Facebook was a necessary evil in her line of work. In addition to her profile for her friends and family, she had a basic business one that pointed visitors to her website. She kept an eye on it, although it was more of a landing page that directed the traffic. She only ever got a blizzard of notifications when she shared a couple's album highlights, with their permission. Harriet never got much activity, unprompted by her. Even if customers uploaded their pictures and tagged her, not very many guests were moved to then shuffle across to thank the photographer. It made her think she was being spammed, except names now listed on her handset looked like real people.

You shouldn't be spreading your dark skank energy round other peoples big days imo, give this up

Harriet read this several times, in bewilderment. She had no idea what "Christian" would know about her energy, dark skank or otherwise. He was a personal trainer from Shadwell who liked "good vibes only." Could've fooled her. She deleted it and blocked him.

Seen your true colours!!

Had she now, and how would Bernadette "I love my Boxer dogs, roast potatoes and three grandkids" know what they were?

Delete, block. Had she got mixed up with a notorious drunk driving case featuring someone of the same appellation in Birmingham, or been twin-named in a petition in an acrimonious custody battle in Liverpool?

Good luck with getting work now your known for what you really are lmao

Harriet could comment "*you're* known" under Niall's post, but she had more pressing issues with it than his grammar. What were they talking about? Was she being targeted in some sort of prank? She felt a queasiness, a certainty that something dreadful had happened somewhere, and that the solution to this mystery would not be as trivial or painless as a case of mistaken identity.

Bitch

This was accompanied by the litter bin drop emoji. She deleted and blocked Damon, a "proud dad" and "father of three perfect girls," with sweating hands. She moved to the search term space on the site and typed in "Harriet Hatley."

It returned her personal profile, her business page, someone at King's College, and a Harriet Hately. It did not contain anything that pointed to the source of the Harriet hate. It was so unsettling that her antagonists were flying in from outer space; these weren't people who'd Liked her page or had any obvious connection to her whatsoever. It was like being shouted at from the window of a speeding car, except it was every other passing car.

As she was frowning in confusion, someone posted to Harriet's business page again. This time with screenshots, captioned: *THIS YOU?* ☺

Even in tiny-size lettering, Harriet could make out Scott's name at the top of the thumbnail and her stomach lurched. She had known, in some part of her brain, he must be behind this. She hadn't wanted to outright think it until she absolutely had to.

She saved the picture to her photos, deleted the comment, and disabled commenting on her page. She opened the screenshot in full on her phone screen.

It was from Scott's personal Facebook, set public. There was a photograph of him in a polo shirt under a tree in a park, hugging his knees and smiling winningly, like he was the former lead singer on the cover of his much-anticipated first solo album.

Underneath, lots of text.

My name is Scott Dyer and I'm a victim of an emotional abuser.

Even now as I type those words, I want to run the cursor back and delete them, make them untrue. I thought I had the power to make it untrue by denying it. I thought it made me weak to admit I was scared of a woman, let alone one who I'd wanted to share my life and my bed with. Someone who I'd been in love with. How pathetic is that, to think her behaviour attacked my masculinity? Fear is fear.

The truth is, if I deny my experiences, I can never heal, and I can never help anybody else. We don't talk about this enough, because society tells men to be strong. We shouldn't show vulnerability and we shouldn't complain if we're going through hell at the hands of our wife or girlfriend. We can all joke among the lads in the pub about "bunny boilers," but we don't know how to talk about it seriously. How to reach out and admit when we're being terrorised by someone who is meant to be our lover, not our enemy.

I will call my ex H, because her identity isn't the point. She knows what she did, even if she can't accept its impact.

What I suffered was a form of domestic violence, but it was emotional, psychological warfare—apart from the objects hurled at me when she was drunk, there was no physical threat.

The trouble is, we have a stereotypical image of an abuser: usually a well-built man, over a certain age, load of tattoos. We don't think it'll be a sarcastic girl with strawberry-blond hair in a plait, and the face of an angel. Because H couldn't dominate me physically, people don't understand how she undertook the demolition of my self-worth and my self-belief.

We met at a party and hit it off. H made it clear she liked me from day one, and I dug that. I thought to myself, she didn't play games, proper salt-of-the-earth Huddersfield lass. Things moved fast—I now see too fast—at her urging. She'd had a very damaging childhood—I won't be more specific to protect privacy—which she insisted hadn't affected her. With hindsight, I can see her refusal to discuss it, or consider that it might have harmed her, was a huge warning sign. She could never be in the wrong, from the start. Any problems we had must have come from me, even though I was from a stable, loving background and wasn't used to drama.

We moved in together and soon, out of nowhere, the attacks on my peace of mind began. If we went out with her friends she would spend the evening finding ways to run me down, mocking me and needling at me in front of them. When I asked why, when we were alone, she'd play dumb.

She would openly come on to other men in front of me, a power play to see if I would step in or sit and take it. Sometimes I'd ask my mates if they'd noticed, and they'd be too embarrassed to admit what they'd seen too. They'd say: "I'm sure she loves you." This became like a mantra from H: I love you, of course I wasn't doing what you say I was doing. To be with her, I had to deny the evidence of my own eyes and ears.

She was secretive about what was on her devices, another huge tell that I was being played. One time I found provocative, half-dressed photos, clearly meant for someone else, on her phone. She said she didn't know what I meant, insisted they were taken only for her.

I had to be very careful about humour, or anything she might find insulting—she was on a hair trigger, and it could provoke days, or even weeks, of sulking if I said the wrong thing. Her insecurity was a deep hole I could never fill, but it was made clear that I had to try anyway. I reassured her that her weight didn't bother me, but she'd pick at her food to punish me for saying I thought someone who happened to be thinner than her was attractive.

She needed constant reassurance, promises from me. She would demand sex, and if I didn't have sex with her, then I didn't love her, she said. If I resisted, she would literally beg me. I knew the unspoken threat was that she'd sleep around if I didn't comply. Consent when someone's put you in a dilemma like that—it isn't really consent.

My friends grew concerned. H was always on her best behaviour and acted sweet as sugar in their company, but they weren't fooled. When I came out without her, I was tired, jumpy, worn down. They dragged it out of me, but even then I lied, I said I was worried for her safety when she had a drink in her. I was more intimidated and worried about mine.

Eventually, some survival instinct kicked in, and after four years, I finally got free. She'd come home late and drunk and thrown things around, and we had an argument about it the next day. She told me she was leaving me, something she did to pull me into line.

For once, I agreed. I don't think she expected me to call her bluff and go. She stood watching me in shock as I hastily loaded up my things and ran for my life. As I left, I begged her to get professional help before she put anyone else through similar. I already felt for the next guy who fell for her as innocently and trustingly as I had.

I had been the problem, my failure to care for her the way she wanted, while she trampled on every feeling I had.

After we split, she stalked me. I blocked her on every platform because I knew she'd check up on me constantly if I didn't; my friends mentioned she was always hanging round the places we'd gone together.

But I moved on, and I got happy with a great girl.

The reason I'm writing all this now is because a couple of weeks ago, H and I ran into each other at a wedding. It was a beautiful, emotional day and I avoided her as much as I could, not wanting any hint of our past to intrude on the happy couple's special celebration. But I knew she'd rage at seeing me settled with someone else. I dreaded what attack she might launch on me in my new life.

As a result of that encounter, she found out who my fiancée is, and where she works, and targeted her.

She wrote a long, poisonous letter, detailing what a horrible boyfriend I'd been to her. It was full of one-sided inventions about how I'd constantly turned on her for no reason, ranting on about how my fiancée should leave me. Naturally, Marianne was badly upset. It's literally weeks before our wedding, and she's dealing with this nasty rubbish instead of being excited about the best day of her life.

I had no choice but to put my side, something I'd wanted to spare Marianne. Luckily for me, when I sat down and poured it all out, put everything on the line, my incredible partner believed in me.

I don't know if H will see this, and if she'll do more to try to drag me and the people I love down as a response. I don't care, because I won't be scared anymore. I want to speak up for all the people who've had their heads fucked with, and haven't known where or who to turn to, or how to talk about it. You're not weak, you're strong for surviving.

My name is Scott Dyer, and I am a victim of abuse.

Harriet ran to the toilet and threw the bagel up.

33

The worst part of Scott's post wasn't Scott's words, but the response he incited.

Seeing a twisted catalog of defamatory fictions about herself from him was deeply unpleasant, but Harriet already loathed Scott. She knew he had a competing narrative about their years together, which he used as both attack and defense, and she had always accepted versions of this had been relayed to third parties. This was more a refresher course in how Scott Dyer operated than revelation. However, she'd always had an unexamined yet comforting conviction that if they heard her side, they'd start changing their minds.

But maybe not? Because now that he'd gone public, the unequivocal response from the crowd was the truly disturbing dimension. As hot, angry tears slid down her cheeks, Harriet scrolled through a hailstorm of affirmations of Scott's story, in the form of fury, judgment, and disgust toward her. People with no authority to come to their conclusions, who nevertheless knew for sure that she was utterly void as a person. It was like being at her own trial, except the charge sheet kept lengthening, the jury had already returned a Guilty verdict, and none of the witnesses knew her.

The post was twenty-four hours old and had 1.4k Likes, 960 shares, and hundreds upon hundreds of comments. Many of those had hundreds of Likes, other men pouring their hearts out about their ordeals with abusive women, other women saying what an impressive, emotionally self-aware man Scott was.

She could see it unfold, as when Harriet read the essay again, she noticed the line "I don't even know if H will see this" and recognized it, with a noise of strangled fury, as coded provocation. Scott was always more savvy about the socials than her. It dawned on Harriet that he'd have purposely designed it so she could view it, like cheese crumbing the mouse to the trap. Harriet figured he'd have looked her up, seen that she had two accounts but had blocked him only on the personal. Sure enough, via her photography profile, she had free access. What an unfortunate oversight. Her hands shook as she scanned the thread.

Of course Scott wouldn't want to risk Harriet not spectating this tsunami of ill will toward her—that was the point.

The level of thought anyone gave a viral post, amid pratfalling pet videos and memes, wasn't considered. It shouldn't be a surprise that Scott's story had been bought hook, line, and sinker by a vast army of morally vehement unknowns, most of whom liked to use half a dozen emojis. Their not knowing Scott clearly didn't matter to them. Their not knowing Harriet *definitely* didn't matter to them.

That he might be unreliable, that there could be another side to this story—it wasn't even a distant consideration. Scott appealed for sympathy, in the language of a sensitive person, and he received sympathy back, as if he was one. He *said* he was being starkly, laceratingly honest—ergo, he *was*. Infuriatingly for Harriet, the blind trust was touching; it's what you'd want anyone sharing their pain to receive. Except of course he didn't deserve it.

Not one comment that Harriet could see, doomscrolling, was anything less than full throttle behind him. She watched the interpretations of his accusations against her morph and grow as the thread got longer, Harriet in the retelling becoming more extreme and dangerous.

You should go to the police about her. Worth making a formal complaint so they've got her name on record if she tries anything else. For all you know she might try to disrupt your wedding

What she said, also if she threw things when drunk, that IS violence and she can be prosecuted

I've been here. Two years out of a toxic relationship myself. The way you have to shore up THEIR self-esteem while they're destroying yours—so many bells ringing for me. Fwiw your ex lashed out because she knows you're winning at life and she's stuck in the prison yard of her ugly mind. I wish you and your beautiful fiancée many good years together, have a great wedding day!

Hi Scott <3 as a woman I can tell you now, no one has nudes on their phone they "took for themselves" and keep from their bf. She was def working other angles when she was with you, sorry to say. Grotty hoe

Never stick your dick in crazy 😂

Halfway down, Scott had posted again, in a comment boosted to visibility in the thread by gaining a sweltering 521 reactions, many clicking Love:

Hey everyone. I was absolutely shitting myself about posting this and I almost didn't. I can't tell what your support means to me. I showed it to my fiancée and she was in tears, saying: "They get it." If this has helped one person, then it's been worth any difficulty or trouble it's cost me. Like I say, I refuse to be ashamed. Peace and light to you all. Love always wins. xxxx

Harriet's eyes then alighted on a much-Liked comment that was so enraging, so ironic, that she gasp-sobbed, then nearly screamed and threw her phone:

When narcissists can no longer control you, they try to control what others think of you.

Yeah, no shit.

Three-quarters of the way in, inevitably, in the Wild West frontier that was online debate, she'd been outed. Scott had knowingly cued up a guessing game and provided enough clues. There was a comment with a link to her photography site, which explained why she'd started getting trolled.

FFS, I know who this is. Harriet Hatley? She's a wedding photographer (er, LOL) This is her . . .

That sparked a subthread, a feeding frenzy of excited delight at being able to pull the mask from evil "H."

No way, she photographed my cousin's friend's wedding?!

Seriously this is her? Looks like butter wouldn't melt. Always the way, isn't it

I would NOT want her at any wedding. For one thing, imagine if she takes a liking to the groom

I remember her from school. She dated my brother's friend and was totally weird with him too

She checked this person's profile. They hadn't been to her school and definitely didn't know anyone she'd dated.

Harriet's trembling fingers hovered over the screen. Maybe she should comment, say something back? Say that this was a misrepresentation, that there were many, many things this mob didn't know.

But she knew better: it would be like wading into a gunfight armed with only a spoon, and a target on her forehead. The world at large had picked a side, as Scott had fully anticipated. No one believes the person who goes next.

She pushed her face into the sofa cushions, and howled.

34

"Hats off to the prick, I genuinely find it hard to choose a favorite line. I can't decide between 'selfies on her phone which I had a God-given right to scour, to prove she was unfaithful,' or 'my parents being alive mean I am a more balanced person than her.' Can you imagine not picking up on any of the red flags in that? More red flags than a communist parade. His creepster cocksureness is coming off it like steam. '*I was being played!*' You used to drive a fuckin' Nissan Micra, you're not Drake."

Harriet opened her mouth, but Lorna continued: "WAIT, no, I do have a favorite. 'Her identity isn't the point—but here's her first initial, a detailed physical description, an event she recently attended, and where she's from.' I would honestly like to feed him feetfirst into an airline propeller."

Lorna paused to breathe. She was in a dress with fuchsia chiffon balloon sleeves, which set off her expressive arm waving beautifully. The day of Scott's post was, coincidentally, also their after-hours date at the Dive, and Harriet had never been so brokenly grateful for it. Candles flickered and Lorde's *Melodrama* played from somewhere behind a towering Swiss cheese plant. She'd WhatsApped the sorry mess to the Fleaslags to disbelief, and a cyclone of messages all afternoon. It helped her weather the storm of the kind of alternate raging and impotent weeping that had left her feeling hollowed out.

Lorna had plenty more to say. Roxy had a Tinder date, and had asked if this was a real definite total crisis, or if Harriet minded if she still went . . . ? Lorna, she knew, would've sacked anyone or anything off to provide this moral support, and a therapeutic Scott Dyer deconstruction.

"I don't think anyone analyzes these things, you know," Harriet said morosely, examining her glass of red. Her throat was still sore and her voice sounded scratchy and dry. "They go by the feelings they get from it. It's an outlet for their own aggro. They can smack the Harriet piñata in a frenzy and hug each other and have a cathartic wail. At first, I thought, *If only they knew it isn't true,* and then I worked out that they don't care if it's not true. It's just a vessel. Scott himself used to say social media is only another type of computer game, and for once I think he was right."

She paused, looked at the ceiling, blinking. "Remember I said Cal, my landlord, couldn't have a decent reason for walking out of his wedding? He did, and I didn't know what it was. I didn't have the full context. I said there couldn't be a reason, because I couldn't think what it would be. This isn't that different, the arrogance of assumption. All these people would say, *Well, Scott's got no reason to lie*. But he has, it's just unknown to them. We've all lost respect for the fact *there's things we don't know,* and I fully include myself in that." She swiped again at her wet cheeks. God, she was sickened by how Scott had so thoroughly turned her inside out, again.

"I dunno how you're being so fair-minded and philosophical, to be honest," Lorna said.

"Hah. Kind of you to see it that way. I was thinking this was more fatalistic acceptance. I've not got anything else to be, have I?"

". . . So, what was Cal's reason for absconding?"

Harriet was relieved to briefly break off to outline someone else's piece of private life theater, to "oohs" and "oh my Christ, no way!"

"He came in, I meant to say!" Lorna said. "With a girl, a very sleek girl. He left a generous tip, so probably was impressing a date, hah."

Harriet made an *oh really* face and stuffed her feelings down. Of course the fabulous life of Cal Clarke continued, outside her remit—why would she expect it not to? He hadn't brought anyone home, but then again, she wasn't always sure when he was home. She wasn't his keeper. Perhaps social media Gatsbys with lodgers sprung for a suite at the Malmaison.

Courtship could be costly: she'd had to duck behind a letterbox in town the other day when Jon had strode past her bearing a turquoise Tiffany bag; mercifully, he'd not seen her. Harriet thought, *Lavish gift for early-doors dating?* Then realized: it'd likely be a Make It Up to Mummy present. Once she'd finished reviling Harriet for their face-off, Jacqueline was probably quite irascible toward her son. All that spite had to go somewhere; Jon's checkbook as Band-Aid.

"Surely there's something you can do legally?" Lorna said, as they returned to the main subject. "That piece of shit has as good as accused you in a public forum. There are Twitter libel trials nowadays."

"No, there isn't. Apart from the fact I don't have the money to take him to court, couldn't afford losing, and couldn't stand the thought of them picking over the evidence of whether I did the things he's saying I did, which would be a he said, she said . . . Apart from all of that, even if I won, 'Harriet Hatley—wedding photographer who was embroiled in the emotional abuse case' doesn't have a very Would Hire ring to it, does it? People don't even need to buy Scott's version. They just won't want to buy into it at all."

Lorna made an air-escaping noise.

"And, if I did my own post, refuting Scott, it'd have the Streisand Effect, wouldn't it? You know, where an attempt to shut something down only means tons more people hear about it."

"This can't be the end." Lorna smacked her hand on the table in emphasis. "You can't behave like him and come out on top. Much more of this and I'll start thinking karma is spiritual woo for Pollyannas."

"Ha. By the way, I don't want you to think I resent you at all for being completely right in your advice to me. I should've known to listen, your advice is never wrong," Harriet said. "I was a woman possessed about sending that letter. I was in denial that I was rattling the cage bars of a . . . maniac, I guess."

She swigged her wine. Once again, it was a failure of imagination as intellectual protection: she couldn't predict how Scott could harm her, therefore he didn't have a way to harm her. *Wrong.*

"Funny you should say that, because I have FULLY come ON FUCKING BOARD with your letter. The fact he could do this shows you have to DESTROY THE APPALLING SHIT. We need to work out how."

"Hahahaha. I love you," Harriet said, and leaned over to hug her. Scott could take Harriet's reputation, and very possibly her livelihood, but he couldn't ever take her best friend again, and that was something.

"The way he used all the elements of the letter and twisted each thing I'd described to sound like it was my crime is so mad . . ." Harriet said. "I've asked myself, *Does Scott really believe himself?* I think he does, you know. He tells himself his version so many times, he thinks it's the truth. His self-righteousness is like a mind-altering drug."

Harriet took a deep breath. She'd been limbered up by wine, so she hoped she'd not regret saying this next thing, in the morning. Admitting to it was counterintuitive—she didn't want to, but if she didn't voice it, she'd feel like she was carrying the horrifying shame of it alone. She inadvertently recalled Cal telling her about Lily and his dad. She'd vaguely wondered at the time why he had, given he was obviously stricken at it being gross. Could it be, as it was for Harriet here, because some people were important enough that they needed to know the whole of you . . . ?

Harriet needed to be swift, because if Lorna cast it up as another example of Scott's ridiculous falsehoods, she'd lose her nerve. The most sadistic ploy in the whole thing was to casually toss in Harriet's most private humiliation, and for it to be genuine.

"Lorna. One thing, though. The sex thing, the begging," Harriet said, nervously. "That part's true. It wasn't true I threatened to cheat on him, but the rest of it . . . That's where he got me to: it was squalid. I honestly didn't think even he'd be so savage as to tell the world." She closed her eyes, shook her head. "It was like role-play, it's what he *wanted* me to do, you know? So it could be clear he held all the cards. What I hate most about Scott is what he turned me into. But it's not like I emerged from four years with him with nothing but credit."

"Oh God, don't sweat that," Lorna said, seeing how mortified Harriet was. Harriet forced a grateful smile back.

"That reminds me, how was the Gethin date?!"

"I am experiencing a profound disquiet regards Gethin."

"Oh no, why?"

"He's great. It's great. We are officially seeing each other and deleted our dating apps. It could not be going better."

"And . . . ?"

"That's it. When's the other shoe gonna drop?!"

"What if there's no shoe!"

"Hmmm. Bubbles Hussein hates me, but Bubbles the devil prince hates everyone. Anyway, yes. For the time being, I will concede Gethin seems really sound."

Harriet smiled as Lorna looked sheepish.

"What if he just is, exactly what he seems?" Harriet said, remembering Sam's ode to Cal.

"I guess so. It's the hope that kills you!" Lorna said, returning herself to Lorna mode. "I'm really quite irked at Rox for not being here," she added, getting up to close a window. "I know you won't hold it against her. But she knows the deal with Scott. With your closest friends, you don't expect to get passed over for Mr. Dick Appointment."

"Oh no, in a way I like her going on her date. I like you two finding love; it gives me hope. Even if I've fully given up on that, I'd settle for peace," Harriet said. Ending up a single old lady, living by the seaside, pottering around with lots of cats and dogs? It'd do her. If no good man would.

As she traveled home in her taxi, the driver's radio blasting Billie Eilish's "Bad Guy," Harriet rested her head on the vibrating glass and admitted to herself: if anything, she'd downplayed what Scott had done, tonight. The effects of this would involve hard practicalities, and she'd deliberately not dwelled upon them. Quite possibly, Lorna had realized this too, and not thought it politic to say so.

It wouldn't simply be a case of finding the right moment to divulge to prospective menfolk that she was That Girl Called Out as an Abuser. Assuming they didn't get warned off beforehand, that this didn't cause the love of her life to swipe left.

Moreover, her job wasn't in a bank or office, safely behind the frontage of a larger logo. She *was* her company, and it relied in part on word of mouth. As she'd said about the perils of going to court, her line of work was vulnerable to public opinion. Like Christian the personal trainer, it wanted *good vibes only*. Harriet didn't doubt she was about to see a mysterious and steep drop-off in bookings.

She had gone over and over her remaining options, and truly there was nothing she could do. As the saying went, the lie was halfway around the world before the truth could get its boots on.

35

Harriet needed to spend time around humanity without Wi-Fi mediating. Knowing there was a virtual toilet wall out there, covered in graffiti about her, fresh scrawls by unknown enemies adding to it, hour on hour: it was petrifying and wearying. She was grateful for small mercies, and at least her current workload depended on gigs she'd long since secured. That Saturday, the union of fifty-somethings Ross and Betty at the Faversham was a balm to her soul, once she'd got past the feeling of raw exposure when entering a busy room. It was restorative, socializing in physical space and not with individuals using one-word epithets and litter bin emoticons.

Life goes on. Everyone treated her as a wedding photographer, bar—she couldn't be sure—a few twenty-somethings, who she felt might be looking in her direction a little too much during one section of the reception, heads bent together, phones in palms.

She knew people of the older generation would say, *It's not the real world, it'll blow over.* Harriet had deactivated her little-used personal Facebook. At some stage, what Scott had done would pass into dim recollection, it would collect dust in the archives and be mostly forgotten. It wasn't as if successive generations would hand down the folk story.

Yet she also knew that there were scores of people "unmasked" for wrongdoing who could never come back online in the way they had existed on it before, because of a kind of war of attrition. They became a magnet for a single issue from crusaders who felt they should never be allowed to shake it off. To those people, she wasn't Harriet Hatley Photography but Harriet Hatley Abuser.

Therefore, it wasn't yet safe to enable comments on her business page, and Harriet couldn't forecast when it would be. She had to put out of her mind that in the three days since Scott had posted, she'd not had a single booking inquiry. This was unusual, in high season.

Whether she'd be able to make a living from the amount in her diary in a year's time, she didn't know. She'd panic-signed for a room in Chapel Allerton yesterday, trying to get ahead of any potential landlords making the connection between the Harriet Hatley looking for a room and Harriet Hatley, Annihilator of Men. She couldn't hide what she did for a living, given it was key to her ability to meet her rent. Fortunately, this landlord seemed unconcerned with her identity, to the point of referring to her as "Heidi."

How far Scott's poison had spread, and how long it would linger in the system: these were unknowns. Only time would tell whether she could weather the whispers, or if she'd have to fold her firm and phoenix it from the ashes, under a different title. It'd take years to rebuild. How could he take so much from her, at this distance? It shouldn't be possible.

What a stupendous victory for Scott, stealing her name. Associating it with something hideous.

What had it all been for? Harriet had passed through many places on her journey, still indulging in hot tears most nights before sleep, and had arrived at the minor market town of defeatist self-reproach. Perhaps all her lofty ideals about rescuing another woman had been self-deceiving bullshit. Perhaps, as Lorna had tried to make her see, it had been about unmaking her own choices. Maybe Scott was right—maybe she couldn't bear to see him thriving and had senselessly lashed out.

She let herself into the house, in early evening, and Cal was in the sitting room, in a beguilingly slightly tight T-shirt and with pleasingly rumpled hair, drinking a beer. Harriet felt an urge to smooth his hair back into place, followed by an emotional rush that at least here, she was safe. This was what she yearned for: nights in front of the television, talking about nothing in particular. Comfort, and company.

"Hello! Good wedding?" he said. "I'm watching a shite film with Ben Affleck, kicking back in my Sonic the Hedgehog slippers. And I've got plenty more of these." He held up a can of something that looked trendy, foamy, and sour. "Care to join?"

Harriet checked if he was joking as regards the slippers. He was.

"I can't believe you looked," Cal said.

Harriet laughed.

"Up for a beer, thank you. I'll drop my things first."

She threw her bag into her bedroom and joined him with her own beer. After a few minutes of Affleck discussing a nuclear bomb with a radiation-assessment team on-screen, Cal cleared his throat.

"Harriet?"

"Yes."

"You know when you first phoned me about the room?"

"Yeah?"

"How did you know about it, before it went online?"

"My friend is an estate agent. She said, 'Oh, hey, you'll love this room, I'll give you first dibs.' I know it was a bit cheeky."

"Ah! Right."

"Why do you ask?" Harriet set the can back down.

"Uhm . . ."

There was a heavy pause where Harriet tried to make sense of the non sequitur, and the usually breezy Cal's slightly unnatural tone.

". . . Oh my God." She gulped, suddenly sweating.

Looking at him, it was all over his face. He'd seen Scott's post. He'd been discussing it with third parties. He was wondering if she was a wrong 'un, and if so, her unusual method of arrival indicated he was the next project.

She'd known there was a risk Cal would hear about it, but hoped he was distant enough from Scott Dyer that it might take a while. Not only was Harriet hurt that Cal was doubting her, it was a hammer blow, after the false ease of today's wedding, and she felt the ever-present threat of tears begin to rise again.

Everyone knew. This was going to follow her everywhere. Perhaps, given she was unsackable at the last minute, they'd all been in on it at today's wedding, and had a collective agreement not to mention it.

At Cal's continued silence, which was seconds and felt like minutes, Harriet said slowly, "OK, you know about Scott

Dyer, and this is your response? Sounding me out on whether I schemed to move in with you, to check if he was giving you a useful caution about me?"

"No! What happened was . . ."

Suddenly, she was furious. Furious that of all the shit things that had happened in the last few weeks, Scott had ruined this—*this*—as well, and her fury nearly choked her. Some blistering reality was in order. "*Scott* is a liar, a gaslighter, and a coercive controller. In our time together, he nearly broke me. If you read what he wrote and think that might be an accurate description of me, then you can go to hell along with him. Good thing I'm moving out in four weeks."

Harriet hadn't given Cal the date, yet now seemed a good time.

She jumped up, with the sudden animation of anger suffused with self-consciousness, and pounded upstairs. She slammed her bedroom door shut and locked it, chest heaving.

"Harriet! Harriet?" Cal said, moments later, on the other side of the door. "Please let me explain why I said what I said!"

She didn't reply, lying down and putting a pillow over her head. Scott's victory over her felt as good as total. She'd thought Cal might be an island away from it, a place of escape. She'd even thought they might have a newfound affinity.

Harriet breathed into the material in the darkness and felt a despair that was new, a hopelessness that felt all-encompassing. She imagined she'd escaped, the morning of the B&Q fight, but had she?

She could see, for the first time, that her life post-Scott had been heavily shadowed by Scott, something she'd never have admitted if she wasn't, as Lorna would say, on her arse. She had moved on from him but she'd never really got past him, and it turned out to be a very meaningful distinction.

It wasn't only that he'd followed her here. He'd never been fully out of her life.

Bruised, still hiding from it, and psychologically jumbled, Harriet could finally admit that, subconsciously, she'd used Jon as a rehab center. It wasn't fair. One broken heart and one broken engagement later, both of which she inflicted on him, it was rightfully her turn.

Thanks to her doomed fixation upon interfering in something that didn't concern her, her job was in jeopardy, and she'd been tarred as the perpetrator of the very thing of which she was victim.

Harriet lifted the pillow slightly as she caught the soft step of Cal leaving his post and going back downstairs. She rolled onto her back and heaved a sigh, tremulously.

She had been resigned to the fact no one would ever know what went on between herself and Scott. In the words of the song, that wasn't right, but it was OK. They both had to live with themselves, and Harriet could. For a vast multitude to now have an opinion on their relationship, but have *her* down as the abuser—it was unbearable. It was Scott's gaslighting writ large. He might not care about other people's feelings, but he was nevertheless an absolute master of identifying weak spots, where to turn the screw. *A narcissist has empathy,* she once read, *they know it affects you—they just don't care.*

Cal's altered manner with her was a stark reminder—those closest to her knew the truth, but she could count them on the fingers of one hand. To the world at large, she'd have a question mark hanging over her head.

None of this needed to happen. Harriet felt like the contestant on the game show who isn't content with their modest gains and gambles it all, only to walk away with nothing. She itched to throw things and smash furniture and pummel something into submission. Instead, she lay motionless on the bed, limp and defeated.

She'd wanted to demonstrate Scott Dyer no longer had any power over her. She'd ended up proving the exact opposite.

36

An hour or so later, there was a cautious knock.

"Harriet," Cal called. "Are you OK?" A long pause. "Please know I'm so, so sorry. That was a stupid way to broach something you must be in bits about. I'm totally and completely on your side and I should've been up front."

Even in the teeth of her anguish, she had to concede he was charming. Perhaps it was even . . . emotional intelligence?

"Go away," she said, half serious, like a sullen teen. She was lying on the bed, staring at the ceiling, eyes swollen but dry now, all cried out again. She knew her behavior was unbecoming, but somehow she had to go through it to get to the other side. If Cal was truly sorry, if he really liked her, he'd withstand it.

"Please, can I grovel my explanation and apologies face-to-face?" Cal said.

"No. Grovel them through the door."

"OK, I will. Hang on, I'll sit down first."

She heard the sound of Cal's T-shirt brushing against the wall.

"There's a German word, *zugzwang,* to describe a situation where any move a chess player makes makes things worse for them. I feel that way right now, because my reasons for saying what I said aren't what you think; I wasn't doubting you. But they're still quite shit."

Harriet said nothing. She throbbed with the indignity of what he knew. Cal Clarke—irrepressible, haloed, priority-boarding-pass-for-life Cal—had read about her begging for sex. She wanted to die. She rolled onto her side and blinked at the light coming under the door, then closed her eyes against her humiliation. She felt as if she'd been stripped in the town square, and Cal had turned out to see the Walk of Shame. It wasn't possible to be calm and gracious when she was naked and he was not—even if it wasn't his fault.

"A colleague showed me the Facebook thing."

"How did she know you knew me?"

"I've talked about you. Some of them met you at my birthday. She didn't know your last name, but enough to make the connection."

"Why *have* you talked about me?"

Harriet knew she sounded peevish to the point of silly, but then again, what exactly was there to preserve, of anything, at this juncture.

"As my friend. I think you initially came up as a wedding recommend."

"Hmmm."

"She was winding me up, saying perhaps I didn't know the nature of the person renting a room in my house. I said of course I did. She said, 'Don't you think it's unlikely, how she turned up by coincidence when she'd photographed your wedding,' and . . ."

She heard Cal hesitate.

". . . that you knew I must be single, and targeted me."

Harriet flinched. She thought about Cal pondering this, scrolling back through memories of their interactions for clues of a seduction.

"I said, 'Don't be daft.' She'd remembered what I'd said about how you and I agreed to this arrangement, sight unseen. She said, 'Wasn't she the first call you got—you said the room wasn't even online? How did she know to call you before the room was online, if she didn't know you?' I didn't have an answer for that. Obviously, I knew it wasn't because you'd plotted anything. I wanted to have the answer ready for next time if she raised it, that was all. I should've told you why I was asking and not fished like a clumsy wanker. I didn't want to mention Facebook before you did. Obviously, because you're not an idiot and hadn't drunk as much six percent IPA, you made the connection immediately. And here we are."

"You weren't gossiping: *Oh God, yes, what IF my lodger's unhinged?*"

"No, of course I wasn't!" Cal said, with what sounded like real indignance. "For what it's worth, even if I hadn't known you, I'd have thought it read like absolute horseshit. There were about a dozen weird leaps of logic. Like, why was he snooping at your phone?"

Harriet twinged again at this outsider's perspective that she had been traduced: she was simultaneously grateful and freshly humiliated at his being informed.

"Not that it would've mattered if it had been revealing," she forced herself to say, unable to let him think less of her in any way, "but Scott lost it at a photo of an ordinary dress in a Topshop changing room. It was only 'provocative' to an Edwardian grandfather."

"I don't doubt you. He's one of those blokes who doesn't even know when his entitlement's showing. He kept giving himself away."

Harriet was somewhat mollified at this. It matched up neatly with what Lorna had said. It gave Harriet hope that some had seen through him.

"Great to know news of my great unveiling as a pissed-up bully has reached the newsroom of the *Yorkshire Post*." Then, quieter: "It's so . . . embarrassing, Cal."

"Will it help if I embarrass myself?"

"I don't know. Try."

"I think partly why I blurted that question like an idiot was . . . when I read it, I felt protective of you, but also a bit . . . possessive, I guess?"

Harriet's heart rate increased, and she sternly instructed herself not to be affected by it.

"You're my friend, and there's this ex saying bizarre, nasty things about you. I knew he was making it up. But he was describing a time in your life when I didn't know you. It gave me a sort of disorientation, like . . . jealousy. Then my colleague starts accusing me of not knowing you, when I'm so sure I do. It got to me."

Harriet swallowed, hard.

"I know how self-absorbed and gruesomely inappropriate this sounds. Not least cos you're thirty-four, so of course you had a life before Travel Iron Jon, and moving in with me . . . and . . . Oh God, stop talking, Cal . . . Yeah, well, there it is. My feeling on reading it was *Who the fuck are you to her, and how dare you*. Nothing else. I've made myself look worlds worse, haven't I?"

In actual fact, Cal had unwittingly struck a chord. Harriet remembered that she'd felt a stab of irrational possessiveness about the casual fling Cal had, thirteen years ago. Were they . . . *both . . . falling* . . . ?! Surely not. No. Fact check: he was going on dates that he wasn't mentioning. Still, it was nice that he felt defensive. It was a teaspoon of sugar stirred into the very bitter, cold black coffee that was her life.

"No. And I think you'll agree: in Scott, I have now decisively won the awful exes competition. Close the phone lines, your vote won't count," Harriet said, in a conciliatory tone.

"Oh, I don't know about that . . ."

Harriet got up, pushed the hair out of her face, checked herself in the mirror (nothing to be done about those eyes), dug in a drawer to find a particular piece of paper. She opened the door to him. Cal was still sitting down, socked feet braced against the opposite wall. He looked up, apprehensive.

"Long story short, you're blaming this on a woman?" Harriet said.

"*Zugzwang!*" Cal grinned.

"You're a massive *zugzwang*."

Harriet handed Cal the florist's card, as he stood up.

"Remember when you thought I'd got flowers from a client? It was Scott. I ran into him and his fiancée at a wedding shortly before, and she looked as down-beaten as I once did. I wrote her a letter about what he'd done to me, saying 'you're not alone.' That bouquet was him promising he'd get me back for it. The Facebook post was the getting me back."

Cal frowned at it. "This is really creepy, Harriet. You should've said at the time. We could've gone to the police, even."

"There wasn't anything you, or they, could do, and I didn't know what he'd do as retaliation. After Jon's antics, I didn't know how you'd take it. What a dream lodger I am."

Cal gave it back. "I'd have installed machine-gun turrets."

She flushed, unbidden.

"Seriously, Harriet. I think this Scott is scum. I honestly, on Sam's life, didn't need you to tell me you'd not behaved like that. I was only looking for confirmation of a minor practicality, nothing more."

Harriet thought on her rant about disrespecting things you didn't fully understand. At least Cal asked.

"Accepted and forgiven," Harriet said, shoulders slumping. Then: "Hey, I have a question. Why is there writing on the wall in there by someone saying they hate you?"

"Uh?"

She showed Cal into the room and pointed to it.

"Urrrgh, Naked Ned. Your predecessor. The guy who walked around nude and used toilets with doors open. He was Mr. Chilled Hippie until I said to him I didn't think it was working out, and could he perhaps go? He flipped at me. I found little notes shoved down the sides of bookcases and folded up in the coffeepot afterward, questioning my mother's family background, shall we say. I feel lucky he didn't beat me to death with his pimped didgeridoo while I slept. Not a euphemism."

"Hahaha. Yet you didn't even want to meet me?"

"I liked your voice," Cal said, shrugging, and smiling, and, in some small way, helping to mend Harriet's heart.

37

"All right, babe, sorry to shout, I'm hands-free on the road!" Bryn said, over acoustics like he was standing on the top of Scafell Pike in a gale. Given her industry rival was always loud anyway, speakerphone Bryn was football-terrace-during-a-goal volume.

"Hi, Brinners, how are you?" Harriet said, holding the handset slightly away from her ear, with lead in her boots. Her mobile had been peppered with five missed calls from him already this morning.

It was the following Sunday, over ten days since Scott's post, and there had been no inquiries—unless she counted an email direct to her site, asking for her cheapest possible price, which had clearly been copied to every other wedding snapper in the region. It was no longer possible to rationalize that Scott might or might not have damaged her living: it was fully evident he had.

Walking to lunch with Lorna at Kadas in the city center, she thought she'd get Bryn out of the way en route and answered on his sixth attempt. From anyone else, this level of pursuit could look frantic to the extent of browbeating, but Bryn was like a puppy Labrador retriever—hyper and harmless. Put your fragile china out of reach, though. The fragile china in this case being Harriet's delicate psyche.

"Not bad, babe, not bad. Yeah, so I wanted to warn you there's some sort of scurrilous rumor doing the rounds about you."

Harriet screwed her eyes closed and said, "Yeah, I know."

"Ah, right, I wondered if you did. About how you whacked an ex-boyfriend around? I don't go on citizen Facebook myself, but when people told me about it, I said, 'How big is the ex-boyfriend? Harriet looks about as intimidating as Minnie the Minx from *The Beano*,' ahahaha. Sorry, not very politically correct. Violence is never the answer. Though some people beg the question, hahahaha."

"No one hit anyone, I assure you," Harriet said, trying to sound calm and firm as she writhed in agony. "Scott made it all up from start to finish because he's a spiteful shit holding a grudge. I appreciate people will still spread it."

"Absolutely, babe, but you don't need to convince me. You're a gem and I've always said so. Thing is, your couple at Oulton Hall, in a couple of weeks? Felix and Margaret? They want to swap to me as a result. I said I'd only do it if you were all right with it, and they'd have to write off their deposit. You know me, I play fair. I don't want any part of thieving your bookings during a downturn."

Downturn.

This hurt. Harriet knew she'd lose prospective customers, but forfeiting those who'd already employed her? Who'd met her?

She tried to keep her tone light, despite the turmoil inside. "They really want to bin me off thanks to one rant online where I wasn't even named, by an ex-boyfriend? It's brutal out there, isn't it? I never knew my good name was this flimsy."

Harriet wanted to land the point to Bryn that this could happen to anyone, though when she looked back over the baroque history between herself and Scott Dyer, that was pushing credulity.

"Yeah, as I said to Margaret, I doubt any of us want our exes doing our character references. My first wife calls me Bryn Laden, hahaha. I don't think they think you'd be Tasmanian-deviling about the place. Margaret said they don't want it overshadowing anything. I said it wouldn't, but you know when a bridezilla gets a notion . . ."

This was it, as she'd foretold. They'd not need to think Scott spoke gospel, only to feel enough of an odor now hung around Harriet to be deterred. Infamy was what she'd gained, and it was very much not wanted from a big-day bit player.

"Sure, take the job, don't worry. It's not as if I want to do it if they don't want me there." She swallowed a lump, stayed breezy. "Thanks for being so principled as to tell me, Bryn. I appreciate it. I've got a feeling I'm going to need friends in the coming months."

Or years.

"No biggie. Tomorrow's chip wrap, babe. Got a call on line two, gotta hustle! Speak soon."

She rang off with a wan smile at Bryn's manner. When he employed one person as an admin assistant, he started naming himself as CEO on his email boilerplate.

Harriet appreciated the sentiment, but she wasn't sure "tomorrow's chip wrap" scaled up to Mark Zuckerberg's website in the twenty-first century. The internet was written in a kind of ink that didn't become illegible while it kept greasy haddock warm.

Harriet arrived at Kadas to find that Lorna had already ordered the mezze: it was a favorite spot and the menu was an old friend, so they didn't have to think their way around any logistics.

Lorna pushed a plate of stuffed grape leaves toward Harriet.

"I've had a splendid idea," Lorna said, full distraction mode employed as she outlined plans for a girls' holiday in Cornwall.

Harriet gritted her teeth. "Such a lovely idea, but I can't really do that while my income's tanking, and Roxy may be about to go self-employed." She cupped a hand underneath her dolma, to catch stray rice.

"Pish. It'll cost next to nothing because I'm going to cover the accommodation. Hang on, rather than explain it twice, I'm going to call Rox."

Lorna prodded the relevant buttons on her phone and stuck it on speakerphone on the table, propped against a beer bottle. Kadas was busy enough that it wasn't too much like sodcasting.

"Rox, Fleaslags conference meeting. I vote we cheer Harriet up by going away for a long weekend. I know neither of you are flush at the moment, but I have leftover comp money which I'd been saving for the right moment. I'd like to spend it on hiring a cottage for a long weekend. What say you? Do you even own any wellies? Or maybe a villa, somewhere hot. Fuck it, if all we can manage is marauding round Legoland Windsor with gin cans, frightening kids, it'll be a laugh."

"Aw, I would, but me and New Man were thinking we'd go away. I kinda want to keep my diary clear."

The Tinder date had been a blast, she'd reported, and Harriet was glad she'd not insisted Roxy miss it to witness her miseries over Scott. Committed online dating was like the lottery, she supposed: you always thought the time you didn't bother was when your numbers would come up.

"Lol, what? You won't do anything with us on the off chance he proposes something? Book us in and book him in around us. Or vice versa, if you wish to dwell in a Gilead of your own creation."

"It's more complicated than that, it depends on when he can get the time off work."

"Doesn't High-Finance Joseph the Broseph call his own shots on annual leave?" Lorna added an eye roll. "Also. We need you. Harriet here needs you."

"That's rather emotional blackmail-y. Thanks, but it's a no thanks for the time being," Roxy said, tartly.

Lorna frowned at Harriet. Harriet frowned back. This was new.

There'd been a few minor rejections by Roxy recently, an apparent indifference to the meaning of certain moments. Harriet had been determined to read nothing into them. Life always got in the way, friends shouldn't act like they were trying to catch friends out, etc., etc. Yet this was a pretty stark announcement of priorities, and in the face of Lorna offering to treat them both, it felt ungrateful too.

"Also," Roxy continued blithely, into their unspoken dismay, "I'm not being funny, but Harriet did bring all of this down on her own head. She wrote a letter to her ex's fiancée saying he was an arsehole. I mean, who does that?! Of course he's defended himself? It's not rocket science. I can see why he's annoyed, to be quite honest with you."

Lorna glanced at Harriet, her stunned expression surely matching Harriet's own. It was obvious Roxy hadn't caught the fact that Harriet was present, and it was too late to say so without making everything more excruciating for all concerned.

"You can't seriously be defending Scott Dyer? What next, the case for wasps in your lager?"

"He's always been awful; I agree he's horrible. But Harriet has a way of making herself the victim even when she's at fault."

Harriet set her falafel down, having abruptly and completely lost her appetite.

"She's not at fault. Scott's an abuser," Lorna said, awkwardly, lacking any way to tell Roxy to tone it down.

"Yes, but she knew that before she decided to wind him up. For no reason whatsoever."

Harriet's mouth went dry and her heart beat loudly in her chest. This was so wholly devastating that she couldn't separate what was cruel and what was unwelcome home truth.

"She was trying to help his fiancée," Lorna said faintly.

There was a disbelieving snort from down the receiver.

"Oh, come on, Lore. She wanted that girl to leave Scott, to get him back. Now that it's blown up in her face it's *poor Harriet.* I'm not saying it's not grim for her, but do the crime, do the time."

Lorna made noises of objection and, after garbling an "I'll get back to you," hung up, hastily.

"Fuck. That was my fault. She's an idiot and I'm going to give her seven bells of hell next I see her, but the fact I put you both through that, that was my fault."

"She's right, though, isn't she?" Harriet said, trying to keep her lip from trembling. "I brought this on myself."

"No, she isn't, she's being selfish and careless and . . . *hard,* and I'm really disappointed in her," Lorna said, looking almost as if she might cry herself. "The number of times you've helped scrape her off the floor when some shithouse boyfriend mistreated her, and then this? Because she thinks she's on to a good thing with this bloke, this Joseph? The trouble is, Roxy genuinely wouldn't understand why you'd do something out of nobility, to help someone else. It's not a feature in her landscape. I always thought her lack of scruple was funny, but maybe age thirty-four is when you stop finding it funny, and start finding it . . . Well. Start finding it." She paused. "*Estate agents.*"

Harriet could barely raise a smile, and Lorna looked glumly at her bowl of paprika-dusted hummus. Harriet wasn't ready to psychoanalyze Roxy, or minimize with humor.

Harriet has a way of making herself the victim.

It was a bucket of cold water when Harriet could've really used a dose of unshakable conviction in herself, the sort she had when she and Lorna had walked around the park that other, optimistic Sunday morning. However, the moment had gone, and she didn't know if she *had* wanted to ruin Scott's life and concealed the motive, even from herself.

It was too soon to assess the damage, but could she ever feel the same way about Roxy again, knowing she thought Scott Dyer had a point? Even if Roxanne was some degree of right, if your friend could see you attacked like that and shrug and sarcastically pronounce "*poor Harriet,*" was she your friend? God, the irony. Harriet spent so many years wishing her friends could see Scott's point of view. What a shattering time for Roxy to oblige.

She and Lorna mutually pretended to think and speak of other topics, but lunch had been ruined, her stomach in a tight knot. It was unheard of for Lorna to be at a loss for things to say.

As they parted, Lorna said, "I will inevitably be having it out with our Roxanne over this. Should I tell her that you heard her opinions? I will make it clear that responsibility for that disaster is on me."

"Oh no," Harriet said. "What will it achieve? She'll be crucified and it's not as if she can take it back. She thinks what she thinks."

"My intuition tells me there's more to this," Lorna said. "It didn't even sound like her speaking. Why did she sound like that?"

For once, Harriet thought Lorna's intuition was purely wishful.

She hoped not to be intercepted by Cal once she got home, but he bounded out of the sitting room as soon as he heard the front door close.

"Just wondered. Need a hand? When you move?"

"No, thanks. Think I've got it covered," Harriet said, with the kind of brittle, concertedly perky brightness that hovers right on the edge of primal screaming.

"Are you sure you want to go? There's no rush."

"Yes! Honestly. It's fine."

"OK." Cal opened his mouth and then shut it again. He looked at her from under his brow but—perhaps detecting her turbulence—was deterred.

She nodded by way of a conclusion and made her way past him and up the stairs.

"Are you all right?" Cal said, frowning after her, and part of her yearned to fall into his arms, sobbing. NOPE. She'd put too much on him already. He was her *landlord,* for God's sake, not her Emotional Support Turkey.

"Yes! Fine," Harriet said, unconvincingly. She glanced back and smiled, a forced, closed-mouth, brave-soldier smile. A smile that was as much a *KEEP OUT* sign.

She got upstairs, closed her door gently, turned the key, and put music on softly as a muffling device, then, when it was safe, burst into near-silent tears. Empty, hopeless, jaw-stretching tears, tears that came from the chest, a borderline howl that pulled her face into strange shapes. She covered her eyes with her hands and let it out: the isolation, the hopelessness, her own sheer ludicrousness.

It was as if she'd made her home on the edge of a cliff and was watching it fall, piece by piece, into the sea.

Harriet has a way of making herself the victim.

She'd lost Roxy, or at least, there was now a distance between them that was likely permanent.

She needed her closest friends to understand—or if not understand, respect—that Scott wasn't *just* an ex and they didn't *just* end on bad terms.

When she finished it with Scott, Harriet interrupted a process where, had it continued, eventually would have led to no Harriet to rescue.

HARRIET CRIED HERSELF to sleep, and when she awoke, after an anxiety dream about being naked in the middle of the Reliance, she could tell the house was empty. Cal must be off seeing Nameless Girl Pal.

She wasn't hungry, and alcohol would only lower her further into the well. She lay in the gloom and scrabbled for her phone. If nothing could help, if all was lost, why not succumb to the temptation of the absolute worst thing she could do? She navigated back to Scott's post.

It was like picking a scab, except that didn't get close to the sense of self-harm—picking a scab, as you lay in a ditch waiting for the paramedics.

The shares and Likes had plateaued, but Harriet saw reams of fresh theorizing about her specific, colorful mental problems and vicious nature. She'd now stage-managed attending the same wedding as Scott in order to "try to blow up his life," and those schooled in the law on harassment offenses were advising how to handle stalkers, because H would definitely strike again. Harriet was starting to wish she went by the mononym H, avenging wronged women while dressed in Lycra.

Her eye was drawn to a recent comment, only an hour old, sitting a few places from the end of the thread.

Nina Jackson

*Hi everyone! I'm not "H" and I have no idea if any of this is true, but for what it's worth, I dated Scott Dyer for almost 3 years out of college, and they were by far the worst years of my life. TBH everything he's describing here sounds like the way *he* behaves in a relationship, so I'm wondering if he's having a full Edward Norton/Brad Pitt Fight Club meltdown. Either way, he's not your hero of abused men, of that I'm sure. You've all got yourselves an unreliable narrator. Nina xoxo*

As Harriet blinked in wonder at this burst of pure magic, it vanished.

38

Where did it go? Where was it?! Harriet hit refresh like a demented woodpecker and it remained stubbornly not present, as if she might have conjured it as a comforting mirage.

Except she hadn't, as she now scanned the few responses to Nina, all displaying the online trademark of bullish confidence:

Bye "Nina," ya troll

Hey everyone, H has got herself a sock puppet! 😂

Believe it or not, you don't have to be perfect to be a victim. This is victim blaming. I Stand With Scott

Scott must have deleted Nina's post. The fucker had deleted it, and here was the thing—the very fact he'd deleted it told Harriet it was genuine. It was good to think of him rattled, attacked by a raptor in this Jurassic Park of hostility he'd created artificially in a lab.

However, in the nick of time, Harriet had seen Nina's name—which was sufficiently unusual it wouldn't return a thousand search results—and a profile photo. She'd had no time to open the picture, but she'd recognize it if she saw it in miniature again: it was two-thirds blue sky.

She tapped "Nina Jackson" into the search bar and there she was, fourth option down. The profile in full was an attractive thirty-something woman casting her eyes up humorously at a Virgin logo hot-air balloon above her, in a quirky sort of selfie. "Lives in Prestwich."

God, she hoped Nina wasn't a fantasist or a troll. She could be neither of those things and simply not very agreeable to an approach, of course. Harriet found herself in the trippy space of hoping Scott chose nice girlfriends.

Harriet was desperate to talk to this woman, desperate for corroboration and connection. "3 years out of college." Harriet and Scott had met when Harriet was twenty-five. Nina must be the "bad breakup," surely?

Harriet was further emboldened that Nina was an ex by the unscientific evidence that she had large eyes and a kind of younger-than-her-years, sunny aspect that she had gleaned was Scott's type.

Harriet opened her laptop, reactivated her personal profile, and sent her a friend request. The wedding business had schooled her that if you messaged someone who wasn't in your network, it'd go into a Requests folder that nobody ever checked. She couldn't risk that, so she had to go balls out and brazenly befriend Nina. She had to pray that she would both work out this Harriet Hatley in Leeds was the dreaded H and still want to talk to her.

She saw Request Sent under Nina's profile, and checked it said the same on her phone. She lay back down on the bed, handset gripped in her clammy hand like it was a detonator.

She felt certain that Scott's censorship of Nina proved it was real. Harriet knew only too well that the testimonies on that thread weren't to be trusted, and veracity, accuracy, or good taste had never been a concern for the moderator before. Only two people had the ability to delete it, Scott or Nina. Or Facebook, she supposed, yet it hadn't broken any "community guidelines," unless contradicting someone was a hate crime.

Harriet recalled Scott blocking Lorna at the outset of this—it might not have been because of her Marianne research, it was more likely that Scott realized he had to neutralize anyone who had firsthand, unflattering intel.

Hah, and not only that, his erasure of exes wasn't simply "scorn" or sublimated guilt, as she'd said in her letter to Marianne, was it? It was a deep-seated instinct of self-preservation. Of course none of them should compare notes. Of course Scott should be free to invent, and self-mythologize, and control the story. The man with no past. Divide and conquer.

Harriet cast her mind back to the Danny and Fergus wedding: Scott as best man had been an acquisition made on a bachelor do, a few years prior. All the gang that Harriet met, when they were first dating, were from his then workplace. She was never introduced to anyone from further back than a couple of years. His friends as well as his lovers needed to be in the intensity and inexperience of a honeymoon period, of fast-tracked, *look at my new shiny toy!* false intimacy.

There was no Lorna to his Harriet, no Sam to his Cal. No continuity. For a reason.

She checked her phone. It still said Request Sent.

How long should she give Nina to accept it, before it implied she wasn't welcome? Some people, sensible people with lives, ignored social media for days or even weeks on end. Harriet saw her screen light up.

She had a notification.

Nina Jackson Accepted Your Friend Request

Harriet's heart went boom. As she opened the app, she received a message.

Hi! Are you "H"? Nina x

Harriet typed at light-speed.

Hi! Unfortunately, yes. x

The dots rippled to indicate Nina was typing back, and then three words landed. Unexpected words that completely blindsided Harriet, words that made her weep afresh.

Are you OK?

39

Harriet had solid practice in her life at being alone, feeling alone, and yet she had never experienced such aloneness until these last few weeks. And she was a woman who had, somehow, been made an orphan twice over.

The aftermath of Scott's post felt as though she were drowning while a group of spectators on dry land jeered and cheered. Even one of her best friends had stood there filing her nails, declining to help, mouthing, *What did you expect?*

And then a complete stranger strode through the crush, stuck out her hand to her, and pulled her out. A good Samaritan. Harriet typed:

I'm not great to be honest, but so grateful for your comment under that post, and accepting my friend request! Thank you.

A reply pinged back instantly again. Nina was more than she'd have dared hope for.

Oh no problem—he's a massive bullshit artist, I couldn't believe my eyes when it popped up in my timeline. I knew he'd delete my com-

ment. He's blocked me too! You got together with Scott in his late/ your mid-twenties, is that right? Thinking you're around my age? (I'm thirty-five)

Yes, thirty-four! How did you know when we got together?

Hah cos he massively rubbed my face in it! We've got some catching up to do. I don't want to be that pushy duck but do you want to chat on the phone? Thinking this is a lot for messages. I'd offer you FaceTime but I'm not dressed and look like a haystack today x

PS DICK! Ducking autocorrect

This was more than Harriet could've hoped for.

YES! Thank you. x

They swapped numbers, and Harriet called. A woman with a youthful, musical voice with a northern accent answered.

"Hello! Harriet?"

"Hi, yes—Nina?"

"OK, this is surreal, isn't it," Nina chortled. "Welcome to the Scott Dyer Survivors' Club. Membership two, and counting."

Harriet laughed, with a vaguely hysterical edge.

"You're wicked H? Tell me more," Nina said. "Please ignore any nibbling noises, I was mid-snack."

She had a laid-back manner, and even down phone lines, Harriet felt at ease in her company immediately.

Trying not to gabble, Harriet summarized her years with Scott, the wedding encounter, the letter, and the viral-post retribution.

"Oh, this sounds so much like the Scott I remember, it's almost giving me the willies, Harriet. I always wondered if he'd fixed his shit after me, but sounds like he got progressively worse. I'll tell you how I know when you met him. After we broke up, Scott made sure I saw a photo of you and him together on group messages, which was very *finally found me a good one, blah blah* gloating. All I heard from friends after was how great you were for him and 'chilled him out,' as if *I'd* been the problem. I wouldn't say I was jealous of you, as I was so relieved to be shot of him. I definitely had you on a pedestal as the intimidating, beautiful, cool goddess who could handle him, though."

"That's extraordinary to hear, given the reality," Harriet said.

Harriet described the dinner party meet-cute and the fact she was later told of a "bad breakup."

"Oh yeah, that must've been me. It was bad for him, in as much as my mum and dad staged an intervention. They came round and outright accused him of being my fucking captor, which he was. I was like a boiling frog, you know," Nina said, with a bark of a laugh. Harriet did know. "I'm so impressed at how you called time on him in the end. If my parents and I weren't so close and they hadn't spotted what was going on, I don't know what I'd have done."

No one had said they were impressed by Harriet in her private life in a long time, and she didn't know what to say, other than thanks, and absorb it. She never allowed herself to wonder how she and Scott would've gone differently if her parents had been alive; firstly, because it was her responsibility, and secondly, because it was too painful.

"We were at the same university in Cardiff, and in the third year we both did the same art module," Nina said. "He was giving it all Mr. Sensitive and culture appreciator and blah blah and catching my eye during the life drawing. Now I can see he homed in on me and took an interest in all my interests. When I was twenty-one and naive, I didn't spot the grooming, I was like, *Wow, look, spooky, we're soul mates.* After graduating I was going to get a place with friends, and he convinced me to get a flat together instead. Then it was like we were married and the temper tantrums started and, well, you know how he operates. It was like quicksand. Even now I sometimes say to my girlfriend, Daisy, that I overreact to trivial shit with her as I still think relationships mean someone's going to check the soles of my shoes when I say I've been for a walk in the park. Oh yeah, that's another thing, I like to say Scott turned me on to women. He didn't, I'm not giving him any credit for anything except why I go to kickboxing, haha."

Harriet had been silently critical of people who felt they knew Scott based on the briefest of acquaintances; however, she had known Nina for seventeen minutes, and she sincerely loved her.

"This Marianne's going to marry him?" Nina said. "Good luck with that! My heart goes out to her."

Harriet sighed. "I was gutted she sold me out and showed him the letter. Having said that, back then, I let him delete my best friend's number out of my phone. I was the same, I know what he does to your head."

Harriet would never forget how it felt to turn up on Lorna's doorstep, post-Scott. She thought she might get a slammed door or shouting; instead, Lorna burst into tears and hugged her. "I'm sorry I pushed you away," Harriet had said, and Lorna replied, stoutly, "It wasn't you who pushed me away."

"Yeah, it's a cliché, but you have to see it for yourself, don't you? You have to see him for what he is, and that takes time," Nina said, and Harriet's heart simply soared at having someone to share this with. "I was still in denial when my parents steamed in. Almost as soon as I was out of that atmosphere, I started to realize how messed up it was. That's the thing. What you need more than anything is distance and perspective and you don't have them, he makes sure of that."

"It becomes your normal," Harriet agreed. "I want to block him and forget about it, but I'm losing work because of it. Everyone thinks I'm the *Fatal Attraction* girl who they don't want lurking round their wedding."

"That's so out of order. The reason I commented was to scare him. He needs to realize there are people out here who know the truth, and to wind his neck right fucking in. I wish I could help you."

"You have helped, you've restored my sanity," Harriet said, feeling a little wobbly. "Truly, Nina. You're like a guardian angel."

"Your guardian angel probably wouldn't be eating a vegan Magnum and wearing stretch jorts."

They both laughed, in nervous exhilaration.

"Keep my number, let's stay friends! I hope Scott sees! Except he can't, if we're both blocked," Nina said.

"How shit is it that the two of us together, backing each other up, probably still aren't worth the word of one Scott?" Harriet said.

"You never know who else is out there," Nina said. "Perhaps others will call out his BS, like I did."

This was a very good point.

"If there's anything I can do, you'll let me know?" Nina said. "I'm in Leeds pretty often. We could meet to brainstorm the perfect murder. Actually, no, I'm not having him relaxing in a nice burial plot, everyone crying and saying nice things about him. Chiseling 'TOP LAD' on his headstone. I want Scott to face up to what he does."

Harriet said, "Amen," while thinking, *Men like Scott never get their comeuppance.*

However, she had also believed there was no flaw in Scott's plot to turn the tables on her, and in fact, there was, and here it was.

Without his attack on "H," she and Nina would never have found each other. His newfound micro-fame was his undoing—like when the police reported an arrest to get other accusers to come forward.

Minutes later, she discovered Scott Dyer might be thinking the same way: the whole post about "H" had been deleted. It was too late to save Harriet's reputation, but it was something.

40

"Whose prick idea was it to have a picnic again?" said Lorna, as they nibbled dejectedly on soggy spinach and feta empanadas in Roundhay Park, the following Friday at dusk.

"I recall some hectoring over it being your thirty-fifth birthday," Harriet said, as the rain spattered on the picturesque wicker basket with leather buckles, and diluted their drinks like a splash of meteorological soda. "Despite Roxy pointing out the forecast was . . . uneven."

"The tea lights were pure hubris." Lorna nodded at the smoking holders nestled in the grass, which had flickered for all of a minute.

"I hope this doesn't affect the glue on my fresh set of lashes," Roxy said, from under her frilly umbrella. She looked like a smartphone-generation Eliza Doolittle. "At least the tiny Cornish pasties are nice."

"I got into my al fresco street-food recipes and wouldn't hear sense." Lorna sighed, wrapping her rainbow angora cardigan around her pencil dress more tightly. She picked up the pink cava from its forty-five-degree angle in the grass, topping up their plastic cups.

It was an inconveniently timed birthday, if Harriet was honest: obliging Roxy to spend time in their company less than a week after the disastrous phone call, when it was hardly a sign of affection to attend, more an act of war not to. Harriet could've done with a little longer for her feelings to heal. Plus she'd taken no wedding bookings this weekend to keep it clear for this, and in her larger *downturn,* she regretted it.

"You should know our Roxanne was totally, totally different when I called back and said, 'What the hell,'" Lorna said, before she arrived at the picnic spot. "She was hormonal, she said, and I'd caught her at a wicked moment. We all have them. I reminded her of some of Scott's greatest hits and she was very remorseful."

Although Harriet trusted Lorna implicitly, she suspected some PR management. Lorna felt at fault for engineering a situation where Harriet got Roxy's unvarnished views, ergo, this was the patch-up of the torn hull. She also noticed there was no mention of the girls' holiday being resurrected.

"You didn't tell her about the speakerphone bork, did you?" Harriet said, warily.

"Absolutely not, framed it all as what I thought."

The sky was a foreboding gunmetal gray. Lorna had resolutely refused gifts or treats, at a generally skint time, and catered: there was no way of fighting the picnic plans.

There was also no Gethin to provide distraction from their wonky triangle: he had a formal work do, so was splitting the difference and meeting them at the Dive later.

"House rules," Lorna had announced, as opener. "Discussion of the world's shittiest little tinpot ruler with the mop top hair is banned. No mentions of Pol Pot Noodle, please."

Both Harriet and Roxy avoided each other's eyes and mumbled assent.

After a short squall, the sun came out and their respective pieces of outerwear came off, somewhat ambitiously.

"How's it going with the new man, Rox?" Lorna said.

"Oh, you know," Roxy said, tucking her hair behind her ear and stretching out her legs in her maxi dress. They might be in a park, but she was in delicate heels, as always. "Fabulous, but it's early days."

"What does he do for a living again?"

"Something important for banks. I don't really understand it."

"That's a nice little bauble. Joseph gift, was it?" said Lorna, nodding to a slim white-gold bangle that Roxy had pushed up her now-exposed slender arm, like Cleopatra.

"Oh yes," Roxy said, as if she'd forgotten she'd put it on, playing with it. She looked unusually sheepish, possibly because it looked over the top for early days, even by the standards of men she dated. "White gold. Tiffany's."

"Huh. That's a coincidence," Harriet said. "I saw Jon with a Tiffany's bag in town, a few weeks back. It's the loaded man's gifting choice of the season. I have a feeling Jon's was destined for his horrendous mother."

Roxy flushed scarlet, an extraordinary shade of claret grape that was so striking as to be impossible to politely ignore. Harriet had never seen someone change color like that before. Roxy dropped her eyes down to her lap.

"Are you OK?" Harriet said anxiously, into her continuing silence. "Did I say something wrong?"

"Oh God, is it a push present? A pre-push baby mama present?

Are you up the stick?" Lorna said, then frowned at the frothy second mug-measure of cava in Roxy's cup.

Harriet replayed her own words. *Jon had a Tiffany's . . .*

Her body froze, plummeting to an icy temperature, as a terrible (im)possibility occurred, and Roxy raised her eyes to meet Harriet's. The look in them was a curdled mixture of guilt and a sort of petulant hostility, like a little girl who's been caught with her hands in the Christmas trifle.

"Holy shit," Harriet said. "That bracelet's from *Jon*?"

"Wait. I don't understand. Your fella is Joseph?" Lorna said.

For Harriet, there was a terrible clang.

"Oh. He's Jonathan *Joseph* Barraclough. JJ." Harriet paused, licked dry lips, heart racing. "I see what you did there."

"Please tell me this is a sick joke? Joseph is Jon?" Lorna said. "You're shagging JON?"

The rain started spitting at them again, but now they couldn't be more indifferent.

"I knew you'd not take it well. I didn't know when to mention it . . ." Roxy said, in a tiny, hoarse voice, pulling at a blade of grass with a shaky hand.

"You're serious? You're involved with Jon?" Harriet said. She didn't want to believe it until utterly forced.

"Yeah, I am," Roxy said, smoothing her hair decorously behind her ear again, as if this was a delicate, sensitive admission being made by a fragile person. As opposed to the most unseemly and violent act of treacherous ugliness that Harriet could currently imagine.

"He was thinking about putting his house on the market, and I went round for a valuation. We always got on great when you two were dating," Roxy appealed to a stunned Harriet, as if this were clear mitigation. "I think we really work well together."

"I feel sick," Harriet said. "I can't believe you've done this. What part of sleeping with my ex behind my back, right after we've finished, seemed OK to you? You realize he's trying to get back at me?"

"It's *not* to get at you," Roxy said, in a tone of teacherly admonishment. "I'd not do that. *Jon* wouldn't do that."

Harriet jumped to her feet. She had taken a lot; so much, too much. But being *chided* by her friend—scratch that, her enemy—was so extreme as to finally provoke her to full battle cry. "Don't fucking tell me what he would or wouldn't do, based on a few weeks of giving him blow jobs in his hot tub!"

A family with young kids ambling past suddenly sped up, as if they'd hit fast-forward in a comedy skit.

"This is properly DISEASED, what is wrong with you?! What part of Jon being off-limits as your latest boyfriend slash benefactor wasn't obvious to you?" Harriet cried. She didn't like fights, but this wasn't any old fight; there was no time to assess anything in the tumult of her feelings—Harriet had lost all inhibition.

Roxy stood up too, brushing grass from her legs, and Lorna realized she had to follow suit.

"Look. Lorna's thirty-five today," Roxy said, pointing at Lorna, switching tack from Little Girl Lost to drill instructor. "We're almost thirty-five. We're not kids anymore, we're supposed to be having kids! There's no point acting like we can play by cute little rules we had when we were twenty-two in nightclubs."

"'Cute little rules'?" Harriet echoed, blankly.

"Jon might not have been right for you, Harriet, but he is a genuinely *lovely* man, who, if you're honest with yourself for once, you'd admit you didn't treat the best. He wants the things I want. Am I meant to throw that opportunity for happiness away?"

"Wants the things you want! Wants to pay for things and you want to let him?" Lorna chipped in.

"Oh, for fuck's sake, Lore," Roxy spat. "Stop acting like you're in charge of us, and know all the right answers to everything. You've found Gethin now, but it was more luck than anything. And look at Harriet, still hankering after the bad boy from her twenties. Yeah, girl power, and we're all going to end up very bitter and poor and alone."

Harriet did a double take at the word "hankering." One tiny, microscopic mercy: she was no longer fearful of Roxy's take on the Scott years. Roxy had misread them, and her, and him, at a profound level. In turn, Harriet had misread Roxanne.

"When were you going to tell me?" Harriet said, breathlessly.

"I wanted to be sure Jon and I were serious first."

"Oh yes, if it was only loads of naked horseplay, better to leave me in the dark," Harriet said, with a shout of unlaughter.

"This is really proving that telling you from the start would've gone well," Roxy said, rolling lashed eyes.

Harriet had always known Roxy could be careless, but this nihilistic lack of any concern beyond herself whatsoever was knocking the breath out of her. They'd always indulged Roxy, without ever thinking she was spoiled. It turned out they were also indulging themselves. They'd created a whole notion of who she was and what their friendship meant that wasn't shared by Roxy. It felt like the tearing up of a contract, except Harriet was now grasping that there had never actually been one.

"You can't have thought you could do this, and it not mean choosing him over us?" Harriet said. "Did you think whether you stay with Jon or not, we'd come back from this?"

"That's up to you, isn't it," Roxy said, piously.

She wasn't even going to have the decency to cop to the consequences. It was *Harriet's* intolerance estranging them.

"Right, thanks. You're putting the responsibility on me? Then I'm never having anything to do with you ever again." She gathered her few things, heart stuttering.

"So be it," Roxy said. She added, "You've got to do what feels right too," in a resigned yet generous tone, as if she were the sole white-gloved churchgoer in a den of vice, who hoped for better but knew better. Harriet clutched her coat, afraid that if she loosened her grip she'd slap her.

"Same here, I'm afraid." Lorna had stuffed everything back into the basket in seconds flat and linked her arm with Harriet's.

A grisly additional realization had dawned on Harriet.

"The night at the Dive? The night of Scott's post, when you sacked us off for a date? That was seeing Jon, wasn't it?" she said.

Roxy gave a small pout and shrug that was reluctant concession. Lorna let out a low whistle.

"Wow. You are legitimately horrific," Harriet said.

"You don't choose who you fall in love with," Roxy said, and Lorna hooted.

"Barbara fuckin' Cartland here."

"That's exactly what you did," Harriet said. "You made a very clear choice. Now I'm making mine."

They strode out of the park in lockstep, leaving Roxy staring after them. Harriet didn't look back.

41

"Never seen the appeal of hot tubs. Glorified paddling pools for swingers," Lorna said. "A bubbling cauldron of suburban pervs. You always ponder what percentage of that tepid water is covert wees. You'd never get into a *bath* with your neighbors, would you? Brrrr."

Harriet laughed, in a broken way.

After fleeing the park massacre, they'd got a cab to the Dive earlier than planned and installed themselves in a discreet corner. Harriet knew unfettered access to a liquor cabinet was going to make them lordly, revoltingly drunk, and she said, *Bring it on.*

They'd made light work of some red wine and moved on to Lorna-shaken cocktails. Harriet was feeling blurry, and both heavy and light at the same time.

"The girl in the backless dress," Lorna hissed, chin tucked into the side of her neck, as the last customers clattered past to the exit. "Big earrings. She's the one who was in with your housemate. Cal?"

"Oh!" Harriet suppressed the potent churn she felt watching the graceful thirty-something-year-old, with long ombre hair gathered clear of her swan neck in a loose knot, disappear into the night. She was giggling and chattering and being casually fabulous, in a way that Harriet could never hope to be. Yes, she was Cal-equivalent.

"Given how I feel about this turn of events with Roxy, I can't imagine how you feel," Lorna said, as Harriet turned back. "Explains where all the hard-ass She Brought It on Herself stuff came from over Scott, though, eh? Jon was probably in the fucking room."

Quite. Harriet recognized that for Roxy to make the transition to Jon's girlfriend, Harriet had to be Othered, distanced, recast as a serial destroyer of men's minds. *If you're honest with yourself for once, you'd admit you didn't treat him the best.* Pillow talk with Jon, pulling Harriet to pieces, Roxanne trading on her insider knowledge. Harriet imagined this was akin to how you'd feel working for British intelligence and discovering your desk mate was a Russian spy: a disorientating instability, and a review of every exchange you'd had with them over the pertinent period.

"I didn't want to say anything at the time, as I hoped I was wrong and I didn't want to add to your worries, but for what it's worth . . ." Lorna said.

"Oh no, what?"

Lorna bit her lip. "Handing your address over to Jon. She played it off as ditzy Roxy, but I didn't buy it. It would've been the work of seconds to sense check it with you, I would have, the timing didn't even make sense. I wouldn't be surprised if she was sitting next to you at the cinema that night, texting him back. She was . . . disrupting, to see where it led."

"She was eyeing Jon's potential as soon as we split?"

"Yeah, I reckon. Sorry. Obviously, had I thought for a second she was capable of this back then, I'd have spoken up. I assumed it was idle stirring."

"I guess she's scheming being supported through the next phase of her career too," Harriet said, glumly.

When the thunderbolt of this receded, Harriet knew she'd simply be very, very sad. The times they'd shared, for what? To end like this. A friend she'd cried her mascara off with, in laughter and tears, and would drive hundreds of miles for in the middle of the night (and had done). Roxy had held her other hand, the night her grandma died.

"Oh, it *all* comes down to money," Lorna said. "Rox is approaching a crunch point, wants her own company, wants a family. She was on the hunt for a man who can bankroll it, and if we're the price, she'll pay it."

Harriet shook her head.

"There are wealthy men out there who aren't my ex. It's not every night you discover a friend you've had for almost half your life doesn't care about you versus presents in blue bags."

"Money is a drug, it's toxic. Quincy Jones says of creativity: 'God walks out of the room when you're thinking about money,'" Lorna said, picking at a salvaged picnic empanada.

"I hope for God's sake He leaves rooms with Jon and Roxy," Harriet said. She covered her eyes, fresh hell hitting her. "Oh no. They're having sex. I don't know how to compute this. I know what fifty percent of it looks like!"

"I refuse to imagine any percent of it. Fair play to Jon; if you'd asked me which man would blow us apart, I'd never have picked him. How are we going to live down our Yoko being Les Dennis?"

"Think she'll regret it? He's doing this to hurt me. Tons of men would like Roxy for herself, not use her as a pawn."

"Hmmm." Lorna chewed contemplatively. "I don't think Rox was ever *looking for lurve,* she's not made that way. As we can see, cos she doesn't love us. I don't think the depth of Jon's feelings will matter to her. But yes, I think she might miss us, in the future. She's never understood the value of things that can't be bought."

The Tiffany bangle that had been Roxy's undoing—while Roxanne would have been incapable of refusing such a bribe, Jon must've known that her suddenly dripping in jewelry that cost a month's whole salary could have alerted her friends that something was up. It was a risk he was happy to take on her behalf, he was using her as a billboard. The manipulation made Harriet seasick. It was a paler shade of Scott.

There was a knock on the misted glass of the door and Lorna shouted, "We're closed," and then: "Bollocks, it's Gethin. Sorry, dear." She laughed.

He'd ascended to "dear." They were really real.

Harriet considered what a lie it was that frivolous behavior led to romantic ruin. She had been the timid serial monogamist; Lorna had only ever, unapologetically, pursued fun. She had carved her way through Tinder like a Mongol warlord annexing feudal kingdoms. Yet Lorna had found love, or love had found her—and Harriet hadn't.

"Hi, I hope I'm not interrupting anything . . . ?"

Gethin was in a suit, clasping a box of flowers, a profusion of green and pink-tinged hydrangeas.

"You're not, but actually, I was about to go," Harriet said. "No offense to you, Gethin. I'm swimming in booze and it's been a day. I'll let your girlfriend explain. Happy birthday, Lorna!"

As Harriet's taxi pulled away, she saw them embracing in the moodily lit window of the deserted restaurant, looking like a Jack Vettriano painting.

HARRIET STUMBLED THROUGH the front door, stood in the hallway, and announced, "Blurgh," to no one in particular. She assumed her landlord would be in bed.

Cal emerged from the sitting room. He was gleaming, as per usual, like a Cadillac, to Harriet's eyes—fantastically attractive, at least in part due to being refreshingly sober. He was the human equivalent of a bed of crisp white linen after a day of sweaty toil and wheel grease.

"Nice night?"

She got the faintest sense he'd been waiting up for her, but dismissed it with a wave of the hand that encompassed the whole day.

"No. I found out Jon is sleeping with one of my best friends, Roxanne. As revenge. Well, ex–best friend."

"God, really?" he boggled.

"Yes. Gross," Harriet said, except it came out "Grosh."

"You need sleep," Cal said, making a swift assessment as Harriet swayed, gently. He went to the kitchen, returned with a pint of water. He put his hand in Harriet's to lead her upstairs.

She was aware of a huge tidal wall of wine between her and experiencing this moment properly, but Drunk Brain sent a message to Future Brain, saying, *This is very pleasant.*

"Have you got your phone?" Cal said, in the bedroom, and Harriet handed it to him as she sat down on her bed. "Here it is, I'm going to put it in the charger. No contacting anyone until tomorrow when you feel clearer. Drink that water, take the aspirin next to it, get some rest."

Harriet was trying and struggling with reduced motor skills to remove her shoes. Cal knelt down and unlaced them for her, helped pull them off. She gazed at the top of his head and inhaled the sea-salty aftershave he wore. Ugh, he was *so hot.* She might not be able to afford him, but she wouldn't mind a borrow. A designer rental.

"Are you going to help me with the rest too?" She grinned. Somewhere, in a room beyond a thick door in her Drunk Brain, a voice screamed, *Dooooon't say that!* Harriet laughed at it, and herself.

"That feels like something the inebriate should do for herself. Sleep well."

"Calvin?"

"Yes."

"You have a lovely face," Harriet said, as he opened the door and she flopped backward onto the bed. Cal grinned.

"Thank you."

"You could even be the Deceased Perfect Husband in the montage at the start of a film." Harriet's speech had untethered from her mind's checks and balances entirely, and was running its own show.

". . . You what?"

"You know in a film when there's a scene with the Tragically Deceased Wife dancing on the beach, laughing, in a home movie. Or Deceased Hot Husband at Christmas, with a dog. Their only job is to look like the nicest, most picture-perfect spouse ever. They show why your main character is so sad as the story starts."

"So they're conventionally attractive but ultimately irrelevant?" Cal said, hand on the door handle.

Harriet whooped. "Yeah. It's a nonspeaking role. But you get the whole plot going."

Cal laughed and shook his head.

"That's the most cunning put-down I've ever received."

Harriet gurgled with laughter, a few units beyond expressing that it really wasn't a put-down.

42

Harriet woke at dawn and, despite a head full of bees, had perfect clarity about what she'd do next.

Harriet knew that Jon (a) habitually got up at bastard early o'clock ("One of the habits of highly effective people, Hatmandu!"), and (b) would've been warned by Roxy that she knew, and would be waiting for her to make contact.

That was the point of what he'd done, after all, she thought, as she scrubbed at her furred tongue with her toothbrush.

How Roxanne could be participant in her exploitation, and not really care, was baffling to Harriet. She'd not want to be used by a man as a weapon. Harriet was confident this wasn't her ego speaking: she was sure Jon thought Roxy a glittering trophy, most men did. But Jon was distraught about Harriet, only weeks ago. Of course he'd not spontaneously fallen for one of her best mates in the time it takes milk to turn.

As she rinsed and spat, she was reminded of a phrase of Cal's, to Kit: *That's not how human beings work.*

The one benefit to the agony of being awake at this hour was not having to see Cal before she left the house. The idiocies of her behavior last night kept revisiting her, in agonizing flashbacks. The Deceased Husband montage, aaaaaaargh.

She rationalized—Cal couldn't not know he was good-looking, and he could've reasonably guessed Harriet thought he was good-looking. She hadn't given *that* much away, if you were going to be hyper-logical about it. Yet her having told him this, in so many words, was exquisitely embarrassing. "You have a lovely face"?! God, NO.

Oh God, oh God—wait, did she make a joke about him undressing her?! That was halfway to a real come-on? Oh God. BRING ON DEATH. Which, inspecting her reflection, looked as if it was on its way and stuck in traffic. Bloodshot eyes were magnified by glasses.

She didn't want to risk waking him with a phone ping, so Harriet scrawled Cal a message, which she propped next to the kettle.

SORRY FOR BEING SUCH A PISS ARTIST and thanks for putting me to bed. ☹ If you fancy an apology take-away later, it's on me. H x

Then she sent a WhatsApp:

Hi Jon. I'm coming round to see you in an hour, if you're in?

Near-instant response, as she anticipated.

To what do I owe the honour, etc. etc. Be great to see you.

Harriet didn't have to ask whether Roxy would be there. She felt sure that as soon as Jon told her that Harriet was steaming over, Roxy would be out of Roundhay Towers as fast as her LK Bennett ruby suede courts with scallop detailing could carry her.

Harriet bought herself a drive-through McDonald's en route, wolfing down McNuggets and a large fries in goblin fashion, before wiping her hands on paper napkins and checking for stray ketchup in the side mirror. She noisily gurgle-drained the Coke and threw the bag in the bin with a bull's-eye shot as she drove past, feeling like a maverick detective in a TV drama who got casework results at the expense of a functional family life.

She parked up on Jon's drive in her VW Golf with an assertive crank of the hand brake, then marched to the door and rang the bell, which came complete with Ring video. Harriet always thought that was needlessly showy. As if Jon thought he might have the kind of demise to feature in an award-winning murder podcast, and instead recorded hours of footage of delivery drivers and next door's cat defecating.

"Hey, Hats! I wonder what you want to talk about," Jon said with faux jollity, crackling through the intercom. He opened the door, dressed for squash and looking inordinately pleased with himself.

"That would be you involving yourself with one of my closest friends."

"Oh, do you have an opinion about that? That's a shame for you." Jon folded his arms. "Do come in."

Harriet stepped into the hallway.

"What's got into you?" she asked.

"You. You got into me. Then you left. You made it clear you weren't coming back. No more Mr. Nice Guy, I'm afraid."

"You're admitting this is about interfering in my life?"

"Your life? I'm an adult. Roxanne is an adult."

"I'm not saying I can legally prevent you, Jon. But it's a horrible way to behave, and you know it."

Jon leaned against the wall and looked her up and down. Harriet had a feeling he'd been scripting this showdown in his mind for a while. What he'd needed was her attention, and now he had it.

"Gav made the observation recently, all women on dating sites say they're looking for the click, the spark, good sense of humor, *personality*. Yet mysteriously, there's no dull man on £100k a year who 'can't find love.'"

Harriet frowned: "What's that meant to—"

"It got me thinking about how everyone else goes after exactly what they want, in this game. They just don't own it. I've always been so low on confidence, held myself to such high standards. Why not have what I want? Your friend flirted with me, and I thought, *Why not?*"

"Because it's treacherous, insulting to me, and has blown apart a friendship I've had for over fifteen years? Plus you're cynically using Roxanne to injure me."

"Oh, and no women have cynically used me, I suppose?"

"Jesus Christ, Jon, listen to yourself! You're going to end up on talk radio saying women are the real Taliban. If I'd left you and immediately started sleeping with Gavin, *that's* equivalent. That'd give you some idea of how despicable this is."

"The man you DID immediately start sleeping with causes me no less anguish."

"I'm not sleeping with anyone! I told you, I didn't know Cal. I'd have thought your girlfriend could confirm that, given she introduced us."

"Very much not the impression my mother was given."

"Ah, yes, your mum. You handed her my address, you didn't warn me or ask my permission. You were perfectly happy for her to turn up and verbally lambast me."

"From what she said, you gave as good as you got."

Harriet exhaled sharply at the futility of holding Jon to account. Nothing was ever his fault. If he didn't want to see something, he simply didn't. *The Eternal Sunshine of the Spotless Jon.*

"And are you forgetting that your pal stuck his oar in? No euphemism, though maybe it should be," Jon said. She could see, under the "Patrick Bateman of racquet sports" routine, how angry he still was.

He was so warped by intervening events, he even looked changed: his eyes and the bones of his face were sharper and harder, the lines deeper. Or then again, perhaps he'd played tons of squash and lost weight.

"Cal overheard her fulminating about how I'd die a spinster after breaking up with you. He was incensed on my behalf. Given how you'd behaved, you can hardly blame him for not being a fan of the Barraclough dynasty."

"Oh, what convoluted crap. He's only doing that because he's got what we quaintly call the *major hots* for you."

"You deduced that on a visit where you turned up steaming drunk and smacked him in the face?!"

"No. I deduced that when I called him at his place of work, to apologize for said incident."

Jon blinked and looked away, and Harriet kept her face straight while thinking, *What?*

"You . . . you called him?" she asked, trying to remain dispassionate while unsure of her ground.

"Well. It was only right that I apologized. It was the right thing to do." He looked uncomfortable, and Harriet sussed that it was a "getting out in front of the situation" in order to protect his employment, and his masculinity couldn't bear for her to know he'd done some tactical groveling. He shifted his weight. "We both agreed to keep the conversation between us. He said he'd not press charges if I stayed away from you. I hardly think that's a pact you'd make if you weren't pretty keen on the lady involved."

"I think Cal was trying to keep things calm around his property," Harriet said, uncertainly.

"Hah. The property being a redhead. I know my enemy when I encounter him. I'll start practicing my surprised face for when news of your marriage reaches me. Despite your trenchant objections."

He rolled his eyes. Harriet didn't know how to respond to this lunacy.

"The bottom line here, *Hats,* is I don't care if you've finally experienced some agonies, or if I've stepped over imaginary lines you've drawn. If you've come here to ask me to feel remorseful for exercising my single-guy freedoms, you're shit out of luck."

Harriet's hangover, the effective loss of a dear friend, the upheavals of Scott Dyer: her response was more of an exhausted outburst.

"OK then! Congratulations on being a shitty person with some seriously twisted, misogynistic justifications for hate-shagging one of his ex's best friends, weeks after our breakup. My respect for you is entirely gone," Harriet said.

"It was never there in the first place," he shot back.

"That's not true. What happened to your goodbyes to me, saying you wanted to stay on good terms, be there for me if I ever wanted to talk?"

Jon looked uneasy. "I realized it wasn't being reciprocated."

"Translation: that offer wasn't without strings, I was supposed to start rewarding it somehow. You think you treat women as equals, but you don't. You liked and respected me for as long as I was your girlfriend. When I didn't want a relationship anymore, it was apparently inconceivable to you to both be sad *and* carry on liking me and respecting me. You using Roxy is part of the same contempt."

"Roxanne is a fling. That's all."

God, was she supposed to be jealous, to fight to win Jon back?

"Cool. Whatever. It makes no difference to me, though you should probably tell her."

Harriet turned to leave, and Jon said, "Wait. There's something I want to say."

He cleared his throat. When he spoke, he was level, the cocky register had gone.

"I always knew you weren't in love with me."

These words hung in the particularly velvet silence of a cavernous house full of purring appliances.

"I knew I had you on the rebound—I know now from *who*—and I decided not to question my luck. Because I knew from our first date that I was an absolute goner. You weren't anything like the women I'd been out with before, or what I'd have said I was looking for. Then there you were. Everything I didn't know I wanted, and somehow that is the most addictive thing of all. With your dry humor and your modesty and that face and that laugh. That vulnerability you're so determined not to display. I decided to be the best partner I could be, to throw my energies into that and hope either that would be enough, or that you'd fall in love along the way. But as you said, you didn't feel what you needed to feel, and I think you knew that very early on. So what I think now is . . . it wasn't fair for you to carry on. You're too emotionally intelligent not to have known how far apart our expectations were. And"—he paused here, distress crossing his face—"I think with that proposal, I *was* subconsciously trying to trap you. I knew I'd not get a yes, fair and square. Which is an awful culpability to have to admit on my part. But getting to that point? I think you have to admit it's both our faults."

Harriet's stomach clenched. This was deeply uncomfortable to hear, because it was mostly, if not wholly, accurate.

"I'm told the character, your ex who posted on Facebook, is a truly nasty piece of work. I certainly didn't recognize the person he described," Jon added.

Harriet folded her arms, across the pain behind her ribs.

"In summary. I'm truly sorry for the ordeal you had before you met me, a lot makes more sense now that I know about him. But my God, you made us both pay for it," Jon said, his voice raw.

Harriet swallowed and forced herself to meet his eyes, as they welled up. She weighed her words, before she spoke, and willed her voice to stay steady.

"You're right. But I didn't fail to tell you about Scott to purposely shut you out; I shut myself out from it too. I wanted to carry on with my life without it being important to me, so I acted like it wasn't. Maybe it was the same coping mechanism I had with my parents. If you give something bad an importance, then you let it define you. *You've given it power,* that's what I thought. But in fact, by not facing it, I was giving it power over me." She took a deep breath, as the next words weren't easy to say. "I didn't set out to hurt you, Jon. I felt safe with you, and in the end that wasn't enough. I'm sorry."

Harriet's eyes shimmered, and Jon nodded. He waited for her to continue. She sensed in the ensuing pause he wanted more discussion about Scott: no way, not now. Not with Roxy's caramel-colored hair in his shower drain.

This was the crux of it: Jon had legitimate complaints, but his recent behavior had blown them out of the water. Expecting her full disclosure now, it was the equivalent of breaking the lock on someone's diary and then hoping they trust you with their innermost secrets. Some lines crossed can't be walked back.

She went to let herself out.

"Harriet?" he said, as she left.

Jon leaned on the wall and smiled a broken smile.

"The thing is, I'd still take you back."

"Yes," Harriet said, "I know. Treat Roxanne well, won't you? She's not got friends looking out for her anymore."

43

"Something interesting on your phone? You're engrossed," Sam said, watching Harriet type, before manhandling a slice of mushroom, thyme, and coppa into his mouth, with mixed results.

"'Interesting' isn't exactly the word," she said. "More astounding, yet completely predictable."

Cal gave Harriet a brooding look.

Harriet looked back at her handset.

Roxanne

Harry, I feel awful for how that came out. You know how I am, I jump and don't think. I've ended it with Jon. Can we talk? I want to make this up to you. R xxx

Harriet wasn't sure how she felt about this: Schadenfreude? Some. Mostly still pretty devastated. She forwarded it to Lorna.

Lorna

Well well well if it isn't the consequences of Roxanne's own actions. Hope pawning that bracelet makes it worth it. You going to reply?

Harriet

Nope. Nothing left to say, is there?

Harriet noticed that Cal's look remained inscrutable. What did it convey . . . ? She tried to categorize it. Wary? Almost suspicious.

"Anyway," she said to Sam, turning her handset facedown. "The situation has now concluded."

"That's a hell of a yarn!" Sam said. "Vivid storytelling."

"All true," Harriet said.

"Jon's involved, I'm guessing?" Cal said.

"He was."

Harriet and Cal exchanged another atypical and loaded glance. She remembered Cal's pact with Jon and Jon's feverish obsession ("when news of your marriage reaches me," *dear lord*). Did Cal think . . . she might get back together with him? Did Cal care?

Cal had accepted Harriet's offer of a takeaway, with the caveat that he'd said he'd see Sam, and was it all right for him to join? Harriet said of course, after the usual "as long as I'm not spoiling anything more interesting you had planned" bargaining.

"They've forgotten my mozzarella sticks," Sam said, flipping the lids on all the boxes in turn. "It's at times like this it's lucky I'm such a spiritual person. I am able to see the bigger picture. Free pizza."

"You draw great strength from your faith, it's good to see," Cal said. "I forgot to say, Harriet, I went to your friend's restaurant! Lorna's. The place in Headingley?"

Aye, did ye now, Harriet wanted to say, waggling her specs. Cal didn't offer who with, as Harriet expected. Maybe she was a few women ago.

"Good, isn't it?"

"Great. Already making plans to go back."

I bet you are.

"You can take me," Sam said.

"Was hoping for someone less likely to wear pool slides with socks."

I bet you are.

"I forgot to say, the paperwork's finally done for my flat," Harriet said. "I move out two weeks on Sunday."

"Oh, right," Cal said. He looked vaguely flummoxed, as if he'd forgotten the imminence of Harriet vacating. "Thanks."

"We'll stay in touch, won't we?" Sam said, ferreting around the garlic bread.

"For sure." She beamed at Sam. Cal said nothing.

The doorbell bonged, and beyond closed curtains, they couldn't see who it was.

"My mozz sticks! The arc of history bends toward justice," Sam said.

Cal went to get it, and after a few seconds, Sam twitched a corner of the curtain to see whom Cal was talking to.

"Aw, fuck no, it's Kit."

Sam slumped down in his seat as Harriet sat up straighter.

"I wonder what she wants?" Sam said. "Apart from Cal's balls and soul trapped in a haunted jam jar."

"Look, I'll prove it to you," Cal said, entering the room with Kit in tow. She was in a turtleneck jumper and slim-cut trousers and looked, as per usual, like a mini-supermodel.

"Hiiiii, everyone." She raised a palm. "Hold on, it's my best man, my photographer, and my groom. Is the vicar in the kitchen, flipping pancakes?"

Harriet knew Kit to be terrifying, but she had to admit: stylishly so.

"There." Cal produced his phone from the far corner of the room and flashed the screen at Kit. "Missed and unread WhatsApps from you."

He threw it down on the sofa, next to Harriet, and Kit glared at the phone and then at Harriet, before tossing her hair and looking back to Cal.

"All right, I accept you didn't get my news." She addressed the room. "Come to say goodbye. Got a job in Qatar."

"Congrats," Sam said, flatly. "And goodbye."

"Congratulations," Harriet mumbled, as Kit stared at her as if it was required.

"I didn't mean you; I don't know you," she said. "All I know about you is you treated my so-called wedding day like it was the search-engine function on fucking Craigslist."

"Don't pick on her, she's done nothing wrong," Cal said, hotly.

Nevertheless, Harriet squirmed at Kit having a point.

Cal and Kit moved to the hallway, where they had a muttered conversation, which Sam accompanied by extravagant eye rolls and a yanking-noose-to-neck gesture. Harriet sensed both she and Sam were listening for any audible clues about what was happening while also trying not to listen in, *and* find their own conversation, and therefore failing on all three fronts.

"Another beer anyone?" Cal put his head around the sitting-room door, after they heard the front door close. "Sam? Hats?"

"Taking it easy, thanks," Harriet said, holding up her tea, liking her new nickname status.

"What was that about?" Sam said, jerking his head toward the window.

"I was having it gently broken to me that Kit is now with Sebastian," Cal said. He pointed at himself. "This is my surprised face."

"Haha. What did she think you were going to say to that?"

"I have no idea. I think Kit always has to win, and in her mind, that was her winning."

"Chilling. Wish she had been a mozz stick. Beer would be welcome, ta."

Cal withdrew. Kit's car had yet to accelerate away. Cal's phone, next to Harriet's leg, lit up with another WhatsApp.

Kit

If you want me to accept we're over for good, maybe you should stop sleeping with me? Just a thought

Harriet gulped. Oh, wow. His love life was even more tangled than she thought? Her stomach churned and her heart rate jumped: she felt so old, and so square, for this not being a thing she even considered could be happening. But Kit was with Sebastian? Exactly how labyrinthine was this bed-hopping?

She raked back over everything Cal had said about the severing of the ties with Kit and wondered if *Oh, but I totally still slide her one from time to time! That's life!* was always an unspoken likelihood among the Gatsbys. Every time she thought she had the measure of Cal, he changed and moved. She had to let her idea of him go—it was partly a fantasy, yet one that had taken quite deep root.

When Cal returned, he picked his phone up, paused for a second, stabbed some sort of riposte into it, and then stuffed it firmly out of sight. He squinted at Harriet as he sat down, but said nothing.

No sooner had they agreed to watch *2 Fast 2 Furious,* when the doorbell went again.

"When did we get so popular?" Cal said, sighing.

He got up to get the door and, after a brief conference she couldn't hear, called, "Harriet. It's for you."

Harriet got to her feet with a frown, and as Cal passed her at the sitting-room door, she caught an unsettled look on his face. She returned his look, unable to ask, *Who is it?* without being overheard.

It couldn't be Jon or Scott, as she instinctively knew Cal would've stayed by the door if so. The thought gave her a pang of adoration, which she acknowledged and forced herself to dismiss.

Outside stood a young woman. She was probably eight stone wringing wet, which she was, even though the rain had stopped a while ago. Her delicate features were framed and anonymized by the tight hood of an elasticated khaki raincoat.

"I'm really sorry to turn up on you like this. He checks my phone and my Uber history, so it was a bus or nothing. I did think about calling you from a telephone box, but the one nearest was full of dog piss and I don't have a burner phone like a drug dealer. Then I thought, *I don't have your number anyway!* What a twat. Sorry, I talk a lot when I'm nervous. I hope you don't hate me, because I've got nowhere else to go for the next two hours. Your boyfriend seemed a bit dubious! Fair enough."

She pulled her hood down, revealing damp blond hair.

"I should've said. It's Marianne."

44

Of all the VIP callers that Harriet never thought she'd have. She was as nervous as if the Pope had disembarked from the bulletproof Popemobile for a Supreme Pontiff's special tour, cutting about in his cassock.

"Drink?" Harriet said, holding up a box containing a bottle of champagne slightly deliriously. She'd shown Marianne into the kitchen, after putting her head around the sitting-room door and garbling a quick explanation to a nonplussed Cal and Sam. "If you want a proper drink, this is the only thing I've got, I'm afraid."

The occasion felt momentous enough for alcohol, despite the clouds from Harriet's last session only recently lifting, yet all she had to offer was a bottle sent to her as a thank-you by a wedding couple.

"If you don't mind wasting it on me!" Marianne said.

"Not a waste at all."

She looked so young and small, and Harriet felt maternally protective.

"You smoke, right?" Harriet said. "Shall we have this in the garden, or do you want to get drier?"

"Oh my God, yeah, gasping for a cigarette! If that's all right?"

She could tell that, having been uncertain of her reception, this sort of welcome was beyond Marianne's dreams. At the gesture of offering nerve-calming nicotine, she gazed upon Harriet as if she were her fairy godmother.

They took the Moët, glasses, and an IKEA candle holder of Harriet's as an ashtray, and sat at the picnic table with the string light canopy.

As Harriet popped the cork, Marianne pulled Marlboro Lights from her raincoat pocket. She lit up and took a deep drag, leaning her head back as she exhaled the smoke like a train whistle.

She waved a small hand, bearing that engagement ring, to ineffectually clear it, and said, "He thinks I'm at my mum's. I told her I was coming to see you so he can't catch her out, but he'd not call her anyway. They hate each other."

Harriet nodded. She had a sense that letting Marianne do the talking was the smartest course of action. She didn't know what she was here to say, and half suspected Marianne didn't know what she was here to say either.

"First of all"—Marianne leaned forward, fixing her huge Tweety eyes on Harriet's—"I feel awful for what Scott put on Facebook. I asked him about your letter, and he acted like he'd take it seriously, if he knew what was in it. He was really nice to me until I gave it to him. I should've known better. Next thing I know, he's showing me that post . . ." She looked down, frowned. "Sorry."

"It's OK, honestly. I know exactly what he's like."

"Everything you said in the letter. Was it true?" Marianne said, flicking her cigarette ash into the candle holder. "He says you were crazy, but . . ."

She glanced up guiltily, and Harriet understood what the problem was. Marianne didn't want to accuse her, yet also needed to hear Harriet outright deny it.

She could empathize so easily—the push-pull of wanting Scott convicted and exculpated, at the same time.

"In short: yes. Everything was true. But if it helps to put it another way, if you and Scott ended, what do you think he'd say about you? That you were lovely, but wanted different things? He has to trash me because of the things I know. Because of what I told you. He doesn't have any other defense than calling me a liar."

Marianne's blue eyes widened. "Yeah. Like he always runs me down for being a hairdresser, says I don't have a degree in anything except 'scissors.' Tells me I can't keep up with him." She tapped her temple. "He said because my dad left when I was small, I didn't have a 'male role model' and I take it out on him. When you said that he said your upbringing was . . . unstable . . . I was like, *Oh. Ding. Recognize that.*"

Marianne swigged her drink, a tremble in her lip.

"It's like we're the issue and he's trying to fix us," Harriet said. "But like I say: in straight answer to your question, I didn't do any of those things he said. The lying is so strange, because he's so vehement, and you start to think, *Do you actually believe this?* I think he convinces himself first. He gets so angry and poisonous and he thinks, *Well, it must be true, she must be hurting me, because I feel so strongly*? The emotion finds the reason."

This was as far as Harriet had ever managed to explain Scott to herself, and she offered it to Marianne for what it was worth. If it had any value, then she doubted she'd ever have a better use for it.

Marianne nodded and took a drag on her cig. She knew everything in the letter was true, Harriet realized; she just had to accept it. These were two different things.

"I can tell you're not like that, just from this . . ." She flapped a small hand at the space between them and smiled.

"Marianne," Harriet said, "feeling scared about what he'll say or do, him checking your phone—it's not normal. It's not OK. It's not that he's so into you that he gets possessive, or needs more reassuring than other men. It's abuse. I don't know how we get ourselves, or rather, how *he* gets *us,* to a place where we tell ourselves it's our fault all the time. It's as if he creates this twisted tiny world only we live in, and then it's like a foreign country with its own language we can't explain to anyone else. However horrible it is, it's our home and we fiercely protect it. Our world is just Scott, so if we lose him, we have nothing."

"*Yes,*" Marianne said, with so much emotion in one syllable. "Yes, that's exactly it!"

Harriet nodded.

"It's mad that until recently I thought I still loved him," Marianne said, haltingly, rubbing her forehead. "When I read your letter, it was like all the things in my head I'd never said out loud. I'd not even said it properly to myself."

"I understand," Harriet said, quietly, and she did. She could have no better or more thorough preparation for understanding this, from the other side of the picnic table. She looked at the droplets of rain still clinging to the dangling fairy lights in the indigo of late evening, glanced at the lambent glow from the kitchen. She sipped her drink and let a comfortable silence develop. Marianne shivered.

"Are you cold? Want to go inside?"

Marianne shook her head.

"We'd had the worst row before Danny and Ferg's wedding. Like, I'm surprised the neighbors didn't call the police. I had to put so much makeup on to cover up my crying, I had eyes like two crows had crashed into a chalk cliff, as my mum says. He never said he knew you. At the wedding, I mean. I didn't even know he'd lived with someone before me until one of his mates mentioned you."

"He wouldn't tell you about me, not if he had no need to. It took me time to work out that Scott never wants connections, never wants people to share notes. Thanks to his attack on me, I'm in contact with one of his exes. She commented, calling him out on the Facebook post, and I saw it before he deleted it."

"Really?"

Marianne's eyes widened again, and Harriet felt a rush of wanting to use Nina as definitive corroboration, while considering that Marianne might take every last word of this back to Scott.

Harriet said, carefully, "Yep. Nina had lived with him before me and had a very similar experience. She said her parents did a 'carefrontation' in the end."

"So he's done this loads of times. I'd been telling myself he'll be different when we're married." She dragged on her cigarette again. "Maybe Scott's right, maybe I am stupid! Hahaha. Cos that's the stupidest idea, isn't it? I'm twenty-seven going on fifteen."

"You're not stupid," Harriet said, reaching over to hold and release Marianne's hand. "I know what you're feeling. I thought I was a good judge of people before I met Scott. The way he undermines you gradually: it's so hard to explain until you've been through it. He waits until you're in love and completely vulnerable and then it starts, and you have no defenses."

It was so starkly obvious to her now that she'd said it in so many words—this was why she'd picked someone, in Jon, she'd not fall in love with. Jon was right, she'd gone in with a full suit of armor. It was so sad this self-knowledge came too late.

"My dad used to knock my mum around," Marianne said, stubbing out her cigarette. "Before he went—I've not seen him since I was three—I used to ask her why she put up with it." Marianne looked at Harriet with shining eyes, full of fast-consumed champagne and sincere feeling. "I'd have a go at her when I was a teenager, I told her *I'd* never stand for it! I honestly thought it couldn't happen to me. All these years before I met Scott, thinking I'm some sassy warrior bitch . . . Know what my bachelorette was?"

Harriet shook her head.

"*Afternoon tea.* I hate afternoon tea. Cucumber and egg sandwiches are rank."

Harriet couldn't help herself, she laughed.

"Stupid custard cake slices, back home in my Ugg Scuffettes by six o'clock. Because Scott would've kicked off at the weekend in Croatia I wanted. All my friends are bad influences, rah

rah. I don't recognize myself anymore. Where's the girl who got barred for life from Revolución de Cuba gone?"

Marianne picked up her glass and swigged. Harriet clinked her glass and said, "I promise you, you're still there."

"I know from your letter that you're tons smarter than me, so I thought I'd admit that I don't have a plan. I don't have anything."

"A plan?"

"Of what we do next."

Harriet frowned. "You want to leave him?"

"Of course."

Marianne looked perplexed, as if that was obviously why she was sat in his ex-girlfriend's garden, on her second cigarette.

45

Harriet's head was spinning. "Don't you get married soon?"

"Next Saturday."

"Do you want someone with you when you tell him?"

Harriet was thinking, *Please don't say it has to be me, I won't feel I can say no, but it'd be carnage.*

"No, I could ask my mum, but that's not my problem. I know how it would go. Reading your B&Q story, I thought, *That's it, that's what he'll do.* Obviously, calling the wedding off is a big deal, but he'll cut me dead. Then he'll tell everyone I was a bad mess."

"I guess so."

"The row before Danny and Ferg's wedding. What he said to me . . ." She sipped champagne and tapped her cigarette tip into the holder, and Harriet saw Marianne gird herself. "He said, 'If we have daughters, I hope they don't turn out like you.'"

Harriet sucked in cold air. "Wow."

"So yeah, I can split up with him. I can cancel the wedding, Harriet," Marianne said, voice rising, gaze now direct. "Then what? He does it all again, doesn't he? To someone who has a family with him. Then it's me writing letters, in a few years' time. I mean to be fair, I'd probably do a voice note because I've not got your way with words."

She smiled wanly and Harriet smiled back.

"It's not enough. I want other women to know who Scott is, so he can't do this all over again. And I want to be *me* again. I want to remind him of who I am. I want to remind me of who I am!"

Of all the twists that Harriet didn't see coming, it was Marianne being gripped by the same sort of fervor she was. The grenade over the high wall was in fact a match flicked at a lake of petrol.

"How? Like a letter we all sign and put online? We'd get all the I Stand with Scott idiots out in force, wouldn't we," Harriet said, pulling a face.

"Those sorts of things melt away, don't they? I don't know." Marianne shrugged.

Harriet wished they melted away a bit faster, but now was not the time to sob about her job.

"Until you came along, I couldn't see anything clearly," Marianne said. "Now it's like I see *everything*. It's a cycle, and you have to break a cycle."

Harriet briefly hoped that Marianne wasn't envisaging a revenge that involved flashlights and tarps and quarry pits.

"His other ex, Nina, she said she'd help me if she could. Should the three of us meet up? She might have some genius idea?"

"Yes!" Then Marianne's face fell: "Although I'd have to tell Scott I'm seeing my mum again. Given there's always wedding things to organize, hopefully he'd buy it."

"What about work? In your breaks? We could meet you for coffee at lunchtime and he'd never know."

"That'd be OK." Pause. "Thank you so much, Harriet. I know you've taken a lot of shit for my sake when you could've walked away."

"I haven't really done anything yet," Harriet said, and Marianne cut her off: "Yes, you have."

Harriet walked Marianne to the bus stop, and as they parted, Marianne added Harriet to her phone as "Heather: Florist."

Harriet had to suppress the thought: *Game On.*

AFTER MARIANNE'S DEPARTURE, a slightly euphoric and frayed Harriet explained to Cal what the visit had been about, Sam having left while they plotted in the garden. To her surprise, he was uncharacteristically subdued, and cautious.

"To all intents and purposes, for now she's still missus to a total demon, isn't she? What if this is part of a plot by what's-his-name—Scott?" he said, stuffing pizza boxes into the recycling bin.

"I know what you mean. She might take it all back and get married anyway. But coming to see me feels like a big enough step that she's actually ready to get out."

Cal looked up and paused, clearly wanting to vocalize something and not knowing how.

"Was he ever violent?" Cal said eventually. As he looked at her, Harriet could sense something had developed between them, though she wasn't quite sure what. They were truly friends, and yet this wasn't a friendship that would outlast being on these premises, of that she was sure. Given the strength of that conviction, she'd expect to have a clear reason to back it up. But she didn't, other than the instinct they were very dissimilar.

Much as she wanted to think they'd meet up from time to time, she couldn't see it.

This rapport with Cal Clarke was time out of Real Life. It was as if she were on a plane where they'd overbooked economy, and she'd been sent to sit next to him in first class. At first, they'd resented the proximity, bickering, then they'd settled in and had a raucous time on the complimentary G&Ts. It was a chance moment of two separate paths, crossing and then diverging again. When they hauled their suitcases from the luggage carousel, and shook hands, that would be that.

"Oh no. No violence. It's emotional torture."

Cal put his hands in the pockets of his joggers. Harriet wondered if he was relieved to only have a week left of this unasked-for commotion. First Jon, now this.

"I don't know why Marianne might lie, but as a journalist I know people *do* lie, all the time, for any reason and no reason. Despite what crime shows tell you, people are not neat boxes of motive you can unpack and fit together like flatpack furniture. Assume nothing, Harriet. She may be doing what he wants. Or she may simply be doing what she wants, and missing some screws."

"Or she could be for real."

"Or she could be for real. I'm not saying this to stop you helping her. I don't want you to have a nasty shock."

"Thanks. I know."

"What about the effect on your work by getting involved?"

"I don't know whether it's not already knackered, to be honest. I might've been more wary of that if Scott hadn't publicly shamed me already. Now the damage has been done there and I have nothing to lose."

Cal didn't speak, a tactful way of doubting this statement.

"Or maybe it's more honest and realistic to say, if I have anything left to lose, I'm prepared to lose it, to see this through."

"You're very selfless."

"Hah, thanks," Harriet said. "I think it's been very much to do with myself throughout. I only hope I haven't been selfish. I hope I haven't set off something that Marianne will later regret. Not that I think it's possible to regret escaping Scott."

"Can't start a fire, worrying about your little world falling apart, as the song says," Cal said, with a flirtatious smile and a shrug of concession, and Harriet swooned, despite herself.

46

"Hello! Evil H, I presume? Enjoying an evil latte. Evilly."

Harriet looked up from her cup to see a young woman with dark brown hair split into two bulky knots above her ears, which Harriet believed were colloquially called "space buns," and a belted tweed coat with faux-fur lapels.

Nina was great. From what Harriet could glean from their social media acquaintance, she was a good-natured, ex-art-school stoner who taught night classes on how to draw seagulls and had signed up to a community scheme where she took infirm pensioners around on outings on a rickshaw.

Nina sent Harriet funny memes every few days, as if they were now mates in general and Scott Dyer was merely an incidental method of introduction. After all the torment of the man, someone who simply hooted at his memory—"*What a fucking nob!*"—was an absolute tonic. Nina was the human equivalent of when golden autumn sun breaks through the clouds on a cold, windy day, unexpectedly warming your chilled face.

"Evil H, that's me," Harriet said, standing up to greet her in the Waterstones café. "Nice to meet you in person! I don't know why I've stood up."

They guffawed and hugged.

"I've got to say, bit disappointed you're not wearing a Hamburglar-type outfit with the black mask across your eyes," Nina said. "You need to lean into your online alter ego."

"I'm going incognito as a regular human woman."

Nina dropped her coat and went to get herself a drink, returning with a pot of loose-leaf tea and round wafer biscuit on a tray.

"There's still no actual plan for this awesome Avengers Assembling of his nemeses, yet?" Nina said.

"Nope. Only we agreed more tit-for-tat Facebook outing isn't the way." Harriet shrugged, and felt a little guilty she'd obliged Nina to get a train from Prestwich on a Wednesday for *yeah, dunno.*

An unbothered Nina nodded, unwrapped her stroopwafel, and balanced a tea strainer on her cup.

"I know I said I wanted him to suffer, but I hope she's not going to suggest hard-core *Dragon Tattoo* shit, because it'll be hard to resist but also, I'm not going to prison for him," she said.

Harriet laughed. She was also starting to sweat a little at what was coming next. Ouija boards were supposed to "work" because everyone pushed the glass as a collective effort and yet didn't detect the pressure they were individually applying. What if they in their own way ended up egging one another on, pouring their joint energies into a plan they'd separately recognize as insane?

In a small flurry of jasmine-heavy perfume, Marianne took the third chair at their table, wearing no coat and holding a phone. Gone was the bedraggled urchin in the raincoat. She was in a black work uniform bearing the Estilo logo, and her butter-colored hair hung in immaculate, curling-ironed ringlets, the sort only an expert could achieve. Harriet believed her when she said the old Marianne was on her way back.

"Hi, sorry I'm late," she said, at a careful volume.

"Marianne, Nina; Nina, Marianne," Harriet gabbled under her breath, and they said hello to each other.

"I'm not going to get a drink. I can't stay long, sorry. I've got a client in foils."

"Of course," Harriet said. Marianne glanced from side to side, no doubt making sure there were no faces she recognized here.

Sensing her inhibition, possibly a reluctance to even be present, Harriet paused.

"You know if you've changed your mind and want to get married, we won't hold you to anything? We can go away and never mention this again, if that's what you want."

There was a pause, which lasted for a couple of weeks.

"That said, don't fucking marry him," Nina said, with a hiccupping laugh, pouring out her tea and breaking the tension beautifully, in a Nina way.

"I'm not going to marry him," Marianne said, calmly, as if she were dismissing the idea of whether she'd have time to go to the big Sainsbury's later. "Also, I've got it. I know what we should do. If you are both up for it. Though I won't mind if you don't want to do it."

She spread both hands flat on the table, for a sense of *focus up*. "I worked out why posting online feels a bit lame. We'd only be telling strangers. Maybe they'd believe us, maybe they wouldn't. To be honest, who cares?"

Harriet's eyes widened. "Go on."

She felt like she was in a courtroom drama, they'd been on the ropes, and now the hotshot maverick attorney was explaining how, against the odds, they were going to switch tactics and win.

"The people who need to know what Scott's like are his friends and family. The ones who take his side and cover things up and think the sun shines out of his harris."

"His enablers," Nina said. "Then there's us, demonstrating the Missing Stair theory."

"What's that?" Marianne said.

"We secretly warn each other to avoid him. We manage the problem, but we don't expose it or fix it. Which I guess makes us enablers too? I don't know."

"His friends and family don't know they're his enablers, that's how good he is at compartmentalizing," Harriet said.

"Yeah. And when are they all going to be in one place? The Queen's Hotel, four p.m., this Saturday," Marianne said.

"Your wedding?" Harriet said, in awed half-whisper.

"Yeah," Marianne said. "My big fat bleak wedding. To which you both have scored an invite, haha."

She sat back and crossed her arms, and were it not for modern restrictions, Harriet felt sure she'd be sparking up a Marlboro Light, in a Lauren Bacall manner.

"We declare Scott's a shit, on your *wedding day*?" Harriet repeated.

"Preferably before 'I do,' or I'll be in a fix. What do you think?" Marianne tucked a curl behind her ear. No wonder she'd got up this morning and fancied a power 'do blow-dry.

Nina let out a low whistle.

"As a concept, it's got impact," Nina said.

"You'd be gathering everyone together, though, wasting all your money on going ahead . . . ?" Harriet said, and as soon as the words left her mouth, she saw Marianne's point. There was nothing to be saved by canceling it, not even face.

"Oh, that expense is gone." Marianne huffed a laugh. "And it was my savings. I made a killing on my flat when I moved in with Scott. Always been good with money," Marianne said, with a wave of her hand as if swatting a fly. "Until now, that is, hahaha. But yeah, dress, venue, the honeymoon in the Caribbean. When I decided to use the wedding instead of calling it off, it was the most massive brain-wave moment," Marianne continued. "Instead of ringing every guest and explaining to them why it's not happening, one by one, in a race before Scott can get to them, I tell them all at once. *The truth.*"

The three of them looked at one another.

OK, maybe Harriet was having the Ouija board "communication from the Hereafter" heightened delusion she feared, but she could actually see a magnificence to this.

"I know it's a lot to ask of you," Marianne said.

A pause.

"You in?" Nina said to Harriet.

"I'm in," Harriet said, even if her stomach was cramping.

"I'm in too."

"Well, you ladies didn't need much convincing. *Legends only*." Marianne nodded, as if this were religious catechism as opposed to social media lol-speak.

Harriet was glad Marianne had suggested this, because it could have only come from the bride-to-be.

"There is that bit in the wedding vows when the person marrying you says, 'If anyone knows any reason why these two should not be lawfully joined . . .'" Harriet said. "Which I always assumed must be an archaic leftover from when bigamy was rife, or something. We could use that as our cue. I don't know. Has anyone ever done that?"

"Fuuu— That's it. Harriet, that's it!" Marianne hissed, leaning forward in excitement.

"Is it?"

"Yeah! The only thing I couldn't work out was how and when. You stand up and say, 'I know a reason.' Then Nina could stand up and say, 'So do I.' Then I say, 'Scott, I'm not marrying you.'"

Marianne mimed a mic drop.

They were briefly silent as they took in the enormity of the proposition. This did not feel within the scope of things that could or should reasonably happen, yet they'd arrived at a place where it not only felt inevitable, but vital. They'd never have this opportunity again.

"That said, they often leave that line out of the service nowadays," Harriet said. She knew her cautious nature was showing, appointing herself the problem finder.

"It's definitely in ours, because I was so antsy about forgetting things or speaking at the wrong time, the celebrant gave me a printout of her whole speech, with X marked for my bits," Marianne said. "I can double-check, but I remember it was there."

"Are you really, really sure you want to do this?" Harriet said. "Once you're in your dress and your guests are arriving, the jitters kick in . . ."

"Yes, I really do. I'd be lying if I said I wasn't scared . . ." Marianne's gaze strayed to Nina's plate. "Is that a stroopwafel? I love them." Then her gaze became focused once more. "It's such a once-in-a-lifetime chance to put a man like him back in his box, isn't it? If you speak, and Nina speaks, then everyone knows who he is, and why I'm doing it. He has to come up with a reason why all three of us are lying. *Dodge this.*" She mimed aiming a sight upon him.

She hesitated. "I can move out to my mum's while we sell the house. I wish I hadn't come to my senses the week before our wedding, but . . . as my boss always says, we are where we are."

Marianne flipped her phone over, faceup, and checked the time.

"Shit, I've got to go, sorry. The only person I'd worry about upsetting on the day is my mum, but she'll be over the moon. She's begged me not to marry him. Only I'm not going to warn her in case she gives us away without meaning to! She can't keep a secret, haha."

This was where Marianne got her steel backbone from, Harriet guessed. With her mum in her corner, she could do this.

"If you're both around this Saturday?" Marianne said, and Nina nodded.

"Funnily enough, I'm free because a wedding couple canceled on me, due to Scott's post," Harriet said.

"If that's not a message from God, I don't know what is," Nina said.

"Let's do this then, ladies," Marianne said. "How do we stay in touch? I can't get WhatsApps in case Scott sees."

She glanced at her handset in embarrassment.

"Are you on Facebook? The Messenger thing?" Nina said.

"Yeah."

"I'll set up a group chat, look out for the request in the Other Messages folder. Change your password and delete the messages whenever you've read something. Then, if he's nosing around, there won't be any notifications or way of him getting in to check it."

"Cool! Thanks."

In another waft of perfume, Marianne was gone.

"She's got the looks of Tinker Bell and the nerves of a cold assassin," Nina said, approvingly. "If Scott's not going to marry her, then I will."

Harriet considered that right enough: Scott's kink was a sweet face and a salty attitude. He had chosen the members of the resistance well.

47

Nina Jackson started a new group chat
Nina Jackson named it
Bride's Side

Nina
Hahahaha! Proud of that name, I can't deny. ☺ *I've thought of a small glitch. Scott's going to recognise me, and Harriet. What if he chucks us out? I've looked up the ballroom online and it's large, but still going to be hard to hide*
Harriet
Oh God, and isn't Danny his best man? Danny and Fergus know me after I photographed their wedding. Ditto some of Scott's friends. Thoughts?! 😬
Marianne
You could turn up minutes before I do? I'll make sure I'm right on time (4pm)
Harriet
Only thing is—with my extensive knowledge of wedding-going—right before you're due to arrive is when everyone starts

concentrating on the grand entrance. We could be picking the exact moment Scott's going to be watching the door like a hawk ☹

Nina

You know where this is headed, don't you? DISGUISES. I LOVE IT. Mrs Doubtfire prosthetics ftw

Harriet

*Bahahaha. Somehow I think two people shuffling in dressed in joke-shop noses and moustaches are going to be *more* conspicuous? Even wigs can be a bit "oh look, someone in a wig." The only hairdresser I know is going to be busy (not) getting married that day*

Marianne

Actually, disguises are not a bad idea! Harriet, you have long hair you wear up in a braid? Nina, yours is mid-length? We know men are really bad at recognising people when they change anything. You could both do something completely different with your hair. Harriet, you could wear it loose, curl it? Nina, how about a hat? Tons of makeup. Boom. If you sashay in late and sit at the back among my salon friends and cousins, Scott won't spot you. There's like two hundred people there, and honest to God, he hasn't bothered to get to know quite a lot of my friends and family. Shoulda been less of a moody bastard! 😂

Nina

Well, I'm convinced. It's our best bet! Plus I love hats. Might go for a kind of Annie Hall vibe

Harriet

OK and I'll try for some uncharacteristic femininity! Also, my friend Lorna made a good point. We don't want Scott to be able to rewrite this bit of history. We should record it. She's volunteered to sneak in the back and film it on her phone for us.

Her idea is to look scruffy and like she might work for the hotel. It's an absolute age since Scott last saw her & she had different colour hair, so I think she's safe. We can stick the clip online later if we want. Or is that too much?

Nina

No

Marianne

No

Harriet

Just checking

48

Courage calls to courage everywhere.

Harriet didn't believe in any Cosmic Architect who directed events, an interventionist God. Given the loss of her parents, it'd be pretty strange if she did. Her jaw muscles tensed when any well-meaning person said, "Everything happens for a reason," and reflected they'd obviously not had anything very bad happen to them.

Nevertheless, the night before the wedding felt like such a huge, psychic game of tetherball, where her refusal to face down and defy Scott and his legacy, her entrenched habit of conflict avoidance, was coming back to haunt her in the most preordained, scripted-drama way.

Standing up and annihilating someone's *wedding ceremony*? Her ex? The Man Who Should Not Be Named for so long? Describing, to hundreds of people, what he'd done to her? Publicly identifying herself with that experience?

It was like asking a nun to streak.

Harriet was contemplating a daredevil stunt, a parachute jump, some sort of towering feat of adrenaline junkiedom.

Telling yourself to hurl yourself out into the thin air at a great altitude, when it went against every survival instinct you had.

It was mind over body, executive function at war with your lizard brain.

No matter how many times Harriet rehearsed—*Marianne wanted this, Scott should be stopped, and Nina would grab her, mid-dive*—it was a completely aberrant thing to do. She might be justly vilified. The nuclear blast might be so big that Leeds would forever be irradiated for her.

This, after a lifetime of going fetal around threat. Yet she finally swore at Jacqueline Barraclough, demanded explanations from Cal, and even steamed around to read Jon his Miranda rights. Maybe change was possible.

What else was she avoiding?

Harriet had been listening to Jazz FM, lying on her bed. She was suddenly galvanized, struck by something that, until now, had never had such a clear and obvious sense of its timeliness. The second it occurred to her, she knew this was it. Hadn't Cal said she'd know? She'd thought that was consoling mysticism, but he was right. She knew.

Or perhaps she was dressing it up in a thunderbolt, but her reasons were incredibly prosaic—there was finally another fear on the horizon that made this fear seem manageable by comparison. Maybe she simply needed a monumental distraction.

Harriet sat up and unthreaded the necklace from around her neck with shaking hands, and put the key pendant in the lock on the jewelry box.

What if the letter had degraded to the point it was unreadable or something? She would have let her mother down? What if the letter contained such a shock that it rendered her unable to function, to go through with tomorrow's promise?

Harriet knew that even so, this didn't matter, as she was going to do it anyway.

She picked the delicate envelope open with great care and pulled out a single page of paper, wrapped around a photograph, an old-style color Polaroid. The notelet was only a few paragraphs long.

Harriet examined the photo first, one she'd never seen before.

Her parents were walking down a tree-lined street she didn't recognize, bundled in padded coats that indicated it was the depths of winter. Her laddish, scarily youthful, dark-haired father had hold of one of her hands, her mother the other, and they were swinging her up in the air. Her mum, with a long strawberry-blond bob, had her lips formed in an openmouthed smile, and Harriet could imagine her making a *wheeee* noise.

Harriet must be about three, her dangling chunky legs in ribbed gray woolen tights and blackcurrant-colored Mary Jane shoes. She was whooping ecstatically, a full set of peg-like teeth on show, pure toddler monkey-delight. Her hair was a rust-colored pageboy cut.

On the back, in her mother's girlish handwriting, was printed:

> This is my favourite one of the three of us. Keep it somewhere safe and close, and we're always with you. Yes, cheesy I know, but if I can't be cheesy now! Lots of love, Mum xx

She stared and stared at the neatly printed handwriting, tried to force herself to accept that the person who had thought those words and held the pen and leaned on the photo to transcribe them wasn't here anymore. Harriet was already streaming with tears, so God knows how she was going to cope with the letter.

She unfurled the sheet of paper and read it, eyes racing across its few sentences in a split second, and gasped a sob. She read it six more times, then a seventh.

Acts of kindness, acts of thoughtfulness: they could echo down the years long after the person who had offered them was gone. This was worth knowing. Her mother wasn't here but this feeling was here with her, in the room. Its effect was real.

Harriet splashed her face with cold water until she was half-way presentable and went downstairs to find Cal, who was stood eating some toast in the kitchen and absentmindedly reading his phone. He glanced up as she came in, his eyes alighting on her face with a lively expression.

"Hey up, it's the wedding crasher."

She had told him of tomorrow's escapade last night.

"It's got a real shit-or-bust feel to it. It's either the best idea or the worst idea, and nothing in-between," Cal had said.

"You think I shouldn't do it?" Harriet had asked.

He'd said, in a lower voice, with directness: "I think you can do anything." She'd had to find something else to say, fast, before it risked becoming A Moment between them, which she had no spare bandwidth to handle.

"Cal," she said now, trying to conceal her chest heaving, as if she'd run a mile. "You know how you said to wait until the right time to read my mum's letter? That I'd know when the right time was?"

He chewed and swallowed. "Yes?"

"It was true. I knew. This evening. I read it. I suddenly needed my mum tonight, so badly, so I read it."

Harriet was stumbling over her words: she'd meant to say *needed to hear from her,* but as soon as she heard herself speak, she knew it was inadvertent honesty. She'd never let herself say she needed her mum before. What was the point in that plea, if it would never be answered? Except maybe it being answered had not been the point. Perhaps there was value simply in admitting it.

"I don't know how, but it said exactly what I needed it to say. I didn't even *know* there was a particular thing I needed to hear from my mum, and there it was . . . How mad is that?" she finished, somewhat anticlimactically.

"Bloody hell, Harriet!" A giant grin lit up his face. "I'm so pleased for you."

"Thank you. I wanted to tell someone. To feel like I'd taken a photograph of this moment, somehow. Recorded it."

"Sure. Glad to have been the person here to tell."

Harriet radiated elation, and Cal smiled again, warmly.

"Do you want some toast?" he said, after a pause.

"Hah, no, I'm all right, thanks. You crack on, I'm going to . . ." She gestured to the door. She wanted to go back upstairs and be with her picture and her letter, and Cal nodded a goodbye, mouth full again. She noticed the class and judgment in the way Cal didn't ask what her mother had said.

She wanted that to stay between the two of them.

49

Today, Harriet's back bedroom in Meanwood was a dressing room for a hell of a show.

The stage was the Queen's Hotel, a vast, historic 1930s Art Deco landmark overlooking City Square, up by the train station. Harriet usually loved the grimy romance and faded glamour of old hotels, the warrens of dimly lit corridors and the mysteries of the closed doors in the rooms beyond. There was always a whiff of scandal, and Harriet supposed today she'd be bringing it. The Queen's even had a private, secret entrance to the station. Harriet half wondered if she'd end up tearing through it.

The costume was the green dress, last seen during a rejected marriage proposal. In place of her glasses, Harriet put in contacts, and for greasepaint, she applied a thick layer of creamy foundation carefully, sweeping blush up her cheekbones. The combination of a cosmetically uniform pallor and fake rosiness, to Harriet's eyes, gave her a slightly open-coffin look. With finger and thumb, she stuck down drag queen–worthy false lashes, like dead flies.

As a finishing touch, she painted her lips with Lorna's favorite Ruby Woo. Her crimson mouth gave her a welcome vixen boldness she didn't feel. She wore her hair down, scrunching it when damp with the serum that Marianne had sent her, and affixed her black net birdcage veil, which fell below her nose.

This accessory had been a fine judgment. On the one hand, it obscured her features and made her look even less like Harriet Hatley. On the other, it drew attention. In the end, trying it on in the department store, she went with it on the basis she really liked it.

She checked the mirror. Harriet didn't recognize the vampy widow, and this felt reassuring. Deep breath. She descended the stairs carefully, unused to heels and a dress that made her totter.

"Fucking hell. When you're done with Scott, can you publicly destroy my reputation too?" Cal said, passing in the hallway, with wide eyes.

Harriet hooted with laughter, in an un-siren-like fashion. He kept looking at her, and she felt it.

She had an involuntary flash image: Cal slightly roughly pushing her against the wall, pulling her dress up her legs in grabbed handfuls, as she clutched at his lapels, him kissing her so hard that he had red lipstick on his mouth.

Ugh, Hatley, she admonished. *Sponge that idea away.* Even though it gave her a pulsing sensation, low in her stomach.

"Wish me luck," Harriet said.

The taxi outside, containing Lorna, beeped. *This was it.*

"Good luck," Cal said. He hesitated, leaned over, and kissed her in chaste fashion on the cheek, his lips pressing against the scratchy fabric of her veil. The spot burned throughout Harriet's walk to the car.

"I presume you know the floor plan," Lorna said, once they were on their way. "The layout? God, I know this wouldn't be happening if Scott Dyer wasn't a scum bucket that hurt women, but fuck me, his reckoning is exciting."

"I know my way to the ballroom. Once through the door I'll have to hope for the best. Obviously the arrangements for each wedding can vary."

Oh God, oh GOD: What if Scott had stationed himself by the door, to guide each arrival to their seat? It was exactly the kind of thing he'd do too—Mr. Performative Attentive Chivalry.

"Where's the other ex going to be? Is it Nina? Are we meeting her?"

"We're only contacting each other through our phones, as we reckon the sight of the two of us together is too risky in terms of Scott realizing something's up." Harriet gazed at the city scenery flying past her window, heart at a slow but increasing gallop, and said, "Even if he does recognize me, if the ceremony is right about to start he'd not have time to make a scene. He might assume I am desolate, spying on the event where I lose him forever."

"How *do* you get to be as big a dildo as Scott Dyer? You sort of wonder, did he attain dildo-hood at any point? Or if you'd met him aged five, he'd have been a little dildo?"

Harriet was wretched with nerves and guilt, and Lorna was still cheering her up.

Guilt: once again it was useful to name the emotion. (*Unnamed fears are the worst fears.* Was that Cal?)

The thing was, she'd instigated all of this: she'd written to Marianne, she'd friend-requested Nina, she'd led directly to Marianne deciding to wreck her own union.

If it all went to hell, it'd be on Harriet.

"You know, supporting someone else like this is really exceptional," Lorna said, as if she could hear Harriet's thoughts.

"Let's hope that's what they say, not that I'm an exceptional piece of work."

"Hang on." Lorna put her hand on Harriet's bare arm. In a role reversal, Lorna was in the plain jeans and T-shirt. It was as if they were playing dress-up as each other. "*Marianne* wanted to do this. You've inspired her, but you've not forced her or cajoled or even suggested this to her. It's a lovely quality that you make other people's feelings your problem, but that can go too far."

"Thank you," Harriet said gratefully. She pulled and snapped at the seat belt across her chest and tried to command her racing pulse to slow down. "Plus, we've invented a secret signal so she can confirm she definitely wants Nina and I to speak."

Marianne had been bewildered by this—Harriet could tell she was almost put out at being doubted. *I've been to so many weddings and know how the emotion can swallow you on the day,* Harriet typed.

If it swallows me, grab my legs and pull me back out! Marianne had responded.

"Really?!" Lorna said. "Oh God, this is too much. This is like a TV series my mum would get the good biscuits out for and call me up to talk about afterward. What's the signal?"

Harriet's stomach lurched as the hotel drew into view.

"Once she's at the altar, she's going to turn round and wave, or blow a kiss, to her mum. That means she's definitely still on board with The Plan and wants us to go ahead."

Harriet wished she'd not said this, as they emerged at the Queen's. It was only when repeating it that she realized that her safety check had in fact added a problem, instead of being a solution. What if Marianne forgot the signal, but remained committed? Then, if it sank everything, she'd feel betrayed by an unnecessary complication of Harriet's making.

Harriet should've thought of that.

It was too late to contact today's bride now, that was for sure. If it was a skydive, she'd already climbed into the plane.

50

Harriet felt the muffled squelch of thick carpet under uncomfortable dainty shoes, and eyes upon her as she crossed the lobby.

Lorna had peeled off to loiter in the bar to separate their arrival out by a few minutes, after Harriet gave her directions to the ballroom.

She was outside the door—signposted by a diner-style noticeboard, SCOTT & MARIANNE, with the date—before she knew it. She commanded herself, *Don't think: walk through it.*

She pulled it open, heart in mouth, to a cathedral of a room. It was filled with neat ranks of white cotton-covered chairs, decorated with yellow satin sashes. The space was flanked by two huge pillars wound with pinprick fairy lights in a maypole pattern. There were looming white-blossomed artificial trees with twisted trunks in planters, also bedecked with white penlight-size lights, running down each side of the seating. The ceiling was almost completely hidden by a canopy of gold helium balloons.

Off to the left, beyond the flower archway under which Scott and Marianne were to be united, was a string quartet.

They were giving a dramatic orchestral rendition of Journey's "Don't Stop Believin'," and Harriet was glad of the background noise.

Somehow, she had expected Marianne's reluctance to marry Scott to translate into low-key event organization. When she'd mentioned she had no bridesmaids as the budget wouldn't stretch, she'd omitted the part where it wasn't a shoestring. The budget had already stretched to the full Liberace goes to Hollywood. If Harriet had to find one word to describe the glamorously lit scene, it would be "cinematic." Its commitment to world-building was akin to walking onto a set.

Not to be selfish or anything, but Harriet would've far rather ruined "a dozen people in a sterile registry office with the EMERGENCY EXITS IN EVENT OF EVACUATION poster prominently displayed" kind of effort.

Making no eye contact, Harriet slunk into the very back row, on the far left-hand side, as per Marianne's instructions. As she sat down, she saw each chair came with a folded piece of card, embossed in gold with:

Welcome to the wedding of
SCOTT & MARIANNE
Order of Service

Harriet opened it.

If you're reading this, it means you're here because we love you!

Thank you for coming.
S&M x

Harriet almost snorted and had to stifle the urge, hurriedly. Any mirth was entirely knocked out of her at the sight of the groom in the middle distance. The brown hair was, as always, expensively tousled; his suit was powder blue, with a narrow floral tie.

Danny as best man was in razor-sharp moonstone gray, and they were both laughing and joking.

Oh, lovely Danny and Fergus. In terms of making an absolute scene of herself, somehow, the thought of their bearing witness injured her more than it should.

"'Scuse me, is this where you sit if you know the bride?" said a late-middle-aged woman in a very loud pink ruffled dress and sequinned shawl, drawing unwanted attention to Harriet.

"Yes, I think so!" Harriet said, in a frantic half-whisper.

She moved along to the very end of the row to make space for her, trying to stay hunched and low.

"Gorge, isn't it," the woman said, nodding upward at the balloons. "Must've cost a packet. How do you know Scott and Marianne?"

Oh God. It was one thing to ruin Scott's day, but Harriet was ruining so many people's day. She wanted to ditch the whole plan, at that very second, for the sake of the nice lady in the bad dress.

"Marianne's my hairdresser," she said, in a moment of desperate inspiration, as she'd not anticipated this question.

"Oh, and you're friends, that's sweet!"

"Yes," Harriet said, every fiber of her being willing her to stop talking to her.

Harriet knew she was supposed to ask pink dress lady how she knew Marianne, but instead she impersonated a rude, phone-fixated millennial, sliding it out of her clutch bag and checking the screen. She had a text.

Nina

Looking HOT, Harriet Hateful! Don't stare but I'm one row to the front of you, to the right. I went for a kind of Jackie O pillbox number in the end. GOOD LUCK OUR QUEEN xxx

Harriet glanced up, clocked an unusually demure Nina from behind, and then glanced away again to check the time. Four minutes to four. Marianne had solemnly sworn her punctuality (*I will literally get there early and sit in the car and pay the traffic ticket if I have to*). Four minutes to go undetected by the groom. A few more late stragglers joined her row, and Harriet thought, *I must be safe in a crowd. If Scott was going to do a glad-handing walkabout, he'd have done it by now, surely.*

Surely makes an ass of you and me: Harriet risked snatching a look in Scott's direction and quickly dropped her eyes with a sharp, silent intake of breath. He was staring, roughly at where she was sitting, and, worse, making an approach.

Oh, so this was it. She'd been made. Harriet felt the change in energy in the force field around her, the increase in air pressure. The tap on her shoulder would come any second, and still make her jump out of her skin. When she couldn't resist checking again, she saw Scott perilously close by, only one row in front. He was leaning down and speaking quietly to someone, beyond Harriet's view.

Whatever was happening wasn't completely benign, because Harriet sensed heads turning and necks craning.

Oh no. It was *Nina* he was speaking to.

She saw a blur of black pillbox hat and dark hair and Nina standing up and being discreetly propelled from the room, Scott behind her with a grim expression.

Head bowed, Harriet peered intently at her Order of Service without seeing a thing, and waited to be ejected next. If Nina was here, he'd know Harriet must be, right? She was suffering the guilty person's inability to assess what they'd given away. How many of their plot twists were now guessable?

Mortifying and ludicrous as discovery would be, more than anything, she'd feel she was abandoning Marianne. She'd have let her down.

More seconds passed. People chattered around her. The string band started "Chasing Cars," which seemed to be cue for Bride on Premises.

She finally risked looking up, and Scott was half jogging down the aisle, back to Danny's side.

Harriet was sat rigid, poker-faced, and in turmoil. He'd not seen her. He thought Nina was a lone shooter? Did it make sense to do this without Nina? She was going to say something, then what? Silence. Booing?

Breathe. *Breathe.*

The celebrant gestured for hush.

"Stand, please, for your bride."

51

Marianne Wharmby was the loveliest bride that Harriet had ever seen, and she'd seen quite a few. An audible gasp-sigh went around the room as she filled the doorway, wearing the composed expression of a born princess.

She wore an oyster tulle gown, with a deep V, that nipped in at the waist and flared out into a soft full skirt, spun through with silver diamante, so the fabric glistened. On her head was a full circle flower crown, the floral halo bursting with white jasmine and yellow roses, lending a pagan cult *Midsommar* feel. It could've been too much, but with her blond curls and innocent face beneath, the effect was enchanting and angelic.

The man on her arm, giving her away, was barely older than her. He was in a canary-yellow velvet suit and large clear-framed glasses, and had an undercut hairstyle, tattoos on both hands. Harriet thought, *Hairdresser.*

When they reached Scott, he was clutching his chest, shaking his head, miming, *I am blown away by this vision.* He got down on one knee and kissed Marianne's hand, to more noisy aahing.

Always the showman. For Harriet's taste, even if she'd not hated him, she'd have thought he was overdoing it. *Stop trying to drag the limelight from her, you wanker.*

"Thank you, everyone, for coming here to witness the marriage of Scott and Marianne," the celebrant said. She was around sixty, with bobbed hair, and in a skirt suit. She had the look of a Labour councillor who would promise to tackle the issues that really mattered to local people. "Please be seated. I'm the celebrant today, and my name is Gwen. To begin today's service, we have a poem, read by Ralph."

The man in yellow velvet who'd given Marianne away stepped forward.

"Hi, everyone. This is Carrie's poem from *Sex and the City.*" He paused. "Scott wants me to point out that Marianne chose it."

Laughter.

Carrie's poem was unknown to Harriet, but very short, and mercifully, had no sex in it, or city for that matter.

"Thank you, Ralph, that was beautiful," Gwen said, as he sat down.

"Now we move on to the exchanging of vows and the exchanging of rings. If I could ask the couple to face each other."

Gwen launched into her spiel, and Harriet started hard-sweating. Where was the signal?! Harriet was terrified by its absence and utterly cursing herself for demanding it.

If Marianne had simply understandably forgotten in the turbulence of being visible up there, Harriet supposed she would have to plow on regardless. She was fairly sure Marianne had not had a transformative epiphany at the sight of Scott in bespoke tailoring, and if she had . . . she could hardly blame Harriet for taking her at her word.

However, it would be excruciating for Harriet to intervene, and discover it wasn't welcome. The whole reason this was survivable was because everyone was going to understand the bride had wanted her to. She recalled Cal's advice. *People* do *lie, all the time, for any reason.*

"Sorry, I've realized I've not said hi to my mum," she heard in the distance, in a tiny, chirruping voice.

"Oh, yes . . . ?" said the politely baffled Gwen.

Marianne faced the audience, scanning the nearest rows. She kissed her hand, waving it at a woman out of Harriet's sight.

As her stomach tumbled down a ravine and her heart rate spiked, Harriet abruptly switched to emergency. *Shit.* OK. This was real. It was going to happen.

Harriet looked at her hands gripping her velvet handbag, her knuckles white.

Gwen's recitation of the formalities was simultaneously dragging on forever and absolutely tearing toward its train-crash conclusion.

A pause, where blood pounded in Harriet's ears. She looked up at the balloons. The urge to run from the room was overwhelming.

"Now." Gwen paused. "We've got to the part where I ask: if anyone here knows a reason why this couple *should not* be lawfully joined together in matrimony, let them speak now or forever hold their peace." Gwen looked out at the assembled company. She accompanied it with the beatific smile that was generally used here, to convey it was an adorable piece of rhetorical silliness. Commanding her limbs to move, Harriet got to her feet, having an out-of-body experience where she was only half aware she *had* stood up.

"Me. I do," she said, in a shaky voice that was apparently hers.

Every head snapped around, and the expectant silence was so taut you could twang it.

Somewhere among the pews, Harriet heard a voice saying, "Who the fuck is that?" and being shushed.

Make. Your. Mouth. Work. Her lips were clamped together, her jaw locked. She cleared her throat. That voice again, which didn't sound like hers.

"Scott Dyer is a coercive controller, a domestic abuser. I was with him for four years and during that time he nearly mentally destroyed me."

The seconds following felt like years. Every face was a mask of riveted, fascinated amazement. Gwen looked as if someone in a clown mask holding a tommy gun had zip-lined into the ballroom.

"I can't believe you'd do this, Harriet," Scott said, eventually, in a hard monotone, like the flat blade of a knife. Every head moved to look at him. It occurred to Harriet he'd be a notch more prepared, having thrown Nina out. The collusion would now be clear. The full extent of it wouldn't, though.

"I can't believe I'd do this either," Harriet said, feeling her courage rise by a tiny degree. There was nothing equally as frightening as jumping, and she had jumped. "It's an extreme measure, to stop you from ruining another woman's life."

"Just because I don't want to be with you doesn't mean I ruined your life," Scott said.

Although he was sheet-white and visibly trembling with fury and embarrassment, he'd calculated she had to be spoken to like a stalker. It was his greatest weapon, his best chance of discrediting her: the suspicion of female hysteria. *That bitch is crazy.*

Undeniably helped along here by the fact interrupting a wedding *was* crazy.

"You know exactly the things I mean, Scott. Monitoring where I was, checking up on me constantly. Calling me a liar so often I started to doubt what was real. Isolating me from my friends, telling me they were our enemies. Falsely accusing me of infidelity, or flirting, of embarrassing myself."

Harriet paused, fully expecting to be interrupted, but the element of surprise was on her side, she had the audience in the palm of her hand. And, she guessed, Scott telling her to shut up was too much like corroborating her.

". . . Viciously criticizing me, calling me worthless. Monstering me if I dared leave the house, until it became easier not to. The sulks, the rages, the accusations, the belittling. Turning me into a dependent, confused wreck, with no one left to turn to, because I'd pushed them all away, to please you. And it's not only me you've done this to, is it, Scott?"

"You seem to be the only person inventing this horrible stuff, Harriet, yes," he said, with an effortful evenness, infusing his tone with a deeply weary regret that implied he'd tried, God knows he'd tried, to help this woman. Scott knew the stakes and was giving the BAFTA-nominated performance of his life. "I've moved on and I'm happy. You're here trying to wreck my wedding. You're wrecking Marianne's day, which is what hurts most of all."

He looked at his bride, who was looking back at him, her sparkling Fiorucci-cherub face blank. Harriet heard the crowd tut and make noises of support.

They were going to believe him? Of course they were. He was always believed. All right, he had an advantage—he was their groom and she was a stranger. Still, what would it take to get people to set aside their preferred version of Scott Dyer, the one they'd bought into? Why did a woman's voice have to be a chorus to count?

"Harriet is NOT the only person saying this!" came a ragged female voice from the back of the room. Harriet turned to see Nina. She'd ditched the hat, and acquired a mini bottle of prosecco.

"Should've locked me out," she added, holding the bottle up to toast Scott. "Hi, everybody, I'm Nina, I'm another ex-girlfriend of Scott's. I've also come here to say, don't do it, Marianne! Everything Harriet said was true. I mean, I didn't hear most of it, but I know what she was going to say. He treated me like dog shit too. I say, HEAR! HEAR!"

She clamped the bottle under one arm and clapped, one small pair of hands sounding tiny in the yawning silence. To Harriet, they were everything.

"What the HELL is going on here?" said a balding older man who'd got to his feet at the front of the room. Harriet recognized Scott's dad. "Get out! Both of you! You're destroying the happiest day of these two young people's lives. Do something!" he said to the traumatized Gwen, as if she were nightclub security.

"I told you! I told you and you wouldn't believe me. Now do you believe me?"

With a rustling noise, another guest got to her feet, near the back on the right-hand side. Now Harriet got to be as surprised as everyone else had been. The unexpected contributor had long brown hair with a curl and a golden tan, and was made up to the nines in a cream tuxedo jacket.

"I had a thing with Scott a few years back, it didn't last very long as he met Marianne," she said in a Scouse accent. "What these two women say is ringing a lot of bells. I couldn't live with myself if I didn't say so. I'm only here because my boyfriend, Martin, is friends with Scott . . ." She cast a look down at a seated partner who, Harriet suspected, was not on board with her decision to speak up. "Behind closed doors, Scott is a vicious little bully. The girl in the veil over there described it perfectly. No one ever believes you, because he's such a charmer when there's other people around."

A collective stunned silence followed this admission, to add to the canon of stunned silences this wedding had produced.

"Three of us now! Have I got any advance on three?" Nina said in an auctioneer impression. "Let's try for a fourth!"

Harriet noticed that a glowering Scott wasn't responding to Nina, or this other woman, because refuting multiple accounts was beyond even his skill set. He'd claim conspiracy, but it was not so easy to paint that in right now.

"Right," said Gwen, struggling to regain control of a hiccup that was absolutely not covered in the How to Officiate Civil Ceremonies handbook. "The person who is marrying Scott today is Marianne. I appreciate feelings are running high here. Given there's no *legal* impediment, which is what I asked for"—she made a pursed-lips scold face, as if she were principally upset at their lack of following instructions—"I'd ask you now to leave these two people to get married in peace."

Hotel staff appeared menacingly, a foot from Harriet. Word of what was happening had left this room, and she was about to be given nonvoluntary escorting from the premises.

"Actually, I asked Harriet and Nina to come today," Marianne said to Scott, in a voice clear and sweet as a bell, dropping her bomb like it was a scented handkerchief.

Harriet swore she could physically feel the room shift from *Well This Is a Hell of a Yarn* to *Oh, OK, History Is Being Made Here, What the Fuck.*

People were urgently whispering their disbelief and, at the same time, trying not to obscure a word of the dialogue.

"Sorry, I can't remember your name," Marianne said to the Scouse girl.

"Paula," she said, half standing again and putting her hand up, as if they were at a cooking demonstration and Marianne was about to call her up to try rolling her dough.

"Paula, that's it. Thank you too."

Marianne turned to her groom.

"Scott, I didn't come here to marry you. I came to tell you it's over. I hate how you've treated me, and I hate how you've treated them." She pointed back at Harriet and Nina.

Marianne didn't sound even slightly nervous. Harriet had never been so impressed by someone in her life.

"There's a reason I've done it in public. What I hate most of all is that everyone here, nice people, good people, our family and friends"—she swung a hand at the stupefied audience—"they all think that you're this devoted good guy who'd never hurt a fly. I started taking beta-blockers last year for panic attacks, because I was so scared of your temper. You've been bullying me to stop seeing my mum for how long? It's not right."

"Oh, this is utter nonsense!" bellowed Scott's dad, off to the right. "I can't listen to another word of this. I don't know why you're all persecuting my son like this. He's got a heart of gold! Shame on you all. Absolutely disgusting."

A large blond woman on the front left stood up.

"Heart of gold, my arse, Keith. I told my daughter he had a mean streak a mile wide from day one. These girls can't ALL be lying, can they? You should care how your son's treating women."

"A mean streak called 'paying off her debts.' A mean streak like 'doing up that spare room while she went out with her friends,'" Keith said.

"Debts?! I clear the balance on my credit card myself EVERY month!" Marianne said, looking dumbfounded for the first time. "He did the back bedroom because he yelled at me for being shit at painting. To be fair, I am quite shit at painting, but that's not the point."

"Wake up and smell the coffee, Keith," said Marianne's mum. "You're sleeping in Starbucks."

Harriet noticed Scott was saying nothing, looking murderous but petrified. Three women's testimony was damning, but Houdini would've still escaped if he had a bride. A cobbled-together, verbal equivalent of a press statement would've circulated at the reception. *Yes, in his day, he'd been a heartbreaker and a lady-killer. Women tended to get hung up on him, he'd picked a few handfuls and got himself in some tangles. Thank God he'd met The One.* His guests might've believed him or might not, but they'd have at least pretended to, in order to eat their chicken Diane without guilt.

"Right, I've said my piece, we're done." Marianne looked Scott directly in the eye. "I'm done. This is over, Scott. Have a nice fucking life and don't fuck up anyone else's life." She turned back to the room. "Now. There are free drinks in the bar. Sorry, everyone, for having a wasted trip today. I know this isn't what you came for, but it was important that we did it. I hope you understand," Marianne said. She turned to the musicians. "Please, can you play my exit music?"

The cowering string quartet looked unsure, having thought their job for the day was definitively over.

"*Please?*" Marianne said, with an intonation that was a command, and they hurriedly turned the pages of their sheet music.

They struck up what Harriet recognized as Lady Gaga's "Bad Romance," and she wanted to laugh, burst into tears, punch the air, and down a dirty martini in one, all at once.

Marianne had certainly reminded Scott of who she was. She gathered her vast *Gone with the Wind* skirts in one hand and made stately progress down the aisle.

When she drew level with Harriet, she stuck out her hand and said, "Join me?"

Harriet ducked around the back of her row, muttering apologies to the two people she had to pull herself past, and Marianne collected Nina on the other side in the meanwhile. They made their exit as a trio, hand in hand in hand.

As they wrenched open the doors, Harriet felt her heart soar. Something had finished, for her, flown out of her. She was cleansed. It was anger. Her anger at Scott had gone. She was free of him.

She was so elated, she had a moment of pure inspiration. Harriet turned back to the groom, who had a face like . . .

It was an expression Harriet remembered well. She'd just never seen it in public before. She cleared her throat.

"Scott. It's like you said. Love always wins."

52

NO WAY: this man gets called out at his wedding ceremony by THREE EX GIRLFRIENDS then his bride DUMPS HIM!!!!
96k views 16k Likes 699 shares

OMFG no

This is sick!!!

Guys this isn't real. If you look at the people on the far left, they're in on it. All actors. Nicely done though

The song the band is playing 😂

I've seen loads of reveal vids like these and this is the best one yet. It's not real but at first you totally believe it might be

This is giving me LIFE

I hope they have a spare bed at the Serious Burns Unit

We've all known a Scott, one way or another. Love to see it. Love this for him

Is that the guy out of that Britpop band

Oh Scott. Gonna need cosmetic surgery before you try to date again. Or at least a hair cut 😂

He's pulled some fit lasses though, I smell a legend

This is kind of like an I am Spartacus for victims of shitbags. Noice!

In the hotel bar, after Lorna hit "post" ("There's a whole sub-culture of these things! 'Man Tells Girlfriend He Knows She's Cheating on Him: You Won't Believe How' and so on."), the footage from the wedding lit her phone up with a blizzard of notifications.

Unsurprisingly, all of Scott's family boycotted the Not Reception, but an interestingly large number of his friends turned up (if not Danny and Fergus: Harriet guessed being a best man conferred special obligations and didn't resent them for it). Presumably they were nursing an uncomprehending, fiery Scott at a secret location. They'd be wondering, however, if they'd known him as well as they thought they did. Everyone would, bar, perhaps, his dad.

There was an adjustment for many to go through: accepting the monster could be your mate.

Marianne was absorbed into the melee as a celebrity, her Estilo gang buzzing around her.

"This feels like one of those huge world events you can't assess until time has passed and you watch the documentaries about it," said Lorna, at their table in the bar. "I'll need to hear what Barack has to say on the matter. Harriet, you spoke SO well. I don't know how you managed that eloquence under pressure. Did you practice?"

Harriet shook her head. "I thought if I did, I'd get hung up on forgetting it, and off the cuff was best."

"Extraordinary."

"I thought we were absolutely screwed when Scott clocked me," Nina said. "I waited and waited for you to come through the doors too."

"He'd obviously never expected a scrubber like me to be so done up. How did he think you'd got in?"

"I said I was in the hotel anyway, saw the sign, wondered if it was him, and decided to have a nosy. He must've known it wasn't true, but he didn't have much time to work out what was up."

Harriet's phone buzzed.

Cal

WELL?! Do I need to come spring you from Elland Road police station? X

Harriet sent the link as response, snap-crackling inside at having his attention.

Well, wow . . .

You are a phenomenal person, Harriet Hatley. xx

She glowed.

Harriet knew she would never know the full effect on Scott Dyer, and she didn't need to. It felt so great to take control, and there was no lust for revenge left in Harriet.

Within half an hour, she was told, he'd disappeared from all social media. Perhaps he'd move to another city and start again. Yet what they'd done would stand as permanent monument; he'd forever risk someone in his new life stumbling across that past. Hopefully it would produce a caution he'd never had before, as well as a heightened awareness among his nearest and dearest. Maybe he'd finally get some of that therapy he was so keen on for Harriet. Emerge reborn, a secular swami of a relationship counselor. A changed and chastened man who'd been to hell and back, whose mistakes other men could learn from.

That progression, Harriet reflected, would be very Scott. He would forever be casting himself as leading man in his chosen story. She could only hope he'd write a better part.

But they changed *this* story, together. If there was a special place in hell reserved for women who didn't help other women, perhaps there were special rewards for those who did. Harriet did not feel alone anymore. They couldn't have achieved this without one another, they couldn't have vanquished this man, except as a team.

As Harriet said to Marianne and Nina as they toasted their success at the end of the night, turns out it wasn't about the treasure of Scott Dyer's takedown: it was the friendships they made along the way.

53

"You know when you say something so stupid that afterward, you get an actual body cringe remembering it? Like . . ." Cal mimed one eye opening wide as a memory occurred, and his body going rigid in response, while sat next to Harriet on the sofa.

"Yes?" Harriet said, tucking her legs underneath herself. It was one week since the exploded wedding, and one day until she moved out to her next digs in Chapel Allerton. For a send-off, Cal had suggested an evening in, sensitively pairing wine and crisps. Harriet was grateful for them when she got back at nine from a hip wedding at Duke Studios.

"When you said you'd read your mum's letter. I said, 'Do you want some toast?'" Cal put a palm over his eyes. "Do you want some TOAST. I am *sunburned* with shame."

"Hahahahaha! I didn't even remember. It was OK."

"I couldn't think of something that would meet the moment, as it were. Instead, I went to the next obvious place. Oven muffins."

"Could've at least offered me a Breville toastie."

Cal looked at her with what looked like acute fondness.

"We're going to stay in touch, right?" Cal said, picking up his glass of red. "This isn't *goodbye*-goodbye?"

Harriet guessed this was coming. She'd already admitted to herself that she had a crush. She knew if she stayed around Cal any longer, it'd be more serious than a crush. It'd go from a crush to a mess. She wasn't going to let that happen.

It was a bittersweet achievement to be the prescient one for a change. The party who could see the oncoming traffic accident, and take the service road.

After Scott, and Jon, she wasn't going to break her own heart by falling for the unattainable popular boy, for the hat trick. Harriet was going to assume control instead. They could meet up, but she already knew how it would go. His friends, bar Sam, would be merely courteous, while not quite knowing why she was there. (*Your ex lodger?* As if she were attending on a scholarship.)

They'd go to the sort of place that microplaned truffles, offered low-intervention wines, and served radishes with their leaves on, to be dragged through things. ("It's called *bagna càuda,* with crudités!" Lorna said of a starter dish to a doubtful Roxy once, who replied, "It looks like my mum's old Weight Watchers tea, without the rolled-up slice of ham.")

Harriet would make half-hearted attempts to befriend the aloof beauty in the Vampire's Wife dress on Cal's arm, who'd wonder exactly how well Harriet knew her boyfriend.

Cal would be anxious she wasn't enjoying herself, that the flatmate badinage he remembered with nostalgia wasn't appearing on cue. He'd end up feeling guiltily baffled, making empty promises of more meetups.

Instead of looking back on a brief, strange, but golden time and rejoicing, they'd both get a squirmy sense of *what happened there?* at the thought of each other.

"Sure, but . . . will we make much sense after I stop being your tenant?"

"What do you mean?"

"I'm not sure our worlds collide all that much, outside these four walls."

Cal's brow knitted. "You can choose the pub."

"The thing is, if I met your next girlfriend and she was another Hot Thatcher, I couldn't stand it. I know too much."

"Ah. Right."

Harriet winced at the sting of her rejection, a poor return for his warmth. She was lying to him, to look cool. It wasn't about his taste in other women. It was about other women, full stop.

"If she was nice, I'd probably hate that even more."

Clunk. Oh, right. She hadn't given herself a heads-up she was going to *sort of tell him.*

Harriet drank her wine, and Cal looked over, gazing at her steadily.

"Yes. I'm not mad keen to shake hands with the next Travel Iron Jon. Assuming he doesn't just knee me in the nuts."

Harriet laughed, glad of the generous rescue.

There was a beat of silence, which Harriet instinctively recognized as one of those split-second moments where everything hangs in the balance.

"And if he's nice, that will be even worse."

Oh. *Oh.*

He was using not only her line, but those eyes on her. She was looking at his mouth. This was bad. Harriet felt as if she were starting to liquefy.

She thought, amid the heavy flirting, she'd best reassert some reality: "You're not still seeing the girl you've been seeing, then?"

Cal squinted. "What girl?"

"Lorna said when you were at her restaurant, it was with a date."

This made it a little too obvious that Cal had been discussed in a certain way, but sod it—there was less than twenty-four hours left around him.

"Er . . ." Cal frowned. "Divertimento . . . ? Ah, that was my sister! Erin."

"Oh, right."

"I've not dated anyone since Kit."

"Right," Harriet said, awkwardly. "And you're not . . . sleeping with Kristina?"

"Oh God, you DID see my phone that evening!"

"Er. Yes," Harriet said.

"That was her idea of a joke and an attempt to fuck me up."

Cal pulled his phone out of his pocket and scrolled to a conversation, turned the screen to face Harriet. "Ignore her jealous gibes about you. I did."

Kit

If you want me to accept we're over for good, maybe it's time to stop sleeping with me? Just a thought

Cal

??? Are you confusing me with someone else?

Kit

LOOLLLLLLL. Lock screen fun. I can tell you're keen on that photographer girl and now I bet she's seen this and you have to work out how to explain it, without showing her THIS message ☺ HEY CAL WANTS TO POUND YOU UNTIL YOU SQUEAK FOR MERCY 😂🍆

Seriously—she's a bit straight-edged for you, somehow, don't you think? A bit "bean bag lap tray supper in front of Countryfile"? You do you, though

"Whoa. I don't always watch *Countryfile*." Harriet was stung, while sensing it was, as Cal said, jealousy.

"Is she moving to Qatar with Seb, or to a hidden island lair to develop a deadly bioweapon?" Cal said, grimacing.

Harriet laughed, nervously. She had leaped without a landing—she'd felt certain that Cal accounting for where she fitted into his furtive tomcatting would create a breathing space.

It would've been for him to describe what he thought was going on here. Instead, she looked like she kept a running tally of rivals. Which she did.

"You're not seeing anyone?" Cal said.

"Hah. Nope."

"If those questions about me were security checks on whether it's unethical for anything to happen between us, it's not."

"OK," said Harriet, blushing and feeling like a total, total idiot, as adrenaline gushed through her veins. "Uhm . . . so . . ."

She hesitated, at a point of no return.

"Say it," Cal said. "Whatever it is."

". . . Was what Kit said true? About your wishes."

Cal took a second to comprehend what she meant.

"For once, what she said was one hundred percent true. Yes. Every word." He paused, while Harriet silently dissolved. "You did say I have a lovely face, which is similar?" Cal added.

"It was exactly that sentiment, in code."

"Really worrying that my gran once said the same, then."

Harriet shrieked with laughter, and in the moment of dropping her guard, Cal leaned forward and kissed her.

Crossing that line had seemed so difficult, and then so easy. All the cagey dance steps leading up to it, the card game of choosing what to reveal, then Harriet's body language trashed it entirely and left him in no doubt. She put her hands in Cal's hair, pulled his mouth to hers, harder. Cal responded to her with as much enthusiasm, his hand gripping her denim-clad upper leg as they tipped backward on the sofa. They laughed at the intensity of the scramble for each other, of the pure joy of it, when they came up for air.

Harriet found her fantasies had been a poor relation to the sensory reality of grappling with Cal, and she'd been quite optimistic in her fantasies. She'd been right that having his undivided attention was a high like no other.

Until this moment, *chemistry* was a concept she'd scoffed at a little, because she'd never encountered it. Maybe he had the gift of making everyone feel this way, but she'd never been kissed like this before: with exactly the right degree of pressure and intent. It was like being with a dance partner who raised your game. Harriet felt like he'd done something to her *spine,* her whole posture changed.

She started unbuttoning his shirt, like she'd only been waiting for permission.

54

"Sleeping with your landlord the night before you move out. It's one way to get your deposit back," Lorna said, when Harriet called her to brag about the best time of her life, and Harriet screamed.

"I knew I shouldn't have told you!"

"I'm thrilled for you. I always had a good feeling about him. And did he feel good?"

It was a night Harriet would never forget. She liked to think that although Cal probably had had many more nights like that than her, he'd rate it in his top five at least.

They had been lying in the sleigh bed that Harriet had previously only seen in the photographs, lit by the streetlamp outside, a tangle of bare limbs and sheets. Cal said, "I've wanted to be here so long. With you."

"*Have* you?" Harriet sat up to face him, head propped on elbow.

"Since Bruce Springsteen at least."

"My singing was erotic?"

"I don't want to objectify you, but it was more your everything else."

"I remember you giving me a look when I sat down. I thought you were worried Sam and I were going to cop off. You were worried he'd spite you by keeping me in your life, remember."

"That *was* my fear, but by that time it was because it would feel like torture, not spite."

"You could've simply made a move. Not to blow smoke, but you're quite sleepable-with."

Cal stroked her hair from her face and said nothing, then kissed her again.

The following morning, their newfound intimacy made loading her car loaded with subtext. She couldn't see his hands on anything without remembering them on her. Cal handed her a coffee and then kissed her neck as she drank it. He took the cup back out of her hands and set it on the side and kissed her in earnest, Harriet's hands sliding under his T-shirt as his body pressed against her. She wondered, amid their fevered grappling—Cal murmuring, "Harriet, you are too much"—if they were about to do it against the sink. She decided if so, she was cool with that. What a house share this had turned out to be. Thank God her next rental was with a librarian called Valerie.

They were interrupted by the doorbell.

Cal paused, his hands holding Harriet's face, then pulled back.

"Fuck my life, I told Sam I'd go to the match with him today!"

Harriet laughed. "It's fine."

"I can't cancel him now he's here."

"No! Probably for the best, else we'd end up back upstairs."

Cal looked at her with dilated pupils.

"Harriet . . ." he began.

The doorbell went again like a fire drill, and Cal shouted, "All right, I'm coming, and sadly not in the way I want!" and as Sam was let in, Harriet was still laughing.

She pushed her hands into her jean pockets, as Cal found his jacket.

"I'll leave my keys in the kitchen," she said to him.

"Sure," Cal said, with a tender smile.

Call her a coward, but Harriet was actually relieved at Sam's presence removing the need to find the way to say farewell. She had accepted from the outset that Cal Clarke was a one-night stand. She knew what Kit meant about her being wrong for him, and she was sure Cal did too. That didn't mean she wanted to face the hard limits here, by confirming it in so many words.

In the hallway, Sam looked suspiciously from one to the other.

"You two seem very pleased with yourselves." He looked at Cal. "He's grinning like a cat with a raspberry-flavored arse."

He looked at Harriet.

"And you are . . . what's the word. Radiant. You're *radiant*."

Pause.

"Waaaaaait. Oh my God, did you . . . ? HAVE YOU TWO . . . ?"

"Come on, Sam, let's get you to the football!" Cal said, in a mock carer-in-an-old-folks-home upbeat voice.

Cal turned and gave Harriet a quick, hard look at her as he followed Sam out the door.

"Goodbye then, Harriet," he said, with meaning.

She raised a hand and steadied her heart.

"Bye, Cal."

55

The room in Chapel Allerton was fine, and the woman, Valerie, she was sharing with was fine, and it was a pleasant enough house and quiet enough street and it was all *fine,* except it wasn't fine.

She'd pronounced that was the end with Cal Clarke, yet her emotions weren't complying. Harriet couldn't stop thinking about him. Actually, thinking about herself too.

Thinking about how Cal's worth to her wasn't one night in his bed, yet she'd let him think that, for fear of looking too keen and foolish. She'd thought she was being so self-aware and self-protective, and as a few days rolled by, she wondered if she hadn't in fact been a bit of a fake.

She could make her lack of expectations to Cal clear, but that wasn't synonymous with acting like she didn't care.

Harriet had drafted a small speech in her head, going over and over precisely what she wanted to say. Not in hope of any reciprocation, but for the value of telling him in itself.

It didn't matter if a Gatsby like him found it slightly overheated, or even gauche, like a plastic rose on Valentine's Day.

What mattered was that she had the bravery—now, in a truly post-Scott world, she understood the value of saying what she meant.

Between bride prep and the ceremony for Jacob and Leah at the Mansion in Roundhay, when Harriet broke off to have her Tupperware of car pasta, she found the opportunity.

It had been nearly a fortnight since she'd starred in a viral video, and booking inquiries had noticeably reenergized: they'd actually started to surpass her usual level, and she'd even referred a few of them on to Bryn. Some asked, "Are you the girl in that thing?"

Derailing a wedding shouldn't be catnip to her demographic, and yet being a very limited kind of famous drove loads to the website. It turned out "having heard of you" was a helpful differential—Oscar Wilde was right. Come for the notoriety, stay for the galleries of superbly lit wedlocking. End up sending an availability query.

Harriet found Cal's name in her WhatsApp and typed.

Hello! I hope you're good and the next lodger doesn't have a pimped didgeridoo. Now that I'm safely out of your way, I wanted to tell you something I was never gutsy enough to say to your face. I thought I'd bash it into a phone instead.

I only realise when looking back how low my expectations had got, by the time I moved in with you. First the Scott trauma, and then the stupid rebound mistake with Jon. I'd started to think that life was mostly to be endured. I'd lost hope that I could ever sincerely feel certain ~feelings~ again.

When I said our worlds wouldn't collide outside your house, I didn't mean it wasn't wonderful that they did, or that I won't cherish that time forever, because I will. I didn't want to become a minor admin responsibility that didn't fit into your next adventures, instead of a good memory.

When I think back to the voyage of self-discovery that was living with you, it's the laughing I'm going to remember the most.

You know the school science project where you dipped a penny in fizzy drink and it came out shining and new? That's how you've made me feel. Thank you for being the off-brand cola to my coin.

You demonstrated that life can be good, Calvin Pants. Better than I ever thought it could be, in fact. For that I will be so eternally grateful. I want every wonderful thing for you, and you'll forever have a place in my heart.

Love always,

Harriet x

There. Her plastic rose, in cellophane printed with tiny hearts. She threw her mobile onto the passenger seat and thought, *A watched pot never boils, so don't look at it again for hours. Don't.* Harriet knew she didn't have the willpower, but suddenly, willpower didn't need to apply. No sooner had she put her fork into her penne, than the mother of the bride was tapping on her car window.

"I'm SO sorry, but we've got an elderly contingent on Jake's side who are going to go straight after the ceremony. I'm wondering if you could take some snaps of them before Leah arrives?"

"Of course!" Harriet said, re-lidding her food, pocketing her phone, and hefting her camera kit from the back seat.

It was a reliable rule of thumb that the flashier the wedding, the heavier the workload, and the reception at Roundhay, with its chandeliers and all-white flower centerpieces, was no exception.

Harriet had just finished pictures of Jacob and Leah waltzing to "Can't Take My Eyes Off You"—why did it suddenly give her a lump in her throat? Harriet must be premenstrual—when she remembered the message.

Her phone! She couldn't get to it fast enough. He'd probably have igno—his name was on her lock screen. It arrived two hours ago. She fumbled it open.

I think the point of the coin experiment was to show us how bad sugary drinks were for us, but I'll take it. I'm not going to pretend "laughing" will be my no. 1 "Things I've Done with Harriet" stand-out memory, but it'll definitely be the second. You don't have a place in my heart. You have it.

Cal xxx

Harriet went hot and cold at the same time, and slightly limp with desire. That . . . seemed quite unequivocally a declaration? Was "you have my heart" ever a sign-off catchphrase? *Catch ya later, Jim! You have my heart.*

Harriet couldn't take the brinkmanship anymore, if that's what it was. She'd get home and call him. Or, all right, maybe not call him but certainly spend an hour crafting a suitably arousing reply, that confessed what he surely already knew.

The DJ had segued into Elton John's "Tiny Dancer."

Harriet's line of sight settled on a handsome man across the disco-ball-lit expanse, eyes fixed on her, his hands in his pockets. His outline was exactly like . . . As he saw her, seeing him, he smiled.

Harriet was rooted to the spot in shock.

"Do you want me?" she mouthed, frowning, pointing at herself, with no idea how she was managing jokes when her heart felt like it was exploding.

Cal nodded. He mouthed back, "Yes."

Harriet felt like her legs were made of rubber bands as she headed over to him and he approached her, and they met in the middle of the half-full dance floor. "Tiny Dancer" was ironically quite hard to dance to.

"Hi," Cal said. "You didn't reply to my message, so I thought I'd turn up in person and say—what the fuck? You send a message like that, then leave me on UNREAD?! Hard as nails. I wasn't spending all evening trying to work out why. You can explain yourself in person."

Harriet grinned from ear to ear.

"Apologies, I meant to reply: 'Good to hear,'" Harriet said, doing a thumbs-up. Cal laughed and they exchanged a look of purest mutual adoration.

He was here. He was *here*?

"How did you get in?"

"If you arrive properly attired, it seems no one stops you. I asked Lorna where tonight's wedding was."

"Ah."

"About that message you sent me."

"Yes."

"I wondered if we might be in one of those situations where I'm madly in love with you and you're at least slightly in love with me, and neither of us are saying so, in case the other isn't. I know you didn't say 'I'm in love with you, Cal' in your message, but it felt like it might be there in the subtext. I'm going to break the deadlock and go first. Harriet, I'm in love with you."

Even though she knew that was what he was here to say from the moment she saw him, the words still practically lifted her off her feet.

"OK then, I admit it. I'm in love with you, Cal."

They gazed at each other in rapt joy as Elton reached a loud part of the chorus and Cal's hands found hers, pulling her a little closer, sliding around and up her back.

"There, was that so difficult? What was so hard about tapping that into WhatsApp, and going on with your day?" Cal said.

Harriet laughed some more.

"And what was 'I don't want to stay in touch' about?" Cal said. "That messed with my head and knocked my confidence, right when I was working up to my big declaration. I've been trying to figure out what to do with that, ever since."

"I thought the offer was as 'friends'!"

"That was my opening gambit, testing the water. My plan was to follow it with *how about dinner next week,* until you realized I was suggesting a date. I was trying to go a sly, lazy route so I didn't end up in a wedding tent having to say things like, *Harriet, turns out I really did feel every second of having you.*"

Harriet slid her bag off her shoulder, reached her arms up around his neck, and kissed him. She kissed him like she owned him, and the moment, and had no fear. She kissed him like they were the only people there.

"Was I imagining that you always ruled me out as a prospect, somehow?" Cal said, as they held each other. "Even after our night together, it was like . . . *thank you for your time.*"

"Erm . . . well, we're so different . . ."

"I should hope so. Why would I want to date myself? The thing is, we're not. I've never felt so understood by someone."

"I agree."

"Then . . . ?" Cal widened his eyes to convey: *I'm at a loss.*

Harriet smiled. There was something else, underneath her conviction he wasn't meant for the likes of her. Something like . . . superstition? She felt like she was opening a final clue envelope.

"I think it was because . . . My life has had good bits, and not-so-good bits. I think I've coped. The one thing I've never been is lucky. I'm generally unlucky. Someone as great as you, loving me back? It's too much luck. *You're* too much luck."

"My loving you isn't luck," Cal said. He kissed her again, under the disco ball, and eloquently made his point that they were perfectly right for each other. Her whole body lit up in response.

"Can I have a photo, with my girlfriend?" he said.

"This doesn't do selfies," Harriet said, indicating her camera bag with her trusty warhorse of a Nikon. "Hang on. Will you take a picture of us?" she asked a nearby guest in a fascinator that looked like an equestrian flower garland. The woman stopped swaying and listened politely to Harriet's explanations of which button did what, before Harriet scurried back into place and the woman balanced it for the shot.

"Here we go . . . *smile*!"

THE FIRST PHOTOGRAPH of Harriet and Cal as a couple shows them with their arms wrapped around each other, on a balloon-scattered dance floor. He's in a suit, but she isn't dressed as if she's at a party, in a black jumper and jeans. She'll notice when they get it framed how much she resembles her mother. They look improbably, deliriously, superlatively happy.

To the right of the frame, unbeknownst to either of them at the time, is a photobombing bridesmaid, pulling a face like a drooling pervert in a trance and making an arse-cupping motion with both palms under Cal's backside.

Two years later, the picture will get a huge laugh in Sam's best man's speech.

Epilogue

Dearest Harriet,

When I realised the hour had come and I finally needed to write this letter, I was full of ideas of things I should say: wise advice and vague aphorisms about growing up, finding love, and making the most of your time. Now that I've got this pen in my hand, it all seems worthless. How can you equip anyone for a future you can't see?

Then I realised, you don't need my advice, you need my encouragement.

You're only a little girl right now, but I already know you have the spirit to lead a happy and full life, without us.

I won't lie to you (I asked your grandparents to save this until you're a little older): I'm scared, and I'm sad at the days I won't get to spend with you. But when I look at you, above all, I feel hope.

Whatever you're doing now, whatever you go on to do—I want you to know this, Harriet.

I am very, very proud of you indeed.

All my love,
Mum x

Acknowledgments

I may be on my eighth book, but the terror of forgetting someone here never goes away. If I've left you out, it's not deliberate. (Apart from Mark Casarotto: I omitted you on purpose so no one knows you're the real life person who's allergic to lettuce.)

So—much gratitude to my editorial team at HarperCollins, my editor Martha Ashby and assistant editor Lucy Stewart, for all their dedicated hard work, and to Lynne Drew for her kind encouragement. And thanks to Keshini Naidoo for a hoot of a copyedit. Well, I was hooting, anyway. Hoot like nobody's listening.

And big shout to my lovely agent, Doug Kean, a more patient man you couldn't find.

Thank you to my first draft readers on this outing, who cheer me on to the finish line—Kristy, Tara, my sister Laura, Katie, and Sean. I really couldn't be without you.

Thanks to female friends, both online and off, who talk to me about life, love, and entertaining catastrophes, and generously reply "of course" when I say: *I may have to use this in a book, please.* This story is about female solidarity, and I couldn't write it if I didn't know it.

Praise be to Rebecca Lucy Taylor, aka Self Esteem, for the quote and the masterpiece of an album that soundtracked my edits and the mood so perfectly. Cheers also to Bruce Springsteen, "Dancing in the Dark," and a line so apposite it's Harriet Hatley's mission statement.

Thank you to the brilliantly witty writer Justin Myers for letting me borrow his peerless description of an Aperol spritz, and to Dominic Grace for allowing his nickname for next door's cat to be repurposed for a demonic chihuahua.

My research squad: huge thanks to the ridiculously talented wedding photographer of Cheshire and Manchester, James Tracey, who talked me through the practicalities of the job, and told me some brilliant anecdotes—please accept my apologies if there are any errors to a professional eye in here!

Thank you to Chris King and also Elaine Campbell for taking the time to explain various Leeds venues to me—much appreciated, and any errors in description are definitely mine.

Thank you to Alex, who knows the writing process ain't always pretty, and who took me for the Fancy Vimto cocktails at the Midland that proved vital to unlocking this plot.

And thank you, once again, to everyone who reads my books: I'm so sincerely amazed and grateful to have your time, and I try my hardest not to waste it.

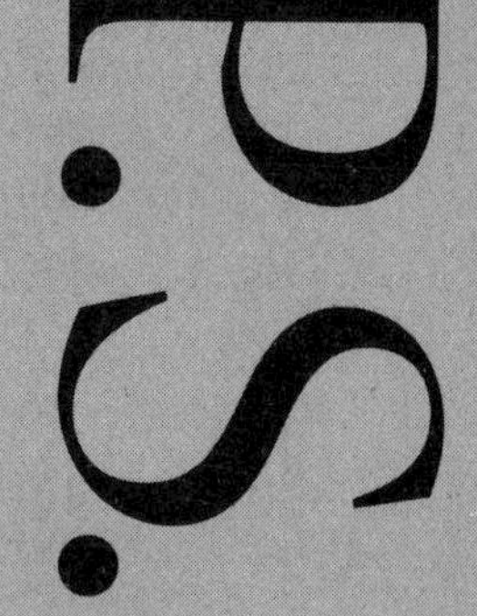

About the author

About the book

Insights,
Interviews
& More . . .

Meet Mhairi McFarlane

Ruth Rose

Sunday Times bestselling author Mhairi McFarlane was born in Scotland, and her unnecessarily confusing name is pronounced *Vah-Ree*. After some efforts at journalism, she started writing novels, and her first book, *You Had Me at Hello,* was an instant success. She's now written eight books, and she lives in Nottingham with a man and a cat.

Dear Reader

Dear Reader,

Thank you so much for picking up *Mad About You,* and I hope you enjoyed it! When I came to write this note, I knew I would feel a little bit of a fraud if I talked grandly about my "mission statement" as I embarked on the book. In truth, writing is quite a messy, unfocused process—I grab inspiration from all kinds of things, and, eventually, the shape of a story emerges from the mist. It's an instinctual, "flail around in the pitch dark while you work out where the furniture is" kind of deal. But I broadly knew two things at the outset: firstly, that I wanted to write about coercive control, and, secondly, that I wanted to explore the bad choices we can make AFTER the first bad choice. The ongoing fallout and impact of a trauma, the way an experience can destabilize you. Fun, huh? Oh, and I also wanted to include lots of weddings, because I absolutely love them.

A surprise to me, as M.A.Y. developed—there are always surprises, however much you plan; there's no substitute for discovering what the story is about by writing it—was the importance of social media. The way it can be raised as a weapon with such ease, and how people enthusiastically join mobs on the shakiest of information. It feels as if we're still very much in the ▸

Dear Reader ***(continued)***

era of both working out its impacts and how to mitigate them. Notice how almost every comment about Harriet or Scott online, however articulate or sassy or outraged, is getting some basic fact or assumption about the situation wrong. Hopefully, the story's never preachy, but I thought . . . yes. This feels too real.

As for the relationship with Scott: perhaps the most significant line in the book is Harriet saying he wasn't the love of her life, he was an abuser, and to confuse the two "seemed impossible." I think we all—myself included—imagine that we could spot the behaviors and the techniques of an abuser and defend ourselves. It's inevitable, if your trust has been abused, that you will doubt yourself and question why you ever trusted in the first place. I wanted to describe the way the treatment escalates, and how being an intelligent and caring person is no protection: in fact, your good qualities can be used against you. I didn't do any dedicated research into coercive control; it's possible this is just superstitious, but I fear that if I dive into textbook analysis and compelling first-person accounts, I'll end up transcribing instead of inventing my own story from scratch. For Harriet's experience, I used things I'd read about and some things I'd witnessed, but I mostly relied on imagination. We all know the dopamine-flooded early rush of new love is when we're at our most susceptible and most unwilling to see problems in the person we're head-over-heels for. We naturally become our partner's defender, PR manager, and co-conspirator, and of course that suits someone like Scott so well.

And as for Jon! It's unseemly to boast, but I admit I'm proud of Jon, the quieter monster. He's the "nicest guy in the room," as they say, and his conviction that he's nice allows him license to behave in abominable ways and STILL remain self-righteous: "Well, clearly I must have been treated terribly if it's made a nice guy like me lash out like this . . ." Never realizing that it's what we do, not who we say we are, that counts.

Harriet accepts Jon had a rough ride after he fell in love with someone who wasn't in love back, but it's important she lands the blow: You think you treat women as equals. You don't. Jon's expectation of control over Harriet is far subtler and less toxic than Scott's; there's (initially) no anger in it. But it's still there.

Obviously, all my novels are about love and its redemptive qualities, and, in each other, Harriet and Cal find a person who's good for them, rather than trying to manipulate them. Cal learns of the letter from Harriet's mum and encourages Harriet to read it when she feels ready, and doesn't ask her to disclose the contents when she has. In Cal, Harriet learns what support with no strings attached truly looks like.

And it felt the right note to finish the novel on: with Harriet finally receiving the one piece of encouragement from another woman who she's never had in her life. I feel quite emotional writing that! OK, on with the Qs . . .

Love,
Mhairi xxx

Reading Group Guide

1. There are some calamities at weddings in *Mad About You.* What's the strangest or funniest thing that you've ever seen at a wedding? You are absolutely allowed to use other people's anecdotes here, too.
2. "It wasn't generosity, it was a messed-up power dynamic," says Lorna of Jon's wealth and his wish to dispense it on Harriet. Do you think one partner earning much more than the other matters? Do you think generosity like Jon's can have a controlling or negative effect? Or should you just enjoy the holidays for as long as you're dating and say sod it?
3. "Unnamed fears are the worst fears," Cal says. He has felt he's been forced to keep secrets about his father's dysfunctional behavior, both from his mum and from the outside world. Can you relate to his resentment at having to accept and live with behavior he doesn't like?
4. "We've all lost respect for the fact *there's things we don't know,*" Harriet says of her Facebook witch hunt by strangers. Do you agree? Passing judgement has always been human nature . . . but has the internet made it worse? Have you ever been either perp or victim?
5. "Getting to that point? I think you have to admit it's both our faults," Jon says. Do you agree? Do you think Roxy had a point when she said Harriet had treated a good man badly? Is your ex sleeping with a close friend after a break-up as completely nuclear as Harriet says—or do you think a friendship could conceivably come back from it?
6. "Why did a woman's voice have to be a chorus to count?" Harriet wonders at one point in the story. Do you feel things are changing, and that women's testimonies about male behavior are being taken more seriously?
7. The book ends with a letter. What's the most important letter you've ever written or received?